PRAISE FOR ROBERT E. HOWARD

"At his best, Howard was the Thomas Wolfe of fantasy."
— STEPHEN KING

"Howard was a true storyteller — one of first, and certainly among the best, you'll find in heroic fantasy. If you've never read him before, you're in for a real treat."
— CHARLES DE LINT
Award-winning author of
Forests of the Heart and *The Onion Girl*

"I adore these books. Howard had a gritty, vibrant style — broadsword writing that cut its way to the heart, with heroes who are truly larger than life. It must be thirty years since I last read Howard, but there are moments from his stories that are as fresh in my mind as if I'd read them yesterday. I heartily recommend them to anyone who loves fantasy."
— DAVID GEMMELL
Author of *Legend* and *White Wolf*

"The voice of Robert E. Howard still resonates after decades with readers — equal parts ringing steel, thunderous horse hooves, and spattered blood. Far from being a stereotype, his creation of Conan is *the* high heroic adventurer. His raw muscle and sinews, boiling temper, and lusty laughs are the gauge by which all modern heroes must be measured."
— ERIC NYLUND
Author of *Halo: The Fall of Reach*

"Howard honestly believed the basic truth of the stories he was telling. It's as if he'd said, 'This is how life was really lived in those former savage times!'"
— DAVID DRAKE
Author of *Grimmer Than Hell* and *Dogs of War*

"That teller of marvellous tales, Robert Howard, did indeed create a giant [Conan] in whose shadow other 'hero tales' must stand."
> — JOHN JAKES
> *New York Times* bestselling author
> of the North and South trilogy

"Most of the fantasy of the past thirty-five years has two main wellsprings: J.R.R. Tolkien and Robert E. Howard. Tolkien himself, who had little use for most contemporary fantasists, rather liked the Conan tales. For headlong, nonstop adventure and for vivid, even florid, scenery, no one even comes close to Howard. If you want a rip-roaring good time, this is the place to start."
> — HARRY TURTLEDOVE
> Author of *Guns of the South*

"[Behind Howard's stories] lurks a dark poetry, and the timeless truth of dreams. That is why these tales have survived. They remain a fitting heritage of the poet and dreamer who was Robert E. Howard."
> — ROBERT BLOCH
> Author of *Psycho*

"The stories have a livingness about them [that's] impossible to fake. . . . Not one of them is boring – there is always some special touch – and most, of course, are rousers."
> — GAHAN WILSON
> Reviewer and author of *I Paint What I See*

"For stark, living fear . . . what other writer is even in the running with Robert E. Howard?"
> — H. P. LOVECRAFT

"Howard . . . brought a brash, tough element to the epic fantasy which did as much to change the course of the American school away from precious writing and static imagery as Hammett, Chandler, and the *Black Mask* pulp writers were to change the course of American detective fiction."

    — MICHAEL MOORCOCK
     Award-winning author of the Elric saga

"In this, I think, the art of Robert E. Howard was hard to surpass: vigor, speed, vividness. And always there is that furious, galloping narrative pace."

    — POUL ANDERSON
     Award-winning author of *Genesis*
     and *World Without Stars*

"For vivid, violent, gripping, headlong action, the stories of Robert E. Howard . . . take the prize among heroic fantasies."

    — L. SPRAGUE DE CAMP
     Author of *Lest Darkness Fall*

"The best pulp [fantasy] writer was Robert E. Howard. . . . He painted in about the broadest strokes imaginable. A mass of glimmering black for the menace, an ice-blue cascade for the hero, betweeen them a swath of crimson for battle, passion, blood – and that was the picture, or story, rather, except where a vivid detail might chance to spring to life, or a swift thought-arabesque be added."

    — FRITZ LEIBER
     Author of *Farewell to Lankhmar*

The fully illustrated Robert E. Howard Library for Del Rey Books

The Savage Tales of Solomon Kane

ROBERT E. HOWARD

ILLUSTRATED BY
GARY GIANNI

BALLANTINE BOOKS · NEW YORK

This book is dedicated to the memory of Father Joseph A. Kelly
"Nulla dies sine linear"

GARY GIANNI

A Del Rey® Book
Published by The Random House Publishing Group
Copyright © 1998 by Solomon Kane LLC
Solomon Kane is a registered trademark of Solomon Kane LLC
Illustrations copyright © 1998 by Gary Gianni
Design copyright © 1998 by Wandering Star Books Ltd.
Design: Marcelo Anciano
Typography: Stuart Williams
Editor: Rusty Burke
Series editor: Rusty Burke

Skulls in the Stars © 1928
by Popular Fiction Publishing Company
for Weird Tales, January 1929
The Right Hand of Doom © 1968
by Glenn Lord for Red Shadows
Red Shadows © 1928
by Popular Fiction Publishing Company
for Weird Tales, August 1928
Rattle of Bones © 1929 by
Popular Fiction Publishing Company
for Weird Tales, June 1929
The Castle of the Devil © 1968
by Glenn Lord for Red Shadows
Death's Black Riders © 1968 by Glenn
Lord for The Howard Collector Vol 2,
No. 4, Spring 1968
The Moon of Skulls © 1930 by
Popular Fiction Publishing Company
for Weird Tales, June, July 1930
The One Black Stain © 1962 by
Glenn Lord for The Howard
Collector, Spring 1962

Blades of the Brotherhood © 1968
by Glenn Lord for Red Shadows
The Hills of the Dead © 1930 by
Popular Fiction Publishing Company
for Weird Tales, August 1930
Hawk of Basti © 1968
by Glenn Lord for Red Shadows
The Return of Sir Richard Grenville
© 1968 by Glenn Lord for Red Shadows
Wings in the Night © 1932
by Popular Fiction Publishing Company
for Weird Tales, July 1932
The Footfalls Within © 1931
by Popular Fiction Publishing Company
for Weird Tales, September 1931
The Children of Asshur © 1968
by Glenn Lord for Red Shadows
Solomon Kane's Homecoming © 1936
by Shepherd and Wollheim for
Fanciful Tales, Fall 1936

Published in the United States by Del Rey Books, an imprint of The Random House
Publishing Group, a division of Random House, Inc., New York, and simultaneously
in Canada by Random House of Canada Limited, Toronto. Originally published in
Great Britain by Wandering Star Books Ltd., London, in 1998.

Del Rey is a registered trademark and the Del Rey colophon is a trademark of
Random House, Inc.

www.delreybooks.com

Published by arrangement with Wandering Star Books Ltd.

Library of Congress Control Number: 2003114908

ISBN 978-0-345-46150-6

Manufactured in the United States of America

Contents

*P*lates

Foreword

I have a confession to make.

I never read any of the Solomon Kane stories before I was asked to illustrate them.

I say this with great reluctance as it's generally assumed artists wish to illustrate the books which have made a lasting impression on them and I fear long-time aficionados might worry about my ability to do justice to Howard's material.

Granted I never knew Kane; but the spirit he embodies – that of the romantic hero – ah! Now I'm on fictional terra firma.

Robin Hood, Long John Silver, Captain Nemo, Tarzan, not to mention Conan – these are the figures I grew up on. I know them well and along with millions of other readers, have thrilled to their exploits.

Solomon Kane is easily part of this tradition. I'm sure Howard would have agreed with me. Kane shares the same ingredients that bring all great fictional heroes to life – action, poetry, drama, rich detailing and most importantly – high adventure.

And who could do it better than Robert E. Howard?

As I finished reading the Solomon Kane stories, I was reminded how I used to feel after reading about some mysterious figure, how I wished I could be him.

And so, if there is still someone out there who hasn't read these wonderful stories, I envy you, you're in for a treat. For the rest of you revisiting Robert E. Howard's grim hero will be *good for your soul*.

Solomon Kane should appreciate that.

Gary Gianni

In Memoriam:
Robert Ervin Howard

The sudden and unexpected death on June 11 (1936) of Robert Ervin Howard, author of fantastic tales of incomparable vividness, forms weird fiction's worst loss since the passing of Henry S. Whitehead four years ago.

Mr. Howard was born at Peaster, Texas, on January 22, 1906, and was old enough to have seen the last phase of southwestern pioneering – the settlement of the great plains and lower Rio Grande valley, and the spectacular rise of the oil industry with its raucous boom towns. His father, who survives him, was one of the pioneer physicians of the region. The family have lived in south, east, and west Texas, and western Oklahoma; for the last few years at Cross Plains, near Brownwood, Texas. Steeped in the frontier atmosphere, Mr. Howard early became a devotee of its virile Homeric traditions. His knowledge of its history and folkways was profound, and the descriptions and reminiscences contained in his private letters illustrate the eloquence and power with which he would have celebrated it in literature had he lived longer. Mr. Howard's family is of distinguished southern planter stock – of Scotch-Irish descent, with most ancestors settled in Georgia and North Carolina in the eighteenth century.

Beginning to write at fifteen, Mr. Howard placed his first story three years later while a student at Howard Payne College in Brownwood. This story, "Spear and Fang", was published in *Weird Tales* for July, 1925. Wider fame came with the appearance of the novelette "Wolfshead" in the same magazine in April, 1926. In August, 1928, began the tales dealing with "Solomon Kane", an English Puritan of relentless duelling and wrong-redressing proclivities whose adventures took him to strange parts of the world – including the shadow-haunted ruins of unknown and primordial cities in the African jungle. With these tales Mr. Howard struck what proved to be one of his most effective accomplishments – the description of vast megalithic cities of the elder world, around whose dark towers and labyrinthine nether vaults clings an aura of pre-human fear and necromancy which no other writer could duplicate. These tales also marked Mr. Howard's development of that skill and zest in depicting sanguinary conflict which became so typical of his work. "Solomon Kane", like several other heroes of the author, was conceived in boyhood long before incorporation in any story.

Always a keen student of Celtic antiquities and other phases of remote history, Mr. Howard began in 1929 – with "The Shadow Kingdom", in the August *Weird Tales* – that succession of tales of the prehistoric world for which he soon grew so famous. The earlier specimens described a very distant age in man's history – when Atlantis, Lemuria, and Mu were above the waves, and when the shadows of pre-human reptile men rested upon the primal scene. Of these the central figure was King Kull of Valusia. In *Weird Tales* for December, 1932, appeared "The Phoenix on the Sword" – first of those tales of King Conan the Cimmerian which introduced a later prehistoric world; a world of perhaps 15,000 years ago, just before the first faint glimmerings of recorded history. The elaborate extent and accurate self-consistency with which Mr. Howard developed this world of Conan in his later stories is well known to all fantasy readers. For his own guidance he prepared a detailed quasi-historical sketch of infinite cleverness and imaginative fertility – now running in The Phantagraph as a serial under the title "The Hyborian Age".

Meanwhile Mr. Howard had written many tales of the early Picts and Celts, including a notable series revolving round the chieftain Bran Mak Morn. Few readers will ever forget the hideous and compelling power of that macabre masterpiece, "Worms of the Earth", in *Weird Tales* for November, 1932. Other powerful fantasies lay outside the connected series – these including the memorable serial "Skull-Face", and a few distinctive tales with a modern setting, such as the recent "Black Canaan" with its genuine regional background and its clutchingly compelling picture of the horror that stalks through the moss-hung, shadow-cursed, serpent-ridden swamps of the American far South.

Outside the fantasy field Mr. Howard was surprisingly prolific and versatile. His strong interest in sports – a thing perhaps connected with his love of primitive conflict and strength – led him to create the prize-fighting hero "Sailor Steve Costigan", whose adventures in distant and curious parts delighted the readers of many magazines. His novelettes of Oriental warfare displayed to the utmost his mastery of romantic swashbuckling, while his increasingly frequent tales of western life – such as the "Breckenridge Elkins" series – shewed his growing ability and inclination to reflect the backgrounds with which he was directly familiar.

Mr. Howard's poetry – weird, warlike, and adventurous – was no less notable than his prose. It had the true spirit of the ballad and the epic, and was marked by a pulsing rhythm and potent imagery of extremely distinctive cast. Much of it, in the form of supposed quotations from ancient writings, served to head the chapters of his novels. It is regrettable that no published collection has ever appeared, and one hopes that such a thing may be posthumously edited and issued. The character and attainments of Mr. Howard were wholly unique. He was, above everything else, a lover of the simpler, older world of barbarian and pioneer days, when courage and strength took the place of subtlety and stratagem, and when a hardy, fearless race battled and bled and asked no quarter from hostile Nature. All his stories reflect this philosophy, and derive from it a vitality found in few of his contemporaries. No one could write more convincingly of violence and gore than he, and his battle passages reveal an instinctive aptitude for military tactics which would have brought him distinction in times of war. His real gifts were even higher than the readers of his published work could suspect, and had he lived would have helped him make his mark in serious literature with some folk-epic of his beloved Southwest.

It is hard to describe precisely what made Mr. Howard's stories stand out so sharply; but the real secret is that he himself was in every one of them, whether they were ostensibly commercial or not. He was greater than any profit-making policy he could adopt – for even when he outwardly made concessions to Mammon-guided editors and commercial critics he had an internal force and sincerity which broke through the surface and put the imprint of his personality on everything he wrote. Seldom if ever did he set down a lifeless stock character or situation and leave it as such. Before he concluded with it, it always took on some tinge of vitality and reality in spite of popular editorial policy – always drew something from his own experience and knowledge of life instead of from the sterile herbarium of desiccated pulpish standbys. Not only did he excel in pictures of strife and slaughter, but he was almost alone in his ability to create real emotions of spectral fear and dread suspense. No author – even in the humblest fields – can truly excel unless he takes his work very seriously; and Mr. Howard did just that, even in cases where he consciously thought he did not. That such a genuine artist should perish while hundreds of insincere hacks continue to concoct spurious ghosts and vampires and space-ships and occult detectives is indeed a sorry piece of cosmic irony.

Mr. Howard, familiar with many phases of southwestern life, lived with his parents in a semi-rural setting in the village of Cross Plains, Texas. Writing was his sole profession. His tastes in reading were wide, and included historical research of notable depth in fields as dissimilar as the American Southwest, prehistoric Great Britain and Ireland, and the prehistoric Oriental and African world. In literature he preferred the virile to the subtle, and repudiated modernism with sweeping completeness. The late Jack London was one of his idols. He was a liberal in politics, and a bitter foe of civic injustice in every form. His leading amusements were sports and travel – the latter always giving rise to delightful descriptive letters replete with historical reflections. Humour was not a specialty, though he had on the one hand a keen sense of irony, and on the other hand an abundant fund of heartiness, cordiality, and conviviality. Though having numerous friends, Mr. Howard belonged to no literary clique and abhorred all cults of "arty" affectation. His admirations ran toward strength of character and body rather than toward scholastic prowess. With his fellow-authors in the fantasy field he corresponded interestingly and voluminously, but never met more than one of them – the gifted E. Hoffmann Price, whose varied attainments impressed him profoundly – in person.

Mr. Howard was nearly six feet in height, with the massive build of a born fighter. He was, save for Celtic blue eyes, very dark; and in later years his weight averaged around 195. Always a disciple of hearty and strenuous living, he suggested more than casually his own most famous character – the intrepid warrior, adventurer, and seizer of thrones, Conan the Cimmerian. His loss at the age of thirty is a tragedy of the first magnitude, and a blow from which fantasy fiction will not soon recover. Mr. Howard's library has been presented to Howard Payne College, where it will form the nucleus of the Robert E. Howard Memorial Collection of books, manuscripts, and letters.

H. P. Lovecraft

Skulls in the Stars

Skulls in the Stars

He told how murderers walk the earth
Beneath the curse of Cain,
With crimson clouds before their eyes
And flames about their brain:
For blood has left upon their souls
Its everlasting stain.

HOOD

I

There are two roads to Torkertown. One, the shorter and more direct route, leads across a barren upland moor, and the other, which is much longer, winds its tortuous way in and out among the hummocks and quagmires of the swamps, skirting the low hills to the east. It was a dangerous and tedious trail; so Solomon Kane halted in amazement when a breathless youth from the village he had just left, overtook him and implored him for God's sake to take the swamp road.

"The swamp road!" Kane stared at the boy.

He was a tall, gaunt man, was Solomon Kane, his darkly pallid face and deep brooding eyes made more somber by the drab Puritanical garb he affected.

"Yes, sir, 'tis far safer," the youngster answered his surprised exclamation.

"Then the moor road must be haunted by Satan himself, for your townsmen warned me against traversing the other."

"Because of the quagmires, sir, that you might not see in the dark. You had better return to the village and continue your journey in the morning, sir."

"Taking the swamp road?"

"Yes, sir."

Kane shrugged his shoulders and shook his head.

"The moon rises almost as soon as twilight dies. By its light I can reach Torkertown in a few hours, across the moor."

"Sir, you had better not. No one ever goes that way. There are no houses at all upon the moor, while in the swamp there is the house of old Ezra who lives there all alone since his maniac cousin, Gideon, wandered off and died in the swamp and was never found – and old Ezra though a miser would not refuse you lodging should you decide to stop until morning. Since you must go, you had better go the swamp road."

Kane eyed the boy piercingly. The lad squirmed and shuffled his feet.

"Since this moor road is so dour to wayfarers," said the Puritan, "why did not the villagers tell me the whole tale, instead of vague mouthings?"

"Men like not to talk of it, sir. We hoped that you would take the swamp road after the men advised you to, but when we watched and saw that you turned not at the forks, they sent me to run after you and beg you to reconsider."

"Name of the Devil!" exclaimed Kane sharply, the unaccustomed oath showing his irritation; "the swamp road and the moor road – what is it that threatens me and why should I go miles out of my way and risk the bogs and mires?"

"Sir," said the boy, dropping his voice and drawing closer, "we be simple villagers who like not to talk of such things lest foul fortune befall us, but the moor road is a way accurst and hath not been traversed by any of the countryside for a year or more. It is death to walk those moors by night, as hath been found by some score of unfortunates. Some foul horror haunts the way and claims men for his victims."

"So? And what is this thing like?"

"No man knows. None has ever seen it and lived, but late-farers have heard terrible laughter far out on the fen and men have heard the horrid shrieks of its victims. Sir, in God's name return to the village, there pass the night, and tomorrow take the swamp trail to Torkertown."

Far back in Kane's gloomy eyes a scintillant light had begun to glimmer, like a witch's torch glinting under fathoms of cold gray ice. His blood quickened. Adventure! The lure of life-risk and battle! The thrill of breathtaking, touch-and-go drama! Not that Kane recognized his sensations as such. He sincerely considered that he voiced his real feelings when he said:

"These things be deeds of some power of evil. The lords of darkness have laid a curse upon the country. A strong man is needed to combat Satan and his might. Therefore I go, who have defied him many a time."

"Sir," the boy began, then closed his mouth as he saw the futility of argument. He only added, "The corpses of the victims are bruised and torn, sir."

He stood there at the crossroads, sighing regretfully as he watched the tall, rangy figure swinging up the road that led toward the moors.

The sun was setting as Kane came over the brow of the low hill which debouched into the upland fen. Huge and blood-red it sank down behind the sullen horizon of the moors, seeming to touch the rank grass with fire; so for a moment the watcher seemed to be gazing out across a sea of blood. Then the dark shadows came gliding from the east, the western blaze faded, and Solomon Kane struck out boldly in the gathering darkness.

The road was dim from disuse but was clearly defined. Kane went swiftly but warily, sword and pistols at hand. Stars blinked out and night winds whispered among the grass like weeping specters. The moon began to rise, lean and haggard, like a skull among the stars.

Then suddenly Kane stopped short. From somewhere in front of him sounded a strange and eery echo – or something like an echo. Again, this time louder. Kane started forward again. Were his senses deceiving him? No!

Far out, there pealed a whisper of frightful laughter. And again, closer this time. No human being ever laughed like that

– there was no mirth in it, only hatred and horror and soul-destroying terror. Kane halted. He was not afraid, but for the second he was almost unnerved. Then, stabbing through that awesome laughter, came the sound of a scream that was undoubtedly human. Kane started forward, increasing his gait. He cursed the illusive lights and flickering shadows which veiled the moor in the rising moon and made accurate sight impossible. The laughter continued, growing louder, as did the screams. Then sounded faintly the drum of frantic human feet. Kane broke into a run.

Some human was being hunted to his death out there on the fen, and by what manner of horror God alone knew. The sound of the flying feet halted abruptly and the screaming rose unbearably, mingled with other sounds unnamable and hideous. Evidently the man had been overtaken, and Kane, his flesh crawling, visualized some ghastly fiend of the darkness crouching on the back of its victim – crouching and tearing.

Then the noise of a terrible and short struggle came clearly through the abysmal silence of the fen and the footfalls began again, but stumbling and uneven. The screaming continued, but with a gasping gurgle. The sweat stood cold on Kane's forehead and body. This was heaping horror on horror in an intolerable manner.

God, for a moment's clear light! The frightful drama was being enacted within a very short distance of him, to judge by the ease with which the sounds reached him. But this hellish half-light veiled all in shifting shadows, so that the moors appeared a haze of blurred illusions, and stunted trees and bushes seemed like giants.

Kane shouted, striving to increase the speed of his advance. The shrieks of the unknown broke into a hideous shrill squealing; again there was the sound of a struggle, and then from the shadows of the tall grass a thing came reeling

– a thing that had once been a man – a gore-covered, frightful thing that fell at Kane's feet and writhed and groveled and raised its terrible face to the rising moon, and gibbered and yammered, and fell down again and died in its own blood.

The moon was up now and the light was better. Kane bent above the body, which lay stark in its unnamable mutilation, and he shuddered – a rare thing for him, who had seen the deeds of the Spanish Inquisition and the witch-finders.

Some wayfarer, he supposed. Then like a hand of ice on his spine he was aware that he was not alone. He looked up, his cold eyes piercing the shadows whence the dead man had staggered. He saw nothing, but he knew – he felt – that other eyes gave back his stare, terrible eyes not of this earth. He straightened and drew a pistol, waiting. The moonlight spread like a lake of pale blood over the moor, and trees and grasses took on their proper sizes.

The shadows melted, and Kane *saw*! At first he thought it only a shadow of mist, a wisp of moor fog that swayed in the tall grass before him. He gazed.

More illusion, he thought. Then the thing began to take on shape, vague and indistinct. Two hideous eyes flamed at him – eyes which held all the stark horror which has been the heritage of man since the fearful dawn ages – eyes frightful and insane, with an insanity transcending earthly insanity. The form of the thing was misty and vague, a brain-shattering travesty on the human form, like, yet horridly unlike.

The grass and bushes beyond showed clearly through it.

Kane felt the blood pound in his temples, yet he was as cold as ice. How such an unstable being as that which wavered before him could harm a man in a physical way was more than he could understand, yet the red horror at his feet gave mute testimony that the fiend could act with terrible material effect.

Of one thing Kane was sure: there would be no hunting of him across the dreary moors, no screaming and fleeing to be dragged down again and again. If he must die he would die in his tracks, his wounds in front.

Now a vague and grisly mouth gaped wide and the demoniac laughter again shrieked out, soul-shaking in its nearness. And in the midst of that threat of doom, Kane deliberately leveled his long pistol and fired. A maniacal yell of rage and mockery answered the report, and the thing came at him like a flying sheet of smoke, long shadowy arms stretched to drag him down.

Kane, moving with the dynamic speed of a famished wolf, fired the second pistol with as little effect, snatched his long rapier from its sheath and thrust into the center of the misty attacker. The blade sang as it passed clear through, encountering no solid resistance, and Kane felt icy fingers grip his limbs, bestial talons tear his garments and the skin beneath.

He dropped the useless sword and sought to grapple with his foe. It was like fighting a floating mist, a flying shadow armed with daggerlike claws. His savage blows met empty air, his leanly mighty arms, in whose grasp strong men had died, swept nothingness and clutched emptiness. Naught was solid or real save the flaying, apelike fingers with their crooked talons, and the crazy eyes which burned into the shuddering depths of his soul.

Kane realized that he was in a desperate plight indeed. Already his garments hung in tatters and he bled from a score of deep wounds. But he never flinched, and the thought of flight never entered his mind. He had never fled from a single foe, and had the thought occurred to him he would have flushed with shame.

He saw no help for it now, but that his form should lie there beside the fragments of the other victim, but the thought held no terrors for him. His only wish was to give as good an account of himself as possible before the end came, and if he could, to inflict some damage on his unearthly foe.

There above the dead man's torn body, man fought with demon under the pale light of the rising moon, with all the advantages with the demon, save one. And that one was enough to overcome all the others. For if abstract hate may bring into material substance a ghostly thing, may not courage, equally abstract, form a concrete weapon to combat that ghost?

Kane fought with his arms and his feet and his hands, and he was aware at last that the ghost began to give back before him, that the fearful laughter changed to screams of baffled fury. For man's only weapon is courage that flinches not from the gates of Hell itself, and against such not even the legions of Hell can stand.

Of this Kane knew nothing; he only knew that the talons which tore and rended him seemed to grow weaker and wavering, that a wild light grew and grew in the horrible eyes. And reeling and gasping, he rushed in, grappled the thing at last and threw it, and as they tumbled about on the moor and it writhed and lapped his limbs like a serpent of smoke, his flesh crawled and his hair stood on end, for he began to understand its gibbering.

He did not hear and comprehend as a man hears and

comprehends the speech of a man, but the frightful secrets it imparted in whisperings and yammerings and screaming silences sank fingers of ice and flame into his soul, and he *knew*.

II

The hut of old Ezra the miser stood by the road in the midst of the swamp, half screened by the sullen trees which grew about it. The walls were rotting, the roof crumbling, and great, pallid and green fungus-monsters clung to it and writhed about the doors and windows, as if seeking to peer within. The trees leaned above it and their gray branches intertwined so that it crouched in the semi-darkness like a monstrous dwarf over whose shoulder ogres leer.

The road which wound down into the swamp, among rotting stumps and rank hummocks and scummy, snake-haunted pools and bogs, crawled past the hut. Many people passed that way these days, but few saw old Ezra, save a glimpse of a yellow face, peering through the fungus-screened windows, itself like an ugly fungus.

Old Ezra the miser partook much of the quality of the swamp, for he was gnarled and bent and sullen; his fingers were like clutching parasitic plants and his locks hung like drab moss above eyes trained to the murk of the swamplands. His eyes were like a dead man's, yet hinted of depths abysmal and loathsome as the dead lakes of the swamplands.

These eyes gleamed now at the man who stood in front of

his hut. This man was tall and gaunt and dark, his face was haggard and claw-marked, and he was bandaged of arm and leg. Somewhat behind this man stood a number of villagers.

"You are Ezra of the swamp road?"

"Aye, and what want ye of me?"

"Where is your cousin Gideon, the maniac youth who abode with you?"

"Gideon?"

"Aye."

"He wandered away into the swamp and never came back. No doubt he lost his way and was set upon by wolves or died in a quagmire or was struck by an adder."

"How long ago?"

"Over a year."

"Aye. Hark ye, Ezra the miser. Soon after your cousin's disappearance, a countryman, coming home across the moors, was set upon by some unknown fiend and torn to pieces, and thereafter it became death to cross those moors. First men of the countryside, then strangers who wandered over the fen, fell to the clutches of the thing. Many men have died, since the first one.

"Last night I crossed the moors, and heard the flight and pursuing of another victim, a stranger who knew not the evil of the moors. Ezra the miser, it was a fearful thing, for the wretch twice broke from the fiend, terribly wounded, and each time the demon caught and dragged him down again. And at last he fell dead at my very feet, done to death in a manner that would freeze the statue of a saint."

The villagers moved restlessly and murmured fearfully to each other, and old Ezra's eyes shifted furtively. Yet the somber expression of Solomon Kane never altered, and his condor-like stare seemed to transfix the miser.

"Aye, aye!" muttered old Ezra hurriedly; "a bad thing, a

bad thing! Yet why do you tell this thing to me?"

"Aye, a sad thing. Harken further, Ezra. The fiend came out of the shadows and I fought with it, over the body of its victim. Aye, how I overcame it, I know not, for the battle was hard and long, but the powers of good and light were on my side, which are mightier than the powers of Hell.

"At the last I was stronger, and it broke from me and fled, and I followed to no avail. Yet before it fled it whispered to me a monstrous truth."

Old Ezra started, stared wildly, seemed to shrink into himself.

"Nay, why tell me this?" he muttered.

"I returned to the village and told my tale," said Kane, "for I knew that now I had the power to rid the moors of its curse forever. Ezra, come with us!"

"Where?" gasped the miser.

"To the rotting oak on the moors."

Ezra reeled as though struck; he screamed incoherently and turned to flee.

On the instant, at Kane's sharp order, two brawny villagers sprang forward and seized the miser. They twisted the dagger from his withered hand, and pinioned his arms, shuddering as their fingers encountered his clammy flesh.

Kane motioned them to follow, and turning strode up the trail, followed by the villagers, who found their strength taxed to the utmost in their task of bearing their prisoner along. Through the swamp they went and out, taking a little-used trail which led up over the low hills and out on the moors.

The sun was sliding down the horizon and old Ezra stared at it with bulging eyes – stared as if he could not gaze enough. Far out on the moors reared up the great oak tree, like a gibbet, now only a decaying shell. There Solomon Kane halted.

Old Ezra writhed in his captor's grasp and made inarticulate noises.

"Over a year ago," said Solomon Kane, "you, fearing that your insane cousin Gideon would tell men of your cruelties to him, brought him away from the swamp by the very trail by which we came, and murdered him here in the night."

Ezra cringed and snarled.

"You can not prove this lie!"

Kane spoke a few words to an agile villager. The youth clambered up the rotting bole of the tree and from a crevice, high up, dragged something that fell with a clatter at the feet of the miser. Ezra went limp with a terrible shriek.

The object was a man's skeleton, the skull cleft.

"You – how knew you this? You are Satan!" gibbered old Ezra.

Kane folded his arms.

"The thing I fought last night told me this thing as we reeled in battle, and I followed it to this tree. *For the fiend is Gideon's ghost.*"

Ezra shrieked again and fought savagely.

"You knew," said Kane somberly, "you knew what thing did these deeds. You feared the ghost of the maniac, and that is why you chose to leave his body on the fen instead of concealing it in the swamp. For you knew the ghost would haunt the place of his death. He was insane in life, and in death he did not know where to find his slayer; else he had come to you in your hut. He hates no man but you, but his mazed spirit can not tell one man from another, and he slays all, lest he let his killer escape. Yet he will know you and rest in peace forever after. Hate hath made of his ghost a solid thing that can rend and slay, and though he feared you terribly in life, in death he fears you not."

Kane halted. He glanced at the sun.

"All this I had from Gideon's ghost, in his yammerings and his whisperings and his shrieking silences. Naught but your death will lay that ghost."

Ezra listened in breathless silence and Kane pronounced the words of his doom.

"A hard thing it is," said Kane somberly, "to sentence a man to death in cold blood and in such a manner as I have in mind, but you must die that others may live – and God knoweth you deserve death.

"You shall not die by noose, bullet or sword, but at the talons of him you slew – for naught else will satiate him."

At these words Ezra's brain shattered, his knees gave way and he fell groveling and screaming for death, begging them

to burn him at the stake, to flay him alive. Kane's face was set like death, and the villagers, the fear rousing their cruelty, bound the screeching wretch to the oak tree, and one of them bade him make his peace with God. But Ezra made no answer, shrieking in a high shrill voice with unbearable monotony. Then the villager would have struck the miser across the face, but Kane stayed him.

"Let him make his peace with Satan, whom he is more like to meet," said the Puritan grimly. "The sun is about to set. Loose his cords so that he may work loose by dark, since it is better to meet death free and unshackled than bound like a sacrifice."

As they turned to leave him, old Ezra yammered and gibbered unhuman sounds and then fell silent, staring at the sun with terrible intensity.

They walked away across the fen, and Kane flung a last look at the grotesque form bound to the tree, seeming in the uncertain light like a great fungus growing to the bole. And suddenly the miser screamed hideously:

"Death! Death! There are skulls in the stars!"

"Life was good to him, though he was gnarled and churlish and evil," Kane sighed. "Mayhap God has a place for such souls where fire and sacrifice may cleanse them of their dross as fire cleans the forest of fungous things. Yet my heart is heavy within me."

"Nay, sir," one of the villagers spoke, "you have done but the will of God, and good alone shall come of this night's deed."

"Nay," answered Kane heavily, "I know not—I know not."

The sun had gone down and night spread with amazing swiftness, as if great shadows came rushing down from unknown voids to cloak the world with hurrying darkness.

Through the thick night came a weird echo, and the men halted and looked back the way they had come.

Nothing could be seen. The moor was an ocean of shadows and the tall grass about them bent in long waves before the faint wind, breaking the deathly stillness with breathless murmurings.

Then far away the red disk of the moon rose over the fen, and for an instant a grim silhouette was etched blackly against it. A shape came flying across the face of the moon – a bent, grotesque thing whose feet seemed scarcely to touch the earth; and close behind came a thing like a flying shadow – a nameless, shapeless horror.

A moment the racing twain stood out boldly against the moon; then they merged into one unnamable, formless mass, and vanished in the shadows.

Far across the fen sounded a single shriek of terrible laughter.

The Right Hand of Doom

The Right Hand of Doom

"And he hangs at dawn! Ho! Ho!"

The speaker smote his thigh resoundingly and laughed in a high-pitched grating voice. He glanced boastfully at his hearers, and gulped the wine which stood at his elbow. The fire leaped and flickered in the tap-room fireplace and no one answered him.

"Roger Simeon, the necromancer!" sneered the grating voice. "A dealer in the diabolic arts and a worker of black magic! My word, all his foul power could not save him when the king's soldiers surrounded his cave and took him prisoner. He fled when the people began to fling cobble stones at his windows, and thought to hide himself and escape to France. Ho! Ho! His escape shall be at the end of a noose. A good day's work, say I."

He tossed a small bag on the table where it clinked musically.

"The price of a magician's life!" he boasted. "What say you, my sour friend?"

This last was addressed to a tall silent man who sat near the fire. This man, gaunt, powerful and somberly dressed, turned his darkly pallid face toward the speaker and fixed him with a pair of deep icy eyes.

"I say," said he in a low powerful voice, "that you have this day done a damnable deed. Yon necromancer was worthy of death, belike, but he trusted you, naming you his one friend, and you betrayed him for a few filthy coins. Methinks you will meet him in Hell, some day."

The first speaker, a short, stocky and evil-faced fellow, opened his mouth as if for an angry retort and then hesitated. The icy eyes held his for an instant, then the tall man rose with a smooth cat-like motion and strode from the tap-room in long springy strides.

"Who is yon?" asked the boaster resentfully. "Who is he to uphold magicians against honest men? By God, he is lucky to cross words with John Redly and keep his heart in's bosom!"

The tavern-keeper leaned forward to secure an ember for his long-stemmed pipe and answered dryly:

"And you be lucky too, John, for keepin' tha' mouth shut. That be Solomon Kane, the Puritan, a man dangerouser than a wolf."

Redly grumbled beneath his breath, muttered an oath, and sullenly replaced the money bag in his belt.

"Are ye stayin' here tonight?"

"Aye," Redly answered sullenly. "Rather I'd stay to watch Simeon hang in Torkertown tomorrow, but I'm London bound at dawn."

The tavern-keeper filled their goblets.

"Here's to Simeon's soul, God ha' mercy on the wretch, and may he fail in the vengeance he swore to take on you."

John Redly started, swore, then laughed with reckless bravado. The laughter rose emptily and broke on a false note.

Solomon Kane awoke suddenly and sat up in bed. He was a light sleeper as becomes a man who habitually carries his life in his hand. And somewhere in the house had sounded a noise which had roused him. He listened. Outside, as he could see through the shutters, the world was whitening with the first tints of dawn.

Suddenly the sound came again, faintly. It was as if a cat were clawing its way up the wall, outside. Kane listened, and then came a sound as if someone were fumbling at the shutters. The Puritan rose, and sword in hand, crossed the room suddenly and flung them open. The world lay sleeping to his gaze. A late moon hovered over the western horizon. No marauder lurked outside his window. He leaned out, gazing at the window of the chamber next his. The shutters were open.

Kane closed his shutters and crossed to his door; went out into the corridor. He was acting on impulse as he usually did. These were wild times. This tavern was some miles from the nearest town – Torkertown. Bandits were common. Someone or something had entered the chamber next his, and its sleeping occupant might be in danger. Kane did not halt to weigh pros and cons but went straight to the chamber door and opened it.

The window was wide open and the light streaming in illumined the room yet made it seem to swim in a ghostly mist. A short evil-visaged man snored on the bed and he Kane recognized as John Redly, the man who had betrayed the necromancer to the soldiers.

Then his gaze was drawn to the window. On the sill squatted what looked like a huge spider, and as Kane watched, it dropped to the floor and began to crawl toward the bed. The thing was broad and hairy and dark, and Kane noted that it had left a stain on the window sill. It moved on five thick and curiously jointed legs and altogether had such an eery appearance about it, that Kane was spellbound for the moment. Now it had reached Redly's bed and clambered up the bedstead in a strange clumsy sort of manner.

Now it poised directly over the sleeping man, clinging to the bedstead, and Kane started forward with a shout of warning. That instant Redly awoke and looked up. His eyes flared wide, a terrible scream broke from his lips and simultaneously the spider-thing dropped, landing full on his neck. And even as Kane reached the bed, he saw the legs lock and heard the splintering of John Redly's neck bones. The man stiffened and lay still, his head lolling grotesquely on his broken neck. And the thing dropped from him and lay limply on the bed.

Kane bent over the grim spectacle, scarcely believing his eyes. For the thing which had opened the shutters, crawled across the floor and murdered John Redly in his bed was a *human hand*!

Now it lay flaccid and lifeless. And Kane gingerly thrust his rapier point through it and lifted it to his eyes. The hand was that of a large man, apparently, for it was broad and thick, with heavy fingers, and almost covered by a matted growth of ape-like hair. It had been severed at the wrist and was caked with blood. A thin silver ring was on the second finger, a curious ornament, made in the form of a coiling serpent.

Kane stood gazing at the hideous relic as the tavern-keeper entered, clad in his night shirt, candle in one hand and blunderbuss in the other.

"What's this?" he roared as his eyes fell on the corpse on the bed.

Then he saw what Kane held spitted on his sword and his face went white. As if drawn by an irresistible urge, he came closer – his eyes bulged. Then he reeled back and sank into a chair, so pale Kane thought he was going to swoon.

"God's name, sir," he gasped. "Let that thing not live! There be a fire in the tap room, sir –"

Kane came into Torkertown before the morning had waned. At the outskirts of the village he met a garrulous youth who hailed him.

"Sir, like all honest men you will be pleasured to know that Roger Simeon the black magician was hanged this dawn, just as the sun came up."

"And was his passing manly?" asked Kane somberly.

"Aye, sir, he flinched not, but a weird deed it was. Look

ye, sir, Roger Simeon went to the gallows with but one hand to his arms!"

"And how came that about?"

"Last night, sir, as he sat in his cell like a great black spider, he called one of his guards and asking for a last favor, bade the soldier strike off his right hand! The man would not do it at first, but he feared Roger's curse, and at last he took his sword and smote off the hand at the wrist. Then Simeon, taking it in his left hand, flung it far through the bars of his cell window, uttering many strange and foul words of magic. The guards were sore afraid, but Roger offered not to harm them, saying he hated only John Redly that betrayed him.

"And he bound the stump of his arm to stop the blood and all the rest of the night he sat as a man in a trance and at times he mumbled to himself as a man that unknowing, talks to himself. And, 'To the right,' he would whisper, and 'Bear to the left!' and, 'On, on!"

"Oh, sir, 'twas grisly to hear him, they say, and to see him crouching over the bloody stump of his arm! And as dawn was gray they came and took him forth to the gallows and as they placed the noose about his neck, sudden he writhed and strained as with effort, and the muscles in his right arm which lacked the hand, bulged and creaked as though he were breaking some mortal's neck!

"Then as the guards sprang to seize him, he ceased and began to laugh. And terrible and hideous his laughter bellowed out until the noose broke it short and he hung black and silent in the red eye of the rising sun."

Solomon Kane was silent for he was thinking of the fearful terror which had twisted John Redly's features in that last swift moment of awakening and life, ere doom struck. And a dim picture rose in his mind – that of a hairy severed hand crawling on its fingers like a great spider, blindly, through the dark night-time forests to scale a wall and fumble open a pair of bedroom shutters. Here his vision stopped, recoiling from the continuance of that dark and bloody drama. What terrible fires of hate had blazed in the soul of the doomed necromancer and what hideous powers had been his, to so send that bloody hand groping on its mission, guided by the magic and will of that burning brain!

Yet to make sure, Solomon asked:

"And was the hand ever found?"

"Nay, sir. Men found the place where it had fallen when it was thrown from the cell, but it was gone, and a trail of red led into the forest. Doubtless a wolf devoured it."

"Doubtless," answered Solomon Kane. "And were Simeon's hands great and hairy with a ring on the second finger of the right hand?"

"Aye, sir. A silver ring coiled like unto a snake.'

Red Shadows

Original title: Solomon Kane

Red Shadows

I
THE COMING OF SOLOMON

The moonlight shimmered hazily, making silvery mists of illusion among the shadowy trees. A faint breeze whispered down the valley, bearing a shadow that was not of the moon-mist. A faint scent of smoke was apparent.

The man whose long, swinging strides, unhurried yet unswerving, had carried him for many a mile since sunrise, stopped suddenly. A movement in the trees had caught his attention, and he moved silently toward the shadows, a hand resting lightly on the hilt of his long, slim rapier.

Warily he advanced, his eyes striving to pierce the darkness that brooded under the trees. This was a wild and menacing country; death might be lurking under those trees. Then his hand fell away from the hilt and he leaned forward. Death indeed was there, but not in such shape as might cause him fear.

"The fires of Hades!" he murmured. "A girl! What has harmed you, child? Be not afraid of me."

The girl looked up at him, her face like a dim white rose in the dark.

"You – who are – you?" her words came in gasps.

"Naught but a wanderer, a landless man, but a friend to

all in need." The gentle voice sounded somehow incongruous, coming from the man.

The girl sought to prop herself up on her elbow, and instantly he knelt and raised her to a sitting position, her head resting against his shoulder. His hand touched her breast and came away red and wet.

"Tell me." His voice was soft, soothing, as one speaks to a babe.

"Le Loup," she gasped, her voice swiftly growing weaker. "He and his men – descended upon our village – a mile up the valley. They robbed – slew – burned –"

"That, then, was the smoke I scented," muttered the man. "Go on, child."

"I ran. He, the Wolf, pursued me – and – caught me–" The words died away in a shuddering silence.

"I understand, child. Then –?"

"Then – he – he – stabbed me – with his dagger – oh, blessed saints! – mercy –"

Suddenly the slim form went limp. The man eased her to the earth, and touched her brow lightly.

"Dead!" he muttered.

Slowly he rose, mechanically wiping his hands upon his cloak. A dark scowl had settled on his somber brow. Yet he made no wild, reckless vow, swore no oath by saints or devils.

"Men shall die for this," he said coldly.

II

THE LAIR OF THE WOLF

"You are a fool!" The words came in a cold snarl that curdled the hearer's blood.

He who had just been named a fool lowered his eyes sullenly without answer.

"You and all the others I lead!" The speaker leaned forward, his fist pounding emphasis on the rude table between them. He was a tall, rangy-built man, supple as a leopard and with a lean, cruel, predatory face. His eyes danced and glittered with a kind of reckless mockery.

The fellow spoken to replied sullenly, "This Solomon Kane is a demon from hell, I tell you."

"Faugh! Dolt! He is a man — who will die from a pistol ball or a sword thrust."

"So thought Jean, Juan and La Costa," answered the other grimly. "Where are they? Ask the mountain wolves that tore the flesh from their dead bones. Where does this Kane hide? We have searched the mountains and the valleys for leagues, and we have found no trace. I tell you, Le Loup, he comes up from hell. I knew no good would come from hanging that friar a moon ago."

The Wolf strummed impatiently upon the table. His keen face, despite lines of wild living and dissipation, was the face of a thinker. The superstitions of his followers affected him not at all.

"Faugh! I say again. The fellow has found some cavern or secret vale of which we do not know where he hides in the day."

"And at night he sallies forth and slays us," gloomily commented the other. "He hunts us down as a wolf hunts deer – by God, Le Loup, you name yourself Wolf but I think you have met at last a fiercer and more crafty wolf than yourself! The first we know of this man is when we find Jean, the most desperate bandit unhung, nailed to a tree with his own dagger through his breast, and the letters S.L.K. carved upon his dead cheeks. Then the Spaniard Juan is struck down, and after we find him he lives long enough to tell us that the slayer is an Englishman, Solomon Kane, who has sworn to destroy our entire band! What then? La Costa, a swordsman second only to yourself, goes forth swearing to meet this Kane. By the demons of perdition, it seems he met him! For we found his sword-pierced corpse upon a cliff. What now? Are we all to fall before this English fiend?"

"True, our best men have been done to death by him," mused the bandit chief. "Soon the rest return from that little trip to the hermit's; then we shall see. Kane can not hide forever. Then – ha, what was that?"

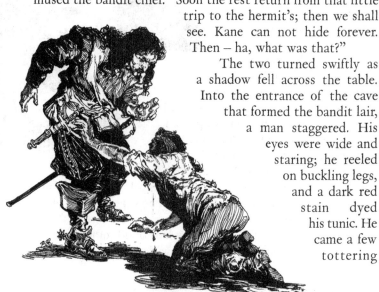

The two turned swiftly as a shadow fell across the table. Into the entrance of the cave that formed the bandit lair, a man staggered. His eyes were wide and staring; he reeled on buckling legs, and a dark red stain dyed his tunic. He came a few tottering steps forward, then pitched across the table, sliding off onto the floor.

"Hell's devils!" cursed the Wolf, hauling him upright and propping him in a chair. "Where are the rest, curse you?"

"Dead! All dead!"

"How? Satan's curses on you, speak!" The Wolf shook the man savagely, the other bandit gazing on in wide-eyed horror.

"We reached the hermit's hut just as the moon rose," the man muttered. "I stayed outside – to watch – the others went in – to torture the hermit – to make him reveal – the hiding-place – of his gold."

"Yes, yes! Then what?" The Wolf was raging with impatience.

"Then the world turned red – the hut went up in a roar and a red rain flooded the valley – through it I saw – the hermit and a tall man clad all in black – coming from the trees–"

"Solomon Kane!" gasped the bandit. "I knew it! I –"

"Silence, fool!" snarled the chief. "Go on!"

"I fled – Kane pursued – wounded me – but I outran – him – got – here – first–"

The man slumped forward on the table.

"Saints and devils!" raged the Wolf. "What does he look like, this Kane?"

"Like – Satan –"

The voice trailed off in silence. The dead man slid from the table to lie in a red heap upon the floor.

"Like Satan!" babbled the other bandit. "I told you! 'Tis the Horned One himself! I tell you –"

He ceased as a frightened face peered in at the cave entrance.

"Kane?"

"Aye." The Wolf was too much at sea to lie. "Keep close watch, La Mon; in a moment the Rat and I will join you."

The face withdrew and Le Loup turned to the other.

"This ends the band," said he. "You, I, and that thief La Mon are all that are left. What would you suggest?"

The Rat's pallid lips barely formed the word: "Flight!"

"You are right. Let us take the gems and gold from the chests and flee, using the secret passageway."

"And La Mon?"

"He can watch until we are ready to flee. Then – why divide the treasure three ways?"

A faint smile touched the Rat's malevolent features. Then a sudden thought smote him.

"He," indicating the corpse on the floor, "said, 'I got here first.' Does that mean Kane was pursuing him here?" And as the Wolf nodded impatiently the other turned to the chests with chattering haste.

The flickering candle on the rough table lighted up a strange and wild scene. The light, uncertain and dancing, gleamed redly in the slowly widening lake of blood in which the dead man lay; it danced upon the heaps of gems and coins emptied hastily upon the floor from the brass-bound chests that ranged the walls; and it glittered in the eyes of the Wolf with the same gleam which sparkled from his sheathed dagger.

The chests were empty, their treasure lying in a shimmering mass upon the blood-stained floor. The Wolf stopped and listened. Outside was silence. There was no moon, and Le Loup's keen imagination pictured the dark slayer, Solomon Kane, gliding through the blackness, a shadow among shadows. He grinned crookedly; this time the Englishman would be foiled.

"There is a chest yet unopened," said he, pointing.

The Rat, with a muttered exclamation of surprize, bent over the chest indicated. With a single, catlike motion, the Wolf sprang upon him, sheathing his dagger to the hilt in the Rat's back, between the shoulders. The Rat sagged to the floor without a sound.

"Why divide the treasure two ways?" murmured Le Loup, wiping his blade upon the dead man's doublet. "Now for La Mon."

He stepped toward the door; then stopped and shrank back.

At first he thought that it was the shadow of a man who stood in the entrance; then he saw that it was a man himself, though so dark and still he stood that a fantastic semblance of shadow was lent him by the guttering candle.

A tall man, as tall as Le Loup he was, clad in black from head to foot, in plain, close-fitting garments that somehow suited the somber face. Long arms and broad shoulders betokened the swordsman, as plainly as the long rapier in his hand. The features of the man were saturnine and gloomy. A kind of dark pallor lent him a ghostly appearance in the uncertain light, an effect heightened by the satanic darkness of his lowering brows. Eyes, large, deep-set and unblinking, fixed their gaze upon the bandit, and looking into them, Le Loup was unable to decide what color they were. Strangely, the Mephistophelean trend of the lower features was offset by a high, broad forehead, though this was partly hidden by a featherless hat.

That forehead marked the dreamer, the idealist, the introvert, just as the eyes and the thin, straight nose betrayed the fanatic. An observer would have been struck by the eyes of the two men who stood there, facing each other. Eyes of both betokened untold deeps of power, but there the resemblance ceased.

The eyes of the bandit were hard, almost opaque, with a curious scintillant shallowness that reflected a thousand changing lights and gleams, like some strange gem; there was mockery in those eyes, cruelty and recklessness.

The eyes of the man in black, on the other hand, deepset and staring from under prominent brows, were cold but deep; gazing into them, one had the impression of looking into countless fathoms of ice.

Now the eyes clashed, and the Wolf, who was used to being feared, felt a strange coolness on his spine. The sensation was new to him – a new thrill to one who lived for thrills, and he laughed suddenly.

"You are Solomon Kane, I suppose?" he asked, managing to make his question sound politely incurious.

"I am Solomon Kane." The voice was resonant and powerful. "Are you prepared to meet your God?"

"Why, Monsieur," Le Loup answered, bowing, "I assure you I am as ready as I ever will be. I might ask Monsieur the same question."

"No doubt I stated my inquiry wrongly," Kane said grimly. "I will change it: Are you prepared to meet your master, the Devil?"

"As to that, Monsieur" – Le Loup examined his finger nails with elaborate unconcern – "I must say that I can at present render a most satisfactory account to his Horned Excellency, though really I have no intention of so doing – for a while at least."

Le Loup did not wonder as to the fate of La Mon; Kane's

presence in the cave was sufficient answer that did not need the trace of blood on his rapier to verify it.

"What I wish to know, Monsieur," said the bandit, "is why in the Devil's name have you harassed my band as you have, and how did you destroy that last set of fools?"

"Your last question is easily answered, sir," Kane replied. "I myself had the tale spread that the hermit possessed a store of gold, knowing that would draw your scum as carrion draws vultures. For days and nights I have watched the hut, and tonight, when I saw your villains coming, I warned the hermit, and together we went among the trees back of the hut. Then, when the rogues were inside, I struck flint and steel to the train I had laid, and flame ran through the trees like a red snake until it reached the powder I had placed beneath the hut floor. Then the hut and thirteen sinners went to hell in a great roar of flame and smoke. True, one escaped, but him I had slain in the forest had not I stumbled and fallen upon a broken root, which gave him time to elude me."

"Monsieur," said Le Loup with another low bow, "I grant you the admiration I must needs bestow on a brave and shrewd foeman. Yet tell me this: Why have you followed me as a wolf follows deer?"

"Some moons ago," said Kane, his frown becoming more menacing, "you and your fiends raided a small village down the valley. You know the details better than I. There was a girl there, a mere child, who, hoping to escape your lust, fled up the valley; but you, you jackal of hell, you caught her and left her, violated and dying. I found her there, and above her dead form I made up my mind to hunt you down and kill you."

"H'm," mused the Wolf. "Yes, I remember the wench. Mon Dieu, so the softer sentiments enter into the affair! Monsieur, I had not thought you an amorous man; be not jealous, good fellow, there are many more wenches."

"Le Loup, take care!" Kane exclaimed, a terrible menace in his voice, "I have never yet done a man to death by torture, but by God, sir, you tempt me!"

The tone, and more especially the unexpected oath, coming as it did from Kane, slightly sobered Le Loup; his eyes narrowed and his hand moved toward his rapier. The air was tense for an instant; then the Wolf relaxed elaborately.

"Who was the girl?" he asked idly. "Your wife?"

"I never saw her before," answered Kane.

"Nom d'un nom!" swore the bandit. "What sort of a man are you, Monsieur, who takes up a feud of this sort merely to avenge a wench unknown to you?"

"That, sir, is my own affair; it is sufficient that I do so."

Kane could not have explained, even to himself, nor did he ever seek an explanation within himself. A true fanatic, his promptings were reasons enough for his actions.

"You are right, Monsieur." Le Loup was sparring now for time; casually he edged backward inch by inch, with such consummate acting skill that he aroused no suspicion even in the hawk who watched him. "Monsieur," said he, "possibly you will say that you are merely a noble cavalier, wandering about like a true Galahad, protecting the weaker; but you and I know different. There on the floor is the equivalent to an emperor's ransom. Let us divide it peaceably; then if you like not my company, why – nom d'un nom! – we can go our separate ways."

Kane leaned forward, a terrible brooding threat growing in his cold eyes. He seemed like a great condor about to launch himself upon his victim.

"Sir, do you assume me to be as great a villain as yourself?"

Suddenly Le Loup threw back his head, his eyes dancing and leaping with a wild mockery and a kind of insane recklessness. His shout of laughter sent the echoes flying.

"Gods of hell! No, you fool, I do not class you with myself! Mon Dieu, Monsieur Kane, you have a task indeed if you intend to avenge all the wenches who have known my favors!"

"Shades of death! Shall I waste time in parleying with this base scoundrel!" Kane snarled in a voice suddenly blood-thirsting, and his lean frame flashed forward like a bent bow suddenly released.

At the same instant Le Loup with a wild laugh bounded backward with a movement as swift as Kane's. His timing was perfect; his back-flung hands struck the table and hurled it aside, plunging the cave into darkness as the candle toppled and went out.

Kane's rapier sang like an arrow in the dark as he thrust blindly and ferociously.

"Adieu, Monsieur Galahad!" The taunt came from somewhere in front of him, but Kane, plunging toward the sound with the savage fury of baffled wrath, caromed against a blank wall that did not yield to his blow. From somewhere seemed to come an echo of a mocking laugh.

Kane whirled, eyes fixed on the dimly outlined entrance, thinking his foe would try to slip past him and out of the cave; but no form bulked there, and when his groping hands found the candle and lighted it, the cave was empty, save for himself and the dead men on the floor.

III
The Chant of the Drums

Across the dusky waters the whisper came: boom, boom, boom! – a sullen reiteration. Far away and more faintly sounded a whisper of different timbre: thrum, throom, thrum! Back and forth went the vibrations as the throbbing drums spoke to each other. What tales did they carry? What monstrous secrets whispered across the sullen, shadowy reaches of the unmapped jungle?

"This, you are sure, is the bay where the Spanish ship put in?"

"Yes, Senhor; the negro swears this is the bay where the white man left the ship alone and went into the jungle."

Kane nodded grimly.

"Then put me ashore here, alone. Wait seven days; then if I have not returned and if you have no word of me, set sail wherever you will."

"Yes, Senhor."

The waves slapped lazily against the sides of the boat that carried Kane ashore. The village that he sought was on the river bank but set back from the bay shore, the jungle hiding it from sight of the ship.

Kane had adopted what seemed the most hazardous

course, that of going ashore by night, for the reason that he knew, if the man he sought were in the village, he would never reach it by day. As it was, he was taking a most desperate chance in daring the nighttime jungle, but all his life he had been used to taking desperate chances. Now he gambled his life upon the slim chance of gaining the negro village under cover of darkness and unknown to the villagers.

At the beach he left the boat with a few muttered commands, and as the rowers put back to the ship which lay anchored some distance out in the bay, he turned and engulfed himself in the blackness of the jungle. Sword in one hand, dagger in the other, he stole forward, seeking to keep pointed in the direction from which the drums still muttered and grumbled.

He went with the stealth and easy movement of a leopard, feeling his way cautiously, every nerve alert and straining, but the way was not easy. Vines tripped him and slapped him in the face, impeding his progress; he was forced to grope his way between the huge boles of towering trees, and all through the underbrush about him sounded vague and menacing rustlings and shadows of movement. Thrice his foot touched something that moved beneath it and writhed away, and once he glimpsed the baleful glimmer of feline eyes among the trees. They vanished, however, as he advanced.

Thrum, thrum, thrum, came the ceaseless monotone of the drums: war and death (they said); blood and lust; human sacrifice and human feast! The soul of Africa (said the drums); the spirit of the jungle; the chant of the gods of outer darkness, the gods that roar and gibber, the gods men knew when dawns were young, beast-eyed, gaping-mouthed, huge-bellied, bloody-handed, the Black Gods (sang the drums).

All this and more the drums roared and bellowed to Kane

as he worked his way through the forest. Somewhere in his soul a responsive chord was smitten and answered. You too are of the night (sang the drums); there is the strength of darkness, the strength of the primitive in you; come back down the ages; let us teach you, let us teach you (chanted the drums).

Kane stepped out of the thick jungle and came upon a plainly defined trail. Beyond, through the trees came the gleam of the village fires, flames glowing through the palisades. Kane walked down the trail swiftly.

He went silently and warily, sword extended in front of him, eyes straining to catch any hint of movement in the darkness ahead, for the trees loomed like sullen giants on each hand; sometimes their great branches intertwined above the trail and he could see only a slight way ahead of him.

Like a dark ghost he moved along the shadowed trail; alertly he stared and harkened; yet no warning came first to him, as a great, vague bulk rose up out of the shadows and struck him down, silently.

IV
THE BLACK GOD

Thrum, thrum, thrum! Somewhere, with deadening monotony, a cadence was repeated, over and over, bearing out the same theme: "Fool – fool – fool!" Now it was far away, now he could stretch out his hand and almost reach it. Now it merged with the throbbing in his head until the two vibrations were as one: "Fool – fool – fool – fool –"

The fogs faded and vanished. Kane sought to raise his hand to his head, but found that he was bound hand and foot. He lay on the floor of a hut – alone? He twisted about to view the place. No, two eyes glimmered at him from the darkness. Now a form took shape, and Kane, still mazed, believed that he looked on the man who had struck him unconscious. Yet no; this man could never strike such a blow. He was lean, withered and wrinkled. The only thing that seemed alive about him were his eyes, and they seemed like the eyes of a snake.

The man squatted on the floor of the hut, near the doorway, naked save for a loin-cloth and the usual paraphernalia of bracelets, anklets and armlets. Weird fetishes of ivory, bone and hide, animal and human, adorned his arms and legs. Suddenly and unexpectedly he spoke in English.

"Ha, you wake, white man? Why you come here, eh?"

Kane asked the inevitable question, following the habit of the Caucasian.

"You speak my language – how is that?"

The black man grinned.

"I slave – long time, me boy. Me, N'Longa, ju-ju man, me, great fetish. No black man like me! You white man, you hunt brother?"

Kane snarled. "I! Brother! I seek a man, yes."

The negro nodded. "Maybe so you find um, eh?"

"He dies!"

Again the negro grinned. "Me pow'rful ju-ju man," he announced apropos of nothing. He bent closer. "White man you hunt, eyes like a leopard, eh? Yes? Ha! ha! ha! ha! Listen,

white man: man-with-eyes-of-a-leopard, he and Chief Songa
make pow'rful palaver; they blood brothers now. Say nothing,
I help you; you help me, eh?"

"Why should you help me?" asked Kane suspiciously.

The ju-ju man bent closer and
whispered, "White man Songa's right-
hand man; Songa more pow'rful than
N'Longa. White man mighty ju-ju!
N'Longa's white brother kill man-
with-eyes-of-a-leopard, be blood
brother to N'Longa, N'Longa be
more pow'rful than Songa; palaver
set."

And like a dusky ghost he floated
out of the hut so swiftly that Kane was
not sure but that the whole affair was
a dream.

Without, Kane could see the flare of fires. The drums
were still booming, but close at hand the tones merged and
mingled, and the impulse-producing vibrations were lost. All
seemed a barbaric clamor without rime or reason, yet there
was an undertone of mockery there, savage and gloating.
"Lies," thought Kane, his mind still swimming, "jungle lies
like jungle women that lure a man to his doom."

Two warriors entered the hut – black giants, hideous with
paint and armed with crude spears. They lifted the white man
and carried him out of the hut. They bore him across an open
space, leaned him upright against a post and bound him there.
About him, behind him and to the side, a great semicircle of
black faces leered and faded in the firelight as the flames leaped
and sank. There in front of him loomed a shape hideous and
obscene – a black, formless thing, a grotesque parody of the
human. Still, brooding, blood-stained, like the formless soul of
Africa, the horror, the Black God.

And in front and to each side, upon roughly carven thrones of teakwood, sat two men. He who sat upon the right was a black man, huge, ungainly, a gigantic and unlovely mass of dusky flesh and muscles. Small, hoglike eyes blinked out over sin-marked cheeks; huge, flabby red lips pursed in fleshly haughtiness.

The other –

"Ah, Monsieur, we meet again." The speaker was far from being the debonair villain who had taunted Kane in the cavern among the mountains. His clothes were rags; there were more lines in his face; he had sunk lower in the years that had passed. Yet his eyes still gleamed and danced with their old recklessness and his voice held the same mocking timbre.

"The last time I heard that accursed voice," said Kane calmly, "was in a cave, in darkness, whence you fled like a hunted rat."

"Aye, under different conditions," answered Le Loup imperturbably. "What did you do after blundering about like an elephant in the dark?"

Kane hesitated, then: "I left the mountain –"

"By the front entrance? Yes? I might have known you were too stupid to find the secret door. Hoofs of the Devil, had you thrust against the chest with the golden lock, which stood

against the wall, the door had opened to you and revealed the secret passageway through which I went."

"I traced you to the nearest port and there took ship and followed you to Italy, where I found you had gone."

"Aye, by the saints, you nearly cornered me in Florence. Ho! ho! ho! I was climbing through a back window while Monsieur Galahad was battering down the front door of the tavern. And had your horse not gone lame, you would have caught up with me on the road to Rome. Again, the ship on which I left Spain had barely put out to sea when Monsieur Galahad rides up to the wharfs. Why have you followed me like this? I do not understand."

"Because you are a rogue whom it is my destiny to kill," answered Kane coldly. He did not understand. All his life he had roamed about the world aiding the weak and fighting oppression, he neither knew nor questioned why. That was his obsession, his driving force of life. Cruelty and tyranny to the weak sent a red blaze of fury, fierce and lasting, through his soul. When the full flame of his hatred was wakened and loosed, there was no rest for him until his vengeance had been fulfilled to the uttermost. If he thought of it at all, he considered himself a fulfiller of God's judgment, a vessel of wrath to be emptied upon the souls of the unrighteous. Yet in the full sense of the word Solomon Kane was not wholly a Puritan, though he thought of himself as such.

Le Loup shrugged his shoulders. "I could understand had I wronged you personally. Mon Dieu! I, too, would follow an enemy across the world, but, though I would have joyfully slain and robbed you, I never heard of you until you declared war on me."

Kane was silent, his still fury overcoming him. Though he did not realize it, the Wolf was more than merely an enemy to

him; the bandit symbolized, to Kane, all the things against which the Puritan had fought all his life: cruelty, outrage, oppression and tyranny.

Le Loup broke in on his vengeful meditations. "What did you do with the treasure, which – gods of Hades! – took me years to accumulate? Devil take it, I had time only to snatch a handful of coins and trinkets as I ran."

"I took such as I needed to hunt you down. The rest I gave to the villages which you had looted."

"Saints and the devil!" swore Le Loup. "Monsieur, you are the greatest fool I have yet met. To throw that vast treasure – by Satan, I rage to think of it in the hands of base peasants, vile villagers! Yet, ho! ho! ho! ho! they will steal, and kill each other for it! That is human nature."

"Yes, damn you!" flamed Kane suddenly, showing that his conscience had not been at rest. "Doubtless they will, being fools. Yet what could I do? Had I left it there, people might have starved and gone naked for lack of it. More, it would have been found, and theft and slaughter would have followed anyway. You are to blame, for had this treasure been left with its rightful owners, no such trouble would have ensued."

The Wolf grinned without reply. Kane not being a profane man, his rare curses had double effect and always startled his hearers, no matter how vicious or hardened they might be.

It was Kane who spoke next. "Why have you fled from me across the world? You do not really fear me."

"No, you are right. Really I do not know; perhaps flight is a habit which is difficult to break. I made my mistake when I did not kill you that night in the mountains. I am sure I could kill you in a fair fight, yet I have never even, ere now, sought to ambush you. Somehow I have not had a liking to meet you, Monsieur – a whim of mine, a mere whim. Then –

mon Dieu! – mayhap I have enjoyed a new sensation – and I had thought that I had exhausted the thrills of life. And then, a man must either be the hunter or the hunted. Until now, Monsieur, I was the hunted, but I grew weary of the role – I thought I had thrown you off the trail."

"A negro slave, brought from this vicinity, told a Portugal ship captain of a white man who landed from a Spanish ship and went into the jungle. I heard of it and hired the ship, paying the captain to bring me here."

"Monsieur, I admire you for your attempt, but you must admire me, too! Alone I came into this village, and alone among savages and cannibals I – with some slight knowledge of the language learned from a slave aboard ship – I gained the confidence of King Songa and supplanted that mummer, N'Longa. I am a braver man than you, Monsieur, for I had no ship to retreat to, and a ship is waiting for you."

"I admire your courage," said Kane, "but you are content to rule amongst cannibals – you the blackest soul of them all. I intend to return to my own people when I have slain you."

"Your confidence would be admirable were it not amusing. Ho, Gulka!"

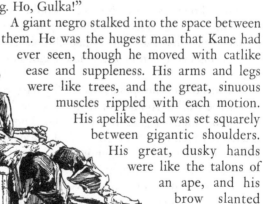

A giant negro stalked into the space between them. He was the hugest man that Kane had ever seen, though he moved with catlike ease and suppleness. His arms and legs were like trees, and the great, sinuous muscles rippled with each motion. His apelike head was set squarely between gigantic shoulders. His great, dusky hands were like the talons of an ape, and his brow slanted back from above bestial eyes. Flat nose and great, thick red lips completed this picture of primitive, lustful savagery.

"That is Gulka, the gorilla-slayer," said Le Loup. "He it was who lay in wait beside the trail and smote you down. You are like a wolf, yourself, Monsieur Kane, but since your ship hove in sight you have been watched by many eyes, and had you had all the powers of a leopard, you had not seen Gulka nor heard him. He hunts the most terrible and crafty of all beasts, in their native forests, far to the north, the beasts-who-walk-like-men — as that one, whom he slew some days since."

Kane, following Le Loup's fingers, made out a curious, manlike thing, dangling from a roof-pole of a hut. A jagged end thrust through the thing's body held it there. Kane could scarcely distinguish its characteristics by the firelight, but there was a weird, humanlike semblance about the hideous, hairy thing.

"A female gorilla that Gulka slew and brought to the village," said Le Loup.

The giant black slouched close to Kane and stared into the white man's eyes. Kane returned his gaze somberly, and presently the negro's eyes dropped sullenly and he slouched back a few paces. The look in the Puritan's grim eyes had pierced the primitive hazes of the gorilla-slayer's soul, and for the first time in his life he felt fear. To throw this off, he tossed a challenging look about; then, with unexpected animalness, he struck his huge chest resoundingly, grinned cavernously and flexed his mighty arms. No one spoke. Primordial bestiality had the stage, and the more highly developed types looked on with various feelings of amusement, tolerance or contempt.

Gulka glanced furtively at Kane to see if the white man was watching him, then with a sudden beastly roar, plunged forward and dragged a man from the semicircle. While the trembling victim screeched for mercy, the giant hurled him upon the crude altar before the shadowy idol. A spear rose and flashed, and the screeching ceased. The Black God looked on, his monstrous features seeming to leer in the flickering firelight. He had drunk; was the Black God pleased with the draft – with the sacrifice?

Gulka stalked back, and stopping before Kane, flourished the bloody spear before the white man's face.

Le Loup laughed. Then suddenly N'Longa appeared. He came from nowhere in particular; suddenly he was standing there, beside the post to which Kane was bound. A lifetime of study of the art of illusion had given the ju-ju man a highly technical knowledge of appearing and disappearing – which after all, consisted only in timing the audience's attention.

He waved Gulka aside with a grand gesture, and the gorilla-man slunk back, apparently to get out of N'Longa's gaze – then with incredible swiftness he turned and struck the ju-ju man a terrific blow upon the side of the head with his open hand. N'Longa went down like a felled ox, and in an instant he had been seized and bound to a post close to Kane. An uncertain murmuring rose from the negroes, which died out as King Songa stared angrily toward them.

Le Loup leaned back upon his throne and laughed uproariously.

"The trail ends here, Monsieur Galahad. That ancient fool thought I did not know of his plotting! I was hiding outside the hut and heard the interesting conversation you two had. Ha! ha! ha! ha! The Black God must drink,

Monsieur, but I have persuaded Songa to have you two burnt; that will be much more enjoyable, though we shall have to forego the usual feast, I fear. For after the fires are lit about your feet the devil himself could not keep your carcasses from becoming charred frames of bone."

Songa shouted something imperiously, and blacks came bearing wood, which they piled about the feet of N'Longa and Kane. The ju-ju man had recovered consciousness, and he now shouted something in his native language. Again the murmuring arose among the shadowy throng. Songa snarled something in reply.

Kane gazed at the scene almost impersonally. Again, somewhere in his soul, dim primal deeps were stirring, age-old thought memories, veiled in the fogs of lost eons. He had been here before, thought Kane; he knew all this of old – the lurid flames beating back the sullen night, the bestial faces leering expectantly, and the god, the Black God, there in the shadows! Always the Black God, brooding back in the shadows. He had known the shouts, the frenzied chant of the worshipers, back there in the gray dawn of the world, the speech of the bellowing drums, the singing priests, the repellent, inflaming, all-pervading scent of freshly spilt blood. All this have I known, somewhere, sometime, thought Kane; now I am the main actor –

He became aware that someone was speaking to him through the roar of the drums; he had not realized that the drums had begun to boom again. The speaker was N'Longa:

"Me pow'rful ju-ju man! Watch now: I work mighty magic. Songa!" His voice rose in a screech that drowned out the wildly clamoring drums.

Songa grinned at the words N'Longa screamed at him. The chant of the drums now had dropped to a low, sinister monotone and Kane plainly heard Le Loup when he spoke:

"N'Longa says that he will now work that magic which it is death to speak, even. Never before has it been worked in the sight of living men; it is the nameless ju-ju magic. Watch closely, Monsieur; possibly we shall be further amused." The Wolf laughed lightly and sardonically.

A black man stooped, applying a torch to the wood about Kane's feet. Tiny jets of flame began to leap up and catch. Another bent to do the same with N'Longa, then hesitated. The ju-ju man sagged in his bonds; his head drooped upon his chest. He seemed dying.

Le Loup leaned forward, cursing, "Feet of the Devil! Is the scoundrel about to cheat us of our pleasure of seeing him writhe in the flames?"

The warrior gingerly touched the wizard and said something in his own language.

Le Loup laughed: "He died of fright. A great wizard, by the —"

His voice trailed off suddenly. The drums stopped as if the drummers had fallen dead simultaneously. Silence dropped like a fog upon the village and in the stillness Kane heard only the sharp crackle of the flames whose heat he was beginning to feel.

All eyes were turned upon the dead man upon the altar, *for the corpse had begun to move!*

First a twitching of a hand, then an aimless motion of an arm, a motion which gradually spread over the body and limbs. Slowly, with blind, uncertain gestures, the dead man turned upon his side, the trailing limbs found the earth. Then, horribly like something being born, like some frightful reptilian thing bursting the shell of non-existence, the corpse tottered and reared upright, standing on legs wide apart and stiffly braced, arms still making useless, infantile motions. Utter silence, save somewhere a man's quick breath sounded loud in the stillness.

Kane stared, for the first time in his life smitten speechless and thoughtless. To his Puritan mind this was Satan's hand manifested.

Le Loup sat on his throne, eyes wide and staring, hand still half raised in the careless gesture he was making when frozen into silence by the unbelievable sight. Songa sat beside him, mouth and eyes wide open, fingers making curious jerky motions upon the carved arms of the throne.

Now the corpse was upright, swaying on stiltlike legs,

body tilting far back until the sightless eyes seemed to stare straight into the red moon that was just rising over the black jungle. The thing tottered uncertainly in a wide, erratic half-circle, arms flung out grotesquely as if in balance, then swayed about to face the two thrones – and the Black God. A burning twig at Kane's feet cracked like the crash of a cannon in the tense silence. The horror thrust forth a black foot – it took a wavering step – another. Then with stiff, jerky and automatonlike steps, legs straddled far apart, the dead man came toward the two who sat in speechless horror to each side of the Black God.

"Ah-h-h!" from somewhere came the explosive sigh, from that shadowy semicircle where crouched the terror-fascinated worshipers. Straight on stalked the grim specter. Now it was within three strides of the thrones, and Le Loup, faced by fear for the first time in his bloody life, cringed back in his chair; while Songa, with a superhuman effort breaking the chains of horror that held him helpless, shattered the night with a wild scream and, springing to his feet, lifted a spear, shrieking and gibbering in wild menace. Then as the ghastly thing halted not its frightful advance, he hurled the spear with all the power of his great, black muscles, and the spear tore through the dead man's breast with a rending of flesh and bone. Not an instant halted the thing – for the dead die not – and Songa the king stood frozen, arms outstretched as if to fend off the terror.

An instant they stood so, leaping firelight and eery moonlight etching the scene forever in the minds of the beholders. The changeless staring eyes of the corpse looked full into the bulging eyes of Songa, where were reflected all the hells of horror. Then with a jerky motion the arms of the thing went out and up. The dead hands fell on Songa's shoulders. At the first touch, the king seemed to shrink and shrivel, and with a scream that was to haunt the dreams of every watcher through all the rest of time, Songa crumpled and fell, and the dead man reeled stiffly and fell with him. Motionless lay the two at the feet of the Black God, and to Kane's dazed mind it seemed that the idol's great, inhuman eyes were fixed upon them with terrible, still laughter.

At the instant of the king's fall, a great shout went up from the blacks, and Kane, with a clarity lent his subconscious mind by the depths of his hate, looked for Le Loup and saw him spring from his throne and vanish in the darkness. Then vision was blurred by a rush of black figures who swept into the space before the god. Feet knocked aside the blazing brands whose heat Kane had forgotten, and dusky hands freed him; others loosed the wizard's body and laid it upon the earth. Kane dimly understood that the blacks believed this thing to be the work of N'Longa, and that they connected the vengeance of the wizard with himself. He bent, laid a hand on the ju-ju man's shoulder. No doubt of it: he was dead, the flesh was already cold. He glanced at the other corpses. Songa was dead, too, and the thing that had slain him lay now without movement.

Kane started to

rise, then halted. Was he dreaming, or did he really feel a
sudden warmth in the dead flesh he touched? Mind reeling, he
again bent over the wizard's body, and slowly he felt
warmness steal over the limbs and the blood begin to flow
sluggishly through the veins again.

Then N'Longa opened his eyes and stared up into Kane's,
with the blank expression of a new-born babe. Kane watched,
flesh crawling, and saw the knowing, reptilian glitter come
back, saw the wizard's thick lips part in a wide grin. N'Longa
sat up, and a strange chant arose from the negroes.

Kane looked about. The blacks were all kneeling, swaying
their bodies to and fro, and in their shouts Kane caught the
word, "N'Longa!" repeated over and over in a kind of
fearsomely ecstatic refrain of terror and worship. As the
wizard rose, they all fell prostrate.

N'Longa nodded, as if in satisfaction.

"Great ju-ju – great fetish, me!" he announced to Kane.
"You see? My ghost go out – kill Songa – come back to me!
Great magic! Great fetish, me!"

Kane glanced at the Black God looming back in the
shadows, at N'Longa, who now flung out his arms toward the
idol as if in invocation.

I am everlasting (Kane thought the Black God said); I
drink, no matter who rules; chiefs, slayers, wizards, they pass
like the ghosts of dead men through the gray jungle; I stand,
I rule; I am the soul of the jungle (said the Black God).

Suddenly Kane came back from the illusory mists in
which he had been wandering. "The white man! Which way
did he flee?"

N'Longa shouted something. A score of dusky hands
pointed; from somewhere Kane's rapier was thrust out to
him. The fogs faded and vanished; again he was the avenger,
the scourge of the unrighteous; with the sudden volcanic
speed of a tiger he snatched the sword and was gone.

V
THE END OF THE RED TRAIL

Limbs and vines slapped against Kane's face. The oppressive steam of the tropic night rose like mist about him. The moon, now floating high above the jungle, limned the black shadows in its white glow and patterned the jungle floor in grotesque designs. Kane knew not if the man he sought was ahead of him, but broken limbs and trampled underbrush showed that some man had gone that way, some man who fled in haste, nor halted to pick his way. Kane followed these signs unswervingly. Believing in the justice of his vengeance, he did not doubt that the dim beings who rule men's destinies would finally bring him face to face with Le Loup.

Behind him the drums boomed and muttered. What a tale they had to tell this night! of the triumph of N'Longa, the death of the black king, the overthrow of the white-man-with-eyes-like-a-leopard, and a more darksome tale, a tale to be whispered in low, muttering vibrations: the nameless ju-ju.

Was he dreaming? Kane wondered as he hurried on. Was all this part of some foul magic? He had seen a dead man rise and slay and die again; he had seen a man die and come to life again. Did N'Longa in truth send his ghost, his soul, his life essence forth into the void, dominating a corpse to do his will? Aye, N'Longa died a real death there, bound to the torture stake, and he who lay dead on the altar rose and did as N'Longa would have done had he been free. Then, the unseen force animating the dead man fading, N'Longa had lived again.

Yes, Kane thought, he must admit it as a fact. Somewhere in the darksome reaches of jungle and river, N'Longa had stumbled upon the Secret – the Secret of controlling life and death, of overcoming the shackles and limitations of the flesh. How had this dark wisdom, born in the black and blood-stained shadows of this grim land, been given to the wizard? What sacrifice had been so pleasing to the Black Gods, what ritual so monstrous, as to make them give up the knowledge of this magic? And what thoughtless, timeless journeys had N'Longa taken, when he chose to send his ego, his ghost, through the far, misty countries, reached only by death?

There is wisdom in the shadows (brooded the drums), wisdom and magic; go into the darkness for wisdom; ancient magic shuns the light; we remember the lost ages (whispered the drums), ere man became wise and foolish; we remember the beast gods – the serpent gods and the ape gods and the nameless, the Black Gods, they who drank blood and whose voices roared through the shadowy hills, who feasted and lusted. The secrets of life and of death are theirs; we remember, we remember (sang the drums).

Kane heard them as he hastened on. The tale they told to

the feathered black warriors farther up the river, he could not translate; but they spoke to him in their own way, and that language was deeper, more basic.

The moon, high in the dark blue skies, lighted his way and gave him a clear vision as he came out at last into a glade and saw Le Loup standing there. The Wolf's naked blade was a long gleam of silver in the moon, and he stood with shoulders thrown back, the old, defiant smile still on his face.

"A long trail, Monsieur," said he. "It began in the mountains of France; it ends in an African jungle. I have wearied of the game at last, Monsieur – and you die. I had not fled from the village, even, save that – I admit it freely – that damnable witchcraft of N'Longa's shook my nerves. More, I saw that the whole tribe would turn against me."

Kane advanced warily, wondering what dim, forgotten tinge of chivalry in the bandit's soul had caused him thus to take his chance in the open. He half suspected treachery, but his keen eyes could detect no shadow of movement in the jungle on either side of the glade.

"Monsieur, on guard!" Le Loup's voice was crisp. "Time that we ended this fool's dance about the world. Here we are alone."

The men were now within reach of each other, and Le Loup, in the midst of his sentence, suddenly plunged forward with the speed of light, thrusting viciously. A slower man had died there, but Kane parried and sent his own blade in a silver streak that slit Le Loup's tunic as the Wolf bounded backward. Le Loup admitted the failure of his trick with a wild laugh and came in with the breath-taking speed and fury of a tiger, his blade making a white fan of steel about him.

Rapier clashed on rapier as the two swordsmen fought. They were fire and ice opposed. Le Loup fought wildly but craftily, leaving no openings, taking advantage of every opportunity. He was a living flame, bounding back, leaping in, feinting, thrusting, warding, striking – laughing like a wild man, taunting and cursing.

Kane's skill was cold, calculating, scintillant. He made no waste movement, no motion not absolutely necessary. He seemed to devote more time and effort toward defense than did Le Loup, yet there was no hesitancy in his attack, and when he thrust, his blade shot out with the speed of a striking snake.

There was little to choose between the men as to height, strength and reach. Le Loup was the swifter by a scant, flashing margin, but Kane's skill reached a finer point of perfection. The Wolf's fencing was fiery, dynamic, like the blast from a furnace. Kane was more steady – less the instinctive, more the thinking fighter, though he, too, was a born slayer, with the co-ordination that only a natural fighter possessed.

Thrust, parry, a feint, a sudden whirl of blades –

"Ha!" the Wolf sent up a shout of ferocious laughter as the blood started from a cut on Kane's cheek. As if the sight drove him to further fury, he attacked like the beast men named him. Kane was forced back before that blood-lusting onslaught, but the Puritan's expression did not alter.

Minutes flew by; the clang and clash of steel did not diminish. Now they stood squarely in the center of the glade, Le Loup untouched, Kane's garments red with the blood that oozed from wounds on cheek, breast, arm and thigh. The Wolf grinned savagely and mockingly in the moonlight, but he had begun to doubt.

His breath came hissing fast and his arm began to weary; who was this man of steel and ice who never seemed to weaken? Le Loup knew that the wounds he had inflicted on Kane were not deep, but even so, the steady flow of blood should have sapped some of the man's strength and speed by this time. But if Kane felt the ebb of his powers, it did not show. His brooding countenance did not change in expression, and he pressed the fight with as much cold fury as at the beginning.

Le Loup felt his might fading, and with one last desperate effort he rallied all his fury and strength into a single plunge. A sudden, unexpected attack too wild and swift for the eye to follow, a dynamic burst of speed and fury no man could have withstood, and Solomon Kane reeled for the first time as he felt cold steel tear through his body. He reeled back, and Le Loup, with a wild shout, plunged after him, his reddened sword free, a gasping taunt on his lips.

Kane's sword, backed by the force of desperation, met Le Loup's in midair; met, held and wrenched. The Wolf's yell of triumph died on his lips as his sword flew singing from his hand.

For a fleeting instant he stopped short, arms flung wide as a crucifix, and Kane heard his wild, mocking laughter peal forth for the last time, as the Englishman's rapier made a silver line in the moonlight.

Far away came the mutter of the drums. Kane mechanically cleansed his sword on his tattered garments. The trail ended here, and Kane was conscious of a strange feeling of futility. He always felt that, after he had killed a foe. Somehow it always seemed that no real good had been wrought; as if the foe had, after all, escaped his just vengeance.

With a shrug of his shoulders Kane turned his attention to his bodily needs. Now that the heat of battle had passed, he began to feel weak and faint from the loss of blood. That last thrust had been close; had he not managed to avoid its full point by a twist of his body, the blade had transfixed him. As it was, the sword had struck glancingly, plowed along his ribs and sunk deep in the muscles beneath the shoulder-blade, inflicting a long, shallow wound.

Kane looked about him and saw that a small stream trickled through the glade at the far side. Here he made the only mistake of that kind that he ever made in his entire life. Mayhap he was dizzy from loss of blood and still mazed from the weird happenings of the night; be that as it may, he laid down his rapier and crossed, weaponless, to the stream. There he laved his wounds and bandaged them as best he could, with strips torn from his clothing.

Then he rose and was about to retrace his steps when a motion among the trees on the side of the glade where he first entered, caught his eye. A huge figure stepped out of the jungle, and Kane saw, and recognized, his doom. The man was Gulka, the gorilla-slayer. Kane remembered that he had not seen the black among those doing homage to N'Longa. How could he know the craft and hatred in that dusky, slanting skull that had led the negro, escaping the vengeance of his tribesmen, to trail down the only man he had ever feared? The Black God had been kind to his neophyte; had led him upon his victim helpless and unarmed. Now Gulka could kill his man openly – and slowly, as a leopard kills, not smiting him down from ambush as he had planned, silently and suddenly.

A wide grin split the negro's face, and he moistened his lips. Kane, watching him, was coldly and deliberately weighing his chances. Gulka had already spied the rapiers. He was closer to them than was Kane. The Englishman knew that there was no chance of his winning in a sudden race for the swords.

A slow, deadly rage surged in him – the fury of helplessness. The blood churned in his temples and his eyes smoldered with a terrible light as he eyed the negro. His fingers spread and closed like claws. They were strong, those hands; men had died in their clutch. Even Gulka's huge black column of a neck might break like a rotten branch between them – a wave of weakness made the futility of these thoughts apparent to an extent that needed not the verification of the moonlight glimmering from the spear in Gulka's black hand. Kane could not even have fled had he wished – and he had never fled from a single foe.

The gorilla-slayer moved out into the glade. Massive, terrible, he was the personification of the primitive, the Stone Age. His mouth yawned in a red cavern of a grin; he bore himself with the haughty arrogance of savage might.

Kane tensed himself for the struggle that could end but

one way. He strove to rally his waning forces. Useless; he had lost too much blood. At least he would meet his death on his feet, and somehow he stiffened his buckling knees and held himself erect, though the glade shimmered before him in uncertain waves and the moonlight seemed to have become a red fog through which he dimly glimpsed the approaching black man.

Kane stooped, though the effort nearly pitched him on his face; he dipped water in his cupped hands and dashed it into his face. This revived him, and he straightened, hoping that Gulka would charge and get it over with before his weakness crumpled him to the earth.

Gulka was now about the center of the glade, moving with the slow, easy stride of a great cat stalking a victim. He was not at all in a hurry to consummate his purpose. He wanted to toy with his victim, to see fear come into those grim eyes which had looked him down, even when the possessor of those eyes had been bound to the death stake. He wanted to slay, at last, slowly, glutting his tigerish blood-lust and torture-lust to the fullest extent.

Then suddenly he halted, turned swiftly, facing another side of the glade. Kane, wondering, followed his glance.

At first it seemed like a blacker shadow among the jungle shadows. At first there was no motion, no sound, but Kane instinctively knew that some terrible menace lurked there in the darkness that masked and merged the silent trees. A sullen horror brooded there, and Kane felt as if, from that monstrous shadow, inhuman eyes seared his very soul. Yet simultaneously there came the fantastic sensation that these eyes were not directed on him. He looked at the gorilla-slayer.

The black man had apparently forgotten him; he stood, half crouching, spear lifted, eyes fixed upon that clump of blackness. Kane looked again. Now there was motion in the shadows; they merged fantastically and moved out into the glade, much as Gulka had done. Kane blinked: was this the illusion that precedes death? The shape he looked upon was such as he had visioned dimly in wild nightmares, when the wings of sleep bore him back through lost ages.

He thought at first it was some blasphemous mockery of a man, for it went erect and was tall as a tall man. But it was inhumanly broad and thick, and its gigantic arms hung nearly to its misshapen feet. Then the moonlight smote full upon its bestial face, and Kane's mazed mind thought that the thing was the Black God coming out of the shadows, animated and blood-lusting. Then he saw that it was covered with hair, and he remembered the manlike thing dangling from the roof-pole in the native village. He looked at Gulka.

The negro was facing the gorilla, spear at the charge. He was not afraid, but his sluggish mind was wondering over the miracle that brought this beast so far from his native jungles.

The mighty ape came out into the moonlight and there was a terrible majesty about his movements. He was nearer Kane than Gulka but he did not seem to be aware of the white man. His small, blazing eyes were fixed on the black man with terrible intensity. He advanced with a curious swaying stride.

Far away the drums whispered through the night, like an accompaniment to this grim Stone Age drama. The savage crouched in the middle of the glade, but the primordial came out of the jungle with eyes bloodshot and blood-lusting. The negro was face to face with a thing more primitive than he.

Again ghosts of memories whispered to Kane: you have seen such sights before (they murmured), back in the dim days, the dawn days, when beast and beast-man battled for supremacy.

Gulka moved away from the ape in a half-circle, crouching, spear ready. With all his craft he was seeking to trick the gorilla, to make a swift kill, for he had never before met such a monster as this, and though he did not fear, he had begun to doubt. The ape made no attempt to stalk or circle; he strode straight forward toward Gulka.

The black man who faced him and the white man who watched could not know the brutish love, the brutish hate that had driven the monster down from the low, forest-covered hills of the north to follow for leagues the trail of him who was the scourge of his kind – the slayer of his mate, whose body now hung from the roof-pole of the negro village.

The end came swiftly, almost like a sudden gesture. They were close, now, beast and beast-man; and suddenly, with an earth-shaking roar, the gorilla charged. A great hairy arm smote aside the thrusting spear, and the ape closed with the negro. There was a shattering sound as of many branches breaking simultaneously, and Gulka slumped silently to the earth, to lie with arms, legs and body flung in strange, unnatural positions. The ape towered an instant above him, like a statue of the primordial triumphant.

Far away Kane heard the drums murmur. The soul of the jungle, the soul of the jungle: this phrase surged through his mind with monotonous reiteration.

The three who had stood in power before the Black God that night, where were they? Back in the village where the drums rustled lay Songa – King Songa, once lord of life and death, now a shriveled corpse with a face set in a mask of horror. Stretched on his back in the middle of the glade lay he whom Kane had followed many a league by land and sea. And Gulka the gorilla-slayer lay at the feet of his killer, broken at last by the savagery which had made him a true son of this grim land which had at last overwhelmed him.

Yet the Black God still reigned, thought Kane dizzily, brooding back in the shadows of this dark country, bestial, blood-lusting, caring naught who lived or died, so that he drank.

Kane watched the mighty ape, wondering how long it would be before the huge simian spied and charged him. But the gorilla gave no evidence of having even seen him. Some dim impulse of vengeance yet unglutted prompting him, he bent and raised the negro. Then he slouched toward the jungle, Gulka's limbs trailing limply and grotesquely. As he reached the trees, the ape halted, whirling the giant form high in the air with seemingly no effort, and dashed the dead man up among the branches. There was a rending sound as a broken projecting limb tore through the body hurled so powerfully against it, and the dead gorilla-slayer dangled there hideously.

A moment the clear moon limned the great ape in its glimmer, as he stood silently gazing up at his victim; then like a dark shadow he melted noiselessly into the jungle.

Kane walked slowly to the middle of the glade and took up his rapier. The blood had ceased to flow from his wounds, and some of his strength was returning, enough, at least, for him to reach the coast where his ship awaited him. He halted at the edge of the glade for a backward glance at Le Loup's upturned face and still form, white in the moonlight, and at the dark shadow among the trees that was Gulka, left by some bestial whim, hanging as the she-gorilla hung in the village.

Afar the drums muttered: "The wisdom of our land is ancient; the wisdom of our land is dark; whom we serve, we destroy. Flee if you would live, but you will never forget our chant. Never, never," sang the drums.

Kane turned to the trail which led to the beach and the ship waiting there.

Rattle of Bones

Rattle of Bones

"Landlord, ho!" The shout broke the lowering silence and reverberated through the black forest with sinister echoing.

"This place hath a forbidding aspect, meseemeth."

Two men stood in front of the forest tavern. The building was low, long and rambling, built of heavy logs. Its small windows were heavily barred and the door was closed. Above the door its sinister sign showed faintly – a cleft skull.

This door swung slowly open and a bearded face peered out. The owner of the face stepped back and motioned his guests to enter – with a grudging gesture it seemed. A candle gleamed on a table; a flame smoldered in the fireplace.

"Your names?"

"Solomon Kane," said the taller man briefly.

"Gaston l'Armon," the other spoke curtly. "But what is that to you?"

"Strangers are few in the Black Forest," grunted the host, "bandits many. Sit at yonder table and I will bring food."

The two men sat down, with the bearing of men who have traveled far. One was a tall gaunt man, clad in a featherless hat and somber black garments, which set off the dark pallor of his forbidding face. The other was of a different type entirely, bedecked with lace and plumes, although his finery was somewhat stained from travel. He was handsome in a bold way, and his restless eyes shifted from side to side, never still an instant.

The host brought wine and food to the rough-hewn table and then stood back in the shadows, like a somber image. His features, now receding into vagueness, now luridly etched in the firelight as it leaped and flickered, were masked in a beard which seemed almost animal-like in thickness. A great nose curved above this beard and two small red eyes stared unblinkingly at his guests.

"Who are you?" suddenly asked the younger man.

"I am the host of the Cleft Skull Tavern," sullenly replied the other. His tone seemed to challenge his questioner to ask further.

"Do you have many guests?" l'Armon pursued.

"Few come twice," the host grunted. Kane started and glanced up straight into those small red eyes, as if he sought for some hidden meaning in the host's words. The flaming eyes seemed to dilate, then dropped sullenly before the Englishman's cold stare.

"I'm for bed," said Kane abruptly, bringing his meal to a close. "I must take up my journey by daylight."

"And I," added the Frenchman. "Host, show us to our chambers."

Black shadows wavered on the walls as the two followed their silent host down a long, dark hall. The stocky, broad body of their guide seemed to grow and expand in the light of the small candle which he carried, throwing a long, grim shadow behind him.

At a certain door he halted, indicating that they were to sleep there. They entered; the host lit a candle with the one he carried, then lurched back the way he had come.

In the chamber the two men glanced at each other. The only furnishings of the room were a couple of bunks, a chair or two and a heavy table.

"Let us see if there be any way to make fast the door," said Kane. "I like not the looks of mine host."

"There are racks on door and jamb for a bar," said Gaston, "but no bar."

"We might break up the table and use its pieces for a bar," mused Kane.

"Mon Dieu," said l'Armon, "you are timorous, m'sieu."

Kane scowled. "I like not being murdered in my sleep," he answered gruffly.

"My faith!" the Frenchman laughed. "We are chance met – until I overtook you on the forest road an hour before sunset, we had never seen each other."

"I have seen you somewhere before," answered Kane, "though I can not now recall where. As for the other, I assume every man is an honest fellow until he shows me he is a rogue; moreover, I am a light sleeper and slumber with a pistol at hand."

The Frenchman laughed again.

"I was wondering how m'sieu could bring himself to sleep in the room with a stranger! Ha! Ha! All right, m'sieu Englishman, let us go forth and take a bar from one of the other rooms."

Taking the candle with them, they went into the corridor. Utter silence reigned and the small candle twinkled redly and evilly in the thick darkness.

"Mine host hath neither guests nor servants," muttered Solomon Kane. "A strange tavern! What is the name, now?

These German words come not easily to me – the Cleft Skull? A bloody name, i'faith."

They tried the rooms next to theirs, but no bar rewarded their search. At last they came to the last room at the end of the corridor. They entered. It was furnished like the rest, except that the door was provided with a small barred opening, and fastened from the outside with a heavy bolt, which was secured at one end to the door-jamb. They raised the bolt and looked in.

"There should be an outer window, but there is not," muttered Kane. "Look!"

The floor was stained darkly. The walls and the one bunk were hacked in places, great splinters having been torn away.

"Men have died in here," said Kane, somberly. "Is yonder not a bar fixed in the wall?"

"Aye, but 'tis made fast," said the Frenchman, tugging at it. "The –"

A section of the wall swung back and Gaston gave a quick exclamation. A small, secret room was revealed, and the two men bent over the grisly thing that lay upon its floor.

"The skeleton of a man!" said Gaston. "And behold, how his bony leg is shackled to the floor! He was imprisoned here and died."

"Nay," said Kane, "the skull is cleft – methinks mine host had a grim reason for the name of his hellish tavern. This man, like us, was no doubt a wanderer who fell into the fiend's hands."

"Likely," said Gaston without interest; he was engaged in idly working the great iron ring from the skeleton's leg bones. Failing in this, he drew his sword and with an exhibition of remarkable strength cut the chain which joined the ring on the leg to a ring set deep in the log floor.

"Why should he shackle a skeleton to the floor?" mused

the Frenchman. "Monbleu! 'Tis a waste of good chain. Now, m'sieu," he ironically addressed the white heap of bones, "I have freed you and you may go where you like!"

"Have done!" Kane's voice was deep. "No good will come of mocking the dead."

"The dead should defend themselves," laughed l'Armon. "Somehow, I will slay the man who kills me, though my corpse climb up forty fathoms of ocean to do it."

Kane turned toward the outer door, closing the door of the secret room behind him. He liked not this talk which smacked of demonry and witchcraft; and he was in haste to face the host with the charge of his guilt.

As he turned, with his back to the Frenchman, he felt the touch of cold steel against his neck and knew that a pistol muzzle was pressed close beneath the base of his brain.

"Move not, m'sieu!" The voice was low and silky. "Move not, or I will scatter your few brains over the room."

The Puritan, raging inwardly, stood with his hands in the air while l'Armon slipped his pistols and sword from their sheaths.

"Now you can turn," said Gaston, stepping back.

Kane bent a grim eye on the dapper fellow, who stood bareheaded now, hat in one hand, the other hand leveling his long pistol.

"Gaston the Butcher!" said the Englishman somberly. "Fool that I was to trust a Frenchman! You range far, murderer! I remember you now, with that cursed great hat off – I saw you in Calais some years agone."

"Aye – and now you will see me never again. What was that?"

"Rats exploring yon skeleton," said Kane, watching the bandit like a hawk, waiting for a single slight wavering of that black gun muzzle. "The sound was of the rattle of bones."

"Like enough," returned the other. "Now, M'sieu Kane, I know you carry considerable money on your person. I had thought to wait until you slept and then slay you, but the opportunity presented itself and I took it. You trick easily."

"I had little thought that I should fear a man with whom I had broken bread," said Kane, a deep timbre of slow fury sounding in his voice.

The bandit laughed cynically. His eyes narrowed as he began to back slowly toward the outer door. Kane's sinews tensed involuntarily; he gathered himself like a giant wolf about to launch himself in a death leap, but Gaston's hand was like a rock and the pistol never trembled.

"We will have no death plunges after the shot," said Gaston. "Stand still, m'sieu; I have seen men killed by dying men, and I wish to have distance enough between us to preclude that possibility. My faith – I will shoot, you will roar and charge, but you will die before you reach me with your bare hands. And mine host will have another skeleton in his secret niche. That is, if I do not kill him myself. The fool knows me not nor I him, moreover –"

The Frenchman was in the doorway now, sighting along the barrel. The candle, which had been stuck in a niche on the wall, shed a weird and flickering light which did not extend past the doorway. And with the suddenness of death, from the darkness behind Gaston's back, a broad, vague form rose up and a gleaming blade swept down. The Frenchman went to his knees like a butchered ox, his brains spilling from his cleft skull. Above him towered the figure of the host, a wild and terrible spectacle, still holding the hanger with which he had slain the bandit.

"Ho! ho!" he roared. "Back!"

Kane had leaped forward as Gaston fell, but the host thrust into his very face a long pistol which he held in his left hand.

"Back!" he repeated in a tigerish roar, and Kane retreated from the menacing weapon and the insanity in the red eyes.

The Englishman stood silent, his flesh crawling as he sensed a deeper and more hideous threat than the Frenchman had offered. There was something inhuman about this man, who now swayed to and fro like some great forest beast while his mirthless laughter boomed out again.

"Gaston the Butcher!" he shouted, kicking the corpse at his feet. "Ho! ho! My fine brigand will hunt no more! I had heard of this fool who roamed the Black Forest – he wished gold and he found death! Now your gold shall be mine; and more than gold – vengeance!"

"I am no foe of yours," Kane spoke calmly.

"All men are my foes! Look – the marks on my wrists! See – the marks on my ankles! And deep in my back – the kiss of the knout! And deep in my brain, the wounds of the years of the cold, silent cells where I lay as punishment for a crime I never committed!" The voice broke in a hideous, grotesque sob.

Kane made no answer. This man was not the first he had seen whose brain had shattered amid the horrors of the terrible Continental prisons.

"But I escaped!" the scream rose triumphantly, "and here I make war on all men. . . . What was that?"

Did Kane see a flash of fear in those hideous eyes?

"My sorcerer is rattling his bones!" whispered the host,

then laughed wildly. "Dying, he swore his very bones would weave a net of death for me. I shackled his corpse to the floor, and now, deep in the night, I hear his bare skeleton clash and rattle as he seeks to be free, and I laugh, I laugh! Ho! ho! How he yearns to rise and stalk like old King Death along these dark corridors when I sleep, to slay me in my bed!"

Suddenly the insane eyes flared hideously: "You were in that secret room, you and this dead fool! Did he talk to you?"

Kane shuddered in spite of himself. Was it insanity or did he actually hear the faint rattle of bones, as if the skeleton had moved slightly? Kane shrugged his shoulders; rats will even tug at dusty bones.

The host was laughing again. He sidled around Kane, keeping the Englishman always covered, and with his free hand opened the door. All was darkness within, so that Kane could not even see the glimmer of the bones on the floor.

"All men are my foes!" mumbled the host, in the incoherent manner of the insane. "Why should I spare any man? Who lifted a hand to my aid when I lay for years in the vile dungeons of Karlsruhe – and for a deed never proven? Something happened to my brain, then. I became as a wolf – a brother to these of the Black Forest to which I fled when I escaped.

"They have feasted, my brothers, on all who lay in my tavern – all except this one who now clashes his bones, this magician from Russia. Lest he come stalking back through the black shadows when night is over the world, and slay me – for who may slay the dead? – I stripped his bones and shackled him. His sorcery was not powerful enough to save him from me, but all men know that a dead magician is more evil than a living one. Move not, Englishman! Your bones I shall leave in this secret room beside this one, to –"

The maniac was standing partly in the doorway of the secret room, now, his weapon still menacing Kane. Suddenly he seemed to topple backward, and vanished in the darkness; and at the same instant a vagrant gust of wind swept down the outer corridor and slammed the door shut behind him. The candle on the wall flickered and went out. Kane's groping hands, sweeping over the floor, found a pistol, and he straightened, facing the door where the maniac had vanished. He stood in the utter darkness, his blood freezing, while a hideous muffled screaming came from the secret room, intermingled with the dry, grisly rattle of fleshless bones. Then silence fell.

Kane found flint and steel and lighted the candle. Then, holding it in one hand and the pistol in the other, he opened the secret door.

"Great God!" he muttered as cold sweat formed on his body. "This thing is beyond all reason, yet with mine own eyes I see it! Two vows have here been kept, for Gaston the Butcher swore that even in death he would avenge his slaying, and his was the hand which set yon fleshless monster free. And he –"

The host of the Cleft Skull lay lifeless on the floor of the secret room, his bestial face set in lines of terrible fear; and deep in his broken neck were sunk the bare fingerbones of the sorcerer's skeleton.

The Castle of the Devil

(Fragment)

The Castle of the Devil

A rider was singing down the forest trail in the growing twilight, keeping time to his horse's easy jog. He was a tall rangy man, broad of shoulder and deep of chest with keen restless eyes which seemed at once to challenge and mock.

"Hola!" he drew his horse to a sudden stop and looked down curiously at the man who rose from his seat on a stone beside the road. This man was even taller than the rider – a lean somber man clad in plain dark garments, his features a dark pallor.

"An Englishman? And a Puritan by the cut o' that garb," commented the man on the horse. "I am glad to see a countryman in this outlandish domain, even such a melancholy fellow as you seem. My name is John Silent and I am bound for Genoa."

"I am Solomon Kane," the other answered in a deep measured voice. "I am a wanderer on the face of the earth and have no destination."

John Silent frowned down at the Puritan in puzzlement. The deep cold eyes gazed back at him unswerving.

"Name of the Devil, man, know you not whither you are bound at the present?"

"Wherever the spirit moves me to go," answered Solomon. "Just now I find myself in this wild and desolate country through which I journey, doubtless hither drawn for some purpose yet unknown to me."

Silent sighed and shook his head.

"Mount behind me, man, and we will at least seek some tavern in which to spend the night."

"I would not overtax your steed, good sir, but if you will permit I will walk along by your side and converse with you, for it is many a month since I have heard good English speech."

As they went slowly down the trail, John Silent still gazed down at the man, noting the stride that was long and cat-like in spite of Kane's lank build, and the long rapier which hung at his hip. Silent's hand instinctively touched the long curved hanger in his own belt.

"Do you mean to tell me that you journey through the countries of the world with no goal in view, caring not where you may be?"

"Sir, what matters it where a man be if he is carrying out God's plan for him?"

"By Jove," swore John Silent, "you are even more wayward than I, for though I rove the world also, I always have some goal in mind. As now I come from the command of a troop of soldiery and am going to Genoa to go on board a ship which sails against the Turkish corsairs. Come with me, friend, and learn to sail the seas."

"I have sailed them and found them to be little to my liking. Many who call themselves honest merchantmen be naught but bloody pirates."

John Silent hid his grin and changed the subject.

"Then since the spirit has moved you to traverse this land, 'tis like you have found something to your liking herein."

"No, good sir, I find little here but starving peasants, cruel lords and lawless men. Yet 'tis like that I have done somewhat of good, for only a few hours agone I came upon a wretch who hung on a gallows and cut him down ere his breath had passed from him."

John Silent nearly fell out of his saddle.

"What! You cut down a man from Baron
Von Staler's gibbet? Name of the Devil, you
will have both our necks in a noose!"

"You should not curse so hotly,"
Solomon reproved mildly. "I know not
this Baron Von Staler, but methinks
he had hanged a man unjustly.
The victim was only a boy and
he had a good face."

"And forsooth," said John
Silent angrily, "you must risk
our lives by saving his worthless
one, which was already doomed."

"What else was there to do?" asked
Kane with a touch of impatience. "I beg you,
vex me no more on the subject but tell me whose
castle it is that I see rising above the trees."

"One which you may come to know much more
thoroughly if we make not haste," Silent answered grimly.
"That is the keep of Baron Von Staler, whose gibbet you
robbed, and who is the most powerful lord in the Black
Forest. There goes the path which leads up the steep to his
door; here is the road which we take – the one that leads us
quickest and furtherest out of the good Baron's reach."

"Methinks that is the castle which the peasants have
spoken to me of," mused Kane. "They call it an unsavory
name – the Castle of the Devil. Come, let us look into the
matter."

"You mean go up to the castle?" cried Silent, staring.

"Aye, sir. The Baron will scarce refuse two wayfarers a
lodging. More, we can ascertain what sort of a man he is. I
would like to see this lord who hangs children."

"And if you like him not?" asked Silent sarcastically.

Kane sighed. "It has fallen upon me, now and again in my sojourns through the world, to ease various evil men of their lives. I have a feeling that it will prove thus with the Baron."

"Name of two devils!" swore Silent in amazement. "You speak as if you were a judge on a bench and Baron Von Staler bound helpless before you, instead of being as it is – you but one blade and the Baron surrounded by lusty men-at-arms."

"The right is on my side," said Kane somberly. "And right is mightier than a thousand men-at-arms. But why all this talk? I have not yet seen the Baron, and who am I to pass judgment unseen. Mayhap the Baron is a righteous man."

Silent shook his head in wonder.

"You are either an inspired maniac, a fool, or the most courageous man in the world!" he laughed suddenly. "Lead on! 'Tis a wild venture that's like to end in death, but its insanity appeals to me and no man can say that John Silent fails to follow where another man leads!"

"Your speech is wild and Godless," said Kane, "but I begin to like you."

"*It has fallen upon me, now and again in my sojourns through the world,
to ease various evil men of their lives.*"

Death's Black Riders

(Fragment)

Death's Black Riders

The hangman asked of the carrion crow,
 but the raven made reply:
"Black ride the men who ride with Death
 beneath the midnight sky,
"And black each steed and grey each skull
 and strange each deathly eye.
"They have given their breath to grey old Death
 and yet they cannot die."

Solomon Kane reined his steed to a halt. No sound broke the death-like stillness of the dark forest which reared starkly about him; yet he sensed that Something was coming down the shadowy trail. It was a strange and ghastly place. The huge trees shouldered each other like taciturn giants, and their intertwining branches shut out the light; so that the white moonlight turned grey as it filtered through, and the trail which meandered among the trees seemed like a dim road through ghostland.

And down this trail, as Solomon Kane halted and drew his pistol, a horseman came flying. A great black horse, incredibly gigantic in the grey light, and on his back a giant of a rider, crouched close over the bow, a shapeless hat drawn low, a great black cloak flying from his shoulders.

Solomon Kane sought to rein aside to let this wild rider go past, but the trail was so narrow and the trees grew so thickly on either side, that he saw it was impossible unless the horseman stopped and gave him time to find an open space. And this the stranger seemed to have no intention of doing.

They swept on, horse and rider a single formless black object like some fabulous monster; now they were only a few strides from the puzzled Kane, and he caught the glint of two burning eyes shadowed by the hat drawn low and the cape

held high about the rider's face. Then as he saw the gleam of
a sword, he fired pointblank into that face. Then a blast of icy
air engulfed him like the surge of a cold river, horse and man
went down together, and the black horse and its rider swept
over them.

Kane scrambled up, unhurt but wrathful, and examined
his snorting, quivering steed, which had risen and stood with
dilated nostrils. The horse, too, was unharmed. Kane could
not understand it.

The Moon of Skulls

The Moon of Skulls

"The wise men know what wicked things
Are written on the sky;
They trim sad lamps, they touch sad strings
Hearing the heavy purple wings,
Where the forgotten Seraph kings
Still plot how God shall die."
                                    CHESTERTON

I
A MAN COMES SEEKING

A great black shadow lay across the land, cleaving the red flame of the sunset. To the man who toiled up the jungle trail it loomed like a symbol of death and horror, a menace brooding and terrible, like the shadow of a stealthy assassin flung upon some candle-lit wall.

Yet it was only the shadow of the great crag which reared up in front of him, the first outpost of the grim foothills which were his goal. He halted a moment at its foot, staring upward where it rose blackly limned against the dying sun. He could have sworn that he caught the hint of a movement at the top, as he stared, hand shielding his eyes, but the fading glare dazzled him and he could not be sure. Was it a man who darted to cover? A man, or –?

He shrugged his shoulders and fell to examining the rough trail which led up and over the brow of the crag. At first glance it seemed that only a mountain goat could scale it, but closer investigation showed numbers of fingerholds drilled into the solid rock. It would be a task to try his powers to the utmost but he had not come a thousand miles to turn back now.

He dropped the large pouch he wore at his shoulder, and laid down the clumsy musket, retaining only his long rapier, dagger, and one of his pistols. These he strapped behind him, and without a backward glance over the darkening trail he had come, he started the long ascent. He was a tall man, long-armed and iron-muscled, yet again and again he was forced to halt in his upward climb and rest for a moment, clinging like an ant to the precipitous face of the cliff. Night fell swiftly and the crag above him was a shadowy blur in which he was forced to feel with his fingers, blindly, for the holes which served him as precarious ladder. Below him, the night noises of the tropical jungle broke forth, yet it appeared to him that even these sounds were subdued and hushed as though the great black hills looming above threw a spell of silence and fear even over the jungle creatures.

On up he struggled, and now to make his way harder, the cliff bulged outward near its summit and the strain on nerve and muscle became heart-breaking. Time and again a hold slipped and he escaped falling by a hair's breadth. But every fiber in his lean hard body was perfectly co-ordinated, and his fingers were like steel talons with the grip of a vise. His progress grew slower and slower but on he went until at last he saw the cliff's brow splitting the stars a scant twenty feet above him.

And even as he looked, a vague bulk heaved into view, toppled on the edge and hurtled down toward him with a great rush of air about it. Flesh crawling, he flattened himself against the cliff's face and felt a heavy blow against his shoulder, only a glancing blow, but even so it nearly tore him from his hold, and as he fought desperately to right himself, he heard a reverberating crash among the rocks far below. Cold sweat beading his brow, he looked up. Who – or what – had shoved that boulder over the cliff edge? He was brave, as the bones on many a battlefield could testify, but the thought of dying like a sheep, helpless and with no chance of resistance, turned his blood cold.

Then a wave of fury supplanted his fear and he renewed his climb with reckless speed. The expected second boulder did not come, however, and no living thing met his sight as he clambered up over the edge and leaped erect, sword flashing from its scabbard.

He stood upon a sort of plateau which debouched into a very broken hilly country some half mile to the west. The crag he had just mounted jutted out from the rest of the heights like a sullen promontory, looming above the sea of waving foliage below, now dark and mysterious in the tropic night.

Silence ruled here in absolute sovereignty. No breeze stirred the somber depths below, and no footfall rustled amid the stunted bushes which cloaked the plateau, yet that boulder which had almost hurled the climber to his death had not fallen by chance. What beings moved among these grim hills? The tropical darkness fell about the lone wanderer like a heavy veil through which the yellow stars blinked evilly. The steams of the rotting jungle vegetation floated up to him as tangible as a thick fog, and making a wry face he strode away from the cliff, heading boldly across the plateau, sword in one hand and pistol in the other.

There was an uncomfortable feeling of being watched in the very air. The silence remained unbroken save for the soft swishing that marked the stranger's cat-like tread through the tall upland grass, yet the man sensed that living things glided before and behind him and on each side. Whether man or beast trailed him he knew not, nor did he care overmuch, for he was prepared to fight human or devil who barred his way. Occasionally he halted and glanced challengingly about him, but nothing met his eye except the shrubs which crouched like short dark ghosts about his trail, blended and blurred in the thick hot darkness through which the very stars seemed to struggle, redly.

At last he came to the place where the plateau broke into the higher slopes and there he saw a clump of trees blocked out solidly in the lesser shadows. He approached warily, then halted as his gaze, growing somewhat accustomed to the darkness, made out a vague form among the somber trunks which was not a part of them. He hesitated. The figure neither advanced nor fled. A dim form of silent menace, it lurked as if in wait. A brooding horror hung over that still cluster of trees.

The stranger advanced warily, blade extended. Closer. Straining his eyes for some hint of threatening motion. He decided that the figure was human but he was puzzled at its lack of movement. Then the reason became apparent – it was the corpse of a black man that stood among those trees, held erect by spears through his body, nailing him to the boles. One arm was extended in front of him, held in place along a great branch by a dagger through the wrist, the index finger straight as if the corpse pointed stiffly – back along the way the stranger had come.

The meaning was obvious; that mute grim signpost could have but one significance – death lay beyond. The man who stood gazing upon that grisly warning rarely laughed, but now he allowed himself the luxury of a sardonic smile. A thousand miles of land and sea – ocean travel and jungle travel – and now they expected to turn him back with such mummery – whoever they were.

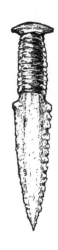

He resisted the temptation to salute the corpse, as an action wanting in decorum, and pushed on boldly through the grove, half expecting an attack from the rear or an ambush.

Nothing of the sort occurred, however, and emerging from the trees, he found himself at the foot of a rugged incline, the first of a series of slopes. He strode stolidly upward in the night, nor did he even pause to reflect how unusual his actions must have appeared to a sensible man. The average man would have camped at the foot of the crag and waited for morning before even attempting to scale the cliffs. But this was no ordinary man. Once his objective was in sight, he followed the straightest line to it, without a thought of obstacles, whether day or night. What was to be done, must be done. He had reached the outposts of the kingdom of fear at dusk, and invading its inmost recesses by night seemed to follow as a matter of course.

As he went up the boulder-strewn slopes the moon rose, lending its air of illusion, and in its light the broken hills ahead loomed up like the black spires of wizards' castles. He kept his eyes fixed on the dim trail he was following, for he knew not when another boulder might come hurtling down the inclines. He expected an attack of any sort and, naturally, it was the unexpected which really happened.

Suddenly from behind a great rock stepped a black man;

an ebony giant in the pale moonlight, a long spear blade gleaming silver in his hand, his headpiece of ostrich plumes floating above him like a white cloud. He lifted the spear in a ponderous salute, and spoke in the dialect of the river-tribes:

"This is not the white man's land. Who is my white brother in his own kraal and why does he come into the Land of Skulls?"

"My name is Solomon Kane," the white man answered in the same language. "I seek the vampire queen of Negari."

"Few seek. Fewer find. None return," answered the other cryptically.

"Will you lead me to her?"

"You bear a long dagger in your right hand. There are no lions here."

"A serpent dislodged a boulder. I thought to find snakes in the bushes."

The giant acknowledged this interchange of subtleties with a grim smile and a brief silence fell.

"Your life," said the black presently, "is in my hand."

Kane smiled thinly. "I carry the lives of many warriors in *my* hand."

The negro's gaze traveled uncertainly up and down the shimmery length of the Englishman's sword.

Then he shrugged his mighty shoulders and let his spear point sink to the earth.

"You bear no gifts," said he; "but follow me and I will lead you to the Terrible One, the Mistress of Doom, the Red Woman, Nakari, who rules the land of Negari."

He stepped aside and motioned Kane to precede him, but

the Englishman, his mind on a spear-thrust in the back, shook his head.

"Who am I that I should walk in front of my brother? We be two chiefs – let us walk side by side."

In his heart Kane railed that he should be forced to use such unsavory diplomacy with a black savage, but he showed no sign. The giant bowed with a certain barbaric majesty and together they went up the hill trail, unspeaking. Kane was aware that men were stepping from hiding-places and falling in behind them, and a surreptitious glance over his shoulder showed him some two score black warriors trailing out behind them in two wedge-shaped lines. The moonlight glittered on sleek black bodies, on waving headgears and long cruel spear blades.

"My brothers are like leopards," said Kane courteously; "they lie in the low bushes and no eyes see them; they steal through the high grass and no man hears their coming."

The black chief acknowledged the compliment with a courtly inclination of his lion-like head, that set the plumes whispering.

"The mountain leopard is our brother, oh chieftain. Our feet are like drifting smoke but our arms are like iron. When they strike, blood drips red and men die."

Kane sensed an undercurrent of menace in the tone. There was no actual hint of threat on which he might base his suspicions, but the sinister minor note was there. He said no more for a space and the strange band moved silently upward in the moonlight like a cavalcade of black specters led by a white ghost. The trail grew steeper and more rocky, winding in and out among crags and gigantic boulders. Suddenly a great chasm opened before them, spanned by a natural bridge of rock, at the foot of which the leader halted.

Kane stared at the abyss curiously. It was some forty feet wide, and looking down, his gaze was swallowed by impenetrable blackness, hundreds of feet deep, he knew. On the other side rose crags dark and forbidding.

"Here," said the black chief, "begin the true borders of Nakari's realm."

Kane was aware that the warriors were casually closing in on him. His fingers instinctively tightened about the hilt of the rapier which he had not sheathed. The air was suddenly supercharged with tension.

"Here, too," the black man said, "they who bring no gifts to Nakari – *die!*"

The last word was a shriek, as if the thought had transformed the speaker into a maniac, and as he screamed it, the great black arm went back and then forward with a ripple of mighty muscles, and the long spear leaped at Kane's breast.

Only a born fighter could have avoided that thrust. Kane's instinctive action saved his life – the great blade grazed his ribs as he swayed aside and returned the blow with a flashing thrust that killed a warrior who jostled between him and the chief at that instant.

Spears flashed in the moonlight and Kane, parrying one and bending under the thrust of another, sprang out upon the narrow bridge where only one could come at him at a time.

None cared to be first. They stood upon the brink and thrust at him, crowding forward when he retreated, giving back when he pressed them. Their spears were longer than his rapier but he more than made up for the difference and the great odds by his scintillant skill and the cold ferocity of his attack.

They wavered back and forth and then suddenly a black giant leaped from among his fellows and charged out upon the bridge like a wild buffalo, shoulders hunched, spear held low, eyes gleaming with a look not wholly sane. Kane leaped back before the onslaught, leaped back again, striving to avoid that stabbing spear and to find an opening for his point. He sprang to one side and found himself reeling on the edge of the bridge with eternity gaping beneath him. The blacks yelled in savage exultation as he swayed and fought for his balance, and the giant on the bridge roared and plunged at the rocking white man.

Kane parried with all his strength – a feat few swords-men could have accomplished, off balance as he was – saw the cruel spear blade flash by his cheek – felt himself falling backward into the abyss. A desperate effort, and he gripped the spear shaft, righted himself and ran the spearman through the body. The black's great red cavern of a mouth spouted blood and with a dying effort he

hurled himself blindly against his foe. Kane, with his heels over the bridge's edge, was unable to avoid him and they toppled over together, to disappear silently into the depths below.

So swiftly had it all happened that the warriors stood stunned. The giant's roar of triumph had scarcely died on his lips before the two were falling into the darkness. Now the rest of the negroes came out on the bridge to peer down curiously, but no sound came up from the dark void.

II
THE PEOPLE OF THE STALKING DEATH

"Their gods were sadder than the sea,
Gods of a wandering will,
Who cried for blood like beasts at night
Sadly, from hill to hill."
CHESTERTON

As Kane fell he followed his fighting instinct, twisting in midair so that when he struck, were it ten or a thousand feet below, he would land on top of the man who fell with him.

The end came suddenly — much more suddenly than the Englishman had thought for. He lay half stunned for an instant, then looking up, saw dimly the narrow bridge banding the sky above him, and the forms of the warriors, limned in the moonlight and grotesquely foreshortened as they leaned over the edge. He lay still, knowing that the beams of the moon did not pierce the deeps in which he was hidden, and that to those watchers he was invisible. Then when they vanished from view he began to review his present plight. The black man was dead, and only for the fact that his corpse had cushioned the fall, Kane would have been dead likewise, for they had fallen a considerable distance. As it was, the white man was stiff and bruised.

He drew his sword from the negro's body, thankful that it had not been broken, and began to grope about in the darkness. His hand encountered the edge of what seemed a cliff. He had thought that he was on the bottom of the chasm and that its impression of great depth had been a delusion, but now he decided that he had fallen on a ledge, part of the way down. He dropped a small stone over the side, and after what seemed a very long time he heard the faint sound of its striking far below.

Somewhat at a loss as to how to proceed, he drew flint and steel from his belt and struck them to some tinder, warily shielding the light with his hands. The faint illumination showed a large ledge jutting out from the side of the cliff, that is, the side next the hills, to which he had been attempting to cross. He had fallen close to the edge and it was only by the narrowest margin that he had escaped sliding off it, not knowing his position.

Crouching there, his eyes seeking to accustom themselves to the abysmal gloom, he made out what seemed to be a darker shadow in the shadows of the wall. On closer examination he found it to be an opening large enough to admit his body standing erect. A cavern, he assumed, and though its appearance was dark and forbidding in the extreme, he entered, groping his way when the tinder burned out.

Where it led to, he naturally had no idea, but any action was preferable to sitting still until the mountain vultures plucked his bones. For a long way the cave floor tilted upward – solid rock beneath his feet – and Kane made his way with some difficulty up the rather steep slant, slipping and sliding now and then. The cavern seemed a large one, for at no time after entering it could he touch the roof, nor could he, with a hand on one wall, reach the other.

At last the floor became level and Kane sensed that the cave was much larger there. The air seemed better, though the darkness was just as impenetrable. Suddenly he stopped dead in his tracks. From somewhere in front of him there came a strange indescribable rustling. Without warning something smote him in the face and slashed wildly. All about him sounded the eery murmurings of many small wings and suddenly Kane smiled crookedly, amused, relieved and chagrined. Bats, of course. The cave was swarming with them. Still it was a shaky experience, and as he went on and the wings whispered through the vasty emptiness of the great cavern, Kane's Puritan mind found space to dally with a bizarre thought – had he wandered into Hell by some strange means, and were these in truth bats, or were they lost souls winging through everlasting night?

Then, thought Solomon Kane, I will soon confront Satan himself – and even as he thought this, his nostrils were assailed by a horrid scent fetid and repellent. The scent grew as he went slowly on, and Kane swore softly, though he was not a profane man. He sensed that the smell betokened some hidden threat, some unseen malevolence, inhuman and deathly, and his somber mind sprang at supernatural conclusions. However, he felt perfect confidence in his ability to cope with any fiend or

demon, armored as he was in unshakable faith of creed and the knowledge of the rightness of his cause.

What followed happened suddenly. He was groping his way along when in front of him two narrow yellow eyes leaped up in the darkness – eyes that were cold and expressionless, too hideously close-set for human eyes and too high for any four-legged beast. What horror had thus reared itself up in front of him?

This is Satan, thought Kane as the eyes swayed above him, and the next instant he was battling for his life with the darkness that seemed to have taken tangible form and thrown itself about his body and limbs in great slimy coils. Those coils lapped his sword arm and rendered it useless; with the other hand he groped for dagger or pistol, flesh crawling as his fingers slipped from slick scales, while the hissing of the monster filled the cavern with a cold paean of terror.

There in the black dark to the accompaniment of the bats' leathery rustlings, Kane fought like a rat in the grip of a mouse-snake, and he could feel his ribs giving and his breath going before his frantic left hand closed on his dagger hilt.

Then with a volcanic twist and wrench of his steel-thewed body he tore his left arm partly free and plunged the keen blade again and again to the hilt in the sinuous writhing terror which enveloped him, feeling at last the quivering coils loosen and slide from his limbs to lie about his feet like huge cables.

The mighty serpent lashed wildly in its death struggles, and Kane, avoiding its bone-shattering blows, reeled away in the darkness, laboring for breath. If his antagonist had not been Satan himself, it had been Satan's nearest earthly satellite, thought Solomon, hoping devoutly that he would not be called upon to battle another in the darkness there.

It seemed to him that he had been walking through the blackness for ages and he began to wonder if there were any end to the cave when a glimmer of light pierced the darkness. He thought it to be an outer entrance a great way off, and started forward swiftly, but to his astonishment, he brought up short against a blank wall after taking a few strides. Then he perceived that the light came through a narrow crack in the wall, and feeling over this wall he found it to be of different material from the rest of the cave, consisting, apparently, of regular blocks of stone joined together with mortar of some sort – an indubitably man-built wall.

The light streamed between two of these stones, where the mortar had crumbled away. Kane ran his hands over the surface with an interest beyond his present needs. The work seemed very old and very much superior to what might be expected of a tribe of ignorant negroes.

He felt the thrill of the explorer and discoverer. Certainly no white man had ever seen this place and lived to tell of it, for when he had landed on the dank West Coast some months before, preparing to plunge into the interior, he had had no hint of such a country as this. The few white men who knew anything at all of Africa with whom he had talked, had never even mentioned the Land of Skulls or the she-fiend who ruled it.

Kane thrust against the wall cautiously. The structure seemed weakened from age – a vigorous shove and it gave perceptibly. He hurled himself against it with all his weight and a whole section of wall gave way with a crash, precipitating him into a dimly lighted corridor amid a heap of stone, dust and mortar.

He sprang up and looked about, expecting the noise to bring a horde of wild spearmen. Utter silence reigned. The corridor in which he now stood was much like a long narrow cave itself, save that it was the work of man. It was several feet wide and the roof was many feet above his head. Dust lay ankle-deep on the floor as if no foot had trod there for countless centuries, and the dim light, Kane decided, filtered in somehow through the roof or ceiling, for nowhere did he see any doors or windows. At last he decided the source was the ceiling itself, which was of a peculiar phosphorescent quality.

He set off down the corridor, feeling uncomfortably like a gray ghost moving along the gray halls of death and decay. The evident antiquity of his surroundings depressed him, making him sense vaguely the fleeting and futile existence of mankind. That he was now on top of the earth he believed, since light of a sort came in, but where, he could not even offer a conjecture. This was a land of enchantment – a land of horror and fearful mysteries, the jungle and river natives had said, and he had gotten whispered hints of its terrors ever since he had set his back to the Slave Coast and ventured into the hinterlands alone.

Now and then he caught a low indistinct murmur which seemed to come through one of the walls, and he at last came to the conclusion that he had stumbled onto a secret passage in some castle or house. The natives who had dared speak to him of Negari, had whispered of a ju-ju city built of stone, set high amid the grim black crags of the fetish hills.

Then, thought Kane, it may be that I have blundered upon the very thing I sought and am in the midst of that city of terror. He halted, and choosing a place at random, began to loosen the mortar with his dagger. As he worked he again heard that low murmur, increasing in volume as he bored through the wall, and presently the point pierced through, and looking through the aperture it had made, he saw a strange and fantastic scene.

He was looking into a great chamber, whose walls and floors were of stone, and whose mighty roof was upheld by gigantic stone columns, strangely carved. Ranks of feathered black warriors lined the walls and a double column of them stood like statues before a throne set between two stone dragons which were larger than elephants. These men he recognized, by their bearing and general appearance, to be tribesmen of the warriors he had fought at the chasm. But his gaze was drawn irresistibly to the great, grotesquely ornamented throne. There, dwarfed by the ponderous splendor about her, a woman reclined. A black woman she was, young and of a tigerish comeliness. She was naked except for a beplumed helmet, armbands, anklets and a girdle of colored ostrich feathers and she sprawled upon the silken cushions with her limbs thrown about in voluptuous abandon.

Even at that distance Kane could make out that her features were regal yet barbaric, haughty and imperious, yet sensual, and with a touch of ruthless cruelty about the curl of her full red lips. Kane felt his pulse quicken. This could be no other than she whose crimes had become almost mythical – Nakari of Negari, demon queen of a demon city, whose monstrous lust for blood had set half a continent shivering. At least she seemed human enough; the tales of the fearful river tribes had lent her a supernatural aspect. Kane had half expected to see a loathsome semi-human monster out of some past and demoniacal age.

The Englishman gazed, fascinated though repelled. Not even in the courts of Europe had he seen such grandeur. The chamber and all its accouterments, from the carven serpents twined about the bases of the pillars to the dimly seen dragons on the shadowy ceiling, were fashioned on a gigantic scale. The splendor was awesome – elephantine – inhumanly oversized, and almost numbing to the mind which sought to measure and conceive the magnitude thereof. To Kane it seemed that these things must have been the work of gods rather than men, for this chamber alone would dwarf most of the castles he had known in Europe.

The black people who thronged that mighty room seemed grotesquely incongruous. They no more suited their surroundings than a band of monkeys would have seemed at home in the council chambers of the English king. As Kane realized this the sinister importance of Queen Nakari dwindled. Sprawled on that august throne in the midst of the terrific glory of another age, she seemed to assume her true proportions – a spoiled, petulant child engaged in a game of make-believe and using for her sport a toy discarded by her elders. And at the same time a thought entered Kane's mind – who were these elders?

Still the child could become deadly in her game, as the Englishman soon saw.

A tall massive black came through the ranks fronting the throne, and after prostrating himself four times before it, remained on his knees, evidently waiting permission to speak. The queen's air of lazy indifference fell from her and she straightened with a quick lithe motion that reminded Kane of a leopardess springing erect. She spoke, and the words came faintly to him as he strained his faculties to hear. She spoke in a language very similar to that of the river tribes.

"Speak!"

"Great and Terrible One," said the kneeling warrior, and Kane recognized him as the chief who had first accosted him on the plateau – the chief of the guards on the cliffs, "let not the fire of your fury consume your slave."

The young woman's eyes narrowed viciously.

"You know why you were summoned, son of a vulture?"

"Fire of Beauty, the stranger brought no gifts."

"No gifts?" she spat out the words. "What have I to do with gifts? I bade you slay all black men who came empty-handed – did I tell you to slay white men?"

"Gazelle of Negari, he came climbing the crags in the night like an assassin, with a dagger as long as a man's arm in his hand. The boulder we hurled down missed him, and we met him upon the plateau and took him to the Bridge-Across-the-Sky, where, as is the custom, we thought to slay him; for it was your word that you were weary of men who came wooing you."

"Black men, fool," she snarled; "black men!"

"Your slave did not know, Queen of Beauty. The white man fought like a mountain leopard. Two men he slew and fell with the last one into the chasm, and so he perished, Star of Negari."

"Aye," the queen's tone was venomous, "the first white man who ever came to Negari! One who might have – rise, fool!"

The man got to his feet.

"Mighty Lioness, might not this one have come seeking –"

The sentence was never completed. Even as he straightened, Nakari made a swift gesture with her hand. Two warriors plunged from the silent ranks and two spears crossed in the chief's body before he could turn. A gurgling scream burst from his lips, blood spurted high in the air and the corpse fell flatly at the foot of the great throne.

The ranks never wavered, but Kane caught the sidelong flash of strangely red eyes and the involuntary wetting of thick lips. Nakari had half risen as the spears flashed, and now she sank back, an expression of cruel satisfaction on her beautiful face and a strange brooding gleam in her scintillant eyes.

An indifferent wave of her hand and the corpse was dragged away by the heels, the dead arms trailing limply in the wide smear of blood left by the passage of the body. Kane could see other wide stains crossing the stone floor, some almost indistinct, others less dim. How many wild scenes of blood and cruel frenzy had the great stone throne-dragons looked upon with their carven eyes?

He did not doubt, now, the tales told him by the river tribes. These people were bred in rapine and horror. Their prowess had burst their brains. They lived, like some terrible beast, only to destroy. There were strange gleams behind their eyes which at times lit those eyes with upleaping flames and shadows of Hell. What had the river tribes said of these mountain people who had ravaged them for countless centuries? *That they were henchmen of death, who stalked among them, and whom they worshipped.*

Still the thought hovered in Kane's mind as he watched – who built this place, and why were negroes evidently in possession? He knew this was the work of a higher race. No black tribe had ever reached such a stage of culture as evidenced by these carvings. Yet the river tribes had spoken of no other men than those upon which he now looked.

The Englishman tore himself away from the fascination of the barbaric scene with an effort. He had no time to waste; as long as they thought him dead, he had more chance of eluding possible guards and seeking what he had come to find. He turned and set off down the dim corridor. No plan of action offered itself to his mind and one direction was as good as

another. The passage did not run straight; it turned and twisted, following the line of the walls, Kane supposed, and found time to wonder at the evident enormous thickness of those walls. He expected at any moment to meet some guard or slave, but as the corridors continued to stretch empty before him, with the dusty floors unmarked by any footprint, he decided that either the passages were unknown to the people of Negari or else for some reason were never used.

He kept a close lookout for secret doors, and at last found one, made fast on the inner side with a rusty bolt set in a groove of the wall. This he manipulated cautiously, and presently with a creaking which seemed terrifically loud in the stillness the door swung inward. Looking out he saw no one, and stepping warily through the opening, he drew the door to behind him, noting that it assumed the part of a fantastic picture painted on the wall. He scraped a mark with his dagger at the point where he believed the hidden spring to be on the outer side, for he knew not when he might need to use the passage again.

He was in a great hall, through which ran a maze of giant pillars much like those of the throne chamber. Among them he felt like a child in some great forest, yet they gave him some slight sense of security since he believed that, gliding among them like a ghost through a jungle, he could elude the black people in spite of their craft.

He set off, choosing his direction at random and going carefully. Once he heard a mutter of voices, and leaping upon the base of a column, clung there while two black women passed directly beneath him, but besides these he encountered no one. It was an uncanny sensation, passing through this vast hall which seemed empty of human life, but in some other part of which Kane knew there might be throngs of people, hidden from sight by the pillars.

At last, after what seemed an eternity of following these monstrous mazes, he came upon a huge wall which seemed to be either a side of the hall, or a partition, and continuing along this, he saw in front of him a doorway before which two spearmen stood like black statues.

Kane, peering about the corner of a column base made out two windows high in the wall, one on each side of the door, and noting the ornate carvings which covered the walls, determined on a desperate plan. He felt it imperative that he should see what lay within that room. The fact that it was guarded suggested that the room beyond the door was either a treasure chamber or a dungeon, and he felt sure that his ultimate goal would prove to be a dungeon.

He retreated to a point out of sight of the blacks and began to scale the wall, using the deep carvings for hand and foot holds. It proved even easier than he had hoped, and having climbed to a point level with the windows, he crawled cautiously along a horizontal line, feeling like an ant on a wall.

The guards far below him never looked up, and finally he reached the nearer window and drew himself up over the sill. He looked down into a large room, empty of life, but equipped in a manner sensuous and barbaric. Silken couches and velvet cushions dotted the floor in profusion and tapestries heavy with gold work hung upon the walls. The ceiling too was worked in gold.

Strangely incongruous, crude trinkets of ivory and ironwood, unmistakably negroid in workmanship, littered the place, symbolic enough of this strange kingdom where signs of barbarism vied with a strange culture. The outer door was shut and in the wall opposite was another door, also closed.

Kane descended from the window, sliding down the edge of a tapestry as a sailor slides down a sail-rope, and crossed the room, his feet sinking noiselessly into the deep fabric of the rug which covered the floor, and which, like all the other furnishings, seemed ancient to the point of decay.

At the door he hesitated. To step into the next room might be a desperately hazardous thing to do; should it prove to be filled with black men, his escape was cut off by the spearmen outside the other door. Still, he was used to taking all sorts of wild chances, and now, sword in hand, he flung the door open with a suddenness intended to numb with surprize for an instant any foe who might be on the other side.

Kane took a swift step within, ready for anything – then halted suddenly, struck speechless and motionless for a second. He had come thousands of miles in search of something and there before him lay the object of his search.

III
LILITH

"Lady of mystery, what is thy history?"
VIERECK

A couch stood in the middle of the room and on its silken surface lay a woman – a woman whose skin was white and whose reddish gold hair fell about her bare shoulders. She now sprang erect, fright flooding her fine gray eyes, lips parted to utter a cry which she as suddenly checked.

"You!" she exclaimed. "How did you –?"

Solomon Kane closed the door behind him and came toward her, a rare smile on his dark face.

"You remember me, do you not, Marylin?"

The fear had already faded from her eyes even before he spoke, to be replaced by a look of incredible wonder and dazed bewilderment.

"Captain Kane! I can not understand – it seemed no one would ever come –"

She drew a small hand wearily across her white brow, swaying suddenly.

Kane caught her in his arms – she was only a girl, little more than a child – and laid her gently on the couch. There, chafing her wrists gently, he talked in a low hurried monotone, keeping an eye on the door all the time – which door, by the way, seemed to be the only entrance or egress from the room. While he talked he mechanically took in the chamber, noting that it was almost a duplicate of the outer room, as regards hangings and general furnishings.

"First," said he, "before we go into any other matters, tell me, are you closely guarded?"

"Very closely, sir," she murmured hopelessly; "I know not how you came here, but we can never escape."

"Let me tell you swiftly how I came to be here, and mayhap you will be more hopeful when I tell you of the difficulties already overcome. Lie still now, Marylin, and I will tell you how I came to seek an English heiress in the devil city of Negari.

"I killed Sir John Taferal in a duel. As to the reason, 'tis neither here nor there, but slander and a black lie lay behind it. Ere he died he confessed that he had committed a foul crime some years agone. You remember, of course, the affection cherished for you by your cousin, old Lord Hildred Taferal, Sir John's uncle. Sir John feared that the old lord, dying without issue, might leave the great Taferal estates to you.

"Years ago you disappeared and Sir John spread the rumor that you had drowned. Yet when he lay dying with my rapier through his body, he gasped out that he had kidnapped you and sold you to a Barbary rover, whom he named – a bloody pirate whose name has not been unknown on England's coasts aforetime. So I came seeking you, and a long weary trail it has been, stretching into long leagues and bitter years.

"First I sailed the seas searching for El Gar, the Barbary corsair named by Sir John. I found him in the crash and roar of an ocean battle; he died, but even as he lay dying he told me that he had sold you in turn to a merchant out of Stamboul. So to the Levant I went and there by chance came upon a Greek sailor whom the Moors had crucified on the shore for piracy. I cut him down and asked him the question I asked all men – if he had in his wanderings seen a captive English girl-child with yellow curls. I learned that he had been one of the crew of the Stamboul merchants, and that she had, on her homeward voyage, been set upon by a Portuguese slaver and sunk – this renegade Greek and the child being among the few who were taken aboard the slaver.

"This slaver then, cruising south for black ivory, had been ambushed in a small bay on the African West Coast, and of your further fate the Greek knew nothing, for he had escaped the general massacre, and taking to

sea in an open boat, had been taken up by a ship of Genoese freebooters.

"To the West Coast, then, I came, on the slim chance that you still lived, and there heard among the natives that some years ago a white child had been taken from a ship whose crew had been slain, and sent inland as a part of the tribute the shore tribes paid to the upper river chiefs.

"Then all traces ceased. For months I wandered without a clue as to your whereabouts, nay, without a hint that you even lived. Then I chanced to hear among the river tribes of the demon city of Negari and the black queen who kept a white woman for a slave. I came here."

Kane's matter-of-fact tone, his unfurbished narration, gave no hint of the full meaning of that tale – of what lay behind those calm and measured words – the sea-fights and the land fights – the years of privation and heart-breaking toil, the ceaseless danger, the everlasting wandering through hostile and unknown lands, the tedious and deadening labor of ferreting out the information he wished from ignorant, sullen and unfriendly savages, black and white.

"I came here" said Kane simply, but what a world of courage and effort was symbolized by that phrase! A long red trail, black shadows and crimson shadows weaving a devil's dance – marked by flashing swords and the smoke of battle –

by faltering words falling like drops of blood from the lips of dying men.

Not a consciously dramatic man, certainly, was Solomon Kane. He told his tale in the same manner in which he had overcome terrific obstacles – coldly, briefly and without heroics.

"You see, Marylin," he concluded gently, "I have not come this far and done this much, to now meet with defeat. Take heart, child. We will find a way out of this fearful place."

"Sir John took me on his saddlebow," the girl said dazedly, and speaking slowly as if her native language came strangely to her from years of unuse, as she framed in halting words an English evening of long ago: "He carried me to the seashore where a galley's boat waited, filled with fierce men, dark and mustached and having simitars, and great rings to the fingers. The captain, a Moslem with a face like a hawk, took me, I a-weeping with fear, and bore me to his galley. Yet he was kind to me in his way, I being little more than a baby, and at last sold me to a Turkish merchant, as he told you. This merchant he met off the southern coast of France, after many days of sea travel.

"This man did not use me badly, yet I feared him, for he was a man of cruel countenance and made me understand that I was to be sold to a black sultan of the Moors. However, in the Gates of Hercules his ship was set upon by a Cadiz slaver and things came about as you have said.

"The captain of the slaver believed me to be the child of some wealthy English family and intended holding me for ransom, but in a grim darksome bay on the African coast he perished with all his men except the Greek you have mentioned, and I was taken captive by a black chieftain.

"I was terribly afraid and thought he would slay me, but he did me no harm and sent me up-country with an escort, who also bore much loot taken from the ship. This loot, together with myself, was, as you know, intended for a powerful king of the river peoples. But it never reached him, for a roving band of Negari fell upon the beach warriors and slew them all. Then I was taken to this city, and have since remained, slave to Queen Nakari.

"How I have lived through all those terrible scenes of battle and cruelty and murder, I know not."

"A providence has watched over you, child," said Kane, "the power which doth care for weak women and helpless children; which led me to you in spite of all hindrances, and which shall yet lead us forth from this place, God willing."

"My people!" she exclaimed suddenly like one awaking from a dream; "what of them?"

"All in good health and fortune, child, save that they have sorrowed for you through the long years. Nay, old Sir Hildred hath the gout and doth so swear thereat that I fear for his soul at times. Yet methinks that the sight of you, little Marylin, would mend him."

"Still, Captain Kane," said the girl, "I can not understand why you came alone."

"Your brothers would have come with me, child, but it was not sure that you lived, and I was loth that any other Taferal should die in a land far from good English soil. I rid the country of an evil Taferal — 'twas but just I should restore in his place a good Taferal, if so be she still lived — I, and I alone."

This explanation Kane himself believed. He never sought to analyze his motives and he never wavered, once his mind was made up. Though he always acted on impulse, he firmly believed that all his actions were governed by cold and logical reasonings. He was a man born out of his time – a strange blending of Puritan and Cavalier, with a touch of the ancient philosopher, and more than a touch of the pagan, though the last assertion would have shocked him unspeakably. An atavist of the days of blind chivalry he was, a knight errant in the somber clothes of a fanatic. A hunger in his soul drove him on and on, an urge to right all wrongs, protect all weaker things, avenge all crimes against right and justice. Wayward and restless as the wind, he was consistent in only one respect – he was true to his ideals of justice and right. Such was Solomon Kane.

"Marylin," he now said kindly, taking her small hands in his sword-calloused fingers, "methinks you have changed greatly in the years. You were a rosy and chubby little maid when I used to dandle you on my knee in old England. Now you seem drawn and pale of face, though you are beautiful as the nymphs of the heathen books. There are haunting ghosts in your eyes, child – do they misuse you here?"

She lay back on the couch and the blood drained slowly from her already pallid features until she was deathly white. Kane bent over her, startled. Her voice came in a whisper.

"Ask me not. There are deeds better hidden in the darkness of night and forgetfulness. There are sights which blast the eyes and leave their burning mark forever on the brain. The walls of ancient cities, recked not of by men, have looked upon scenes not to be spoken of, even in whispers."

Her eyes closed wearily and Kane's troubled, somber eyes unconsciously traced the thin blue lines of her veins, prominent against the unnatural whiteness of her skin.

"Here is some demoniacal thing," he muttered. "A mystery —"

"Aye," murmured the girl, "a mystery that was old when Egypt was young! And nameless evil more ancient than dark Babylon — that spawned in terrible black cities when the world was young and strange."

Kane frowned, troubled. At the girl's strange words he felt an eery crawling fear at the back of his brain, as if dim racial memories stirred in the eon-deep gulfs, conjuring up grim chaotic visions, illusive and nightmarish.

Suddenly Marylin sat erect, her eyes flaring wide with fright. Kane heard a door open somewhere.

"Nakari!" whispered the girl urgently. "Swift! She must not find you here! Hide quickly, and" — as Kane turned — "keep silent, whatever may chance!"

She lay back on the couch, feigning slumber as Kane crossed the room and concealed himself behind some tapestries which, hanging upon the wall, hid a niche that might have once held a statue of some sort.

He had scarcely done so when the single door of the room opened and a strange barbaric figure stood framed in it. Nakari, queen of Negari, had come to her slave.

The black woman was clad as she had been when he had seen her on the throne, and the colored armlets and anklets clanked as she closed the door behind her and came into the room. She moved with the easy sinuousness of a she-leopard and in spite of himself the watcher was struck with admiration for her lithe beauty. Yet at the same time a shudder of repulsion shook him, for her eyes gleamed with vibrant and magnetic evil, older than the world.

"Lilith!" thought Kane. "She is beautiful and terrible as Purgatory. She is Lilith – that foul, lovely woman of ancient legend."

Nakari halted by the couch, stood looking down upon her captive for a moment, then with an enigmatic smile, bent and shook her. Marylin opened her eyes, sat up, then slipped from her couch and knelt before her black mistress – an act which caused Kane to curse beneath his breath. The queen laughed and seating herself upon the couch, motioned the girl to rise, and then put an arm about her waist and drew her upon her lap. Kane watched, puzzled, while Nakari caressed the white girl in a lazy, amused manner. This might be affection, but to Kane it seemed more like a sated leopard teasing its victim. There was an air of mockery and studied cruelty about the whole affair.

"You are very soft and pretty, Mara," Nakari murmured lazily, "much prettier than the black girls who serve me. The time approaches, little one, for your nuptial. And a fairer bride has never been borne up the Black Stairs."

Marylin began to tremble and Kane thought she was going to faint. Nakari's eyes gleamed strangely beneath her long-lashed drooping lids, and her full red lips curved in a faint tantalizing smile. Her every action seemed fraught with some sinister meaning. Kane began to sweat profusely.

"Mara," said the black queen, "you are honored above all other girls, yet you are not content. Think how the girls of Negari will envy you, Mara, when the priests sing the nuptial song and the Moon of Skulls looks over the black crest of the Tower of Death. Think, little bride-of-the-Master, how many girls have given their lives to be his bride!"

And Nakari laughed in her hateful musical way, as at a rare jest. And then suddenly she stopped short. Her eyes narrowed to slits as they swept the room, and her whole body tensed. Her hand went to her girdle and came away with a long thin dagger. Kane sighted along the barrel of his pistol, finger against the trigger. Only a natural hesitancy against shooting a woman kept him from sending death into the black heart of Nakari, for he believed that she was about to murder the girl.

Then with a lithe cat-like motion she thrust the girl from her knees and bounded back across the room, her eyes fixed with blazing intensity on the tapestry behind which Kane stood. Had those keen eyes discovered him? He quickly learned.

"Who is there?" she rapped out fiercely. "Who hides behind those hangings? I do not see you nor hear you, but I know someone is there!"

Kane remained silent. Nakari's wild beast instinct had betrayed him and he was uncertain as to what course to follow. His next actions depended on the queen.

"Mara!" Nakari's voice slashed like a whip, "who is behind those hangings? Answer me! Shall I give you a taste of the whip again?"

The girl seemed incapable of speech. She cowered where she had fallen, her beautiful eyes full of terror. Nakari, her blazing gaze never wavering, reached behind her with her free hand and gripped a cord hanging from the wall. She jerked

viciously. Kane felt the tapestries whip back on either side of
him and he stood revealed.

For a moment the strange tableau held – the gaunt white
man in his blood-stained, tattered garments, the long pistol
gripped in his right hand –
across the room the black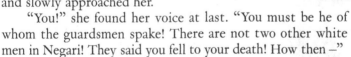
queen in her savage finery,
one arm still lifted to the
cord, the other hand
holding the dagger in front
of her – the white girl
cowering on the floor.

Then Kane spoke:
"Keep silent, Nakari, or
you die!"

The queen seemed
numbed and struck
speechless by the sudden
apparition. Kane stepped
from among the tapestries
and slowly approached her.

"You!" she found her voice at last. "You must be he of
whom the guardsmen spake! There are not two other white
men in Negari! They said you fell to your death! How then –"

"Silence!" Kane's voice cut in harshly on her amazed
babblings; he knew that the pistol meant nothing to her, but
she sensed the threat of the long blade in his left hand.
"Marylin," still unconsciously speaking in the river-tribes'
language, "take cords from the hangings and bind her –"

He was about the middle of the chamber now. Nakari's
face had lost much of its helpless bewilderment and into her
blazing eyes stole a crafty gleam. She deliberately let her
dagger fall as in token of surrender, then suddenly her hands

shot high above her head and gripped another thick cord. Kane heard Marylin scream but before he could take another step, before he could pull the trigger or even think, the floor fell beneath his feet and he shot down into abysmal blackness. He did not fall far and he landed on his feet; but the force of the fall sent him to his knees and even as he went down, sensing a presence in the darkness beside him, something crashed against his skull and he dropped into a yet blacker abyss of unconsciousness.

IV
DREAMS OF EMPIRE

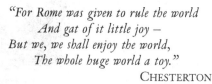

"For Rome was given to rule the world
And gat of it little joy —
But we, we shall enjoy the world,
The whole huge world a toy."
CHESTERTON

Slowly Kane drifted back from the dim realms where the unseen assailant's bludgeon had hurled him. Something hindered the motion of his hands and there was a metallic clanking when he sought to raise them to his aching, throbbing head.

He lay in utter darkness but he could not determine whether this was absence of light, or whether he was still blinded by the blow. He dazedly collected his scattered faculties and realized that he was lying on a damp stone floor, shackled by wrist and ankle with heavy iron chains which were rough and rusty to the touch.

How long he lay there, he never knew. The silence was

broken only by the drumming pulse in his own aching head
and the scamper and chattering of rats. At last a red glow
sprang up in the darkness and grew before his eyes. Framed in
the grisly radiance rose the sinister and sardonic face of
Nakari. Kane shook his head, striving to rid himself of the
illusion. But the light grew and as his eyes accustomed
themselves to it, he saw that it emanated from a torch borne
in the hand of the queen.

In the illumination he now saw that he lay in a small dank
cell whose walls, ceiling and floor were of stone. The heavy
chains which held him captive were made fast to metal rings
set deep in the wall. There was but one door, which was
apparently of bronze.

Nakari set the torch in a niche near the door, and coming
forward, stood over her captive, gazing down at him in a
manner rather speculating than mocking.

"You are he who fought the men on the cliff." The remark
was an assertion rather than a question. "They said you fell
into the abyss – did they lie? Did you bribe them to lie? Or
how did you escape? Are you a magician and did you fly to the
bottom of the chasm and then fly to my palace? Speak!"

Kane remained silent. Nakari cursed.

"Speak or I will have your eyes torn out! I will cut your
fingers off and burn your feet!"

She kicked him viciously, but Kane lay silent, his deep
somber eyes boring up into her face, until the feral gleam
faded from her eyes to be replaced by an avid interest and
wonder.

She seated herself on a stone bench, resting her elbows
on her knees and her chin on her hands.

"I never saw a white man before," she said. "Are all white
men like you? Bah! That can not be! Most men are fools, black
or white. I know most black men are fools, and white men are

not gods, as the river tribes say – they are only men. I, who
know all the ancient mysteries, say they are only men.

"But white men have strange mysteries too, they tell me
– the wanderers of the river tribes, and Mara. They have war
clubs that make a noise like thunder and kill afar off – that
thing which you held in your right hand, was that one of
those clubs?"

Kane permitted himself a grim smile.

"Nakari, if you know all mysteries, how can I tell you
aught that you know not already?"

"How deep and cold and strange your eyes are!" the
queen said as if he had not spoken. "How strange your whole
appearance is – and you have the bearing of a king! You do not
fear me – I never met a man who neither loved nor feared me.
You would never fear me, but you could learn to love me.
Look at me, white man – am I not beautiful?"

"You are beautiful," answered Kane.

Nakari smiled and then frowned. "The way you say that,
it is no compliment. You hate me, do you not?"

"As a man hates a serpent," Kane replied bluntly.

Nakari's eyes blazed with almost insane fury. Her hands
clenched until the long nails sank into the palms; then as
quickly as her anger had arisen, it ebbed away.

"You have the heart of a king," she said calmly, "else you
would fear me. Are you a king in your land?"

"I am only a landless wanderer."

"You might be a king here," Nakari said slowly.

Kane laughed grimly. "Do you offer me my life?"

"I offer you more than that!" Kane's eyes narrowed as the
queen leaned toward him, vibrant with suppressed
excitement. "White man, what is it that you want more than
anything else in the world?"

"To take the white girl you call Mara, and go."

Nakari sank back with an impatient exclamation.

"You can not have her; she is the promised bride of the Master. Even I could not save her, even if I wished. Forget her. I will help you forget her. Listen, white man, listen to the words of Nakari, queen of Negari! You say you are a landless man – I will make you a king! I will give you the world for a toy!

"No, no! Keep silent until I have finished," she rushed on, her words tumbling over each other in her eagerness. Her eyes blazed, her whole body quivered with dynamic intensity. "I have talked to travelers, to captives and slaves, men from far countries. I know that this land of mountains and rivers and jungle is not all the world. There are far-off nations and cities, and kings and queens to be crushed and broken.

"Negari is fading, her might is crumbling, but a strong man beside her queen might build it up again – might restore all her vanishing glory. Listen, white man! Sit by me on the throne of Negari! Send afar to your people for the thunder-clubs to arm my warriors! My nation is still lord of central Africa; together we will band the conquered tribes – call back the days when the realm of ancient Negari spanned the land from sea to sea! We will subjugate all the tribes of the river, the plain and the sea-shore, and instead of slaying them all, we will make one mighty army of them! And then, when all Africa is under our heel, we will sweep forth upon the world like a hungry lion to rend and tear and destroy!"

Solomon's brain reeled. Perhaps it was the woman's fierce magnetic personality, the dynamic power she instilled in her fiery words, but at the moment her wild plan seemed not at all wild and impossible. Lurid and chaotic visions flamed through the Puritan's brain – Europe torn by civil and religious strife, divided against herself, betrayed by her rulers, tottering – aye, Europe was in desperate straits now,

and might prove an easy victim for some strong savage race of conquerors. What man can say truthfully that in his heart there lurks not a yearning for power and conquest? For a moment the Devil sorely tempted Solomon Kane; then before his mind's eye rose the wistful sad face of Marylin Taferal, and Solomon cursed.

"Out on ye, daughter of Satan! Avaunt! Am I a beast of the forest to lead your black devils against mine own race? Nay, no beast ever did so. Begone! If you wish my friendship, set me free and let me go with the girl."

Nakari leaped like a tiger-cat to her feet, her eyes flaming now with passionate fury. A dagger gleamed in her hand and she raised it high above Kane's breast with a feline scream of hate. A moment she hovered like a shadow of death above him; then her arm sank and she laughed.

"Freedom? She will find her freedom when the Moon of Skulls leers down on the black altar. As for you, you shall rot in this dungeon. You are a fool; Africa's greatest queen has offered you her love and the empire of the world – and you revile her! You love the white girl, perhaps? Until the Moon of Skulls she is mine and I leave you to think about this: that she shall be punished as I have punished her before – hung up by her wrists, naked, and whipped until she swoons!"

Nakari laughed as Kane tore savagely at his shackles. She crossed to the door, opened it, then hesitated and turned back for another word.

"This is a foul place, white man, and maybe you hate me the more for chaining you here. Maybe in Nakari's beautiful throneroom, with wealth and luxury spread before you, you will look upon her with more favor. Very soon I shall send for you, but first I will leave you here awhile to reflect. Remember – love Nakari and the kingdom of the world is yours; hate her – this cell is your realm."

The bronze door clanged sullenly, but more hateful to the imprisoned Englishman was the venomous, silvery laugh of Nakari.

Time passed slowly in the darkness. After what seemed a long time the door opened again, this time to admit a huge black who brought food and a sort of thin wine. Kane ate and drank ravenously and afterward slept. The strain of the last few days had worn him greatly, mentally and physically, but when he awoke he felt fresh and strong.

Again the door opened and two great black warriors entered. In the light of the torches they bore, Kane saw that they were giants, clad in loin-cloths and ostrich plume headgear, and bearing long spears in their hands.

"Nakari wishes you to come to her, white man," was all 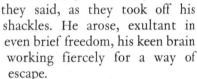 they said, as they took off his shackles. He arose, exultant in even brief freedom, his keen brain working fiercely for a way of escape.

Evidently the fame of his prowess had spread, for the two warriors showed great respect for him. They motioned him to precede them, and walked carefully behind him, the points of their spears boring into his back. Though they were two to one, and he was unarmed, they were taking no chances. The gazes they directed at him were full of awe and suspicion, and Kane decided that Nakari had told the truth when she had said that he was the first white man to come to Negari.

Down a long dark corridor they went, his captors guiding him with light prods of their spears, up a narrow winding stair, down another passageway, up another stair, and then they emerged into the vast maze of gigantic pillars into which Kane had first come. As they started down this huge hall, Kane's eyes suddenly fell on a strange and fantastic picture painted on the wall ahead of him. His heart gave a sudden leap as he recognized it. It was some distance in front of him and he edged imperceptibly toward the wall until he and his guards were walking along very close to it. Now he was almost abreast of the picture and could even make out the mark his dagger had made upon it.

The warriors following Kane were amazed to hear him gasp suddenly like a man struck by a spear. He wavered in his stride and began clutching at the air for support. They eyed each other doubtfully and prodded him, but he cried out like a dying man, and slowly crumpled to the floor, where he lay in a strange unnatural position, one leg doubled back under him and one arm half supporting his lolling body. The blacks looked at him fearfully. To all appearances he was dying, but there was no wound upon him. They threatened him with their spears but he paid no heed. Then they lowered their weapons uncertainly and one of them bent over him.

Then it happened. The instant the black stooped forward, Kane came up like a steel spring released. His right fist following his motion curved up from his hip in a whistling half-circle and crashed against the black giant's jaw. Delivered with all the power of arm and shoulder, propelled by the upthrust of the powerful legs as Kane straightened, the blow was like that of a slung-shot. The negro slumped to the floor, unconscious before his knees gave way.

The other warrior plunged forward with a bellow, but even as his victim fell, Kane twisted aside and his frantic hand found the secret spring in the painting and pressed. All happened in the breath of a second. Quick as the warrior was, Kane was quicker, for he moved with the dynamic speed of a famished wolf. For an instant the falling body of the senseless black hindered the other warrior's thrust, and in that instant Kane felt the hidden door give way. From the corner of his eye he saw a long gleam of steel shooting for his heart. He twisted about and hurled himself against the door, vanishing through it even as the stabbing spear slit the skin on his shoulder.

To the dazed and bewildered warrior, who stood with weapon upraised for another thrust, it seemed as if the white man had simply vanished through a solid wall, for only a fantastic picture met his gaze and this did not give to his efforts.

V
"FOR A THOUSAND YEARS —"

"The blind gods roar and rave and dream
Of all cities under the sea."
CHESTERTON

Kane slammed the hidden door shut behind him, jammed down the spring and for a moment leaned against it, every muscle tensed, expecting to hold it against the efforts of a horde of spearmen. But nothing of the sort materialized. He heard the black warrior fumbling outside for a time; then that sound, too, ceased. It seemed impossible that these people should have lived in this palace as long as they had without discovering the secret doors and passages, but it was a conclusion which forced itself upon Kane's mind.

At last he decided that he was safe from pursuit for the time being, and turning, started down the long, narrow corridor with its eon-old dust and its dim gray light. He felt baffled and furious, though he was free from Nakari's shackles. He had no idea how long he had been in the palace; it seemed ages. It must be day now, for it was light in the outer halls, and he had seen no torches after they had left the subterranean dungeons. He wondered if Nakari had carried out her threat of vengeance on the helpless girl, and swore passionately. Free for the time being, yes; but unarmed and hunted through this infernal palace like a rat. How could he aid either himself or Marylin? But his confidence never faltered. He was in the right and some way would present itself.

Suddenly a narrow stairway branched off the main passageway, and up this he went, the light growing stronger and stronger until he stood in the full glare of the African sunlight. The stair terminated in a sort of small landing directly in front of which was a tiny window, heavily barred. Through this he saw the blue sky, tinted gold with the blazing sunlight. The sight was like wine to him and he drew in deep breaths of fresh, untainted air, breathing deep as if to rid his lungs of the aura of dust and decayed grandeur through which he had been passing.

He was looking out over a weird and bizarre landscape. Far to the right and the left loomed up great black crags and beneath them there reared castles and towers of stone, of strange architecture – it was as if giants from some other planet had thrown them up in a wild and chaotic debauch of creation. These buildings were backed solidly against the cliffs, and Kane knew that Nakari's palace also must be built into the wall of the crag behind it. He seemed to be in the front of that palace in a sort of minaret built on the outer wall. But there was only one window in it and his view was limited. Far below him through the winding and narrow streets of that strange city, swarms of black people went to and fro, seeming like black ants to the watcher above. East, north and south, the cliffs formed a natural bulwark; only to the west was a built wall.

The sun was sinking west. Kane turned reluctantly from

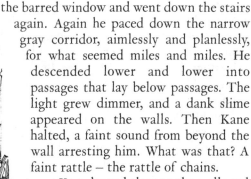

the barred window and went down the stairs again. Again he paced down the narrow gray corridor, aimlessly and planlessly, for what seemed miles and miles. He descended lower and lower into passages that lay below passages. The light grew dimmer, and a dank slime appeared on the walls. Then Kane halted, a faint sound from beyond the wall arresting him. What was that? A faint rattle – the rattle of chains.

Kane leaned close to the wall, and in the semi-darkness his hand encountered a rusty spring. He worked at it cautiously and presently felt the hidden door it betokened swing inward. He gazed out warily.

He was looking into a cell, the counterpart of the one in which he had been confined. A smoldering torch was thrust into a niche on the wall, and by its lurid and flickering light he made out a form on the floor, shackled wrist and ankle as he had been shackled. A man; at first Kane thought him to be a negro but a second glance made him doubt. The hair was too straight, the features too regular. Negroid, yes, but some alien blood in his veins had sharpened those features and given the man that high magnificent forehead, and those hard vibrant eyes which stared at Kane so intensely. The skin was dark, but not black.

The man spoke in an unfamiliar dialect, one which was strangely distinct and clear-cut in contrast to the guttural jargon of the black people with whom Kane was familiar. The Englishman spoke in English, and then in the language of the river tribes.

"You who come through the ancient door," said the other, in the latter dialect, "who are you? You are no black man – at first I thought you one of the Old Race, but now I see you are not as they. Whence come you?"

"I am Solomon Kane," said the Puritan, "a prisoner in this devil-city. I come from far across the blue salt sea."

The man's eyes lighted at the word.

"The sea! The ancient and everlasting! The sea which I never saw but which cradled the glory of my ancestors! Tell me, stranger, have you, like they, sailed across the breast of the great blue monster, and have your eyes looked on the golden spires of Atlantis and the crimson walls of Mu?"

"Truly," answered Solomon uncertainly, "I have sailed the seas, even to Hindostan and Cathay, but of the countries you mention I know nothing."

"Nay," the other sighed, "I dream – I dream. Already the shadow of the great night falls across my brain and my words wander. Stranger, there have been times when these cold walls and floor have seemed to melt into green surging deeps and my soul was filled with the deep booming of the everlasting sea. I who have never seen the sea!"

Kane shuddered involuntarily. Surely this man was insane. Suddenly the other shot out a withered claw-like hand and gripped his arm, despite the hampering chain.

"You whose skin is so strangely white! Have you seen Nakari, the she-fiend who rules this crumbling city?"

"I have seen her," said Kane grimly, "and now I flee like a hunted rat from her murderers."

"You hate her!" the other cried. "Ha, I know! You seek Mara, the white girl who is her slave?"

"Aye."

"Listen, white man," the shackled one spoke with strange solemnity; "I am dying. Nakari's rack has done its work. I die and with me dies the shadow of the glory that was my nation's. For I am the last of my race. In all the world there is none like me. Hark now, to the voice of a dying race."

And Kane leaning there in the flickering semi-darkness of the cell heard the strangest tale to which man has ever listened, brought out of the mist of the dim dawn ages by the lips of delirium. Clear and distinct the words fell from the dying man and Kane alternately burned and froze as vista after gigantic vista of time and space swept up before him.

"Long eons ago – ages, ages ago – the empire of my race rose proudly above the waves. So long ago was it that no man remembers an ancestor who remembered it. In a great land to the west our cities rose. Our golden spires split the stars; our purple-prowed galleys broke the waves around the world, looting the sunset for its treasure and the sunrise for its wealth. Our legions swept forth to the north and to the south, to the west and the east, and none could stand before them. Our cities banded the world; we sent our colonies to all lands to subdue all savages, red, white or black, and enslave them. They toiled for us in the mines and at the galley's oars. All over the world the brown people of Atlantis reigned supreme. We were a sea-people and we delved the deeps of all the oceans.

The mysteries were known to us, and the secret things of land and sea and sky. We read the stars and were wise. Sons of the sea, we exalted him above all others.

"We worshipped Valka and Hotah, Honen and Golgor. Many virgins, many strong youths, died on their altars and the smoke of the shrines blotted out the sun. Then the sea rose and shook himself. He thundered from his abyss and the thrones of the world fell before him! New lands rose from the deep and Atlantis and Mu were swallowed up by the gulf. The green sea roared through the fanes and the castles, and the sea-weed encrusted the golden spires and the topaz towers. The empire of Atlantis vanished and was forgotten, passing into the everlasting gulf of time and oblivion. Likewise the colony cities in barbaric lands, cut off from their mother kingdom, perished. The black savages and the white savages rose and burned and destroyed until in all the world only the colony city of Negari remained as a symbol of the lost empire.

"Here my ancestors ruled as kings, and the ancestors of Nakari – the she-cat! – bent the knee of slavery to them. Years passed, stretching into centuries. The empire of Negari dwindled. Tribe after tribe rose and flung off the chains, pressing the lines back from the sea, until at last the sons of Atlantis gave way entirely and retreated into the city itself – the last stronghold of the race. Conquerors no longer, hemmed in by ferocious tribes, yet they held those tribes at bay for a thousand years. Negari was invincible from without; her walls held firm; but within evil influences were at work.

"The sons of Atlantis had brought their black slaves into the city with them. The rulers were warriors, scholars, priests, artizans; they did no menial work. For that they depended upon the slaves. There were more of these slaves than there were masters. And they increased while the brown people dwindled.

"They mixed with each other more and more as the race degenerated until at last only the priestcraft was free of the taint of black blood. Rulers sat on the throne of Negari who were nearly pure negro, and these allowed more and more wild tribesmen to enter the city in the guise of servants, mercenaries and friends.

"Then came a day when these fierce slaves revolted and slew all who bore a trace of brown blood, except the priests and their families. These they imprisoned as 'fetish people.' For a thousand years black men have ruled in Negari, their kings guided by the captive brown priests, who though prisoners, were yet the masters of kings."

Kane listened enthralled. To his imaginative mind, the tale burned and lived with strange fire from cosmic time and space.

"After all the sons of Atlantis, save the priests, were dead, there rose a great black king on the defiled throne of ancient Negari. He was a tiger and his warriors were like leopards. They called themselves Negari, ravishing even the name of their former masters, and none could stand before them. They swept the land from sea to sea, and the smoke of destruction put out the stars. The great river ran red and the black lords of Negari strode above the corpses of their black foes. Then the great king died and the black empire crumbled, even as the brown kingdom of Negari had crumbled. They were skilled in war – the dead sons of Atlantis, their masters, had trained them in the ways of battle, and against the wild tribesmen they were invincible. But only the ways of war had they learned, and the empire was torn with civil strife. Murder and intrigue stalked red-handed through the palaces and the streets, and the boundaries of the empire dwindled and dwindled. All the while black kings with red, frenzied brains sat on the throne, and behind the curtains, unseen but greatly feared, the brown priests guided the nation, holding it together, keeping it from absolute destruction.

"Prisoners in the city were we, for there was nowhere else in the world to go, but we moved like ghosts through the secret passages in the walls and under the earth, spying on intrigue and doing secret magic. We upheld the cause of the royal family – the descendants of that tiger-like king of long ago – against all plotting chiefs, and grim are the tales which these silent walls could tell. For these black people are not as other negroes. A latent insanity lurks in the brains of every one. They have tasted so deeply and so long of slaughter and victory that they are as human leopards, for ever thirsting for blood. On their myriad wretched slaves they have sated all lusts and desires until they have become foul and terrible beasts, for ever seeking some new sensation, for ever quenching their fearful thirsts in blood.

"Like a lion have they lurked in these crags for a thousand years, to rush forth and ravage the jungle and river people, enslaving and destroying. They are still invincible from without, though their possessions have dwindled to the very walls of this city, and their former great conquests and invasions have dwindled to raids for slaves.

"But as they faded, so too faded their masters, the brown priests. One by one they died, until only I remained. In the last century they too mixed with their rulers and slaves, and now – oh, black the shame upon me! – I, the last son of Atlantis, bear in my veins the taint of negro blood. They died; I remained, doing magic and guiding the black kings, I the last brown man of Negari. Then the she-fiend, Nakari, arose."

Kane leaned forward with quickened interest. New life surged into the tale as it touched upon his own time.

"Nakari!" the name was spat as a snake hisses; "slave and the daughter of a slave! Yet she prevailed when her hour came and all the royal family died.

"And me, the last son of Atlantis, me she prisoned and chained. She feared not the silent brown priests, for she was the daughter of a Satellite – one of the lesser priests, black men who did the menial work of the brown masters – performing the lesser sacrifices, divining from the livers of fowls and serpents and keeping the holy fires for ever burning. Much she knew of us and our ways, and evil ambition burned in her.

"As a child she danced in the March of the New Moon, and as a young girl she was one of the Star-maidens. Much of the lesser mysteries was known to her, and more she learned, spying upon the secret rites of the priests who enacted hidden rituals that were old when the earth was young. For the remnants of Atlantis secretly kept alive the old worships of Valka and Hotah, Honen and Golgor, long forgotten and not to be understood by these black people whose ancestors died screaming on their altars. Alone of all the black Negari she feared us not and she not only overthrew the king and set herself on the throne, but she dominated the priests – the black Satellites and the few brown masters who were left. All these last, save me, died beneath the daggers of her assassins or on her racks. She alone of all the myriad black thousands who have lived and died between these walls guessed at the hidden passages and subterranean corridors, secrets which we of the priestcraft had guarded jealously from the people for a thousand years.

"Ha! Ha! Blind, black fools! To pass an ageless age in this city, yet never to learn of the secrets thereof! Black apes – fools! Not even the lesser black priests know of the long gray corridors, lit by phosphorescent ceilings, through which in bygone ages strange forms have glided silently. For our ancestors built Negari as they built Atlantis – on a mighty scale and with an unknown art. Not for men alone did we build, but for the gods who moved unseen among us. And deep the secrets these ancient walls hold!

"Torture could not wring these secrets from our lips, but shackled in her dungeons, we trod our hidden corridors no more. For years the dust has gathered there, untouched by human foot, while we, and finally I alone, lay chained in these foul cells. And among the temples and the dark, mysterious shrines of old, move vile black Satellites, elevated by Nakari to glories that were once mine – for I am the last Atlantean high priest. Black be their doom, and red their ruin! Valka and Golgor, gods lost and forgotten, whose memory shall die with me, strike down their walls and humble them unto the dust!

Break the altars of their blind pagan gods —"

Kane realized that the man was wandering in his mind. The keen brain had begun to crumble at last.

"Tell me," said he; "you mentioned the white girl, Mara. What do you know of her?"

"She was brought to Negari years ago by raiders," the other answered, "only a few years after the rise of the black queen, whose slave she is. Little of her I know, for shortly after her arrival, Nakari turned on me — and the years that lie between have been grim black years, shot red with torture and agony. Here I have lain, hampered by my chains from escape which lay in that door through which you entered — and for the knowledge of which Nakari has torn me on racks and suspended me over slow fires."

Kane shuddered. "You know not if they have so misused the white girl? Her eyes are haunted and she has wasted away."

"She has danced with the Star-maidens at Nakari's command, and has looked on the bloody and terrible rites of the Black Temple. She has lived for years among a people with whom blood is cheaper than water, who delight in slaughter and foul torture, and such sights as she has looked upon would blast the eyes and wither the flesh of strong men. She has seen the victims of Nakura die amid horrid torments, and the sight is burned for ever in the brain of the beholder. The rites of the Atlanteans the blacks took whereby to honor their crude gods, and though the essence of those rites is lost in the wasting years, yet even as Nakari's black apes perform them, they are not such as men can look on, unshaken."

Kane was thinking: "A fair day for the world when this Atlantis sank, for most certainly it bred a race of strange and unknown evil." Aloud he said: "Who is this Master of whom Nakari spake, and what meant she by calling Mara his bride?"

"Nakura – Nakura. The skull of evil, the symbol of Death that they worship. What know these savages of the gods of sea-girt Atlantis? What know they of the dread and unseen gods whom their masters worshipped with majestic and mysterious rites? They understand not of the unseen essence, the invisible deity that reigns in the air and the elements; they must worship a material object, endowed with human shape. Nakura was the last great wizard of Atlantean Negari. A brown renegade he was, who conspired against his own people and aided the revolt of the black beasts. In life they followed him and in death they deified him. High in the Tower of Death his fleshless skull is set, and on that skull hinge the brains of all the people of Negari. Nay, we of Atlantis worshipped Death, but we likewise worshipped Life. These people worship only Death and call themselves Sons of Death. And the skull of Nakura has been to them for a thousand years the symbol of their power, the evidence of their greatness."

"Do you mean," Kane broke in impatiently on these ramblings, "that they will sacrifice the girl to their god?"

"In the Moon of Skulls she will die on the Black Altar."

"What in God's name is this Moon of Skulls?" Kane cried passionately.

"The full moon. At the full of each moon, which we name

the Moon of Skulls, a virgin dies on the Black Altar before the Tower of Death, where centuries ago, virgins died in honor of Golgor, the god of Atlantis. Now from the face of the tower that once housed the glory of Golgor, leers down the skull of the renegade wizard, and the people believe that his brain still lives therein to guide the star of the city. For look ye, stranger, when the full moon gleams over the rim of the tower and the chant of the priests falls silent, then from the skull of Nakura thunders a great voice, raised in an ancient Atlantean chant, and the black people fall on their faces before it.

"But hark, there is a secret way, a stair leading up to a hidden niche behind the skull, and there a priest lurks and chants. In days gone by one of the sons of Atlantis had this office, and by all rights of men and gods it should be mine this day. For though we sons of Atlantis worshipped our ancient gods in secret, the black people would have none of them and to hold our power we were devotees to their foul gods and we sang and sacrificed to him whose memory we cursed.

"But Nakari discovered the secret, known before only to the brown priests, and now one of her black Satellites mounts the hidden stair and yammers forth the strange and terrible chant which is but meaningless gibberish to him, as to those who hear it. I, and only I, know its grim and fearful meaning."

Kane's brain whirled in his efforts to formulate some plan of action. For the first time during the whole search for the girl, he felt himself against a blank wall. This palace was a labyrinth, a maze in which he could decide no direction. The corridors seemed to run without plan or purpose, and how could he find Marylin, prisoned as she doubtless was in one of the myriad chambers or cells? Or had she already passed over the borderline of life, or succumbed to the brutal torture-lust of Nakari?

He scarcely heard the ravings and mutterings of the dying man.

"Stranger, do you indeed live or are you but one of the ghosts which have haunted me of late, stealing through the darkness of my cell? Nay, you are flesh and blood – but you are a white savage, as Nakari's race are black savages – eons ago when your ancestors were defending their caves against the tiger and the mammoth, with crude spears of flint, the gold spires of my people split the stars! They are gone and forgotten, and the world is a waste of barbarians, white and black. Let me, too, pass as a dream that is forgotten in the mists of the ages –"

Kane rose and paced the cell. His fingers closed like steel talons as on a sword hilt and a blind red wave of fury surged through his brain. Oh God! to get his foes before the keen blade that had been taken from him – to face the whole city, one man against them all –

Kane pressed his hands against his temples.

"The moon was nearly full when last I saw it. But I know not how long ago that was. I know not how long I have been in this accursed palace, or how long I lay in that dungeon where Nakari threw me. The time of full moon may be past, and – oh merciful God! – Marylin may be dead already."

"Tonight is the Moon of Skulls," muttered the other; "I heard one of my jailers speak of it."

Kane gripped the dying man's shoulder with unconscious force.

"If you hate Nakari or love mankind, in God's name tell me how to save the child."

"Love mankind?" the priest laughed insanely. "What has a son of Atlantis and a priest of forgotten Golgor to do with love? What are mortals but food for the jaws of the black gods? Softer girls than your Mara have died screaming beneath these hands and my heart was as iron to their cries. Yet hate" – the strange eyes flamed with fearful light – "for hate I will tell you what you wish to know!

"Go to the Tower of Death when the moon is risen. Slay the black priest who lurks behind the skull of Nakura, and then when the chanting of the worshippers below ceases, and the masked slayer beside the Black Altar raises the sacrificial dagger, speak in a loud voice that the people can understand, bidding them set free the victim and offer up instead, Nakari, queen of Negari!

"As for the rest, afterward you must rely on your own craft and prowess if you come free."

Kane shook him.

"Swift! Tell me how I am to reach this tower!"

"Go back through the door whence you came." The man was sinking fast, his words dropped to whispers. "Turn to the left and go a hundred paces. Mount the stair you come to, as high as it goes. In the corridor where it ceases go straight for another hundred paces, and when you come to what seems a blank wall, feel over it until you find a projecting spring. Press this and enter the door which will open. You will then be out of the palace and in the cliffs against which it is built, and in the only one of the secret corridors known to the people of Negari. Turn to your right and go straight down the passage for five hundred paces. There you will come to a stair which leads up to the niche behind the skull. The Tower of Death is built into the cliff and projects above it. There are two stairs –"

Suddenly the voice trailed out. Kane leaned forward and shook the man but he suddenly rose up with a great effort. His eyes blazed with a wild and unearthly light and he flung his shackled arms wide.

"The sea!" he cried in a great voice. "The golden spires of Atlantis and the sun on the deep blue waters! I come!"

And as Kane reached to lay him down again, he slumped back, dead.

VI
THE SHATTERING OF THE SKULL

"By thought a crawling ruin,
By life a leaping mire,
By a broken heart in the breast of the world,
And the end of the world's desire."
CHESTERTON

Kane wiped the cold sweat from his pale brow as he hurried down the shadowy passage. Outside this horrible palace it must be night. Even now the full moon – the grim Moon of

Skulls – might be rising above the horizon. He paced off a hundred paces and came upon the stair the dying priest had mentioned. This he mounted, and coming into the corridor above, he measured off another hundred paces and brought up short against what appeared to be a doorless wall. It seemed an age before his frantic fingers found a piece of projecting metal. There was a creak of rusty hinges as the hidden door swung open and Kane looked into a passageway darker than the one in which he stood.

He entered, and when the door shut behind him he turned to his right and groped his way along for five hundred paces. There the corridor was lighter; light sifted in from without, and Kane discerned a stairway. Up this he went for several steps, then halted, baffled. At a sort of landing the stairway became two, one leading away to the left, the other to the right. Kane cursed. He felt that he could not afford to make a mistake – time was too precious – but how was he to know which would lead him to the niche where the priest hid?

The Atlantean had been about to tell him of these stairs when struck by the delirium which precedes death, and Kane wished fervently that he had lived only a few moments longer.

At any rate, he had no time to waste; right or wrong, he must chance it. He chose the right hand stair and ran swiftly up it. No time for caution now. He felt instinctively that the time of the sacrifice was close at hand. He came into another passage and discerned by the change in masonry that he was out of the cliffs again and in some building – presumably the Tower of Death. He expected any moment to come upon another stair, and suddenly his expectations were realized – but instead of up, it led down. From somewhere in front of him Kane heard a vague, rhythmic murmur and a cold hand gripped his heart. The chanting of the worshippers before the Black Altar!

He raced forward recklessly, rounded a turn in the corridor, brought up short against a door and looked through a tiny aperture. His heart sank. He had chosen the wrong stair and had wandered into some other building adjoining the Tower of Death.

He looked upon a grim and terrible scene. In a wide open space before a great black tower whose spire rose above the crags behind it, two long lines of black dancers swayed and writhed. Their voices rose in a strange meaningless chant, and they did not move from their tracks. From their knees upward their bodies swayed in fantastic rhythmical motions, and in their hands torches tossed and whirled, shedding a lurid shifting red light over the scene. Behind them were ranged a vast concourse of people who stood silent. The dancing torchlight gleamed on a sea of glittering eyes and black faces. In front of the dancers rose the Tower of Death, gigantically tall, black and horrific. No door or window opened in its face, but high on the wall in a sort of ornamented frame there leered a grim symbol of death and decay. The skull of Nakura! A faint eery glow surrounded it, lit somehow from within the tower, Kane knew, and wondered by what strange art the priests had kept the skull from decay and dissolution so long.

But it was neither the skull nor the tower which gripped the Puritan's horrified gaze and held it. Between the converging lines of yelling, swaying worshippers there rose a great black altar. On this altar lay a slim white shape.

"Marylin!" the word burst from Kane's lips in a great sob.

For a moment he stood frozen, helpless, struck blind. No time now to retrace his steps and find the niche where the skull priest lurked. Even now a faint glow was apparent behind the spire of the tower, etching that spire blackly against the sky. The moon had risen. The chant of the dancers soared up to a frenzy of sound and from the silent watchers behind them began a sinister low rumble of drums. To Kane's dazed mind it seemed that he looked on some red debauch of a lower Hell. What ghastly worship of past eons did these perverted and degenerate rites symbolize? Kane knew that these black people aped the rituals of their former masters in their crude way, and even in his despair he found time to shudder at the thought of what those original rites must have been.

Now a fearful shape rose up beside the altar where lay the silent girl. A tall black man, entirely naked save for a hideous painted mask on his face and a great head-dress of waving plumes. The drone of the chant sank low for an instant, then rose up again to wilder heights. Was it the vibrations of their song that made the floor quiver beneath Kane's feet?

Kane with shaking fingers began to unbar the door. Naught to do now but to rush out barehanded and die beside the girl he could not save. Then his gaze was blocked by a giant form which shouldered in front of the door. A huge black man, a chief by his bearing and apparel, leaned idly against the wall as he watched the proceedings. Kane's heart gave a great leap. This was too good to be true! Thrust in the black man's girdle was the pistol he himself had carried! He knew that his weapons must have been divided among his captors. This pistol meant nothing to the chief, but he must have been taken by its strange shape and was carrying it as savages will wear useless trinkets, or perhaps he thought it a sort of war-club. At any rate, there it was. And again floor and building seemed to tremble.

Kane pulled the door silently inward and crouched in the shadows behind his victim like a great brooding tiger. His brain worked swiftly and formulated his plan of action. There was a dagger in the girdle beside the pistol; the black man's back was turned squarely to him and he must strike from the left to reach the heart and silence him quickly. All this passed through Solomon's brain in a flash as he crouched.

The black man was not aware of his foe's presence until Kane's lean right hand shot across his shoulder and clamped on his mouth, jerking him backward. At the same instant the Puritan's left hand tore the dagger from the girdle and with one desperate plunge sank the keen blade home. The black crumpled without a sound and in an instant Kane's pistol was in its owner's hand. A second's investigation showed that it was still loaded and the flint still in place.

No one had seen the swift murder. Those few who stood near the doorway were all facing the Black Altar, enwrapped in the drama which was there unfolding. As Kane stepped across the corpse, the chanting of the dancers ceased abruptly. In the instant of silence which followed, Kane heard, above the pounding of his own pulse, the nightwind rustle the deathlike plumes of the masked horror beside the altar. A rim of the moon glowed above the spire.

Then from high up on the face of the Tower of Death a deep voice boomed out in a strange chant. Mayhap the black priest who spoke behind the skull knew not what his words meant, but Kane believed that he at least mimicked the very intonation of those long-dead brown acolytes. Deep, mystic, resonant the voice sounded out, like the endless flowing of long tides on the broad white beaches.

The masked one beside the altar drew himself up to his great height and raised a long glimmering blade. Kane

recognized his own sword, even as he leveled his pistol and
fired – not at the masked priest but full at the skull which
gleamed in the face of the tower! For in one blinding flash of
intuition he remembered the dying Atlantean's words: "Their
brains hinge on the skull of Nakura!"

Simultaneously with the crack of the pistol came a
shattering crash; the dry skull flew into a thousand pieces and
vanished, and behind it the chant broke off short in a death
shriek. The rapier fell from the
hand of the
masked priest
and many of
the dancers
crumpled to
the earth,
the others
halting short,
spellbound.
Through the
deathly silence
which reigned
for an instant,
Kane rushed toward
the altar; then all Hell
broke loose.

A babel of bestial screams rose to
the shuddering stars. For centuries only their
faith in the dead Nakura had held together the blood-
drenched brains of the black Negari. Now their symbol had
vanished, had been blasted into nothing before their eyes. It
was to them as if the skies had split, the moon fallen and the
world ended. All the red visions which lurked at the backs of
their corroded brains leaped into fearful life, all the latent

insanity which was their heritage rose to claim its own, and Kane looked upon a whole nation turned to bellowing maniacs.

Screaming and roaring they turned on each other, men and women, tearing with frenzied fingernails, stabbing with spears and daggers, beating each other with the flaming torches, while over all rose the roar of frantic human beasts. With clubbed pistol Kane battered his way through the surging, writhing ocean of flesh, to the foot of the altar stairs. Nails raked him, knives slashed at him, torches scorched his garments but he paid no heed.

Then as he reached the altar, a terrible figure broke from the struggling mass and charged him. Nakari, queen of Negari, crazed as any of her subjects, rushed upon the white man with dagger bared and eyes horribly aflame.

"You shall not escape this time, white man!" she was screaming, but before she reached him a great black giant, dripping blood and blind from a gash across his eyes, reeled across her path and lurched into her. She screamed like a wounded cat and struck her dagger into him, and then the groping hands closed on her. The blind giant whirled her on high with one dying effort, and her last scream knifed the din of battle as Nakari, last queen of Negari, crashed against the stones of the altar and fell shattered and dead at Kane's feet.

Kane sprang up the black steps, worn deep by the feet of myriad priests and victims, and as he came, the masked figure, who had stood like one turned to stone, came suddenly to life. He bent swiftly, caught up the sword he had dropped and thrust savagely at the charging white man. But the dynamic quickness of Solomon Kane was such as few men could match. A twist and sway of his steely body and he was inside the thrust, and as the blade slid harmlessly between arm and chest, he brought down the heavy pistol barrel among the waving plumes, crashing headdress, mask and skull with one blow.

Then ere he turned to the fainting girl who lay bound on the altar, he flung aside the shattered pistol and snatched his stolen sword from the nerveless hand which still grasped it, feeling a fierce thrill of renewed confidence at the familiar feel of the hilt.

Marylin lay white and silent, her death-like face turned blindly to the light of the moon which shone calmly down on the frenzied scene. At first Kane thought her to be dead, but his searching fingers detected a faint flutter of pulse. He cut her bonds and lifted her tenderly – only to drop her again and whirl as a hideous blood-stained figure of insanity came leaping and gibbering up the steps. Full upon Kane's outthrust blade the creature ran, and toppled back into the red swirl below, clawing beast-like at its mortal wound.

Then beneath Kane's feet the altar rocked; a sudden tremor hurled him to his knees and his horrified eyes beheld the Tower of Death sway to and fro. Some horror of Nature was taking place and this fact pierced the crumbling brains of the fiends who fought and screamed below. A new element entered into their shrieking, and then the Tower of Death swayed far out with a terrible and awesome majesty – broke from the rocking crags and gave way with a thunder of crashing worlds. Great stones and shards of masonry came raining down, bringing death and destruction to hundreds of screaming humans below. One of these stones crashed to pieces on the altar beside Kane, showering him with dust.

"Earthquake!" he gasped, and smitten by this new terror he caught up the senseless girl and plunged recklessly down the cracking steps, hacking and stabbing a way through the crimson whirlpools of bestial humanity that still tore and ravened.

The rest was a red nightmare, in which Kane's dazed brain refused to record all its horrors. It seemed that for screaming crimson centuries he reeled through narrow winding streets where bellowing, screeching black demons battled and died, among titanic walls and black columns that rocked against the sky and crashed to ruin about him, while the earth heaved and trembled beneath his staggering feet and the thunder of crashing towers filled the world.

Gibbering fiends in human shape clutched and clawed at him, to fade before his flailing sword, and falling stones bruised and battered him. He crouched as he reeled along, covering the girl with his body as best he could, sheltering her alike from blind stone and blinder human. And at last, when it seemed mortal endurance had reached its limit, he saw the great black outer wall of the city loom before him, rent from earth to parapet and tottering for its fall. He dashed through a crevice, and gathering his efforts, made one last sprint. And scarce was he out of reach than the wall crashed, falling inward like a great black wave.

The night wind was in his face and behind him rose the clamor of the doomed city as Kane staggered down the hill path that trembled beneath his feet.

VII
THE FAITH OF SOLOMON

*"The last lost giant, even God,
Is risen against the world."*
CHESTERTON

Dawn lay like a cool white hand on the brow of Solomon
Kane. The nightmares faded from his soul as he breathed deep
of the morning wind which blew up from the jungle far below
his feet – a wind laden with the musk of decaying vegetation;
yet it was like the breath of life to him, for the scents were
those of the clean natural disintegration of outdoor things,
not the loathsome aura of decadent antiquity that lurks in
the walls of eon-old cities – Kane shuddered involuntarily.

He bent over the sleeping girl who lay at his feet,
arranged as comfortably as possible with the few soft tree
branches he had been able to find for her bed. Now she opened
her eyes and stared about wildly for an instant; then as her
gaze met the face of Solomon, lighted by one of his rare
smiles, she gave a little sob of thankfulness and clung to him.

"Oh, Captain Kane! Have we in truth escaped from yon
fearful city? Now it seems all like a dream – after you fell
through the secret door in my chamber Nakari later went to
your dungeon – as she told me – and returned in vile humor.
She said you were a fool, for she had offered you the kingdom
of the world and you had but insulted her. She screamed and
raved and cursed like one insane and swore that she would yet,
alone, build a great empire of Negari. Then she turned on me
and reviled me, saying that you held me – a slave – in more
esteem than a queen and all her glory. And in spite of my pleas
she took me across her knees and whipped me until I swooned.

"Afterward I lay half senseless for a long time, and was

only dimly aware that men came to Nakari and said that you had escaped; they said you were a sorcerer, for you faded through a solid wall like a ghost. But Nakari killed the men who had brought you from the cell, and for hours she was like a wild beast.

"How long I lay thus I know not. In those terrible rooms and corridors where no natural sunlight ever entered, one lost all track of time. But from the time you were captured by Nakari and the time that I was placed on the altar, at least a day and a night and another day must have passed. It was only a few hours before the sacrifice that word came you had escaped.

"Nakari and her Star-maidens came to prepare me for the rite." At the bare memory of that fearful ordeal she whimpered and hid her face in her hands. "I must have been drugged — I only know that they clothed me in the white robe of the sacrifice and carried me into a great black chamber filled with horrid statues. There I lay for a space like one in a trance while the women performed various strange and shameful rites according to their grim religion. Then I fell into a swoon, and when I emerged I was lying bound on the Black Altar — the torches were tossing and the devotees chanting — behind the Tower of Death the rising moon was beginning to glow — all this I knew faintly, as in a deep dream. And as in a dream I saw the glowing skull high on the tower – and the gaunt black naked priest holding a sword above my heart; then I knew no more. What happened?"

"At about that moment," Kane answered, "I emerged from a building wherein I had wandered by mistake, and blasted their hellish skull to atoms with a pistol ball. Whereupon, all these people, being cursed from birth by demons, and being likewise possessed of devils, fall to slaying one another, and in the midst of the tumult an earthquake cometh to pass which shakes the walls down. Then I snatch you up, and running at random, come upon a rent in the outer wall and thereby escape, carrying you, who seem in a swoon.

"Once only you awoke, after I had crossed the Bridge-Across-the-Sky, as the black people called it, which was crumbling beneath our feet by reason of the earthquake. After I had come to these cliffs, but dared not descend them in the darkness, the moon being nigh to setting by that time, you awoke and screamed and clung to me, whereupon I soothed you as best I might, and after a time you fell into a natural sleep."

"And now what?" asked the girl.

"England!" Kane's deep eyes lighted at the word. "I find it hard to remain in the land of my birth for more than a month at a time; yet though I am cursed with the wanderlust, 'tis a name which ever rouses a glow in my bosom. And how of you, child?"

"Oh heaven!" she cried, clasping her small hands. "Home! Something of which to be dreamed – never attained, I fear. Oh Captain Kane, how shall we gain through all the vast leagues of jungle which lie between this place and the coast?"

"Marylin," said Kane gently, stroking her curly hair, "methinks you lack somewhat in faith, both in Providence and in me. Nay, alone I am a weak creature, having no strength or might in me; yet in times past hath God made me a great vessel of wrath and a sword of deliverance. And, I trust, shall do so again.

"Look you, little Marylin: in the last few hours as it were, we have seen the passing of an evil race and the fall of a foul black empire. Men died by thousands about us, and the earth rose beneath our feet, hurling down towers that broke the heavens; yea, death fell about us in a red rain, yet we escaped unscathed.

"Therein is more than the hand of man! Nay, a Power – the mightiest Power! That which guided me across the world, straight to that demon city – which led me to your chamber – which aided me to escape again and led me to the one man in all the city who would give the information I must have, the strange, evil priest of an elder race who lay dying in a subterranean cell – and which guided me to the outer wall, as I ran blindly and at random – for should I have come under the cliffs which formed the rest of the wall, we had surely perished. That same Power brought us safely out of the dying city, and safe across the rocking bridge – which shattered and thundered down into the chasm just as my feet touched solid earth!

"Think you that having led me this far, and accomplished such wonders, the Power will strike us down now? Nay! Evil flourishes and rules in the cities of men and the waste places of the world, but anon the great giant that is God rises and smites for the righteous, and they lay faith on him.

"I say this: this cliff shall we descend in safety, and yon dank jungle traverse in safety, and it is as sure that in old Devon your people shall clasp you again to their bosom, as that you stand here."

And now for the first time Marylin smiled, with the quick eagerness of a normal young girl, and Kane sighed in relief. Already the ghosts were fading from her haunted eyes, and Kane looked to the day when her horrible experiences should be as a dimming dream. One glance he flung behind him, where beyond the scowling hills the lost city of Negari lay shattered and silent, amid the ruins of her own walls and the fallen crags which had kept her invincible so long, but which had at last betrayed her to her doom. A momentary pang smote him as he thought of the myriad of crushed, still forms lying amid those ruins; then the blasting memory of their evil crimes surged over him and his eyes hardened.

"And it shall come to pass, that he who fleeth from the noise of the fear shall fall into the pit; and he that cometh up out of the midst of the pit shall be taken in the snare; for the windows from on high are open, and the foundations of the earth do shake.

"For Thou hast made of a city an heap; of a defended city a ruin; a palace of strangers to be no city; it shall never be built.

"Moreover, the multitude of Thy strangers shall be like small dust and the multitude of the terrible ones shall be as chaff that passeth suddenly away; yea, it shall be at an instant suddenly.

"Stay yourselves and wonder; cry ye out and cry; they are drunken but not with wine; they stagger but not with strong drink.

"Verily, Marylin," said Kane with a sigh, "with mine own eyes have I seen the prophecies of Isaiah come to pass. They were drunken but not with wine! Nay, blood was their drink and in that red flood they dipped deep and terribly."

Then taking the girl by the hand he started toward the edge of the cliff. At this very point had he ascended, in the night – how long ago it seemed.

Kane's clothing hung in tatters about him. He was torn, scratched and bruised. But in his eyes shone the clear calm light of serenity as the sun came up, flooding cliffs and jungle with a golden light that was like a promise of joy and happiness.

The One Black Stain

The One Black Stain

Sir Thomas Doughty, executed at St. Julian's Bay, 1578

They carried him out on the barren sand
    where the rebel captains died;
Where the grim grey rotting gibbets stand
    as Magellan reared them on the strand,
And the gulls that haunt the lonesome land
    wail to the lonely tide.

Drake faced them all like a lion at bay,
    with his lion head upflung:
"Dare ye my word of law defy,
    to say that this traitor shall not die?"
And his captains dared not meet his eye
    but each man held his tongue.

Solomon Kane stood forth alone,
    grim man of a somber race:
"Worthy of death he well may be,
    but the court ye held was a mockery,
"Ye hid your spite in a travesty
    where Justice hid her face.

"More of the man had ye been,
         on deck your sword to cleanly draw
"In forthright fury from its sheath,
         and openly cleave him to the teeth —
"Rather than slink and hide beneath
         a hollow word of Law."

Hell rose in the eyes of Francis Drake.
         "Puritan knave!" swore he,
"Headsman, give him the axe instead!
         He shall strike off yon traitor's head!"
Solomon folded his arms and said,
         darkly and somberly:

"I am no slave for your butcher's work."
         "Bind him with triple strands!"
Drake roared in wrath and the men obeyed,
         hesitantly, as men afraid,
But Kane moved not as they took his blade
         and pinioned his iron hands.

They bent the doomed man to his knees,
         the man who was to die;
They saw his lips in a strange smile bend;
         one last long look they saw him send
At Drake, his judge and his one-time friend,
         who dared not meet his eye.

The axe flashed silver in the sun,
         a red arch slashed the sand;
A voice cried out as the head fell clear,
         and the watchers flinched in sudden fear,
Though 'twas but a sea-bird wheeling near
         above the lonely strand.

"This be every traitor's end!" Drake cried,
    and yet again;
Slowly his captains turned and went,
    and the admiral's stare was elsewhere bent
Than where cold scorn with anger blent
    in the eyes of Solomon Kane.

Night fell on the crawling waves;
    the admiral's door was closed;
Solomon lay in the stenching hold;
    his irons clashed as the ship rolled,
And his guard, grown weary and overbold,
    laid down his pike and dozed.

He woke with a hand at his corded throat
    that gripped him like a vise;
Trembling he yielded up the key,
    and the somber Puritan stood up free,
His cold eyes gleaming murderously
    with the wrath that is slow to rise.

Unseen to the admiral's cabin door
    went Solomon from the guard,
Through the night and silence of the ship,
    the guard's keen dagger in his grip;
No man of the dull crew saw him slip
    in through the door unbarred.

Drake at the table sat alone,
    his face sunk in his hands;
He looked up, as from sleeping –
    but his eyes were blank with weeping
As if he saw not, creeping,
    Death's swiftly flowing sands.

He reached no hand for gun or blade
    to halt the hand of Kane,
Nor even seemed to hear or see,
    lost in black mists of memory,
Love turned to hate and treachery,
    and bitter, cankering pain.

A moment Solomon Kane stood there,
    the dagger poised before,
As a condor stoops above a bird,
    and Francis Drake spoke not nor stirred,
And Kane went forth without a word
    and closed the cabin door.

The Blue Flame of
Vengeance

Previously published as
Blades of the Brotherhood

The Blue Flame of Vengeance

"Death is a blue flame dancing over corpses."
SOLOMON KANE

I
SWORDS CLASH AND A STRANGER COMES

The blades crossed with a sharp clash of venomous steel; blue sparks showered. Across those blades hot eyes burned into each other – hard inky black eyes and volcanic blue ones. Breath hissed between close locked teeth; feet scruffed the sward, advancing, retreating.

He of the black eyes feinted and thrust as quick as a snake strikes. The blue-eyed youth parried with a half turn of a steely wrist and his counter stroke was like the flash of summer lightning.

"Hold, gentlemen!" The swords were struck up and a portly man stood between the combatants, jeweled rapier in one hand, cocked hat in the other.

"Have done! The matter is decided and honor satisfied! Sir George is wounded!"

The black-eyed man with an impatient gesture put behind him his left arm from which, from a narrow wound, blood was streaming.

"Stand aside!" cried he furiously and with an oath. "A wound – a scratch! It decides nothing! 'Tis no matter. This must be to the death!"

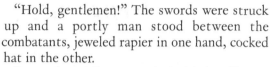

"Aye, stand aside, Sir Rupert," said the victor, quietly, but his hot blue eyes were sparks of steel. "The matter between us can be settled only by death!"

"Put up your steel, you young cockerels!" snapped Sir Rupert. "As magistrate I command it! Sir physician, come and look to Sir George's wound. Jack Hollinster, sheathe your blade, sirrah! I'll have no bloody murders in this district an' my name be Rupert d'Arcy."

Young Hollinster said nothing, nor did he obey the choleric magistrate's command, but he dropped his sword point to the earth and with head half lowered, stood silent and moody, watching the company from under frowning black brows.

Sir George had hesitated, but one of his seconds whispered urgently in his ear and he sullenly acquiesced, handed his sword to the speaker and gave himself up to the ministrations of the physician.

It was a strange setting for such a scene. A low level land, sparsely grown with sickly yellow grass, now withered, ran to a wide strip of white sand, strewn with bits of driftwood. Beyond this strip the sea washed grey and restless, a dead thing upon whose desolate bosom the only sign of life was a single sail hovering in the distance. Inland, across the bleak moors there could be seen in the distance the drab cottages of a small village.

In such a barren and desolate landscape, the splash of color and passionate life there on the beach contrasted strangely. The pale autumn sun flashed on the bright blades, the jeweled hilts, the silver buttons on the coats of some of the men, and the gilt-work on Sir Rupert's vast cocked hat.

Sir George's seconds were helping him in his coat, and Hollinster's second, a sturdy young man in homespun, was urging him to don his. But Jack, still resentful, put him aside. Suddenly he sprang forward with his sword still in his hand and spoke, his voice ringing fierce and vibrant with passion.

"Sir George Banway, look to yourself! A scratch in the arm will not blot out the insult whereof you know! The next time we meet there will be no magistrate to save your rotten hide!"

The nobleman whirled round with a black oath, and Sir Rupert started forward with a roar: "Sirrah! How dare you —"

Hollinster snarled in his face and turning his back, strode away, sheathing his sword with a vicious thrust. Sir George made as if to follow him, his dark face contorted and eyes burning like hot coals, but his friend whispered again in his ear, motioning seaward. Banway's eyes wandered to the single

sail which hung as if suspended in the sky and he nodded grimly.

Hollinster strode along the beach in silence, bareheaded, hat in one hand and his coat slung over his arm. The bleak wind brought coolness to his sweat-plastered locks and it seemed he sought coolness for a turmoiled brain.

His second, Randel, followed him in silence. As they progressed along the beach, the scenery became more wild and rugged; gigantic rocks, grey and moss-grown, reared their heads along the shore and straggled out to meet the waves in grim jagged lines. Further out a rugged and dangerous reef sent up a low and continuous moaning.

Jack Hollinster stopped, turned his face seaward and cursed long, fervently and deep-throated. The awed listener understood the burden of his profanity to be regret at the fact that he, Hollinster, had failed to sink his blade to the hilt in the black heart of that swine, that jackal, that beast, that slanderer of innocence, that damned rogue, Sir George Banway!

"And now," he snarled, "it's like the villain will never meet me in fair combat again, having tasted my steel, but by God —"

"Calm yourself, Jack," honest Randel squirmed uneasily; he was Hollinster's closest friend but he did not understand the black furious moods into which his comrade sometimes fell. "You drubbed him fairly; he got the worst o' it all around. After all, you'd hardly kill a man for what he did —"

"No?" Jack cried passionately. "I'd hardly kill a man for that foul insult? Well, not a man, but a base rogue of a nobleman whose heart I'll see before the moon wanes! Do you realize that he publicly slandered Mary Garvin, the girl I love? That he befouled her name over his drinking cup in the tavern? Why —"

"That I understand," sighed Randel, "having heard the full details not less than a score of times. Also I know that you threw a cup of wine in his face, slapped his chops, upset a table on him and kicked him twice or thrice. Troth, Jack, you've done enough for any man! Sir George is highly connected – you are but the son of a retired sea-captain – even though you have distinguished yourself for valor abroad. Well, after all Jack, Sir George need not have fought you at all. He might have claimed his rank and had his serving men flog you forth."

"An' he had," Hollinster said grimly with a vicious snap of his teeth, "I had put a pistol ball between his damned black eyes – Dick, leave me to my folly. You preach the right road I know – the path of forbearance and meekness. But I have lived where a man's only guide and aid was the sword at his belt; and I come of hot wild blood. Just now that blood is stirred to the marrow by reason of that swine-nobleman. He knew Mary was my beloved, yet he sat there and insulted her in my presence – aye, in my very teeth! – with a leer at me. And why? Because he has monies, lands, titles – high family connections and noble blood. I am a poor man and a poor man's son, who carries his fortune in a sheath at the belt-side. Had I, or had Mary been of high birth, he had respected –"

"Pshaw!" broke in Randel. "When did George Banway ever respect – anything? His black name hereabouts is well deserved. He respects his own desires."

"And he desires Mary," moodily growled the other. "Well, mayhap he'll take her as he's taken many another maid hereabouts. But first he'll kill John Hollinster. Dick – I would not appear churlish but mayhap you'd better leave me for a space. I am no fit companion to anyone and I need solitude and the cold breath of the sea to cool my burning blood."

"You'll not seek Sir George –" Randel hesitated.

Jack made a gesture of impatience. "I'll go the other way, I promise you. Sir George went home to coddle his scratch. He'll not show his face for a fortnight."

"But Jack, his bullies are of unsavory repute. Is it safe for you?"

Jack grinned and the grin was wolfish in spite of his open and frank countenance.

"'Twould be no more than I could ask. But no fear; if he strikes back *that* way – 'twill be in the darkness of midnight – not in open day."

Randel walked away toward the village, shaking his head dubiously, and Jack strode on along the beach, each step taking him further away from the habitations of man and further into a dim realm of waste lands and waste waters. The wind sighed through his clothing, cutting like a knife, but he did not don his coat. The cold grey aura of the day lay like a shroud over his soul and he cursed the land and the clime.

His soul hungered for the far warm southern lands he had known in his wanderings, but a face rose in his visions – a laughing girlish face crowned with golden curls, in whose eyes lay a warmth which transcended the golden heat of tropic moons and which rendered even this barren country warm and pleasant.

Then in his musings another face rose – a dark mocking face, with hard black eyes and a cruel mouth curled viciously under a thin black mustache. Jack Hollinster cursed sincerely.

A deep vibrant voice broke in on his profanity.

"Young man, your words are vain and worldly. They are as sounding brass and tinkling cymbals, full of sound and fury, signifying nothing."

Jack whirled, hand shooting to hilt. He had thought he was alone. On a great grey boulder there sat a Stranger. This man rose as Jack turned, unwrapping a wide black cloak and laying it over his arm.

Hollinster gazed at him curiously. The man was of a type to command attention and something more. He was inches taller than Hollinster who was considerably above medium height. There was no ounce of fat or surplus flesh on that spare frame, yet the man did not look frail or even too thin. On the contrary. His broad shoulders, deep chest and long rangy limbs betokened strength, speed and endurance – bespoke the swordsman as plainly as did the long unadorned rapier at his belt. The man reminded Jack, more than anything else, of one of the great gaunt grey wolves he had seen on the Siberian steppes.

But it was the face which first caught and held the young man's attention. The face was rather long, was smooth-shaven and of a strange dark pallor which together with the somewhat sunken cheeks lent an almost corpse-like appearance at times – until one looked at the eyes. These gleamed with vibrant life and dynamic vitality, pent deep and ironly controlled. Looking directly into these eyes, feeling the cold shock of their strange power, Jack Hollinster was unable to tell their color. There was the greyness of ancient ice in them, but there was also the cold blueness of the Northern sea's deepest depths. Heavy black brows hung above them and the whole effect of the countenance was distinctly Mephistophelean.

The stranger's clothing was simple, severely plain and suited the man. His hat was a black slouch, featherless. From heel to neck he was clad in close-fitting garments of a sombre hue, unrelieved by any ornament or jewel. No ring adorned his powerful fingers; no gem twinkled on his rapier hilt and its long blade was cased in a plain leather sheath. There were no silver buttons on his garments, no bright buckles on his shoes.

Strangely enough the drab monotone of his dress was broken in a novel and bizarre manner by a wide sash knotted gypsy-fashion about his waist. This sash was silk of Oriental workmanship; its color was a sinister virulent green, like a serpent's hide, and from it projected a dirk hilt and the black butts of two heavy pistols.

Hollinster's gaze wandered over this strange apparition even as he wondered how this man came here, in his strange apparel, armed to the teeth. His appearance suggested the Puritan, yet –

"How came you here?" asked Jack bluntly. "And how is it that I saw you not until you spoke?"

"I came here as all honest men come, young sir," the deep voice answered, as the speaker wrapped his wide black cloak about him and reseated himself on the boulder, "on my two legs – as for the other: men engrossed in their own affairs to the point of taking the Name in vain, see neither their friends – to their shame – nor their foes – to their harm."

"Who are you?"

"My name is Solomon Kane, young sir, a landless man – one time of Devon."

Jack frowned uncertainly. Somewhere, somehow, the

Puritan had certainly lost all the unmistakable Devonshire accent. From the
sound of his words he might have been
from anywhere in England, north or
south.

"You have travelled a great deal, sir?"

"My steps have been led in many far countries,
young sir."

A light broke in on Hollinster and he gazed at his strange
companion with quickened interest.

"Were you not a captain in the French army for a space,
and were you not at – " he named a certain name.

Kane's brow clouded.

"Aye. I led a rout of ungodly men, to my shame be it said,
though the cause was a just one. In the sack of that town you
name, many foul deeds were done under the cloak of the cause
and my heart was sickened – oh, well – many a tide has flowed
under the bridge since then, and I have drowned some red
memories in the sea –

"And speaking of the sea, lad, what make you of yonder
ship standing off and on as she hath done since yesterday's
daybreak?"

A lean finger stabbed seaward, and Jack shook his head.

"She lies too far out. I can make naught of her."

The sombre eyes bored into his and Hollinster did not
doubt that that cold gaze might plumb the distances and
detect the very name painted on the far away ship's bows.
Anything seemed possible for those strange eyes.

"'Tis in truth a thought far for the eye to carry," said
Kane. "But by the cut of her rigging I believe I recognize her.
It is in my mind that I would like to meet the master of this
ship."

Jack said nothing. There was no harbor hereabouts, but a

ship might, in calm weather, run close ashore and anchor just outside the reef. This ship might be a smuggler. There was always a good deal of illicit trade going on about this lonely coast where the custom officers seldom came.

"Have you ever heard of one Jonas Hardraker, whom men call The Fishhawk?"

Hollinster started. That dread name was known on all the coasts of the civilized world, and in many uncivilized coasts, for the owner had made it feared and abhorred in many waters, warm and cold. Jack sought to read the stranger's face, but the brooding eyes were inscrutable.

"That bloody pirate? The last I heard of him, he was purported to be cruising the Caribees."

Kane nodded.

"Lies travel ahead of a fast craft. The Fishhawk cruises where his ship is, and where his ship is, only his master Satan knows."

He stood up, wrapping his cloak more closely about him. "The Lord hath led my feet into many strange places, and over many queer paths," said he sombrely. "Some were fair and many were foul; sometimes I seemed to wander without purpose or guidance but always when I sought deep I found fit reason therefor. And harkee, lad, forbye the fires of Hell there is no hotter fire than the blue flame of vengeance which burneth a man's heart night and day without rest until he quench it in blood.

"It hath been my duty in times past to ease various evil men of their lives – well, the Lord is my staff and my guide and methinks he hath delivered mine enemy into mine hands."

And so saying Kane strode away with long cat-like strides, leaving Hollinster to gape after him in bewilderment.

II
One Comes in the Night

Jack Hollinster awoke from a dream-haunted slumber. He sat up in bed and stared about him. Outside the moon had not risen but in his window a head and a pair of broad shoulders were framed black in the starlight. A warning "Shhhh!" came to him like a serpent's hiss.

Slipping his sword from the scabbard which hung on the bed post, Jack rose and approached the window. A bearded face set with two small sparkling eyes looked in at him; the man was breathing deeply as if from a long run.

"Bring tha swoord, lad, and follow me," came the urgent whisper. "'E's got she!"

"How now? Who's got who?"

"Sir Garge!" was the chilling whisper. "'E sent she a writin' wi' your name onto it, biddin' 'er come to the Rocks, and his rogues grabbed she and – "

"Mary Garvin?"

"Truth as ever was, maaster!"

The room reeled. Hollinster had anticipated attack on himself; he had not supposed the villainy of Sir George's nature went deep enough for an abduction of a helpless girl.

"Blast his black soul," he growled between his teeth as he snatched at his clothes. "Where is she now?"

"They tooken she to 'is 'ouse, sur."

"And who are you?"

"No' but poor Sam as tends stable down to the tavern, sur. I see 'em grab she."

Dressed and bare sword in hand, Hollinster climbed through the window. He would not risk awaking his parents by going out the front door.

"I thank you, Sam," said he. "If I live, I'll remember this."

Sam grinned, showing his yellow fangs: "I'll go wi' 'e, maaster; I've a grudge or twain to settle wi' Sir Garge!" His eyes gleamed with hatred and he flourished a wicked looking bludgeon.

"Come then. We'll go straight to the swine's house."

Sir George Banway's huge ancient manor house, in which he lived alone except for a few evil-visaged servants and several more evil cronies, stood some two miles from the village, close to the beach but in the opposite direction from that taken by Jack in his stroll yesterday. A great lowering bulk of a house, in some disrepair, its oaken panels stained with age, many ill tales were told about it, and of the

villagers, only such rowdies and ruffians as
enjoyed the owner's confidence, had ever
set foot in it. No wall surrounded it, only
a few ragged hedges and a few straggling
trees. The moors ran to the back of the house
and the front faced a strip of sandy beach some
two hundred yards wide which lay between the house
and the boulder-torn surf. The rocks directly in front of
the house, at the water's edge were unusually high, barren
and rugged. It was said that there were curious caves among
them, but no one knew exactly for Sir George regarded that
particular strip of beach as his own private property and had
a way of taking musket shots at parties who showed a
curiosity regarding it.

Not a light showed in the house as Jack Hollinster and his
strange follower made their way across the dank moor. A thin
mist had blotted out most of the stars and through it the
great black house reared up dark and ominous, surrounded by
dark, bent ghosts which were hedges and trees. Seaward all
was veiled in a grey shroud but once Jack thought he heard
the muffled clank of a mooring chain. He wondered if a ship
could be anchored outside that venomous line of breakers.
The grey sea moaned restlessly as a sleeping monster might
moan without waking.

"The windy, maaster," came from the man Sam in a fierce
whisper. "'E'll have tha glims doused but 'e be there, just the
same!"

Together they stole silently to the great dark house. Jack
found time to wonder at the silence and the lack of guards.
Was Sir George so certain of himself that he had not taken
the trouble to throw out sentries? Or were the sentries
sleeping on duty? He tried a window cautiously. It was heavily
shuttered but the shutters swung open with surprizing ease.

Even as they did, a suspicion crossed his mind like a lightning flash – all this was too sure – too easy! He whirled, just as he saw the bludgeon in Sam's hand go up. There was no time to thrust or duck. Yet even in that fleeting flash of vision he saw the evil triumph in the little swinish eyes – then the world crashed about him and all was utter blackness.

III
"– DEATH'S WALKIN' TONIGHT –"

Slowly Jack Hollinster drifted back to consciousness. A red glow was in his eyes and he blinked repeatedly. His head ached sickeningly and this glare hurt his eyes. He shut them, hoping it would cease, but the merciless radiance beat through the lids – into his throbbing brain, it seemed. A confused medley of voices bore dimly on his ears. He tried to raise his hand to his head but was unable to stir. Then it all came back with a rush and he was fully and poignantly awake.

He was bound hand and foot with cruel tightness and was lying on a dank dirt floor. He was in a vast cellar, piled high with squat casks and kegs and black sticky-looking barrels. The ceiling or roof of this cellar was fairly high, braced with heavy oaken timbers. On one of these timbers hung a lanthorn from which emanated the red glow that hurt his eyes. This light illuminated the cellar but filled its corners with flickering shadows. A flight of broad stone stairs came down the cellar at one end and a dark passageway led away out of the other end.

There were many men in the cellar; Jack recognized the dark mocking countenance of Banway, the drink-flushed bestial face of the traitor Sam, two or three bullies who divided their time between Sir George's house and the village tavern. The rest, some ten or twelve men, he did not know. They were all indubitably seamen; brawny hairy men with ear rings and nose rings and tarry breeches. But their dress was bizarre and grotesque. Some had gay bandannas bound about their heads and all were armed to the teeth. Cutlasses with broad brass guards were much in evidence as well as jewel-hilted daggers and silver-chased pistols. These men diced and drank and swore terrific oaths, while their eyes gleamed terribly in the lanthorn light.

Pirates! No true honest seamen, these, with their strange contrast of finery and ruffianism. Tarry breeks and seamen's shirts, yet silken sashes lapped their waists; no stockings to their legs, yet many had on silver-buckled shoes and heavy gold rings to their fingers. Great gems dangled from many a heavy gold hoop serving as ear ring. Not an honest sailorman's knife among them, but costly Spanish and Italian daggers. Their gauds, their ferocious faces, their wild and blasphemous bearing stamped them with the mark of their red trade.

Jack thought of the ship he had seen before sundown and of the rattle of the anchor chain in the mist. He suddenly remembered the strange man, Kane, and wondered at his words. Had he known that ship was a buccaneer? What was his connection with these wild men? Was his Puritanism merely a mask to hide sinister activities?

A man casting dice with Sir George turned suddenly toward the captive. A tall, rangy, broad-shouldered man – Jack's heart leaped into his mouth. Then subsided. At first glimpse he had thought this man to be Kane, but he now saw that the buccaneer, though alike to the Puritan in general build, was his antithesis in all other ways. He was scantily but gaudily clad, and ornate with silken sash and silver buckles, and gilded tassels. His broad girdle bristled with dagger hilts and pistol butts, scintillant with jewels. A long rapier, resplendent with gold-work and gems, hung from a rich scroll-worked baldric. From each slim gold ear ring was pendant a sparkling red ruby of goodly size, whose crimson brilliance contrasted strangely with the dark face.

This face was lean, hawk-like and cruel. A cocked hat topped the narrow high forehead, pulled low over sparse black brows, but not too low to hide the gay bandanna beneath. In the shadow of the hat a pair of cold grey eyes danced recklessly, with changing sparks of light and shadow. A knife-bridged beak of a nose hooked over a thin gash of a mouth, and the cruel upper lip was adorned with long drooping mustachios, much like those worn by Manchu mandarins.

"Ho, George, our prey wakes!" this man shouted with a cruel slash of laughter in his words. "By Zeus, Sam, I'd thought you'd given him his resting dose. But he'd a thicker pate than I thought for."

The pirate crew ceased their games and stared curiously or mockingly at Jack. Sir George's dark face darkened and he indicated his left arm, with the bandage showing through the ruffled silk sleeve.

"You spoke truth, Hollinster, when you said with our next meeting no magistrate should intervene. Only now, methinks 'tis *your* rotten hide shall suffer."

"*Jack!*"

Deeper than Banway's taunts, the sudden agonized voice cut like a knife. Jack, with his blood turning to ice, wrenched frantically over and craning his neck, saw a sight that almost stopped his heart. A girl was bound to a great ring in an oaken support – a girl who knelt on the dank dirt floor, straining toward him, her face white, her soft eyes dilated with fright, her golden locks in disarray –

"Mary – oh my God!" burst from Jack's anguished lips. A brutal shout of laughter chorused his frantic outcry.

"Drink a health to the loving pair!" roared the tall pirate captain, lifting a frothing drinking jack. "Drink to the lovers, lads! Meseemeth he grudges us our company. Wouldst be alone with the little wench, boy?"

"You black-hearted swine!" raved Jack, struggling to his knees with a superhuman effort. "You cowards, you poltroons, you dastards, you white-livered devils! Gods of Hell, if my arms were but free! Loose me, an' the pack of you have a drop of manhood between you all! Loose me, and let me at your swines'-throats with my bare hands! If I make not corpses of jackals, then blast me for a varlet and a coward!"

"Judas!" spoke one of the buccaneers admiringly. "The lad hath the good right guts, even so! And what a flow o' speech, keelhaul me! Blast my lights and liver, cap'n, but –"

"Be silent," cut in Sir George harshly, for his hatred ate at his heart like a rat. "Hollinster, you waste your breath. Not this time do I face you with naked blade. You had your chance and failed. This time I fight you with weapons better suited to your rank and station. None knows where you went or to what end. None shall ever know. The sea has hidden better bodies than yours, and shall hide still better ones after your bones have turned to slime on the sea bottom. As for you –"

he turned to the horrified girl who was stammering pitiful pleas, "you will bide with me awhile in my house. In this very cellar, belike. Then when I have wearied of you –"

"Hadst better be wearied of her by the time I return, in two months," broke in the pirate captain with a sort of fiendish joviality. "If I take a corpse to sea this trip – which Satan knoweth is a plaguey evil cargo! – I must have a fairer passenger next time."

Sir George grinned sourly. "So be it. In two months she is yours – unless she should chance to die before that time. You sail just before dawn with the red ruin of a man I intend to make of Hollinster wrapped in canvas, and you sink the remains so far out at sea they will never wash ashore. (Though it's few will recognize the corpse after I am through with him.) That is understood – then in two months you may return for the girl."

As Jack listened to this callous and frightful program his heart shrivelled within him.

"Mary, my girl," he said weakly, "how came you here?"

"A man brought a missive," she whispered, too faint with fear to speak aloud. "It was written in a hand much like yours, with your name signed. It said that you were hurt and for me to come to you to the Rocks. I came; these men seized me and bore me here through a long evil tunnel."

"As I told 'e, maaster!" shouted the hirsute Sam with gloating glee. "Trust ole Sam to trick 'em! 'E come along same as a lamb! Oh, that were a rare trick – and a rare fool 'e were, too!"

"Belay," spoke up a dark, lean saturnine pirate, evidently first mate, "'tis perilous enough puttin' in this way to get rid o' the loot we takes. What if they find the girl here and she tips 'em the lay? Where'd we find a market this side the Channel for the North Sea plunder?"

Sir George and the captain laughed.

"Be at ease, Allardine. Wast ever a melancholy knave. They'll think the wench and the lad eloped together. Her father is against him, George says. None of the villagers will ever see or hear of either of them again and they'll never look here. You're downhearted because we're so far from the Main. Faith man, haven't we threaded the Channel before, aye, and taken merchantmen in the Baltic, under the very noses of the men-o'-war?"

"Mayhap," mumbled Allardine, "but I'll feel safer wi' these waters far behind. The day o' the Brotherhood is passin' in these climes. Best the Caribs for us. I feel evil in my bones. Death hovers over us like a black cloud and I see no channel to steer through."

The pirates moved uneasily. "Avast man, that's ill talk."

"It's an ill bed, the sea bottom," answered the other gloomily.

"Cheer up," laughed the captain, slapping his despondent mate resoundingly on the back. "Drink a swig o' rum to the bride! It's a foul berth, Execution Dock, but we're well to windward of *that*, so far. Drink to the bride! Ha ha! George's bride and mine – though the little hussy seems not overjoyful –"

"Hold!" the mate's head jerked up. "Was not that a muffled scream overhead?"

Silence fell while eyes rolled toward the stair and thumbs stealthily felt the edge of blades. The captain shrugged his mighty shoulders impatiently.

"I heard nothing."

"I did. A scream and a fallin' carcase – I tell you, Death's walkin' tonight –"

"Allardine," said the captain, with a sort of still passion as he knocked the neck from a bottle, "you are become an old woman, in very truth, of late, starting at shadows. Take heart from me! Do I ever fret myself wi' fear or worry?"

"Better if you went wi' more heed," answered the gloomy one direly. "A-takin' o' break-neck chances, night and day – and wi' a human wolf on your trail day and night as you have – ha' you forgot the word sent you near two years ago?"

"Bah!" the captain laughed, raising the bottle to his lips. "The trail's too long for even –"

A black shadow fell across him and the bottle slipped from his fingers to shatter on the floor. As if struck by a premonition, the pirate paled and turned slowly. All eyes sought the stone stairway which led down into the cellar. No one had heard a door open or shut, but there on the steps stood a tall man, dressed all in black save for a bright green sash about his waist. Under heavy black brows, shadowed by a low-drawn slouch hat, two cold eyes gleamed like burning ice. Each hand gripped a heavy pistol, cocked. Solomon Kane!

IV

THE QUENCHING OF THE FLAME

"Move not, Jonas Hardraker," said Kane tonelessly. "Stir not, Ben Allardine! George Banway, John Harker, Black Mike, Bristol Tom – keep your hands in front of you! Let no man touch sword or pistol, lest he die suddenly!"

There were nearly twenty men in that cellar, but in those gaping black muzzles there was sure death for two, and none wished to be the first to die. So nobody moved. Only the mate

Allardine with his face like snow on a winding sheet, gasped:

"Kane! I knew it! Death's in the air when he's near! I told you, near two years ago when he sent you word, Jonas, and you laughed! I told you he came like a shadow and slew like a ghost! The red Indians in the new lands are naught to him in subtlety! Oh, Jonas, you should ha' harkened to me!"

Kane's sombre eyes chilled him into silence. "You remember me of old, Ben Allardine – you knew me before the brotherhood of buccaneers turned into a bloody gang of cutthroat pirates. And I had dealings with your former captain, as we both remember – in the Tortugas and again off the Horn. An evil man he was and one whom Hell fire hath no doubt devoured – to which end I aided him with a musket ball.

"As to my subletly – true I have dwelt in Darien and learned somewhat of stealth and woodcraft and strategy, but your true pirate is a very hog and easy to steal upon. Those who watch outside the house saw me not as I stole through

the thick fog, and the bold rover who with sword and musket guarded the cellar door, knew not that I entered the house; he died suddenly and with only a short squeal like a stuck hog."

Hardraker burst out with a furious oath: "What want you? What do you here?"

Solomon Kane regarded him with a cold concentrated hate in his eyes; yet it was not so much the hatred that was blood chilling – as it was a bleak certainty of doom, a relentless cold blood lust that was sure of satiety.

"Some of your crew know me of old, Jonas Hardraker whom men call the Fishhawk." Kane's voice was toneless but deep feeling hummed at the back of it. "And you well know why I have followed you from the Main to Portugal, from Portugal to England. Two years ago you sank a ship in the Caribees, 'The Flying Heart' out of Dover. Thereon was a young girl, the daughter of – well, never mind the name. You remember the girl. The old man, her father, was a close friend to me, and many a time, in bygone years have I held his infant daughter on my knee – the infant who grew up to be torn by your foul hands, you black devil. Well, when the ship was taken, this maid fell into your clutches and shortly died. Death was more kind to her than you had been. Her father who learned of her fate from survivors of that massacre, went mad and is in such state to this day. She had no brothers, no one but that old man. None might avenge her –"

"Except you, Sir Galahad?" sneered the Fishhawk.

"*Yes, I, you damned black swine!*" roared
Kane unexpectedly. The crash of his
powerful voice almost shattered the ear
drums and hardened buccaneers started and
blenched. Nothing is more stunning or terrible
than the sight of a man of icy nerves and iron
control suddenly losing that control and flaming into
a full withering blast of murderous fury. For a fleeting
instant as he thundered those words, Kane was a fearful
picture of primitive, relentless and incarnate passion. Then
the storm passed instantly and he was his icy self again – cold
as chill steel, calm and deadly as a cobra.

One black muzzle centered directly on Hardraker's
breast, the other menaced the rest of the gang.

"Make your peace with God, pirate," said Kane
tonelessly, "for in another instant it will be too late."

Now for the first time the pirate blenched.

"Great God," he gasped, sweat beading his brow, "you'd
not shoot me down like a jackal, without a chance?"

"That will I, Jonas Hardraker," answered Kane, with
never a tremor of voice or steely hand, "and with a joyful
heart. Have you not committed all crimes under the sun? Are
you not a stench in the nostrils of God and a black smirch on
the books of men? Have you ever spared weakness or pitied
helplessness? Shrink you from your fate, you black coward?"

With a terrific effort the pirate pulled himself together.

"Why, I shrink not. But it is *you* who are the coward."

Menace and added fury clouded the cold eyes for an
instant. Kane seemed to retreat within himself – to withdraw
himself still further from human contact. He poised himself
there on the stairs like some brooding unhuman thing – like
a great black condor about to rend and slay.

"You are a coward," continued the pirate recklessly,

realizing – for he was no fool – that he had touched the one accessible chord in the Puritan's breast – the one weak spot in Kane's armor – vanity. Though he never boasted, Kane took a deep pride in the fact that whatever his many enemies said of him, no man had ever called him a coward.

"Mayhap I deserve killing in cold blood," went on the Fishhawk, watching him narrowly, "but if you give me no chance to defend myself, men will name you poltroon."

"The praise or the blame of man is vanity," said Kane somberly. "And men know if I be coward or not."

"But not I!" shouted Hardraker triumphantly. "An' you shoot me down I will go into Eternity, knowing you are a dastard, despite what men say or think of you!"

After all Kane, fanatic as he was, was still human. He tried to make himself believe that he cared not what this wretch said or thought, but in his heart he knew that so deep was his underlying vanity of courage, that if this pirate died with a scornful sneer on his lips, that he, Kane, would feel the sting all the rest of his life. He nodded grimly.

"So be it. You shall have your chance, though the Lord knoweth you deserve naught. Name your weapons."

The Fishhawk's eyes narrowed. Kane's skill with the sword was a byword among the wild outcasts and rovers that wandered over the world. With pistols, he, Hardraker, would have no opportunity for trickery or to use his iron strength.

"Knives!" he snapped with a vicious clack of his strong white teeth.

Kane eyed him moodily for a moment, the pistols never wavering, then a faint grim smile spread over his dark countenance.

"Good enough; knives are scarce a gentleman's arm – but with one an end may be made which is neither quick nor painless."

He turned to the pirates. "Throw down your weapons." Sullenly they obeyed.

"Now loose the girl and the boy." This also was done and Jack stretched his numbed limbs, felt the cut in his head, now clotted with dried blood, and took the whimpering Mary in his arms.

"Let the girl go," he whispered, but Solomon shook his head.

"She could never get by the guards outside the house."

Kane motioned Jack to stand part way up the stairs, with Mary behind him. He gave Hollinster the pistols and swiftly undid his sword belt and jacket, laying them on the lower step. Hardraker was laying aside his various weapons and stripping to his breeches.

"Watch them all," Kane muttered. "I'll take care of the Fishhawk. If any other reaches for a weapon, shoot quick and straight. If I fall, flee up the stairs with the girl. But my brain is on fire with the blue flame of vengeance and I will not fall!"

The two men now approached each other, Kane bareheaded and in his shirt, Hardraker still wearing his knotted bandanna, but stripped to the waist. The pirate was armed with a long Turkish dagger which he held point upward. Kane held a dirk in front of him as a man holds a rapier. Experienced fighters, neither held his blade point down in the conventional manner – which is unscientific and awkward, except in special cases.

It was a strange, nightmare scene that was lighted by the guttering lanthorn on the wall: the pale youth with his pistols on the stair with the shrinking girl behind him, the fierce hairy faces ringed about the walls, reddened eyes glittering with savage intensity – the gleam on the dull blue blades –

the tall figures in the center circling each other while their shadows kept pace with their movements, changing and shifting as they advanced or gave ground.

"Come in and fight, Puritan," taunted the pirate, yet giving ground before Kane's steady though wary approach. "Think of the wench, Broadbrim!"

"I *am* thinking of her, offal of Purgatory," said Kane somberly. "There be many fires, scum, some hotter than others –" how deadly blue the blades shimmered in the lanthorn light! – "but save the fires of Hell – all fires – may be – quenched – by – *blood!*"

And Kane struck as a wolf leaps. Hardraker parried the straight thrust and springing in, struck upward with the venomous disembowelling stroke. Kane's down-turned point deflected the sweep of the blade and with a dynamic coil and release of steel-spring muscles, the pirate bounded backward out of reach. Kane came on in a relentless surge; he was ever the aggressor in any battle.

He thrust like lightning for face and body and for an instant the pirate was too busy parrying the whistling strokes to launch an attack of his own. This could not last; a knife fight is necessarily short and deadly. The nature of the weapons prevents any long drawn play of fencing skill.

Now Hardraker, watching his opportunity, suddenly caught Kane's knife wrist in an iron grip and at the same time ripped savagely upward for the belly. Kane, at the cost of a badly cut hand, caught the uplunging wrist and checked the point an inch from his body. There for a moment they stood like statues glaring into each other's eyes, exerting all their strength.

Kane did not care for this style of fighting. He had rather trust the other way which was more swiftly deadly – the open free style, the leaping in and out, thrusting and parrying, where one relied on his quickness of hand and foot and eye, and gave and invited open strokes. But since it was to be a test of strength – so be it!

Hardraker had already begun to doubt. Never had he met a man his equal in sheer brute power, but now he found this Puritan as immovable as iron. He threw all his strength, which was immense, into his wrists and his powerfully braced legs. Kane had shifted his grip on his dirk to suit the emergency. At first grips, Hardraker had forced Kane's knife hand upward. Now Solomon held his dirk poised above the pirate's breast, point downward. His task at hand was to force down the hand that gripped his wrist until he could drive the dirk through Hardraker's breast. The Fishhawk's knife hand was held low, the blade upward; he sought to strain against Kane's arresting left hand and braced arm until he could rip open the Puritan's belly.

So there they strained, man to man, until the muscles bulged in tortured knots all over them and sweat stood out on their foreheads. The veins swelled in Hardraker's temples. In the watching ring breath hissed sharply between clenched teeth.

For awhile neither gained the advantage. Then slowly but surely, Kane began to force Hardraker backwards. The locked hands of the men did not change in their relative position but the pirate's whole body began to sway. The pirate's thin lips split in a ghastly grin of superhuman effort, in which there was no mirth. His face was like a grinning skull and the eyes bulged from their sockets. Inflexibly as Death, Kane's greater strength asserted itself. The Fishhawk bent slowly like a tree whose roots are ripped up and which falls slowly. His breath hissed and whistled as he fought fiercely to brace himself like steel, to regain his lost ground. But back and down he went, inch by inch, until after what seemed hours, his back was pressed hard against an oaken table top and Kane loomed over him like a harbinger of Doom.

Hardraker's right hand still gripped his dagger, his left hand was still locked on Kane's right wrist. But now Kane, holding the dagger point still at bay with his left, began to force his knife hand downward. It was slow agonizing hard work. The veins stood out on Kane's temples with the effort. Inch by inch, as he had forced the Fishhawk down on the table, he forced the dirk downward. The muscles coiled and swelled like tortured steel cables in the pirate's slowly bending left arm, but slowly the dirk descended. Sometimes the Fishhawk managed to halt its relentless course for an instant, but he could never force it back by a fraction of an inch. He wrenched desperately with his right hand which still gripped the Turkish dagger, but Kane's bloody left hand held it as in a steel vise.

Now the implacable dirk point was within an inch of the pirate's heaving breast, and Kane's deathly cold eyes matched the chill of the blue steel. Within two inches of that black heart the point stopped, held fixed by the desperation of the doomed man. What were those distended eyes seeing? There

was a faraway glassy stare in them, though they were focussed
on the dirk point which was the center of the universe to
them. But what else did they see? – Sinking ships that the
black sea drank and gurgled over? Coastal towns lit with red
flame, where women screamed and through whose red glow
dark figures leaped and blasphemed? Black seas, wild
with winds and lit with the sheet lightning of an
outraged heaven? Smoke and flame and red
ruin – black shapes dangling at the yard-
arms – writhing figures that fell from a
plank laid out over the rail – a white
girlish shape whose pallid lips framed
frenzied pleas –?

From Hardraker's slavering
lips burst a terrible scream. Kane's
hand lurched downward – the dirk
point sank into the breast. On the
stairs Mary Garvin turned away, pressed
her face against the dank wall to shut out
sight – covered her ears to shut out sound.

Hardraker had dropped his dagger; he
sought to tear loose his right to fend off that cruel dirk. But
Kane held him, vise-like. Yet still the writhing pirate did not
release Kane's wrist. Holding death at bay to the bitter end,
he clutched and as Kane had forced the point to his breast, so
he forced it into his heart – inch by inch. The sight brought
cold sweat to the brows of the onlookers, but Kane's icy eyes
never flickered. He too was thinking of a bloodstained deck
and a weak young girl who cried in vain for mercy.

Hardraker's screams rose unbearably, thinned to a
frightful thin squealing; not the cries of a coward afraid of the
dark, but the blind unconscious howling of a man in his death
agony. The hilt of the dirk almost touched his breast when

the screaming broke in a ghastly strangled gurgling and then ceased. Blood burst from the ashy lips and the wrist in Kane's left hand went limp. Only then did the fingers of the left hand fall away from Kane's knife wrist – relaxed by the death they had striven so madly to hold at bay.

Silence lay like a white shroud over all. Kane wrenched his dirk clear and a trickle of seeping blood followed sluggishly, then ceased. The Puritan mechanically swished the blade through the air to shake off the red drops which clung to the steel, and as it flashed in the lanthorn light, it seemed to Jack Hollinster to glitter like a blue flame – a flame which had been quenched in scarlet.

Kane reached for his rapier. At that instant, Hollinster, jerking himself out of his trance-like mood, saw the man Sam stealthily lift a pistol and aim at the Puritan. Sight and action were as one. At the crash of Jack's shot Sam screamed and reared upright, his pistol exploding in the air. He had been crouched directly under the lanthorn. As he flung out his arms in his death throes, the pistol barrel struck the lanthorn and shattered it, plunging the cellar into instant blackness.

Instantly the darkness crashed into sound, strident and blasphemous. Kegs were upset, men fell over each other and swore soulfully, steel clashed and pistols cracked as men found them with groping hands and fired at random. Somebody howled profanely as one of these blind bullets found a mark. Jack had the girl by the arm and was half leading, half carrying her up the dark stairs. He slipped and stumbled, but eventually reached the top and flung open the heavy door. A faint light which this opening let in showed him a man just behind him and a dim flood of figures scrambling up the lower steps.

Hollinster swung the remaining loaded pistol around, then Kane's voice spoke:

"'Tis I – Kane – young sir. Out swiftly, with your lady."

Hollinster obeyed and Kane, leaping out after him, turned and slammed the oaken door in the faces of the yelling horde which surged up from below. He dropped a strong bolt into place and then stepped back, eyeing his work with satisfaction. Inside sounded muffled yells, hammerings and shots, and in places the wood of the door bulged outward as bullets chunked into the other side. But none of the soft lead went entirely through the thick hard panels.

"And now what?" asked Jack, turning to the tall Puritan. He noticed for the first time that a bizarre figure lay at his feet – a dead pirate with ear rings and gay sash, whose futile sword and useless musket lay beside him. Undoubtedly the sentry whose watch Kane's silent sword had ended.

The Puritan casually shoved the corpse aside with his foot and motioned the two lovers to follow him. He led the way up a short flight of wooden steps, down a dark hallway, into a chamber, then halted. The chamber was lit by a large candle on a table.

"Wait here a moment," he requested. "Most of the evil ones are confined below, but there be guards without – some five or six men. I slipped between them as I came, but now the moon is out and we must be wary. I will look through an outer window and see if I can spy any."

Left alone in the great chamber, Jack looked at Mary in love and pity. This had been a hectic night for any girl. And

Mary, poor child, had never been used to violence and ill treatment. Her face was so pale that Jack wondered if the color would ever come back into her once rosy cheeks. Her eyes were wide and haunted, though trusting when she looked at her lover.

He drew her gently into his arms. "Mary girl –" he began tenderly when, looking over his shoulder, she screamed, her eyes flaring with new terror. Instantaneously came the scrape of a rusty bolt.

Hollinster whirled. A black opening gaped in the wall where formerly had been only one of the regular panels. Before it stood Sir George Banway, eyes blazing, garments dishevelled, pistol leveled.

Jack flung Mary aside and threw up his weapon. The two shots crashed together. Hollinster felt the bullet cut the skin on his cheek like a red-hot razor edge. A bit of cloth flew from Sir George's shirt bosom. With a sobbing gasp of curse he went down – then as Jack turned back to the horrified girl, Banway reeled up again. He was drinking in the air in great gasps as if his breath had been driven out of him, but he did not seem hurt and there was no spot of blood about him.

Aghast and astounded – for he knew the ball had struck squarely – Jack stood gaping, dazed, holding the smoking pistol, until Sir George knocked him sprawling with a hard buffet of his fist. Then Hollinster bounded up, raging, but in that second Banway snatched the girl, and dragging her in a brutal grip, leaped back through the opening with her, slamming shut the secret panel. Solomon Kane, returning as

fast as his long legs could carry him, found Hollinster raving
and bruising his bare fists against a blank wall.

A few gasping words interlarded with wild blasphemies
and burning self-reproaches, gave Kane the situation.

"The hand of Satan is over him," raved the frantic youth.
"Full in the breast I shot him – yet he took no hurt! Oh, fool
and drooling imbecile I am – I stood there like an image
instead of rushing him with the barrel for a club – stood there
like a blind, dumb fool while he –"

"Fool that I am, not to have thought that this house
might have secret passages," said the Puritan. "Of course this
secret doorway leads into the cellar. But stay –" as Hollinster
would have attacked the panel with the dead sailor's cutlass
which Kane had brought. "Even if we open the secret door
and go into the cellar that way, or back through the bolted
stair-door, they will shoot us like rabbits,
uselessly. Now be calm for a
moment, and harken:

"You saw that dark
passageway leading out of the
cellar? Well, it is in my mind
that must be a tunnel which
leads to the rocks along the sea
shore. Banway has long been in
league with smugglers and
pirates. Spies have never seen
any bundles carried into the
house or out, though. It follows
therefore that there needs must
be a tunnel connecting the
cellar with the sea. Therefore,
it likewise follows that these
rogues, with Sir George – who

can never bide in England after this night – will run through
the tunnel and take to ship. We will go across the beach and
meet them as they emerge."

"Then in God's name, let us hasten!" begged the youth,
wiping the cold sweat from his brow. "Once on that hellish
craft, we can never get the girl again!"

"Your wound bleeds again," muttered Kane with a
worried glance.

"No matter; on, for God's sake!"

V
"– INTO THE SUNRISE I GO –"

Hollinster followed Kane who went boldly to the front door,
opened it and sprang out. The fog had faded and the moon
was clear, showing the black rocks of the beach two hundred
yards away and beyond them the long low evil-looking ship
riding at anchor outside the foam line of the breakers. Of the
guards outside the house there were none. Whether they took
alarm at the noise inside the house and fled, whether they had
received a command in some way, or whether they had had
orders to return to the beach before this time, Kane and Jack
never knew. But they saw no one. Along the beach the Rocks
rose black and sinister like jagged dark houses, hiding
whatever was going on in the sand at the water's edge.

The companions raced recklessly across the separating
space. Kane showed no signs that he had just gone through a
terrible gruelling grind of life and death. He seemed made of
steel springs and an extra two hundred yard dash had no
effect on nerve or wind. But Hollinster reeled as he ran. He
was weak from worry, excitement and loss of blood. Only his
love for Mary and a grim determination kept him on his feet.

As they approached the Rocks, the
sound of fierce voices instilled caution
into their movements. Hollinster, almost
in delirium, was for leaping across the rocks
and falling on whoever was on the other side,
but Kane restrained him. Together they crept
forward and lying flat on their bellies on a jutting
ledge, they looked down.

The clear moonlight showed the watchers that the
buccaneers on board the ship were preparing to weigh anchor.

Below them stood a small group of men. Already a long-
boat full of rogues was pulling away to the ship, while another
boatload waited impatiently, resting on their oars, while their
leaders argued out a question on shore. Evidently the flight
through the tunnel had been made with no loss of time. Had
Sir George not halted to seize the girl, in which act luck was
with him, all the rogues would have been aboard ship. The
watchers could see the small cave, revealed by the rolling back
of a large boulder, which was the mouth of the tunnel.

Sir George and Ben Allardine stood facing each other in
hot debate. Mary, bound hand and foot, lay at their feet. At
the sight Hollinster made to rise but Kane's iron grip held
him quiescent for the time.

"I take the girl aboard!" rose Banway's angry voice.

"And I say 'no'!" came Allardine's answering rasp. "No
good'll come o' it! Look! There's Hardraker a-lyin' in his
blood in yon cellar this minute account o' a girl! Women stirs
up trouble and strife between men – bring that wench aboard
and we'll have a dozen slit gullets afore sunrise! Cut her
throat here, I says, and –"

He reached for the girl. Sir George struck aside his hand
and drew his rapier, but Jack did not see that motion.
Throwing aside Kane's restraining hand, Hollinster bounded

erect and leaped recklessly from the ledge. At the sight the pirates in the boat raised a shout, and evidently thinking themselves to be attacked by a larger party, laid to their oars, leaving their mate and patron to shift for themselves.

Hollinster, striking feet first in the soft sand, went to his knees from the impact, but bounding up again, he charged the two men who stood gaping at him. Allardine went down with a cleft skull before he could lift his steel, and then Sir George parried Jack's second ferocious slash.

A cutlass is clumsy and not suitable for fencing or quick clever work. Jack had proved his superiority over Banway with the straight light blade, but he was unused to the heavy curved weapon and he was weakened and weary. Banway was fresh.

Still, for a few seconds Jack kept the nobleman on the defensive by the sheer fury of his onslaught – then in spite of his hate and determination, he began to weaken. Banway, with a cruel cold smile on his dark face, touched him again and again, on cheek, breast and leg – not deep wounds, but stinging scratches which, bleeding, added to the general score of his weakness.

Sir George feinted swiftly, started his finishing lunge. His foot slipped in the shifty sand, he lost balance, slashed wildly, leaving himself wide open. Jack, seeing this dimly through blood-blinded eyes, threw all his waning strength into one last desperate effort. He sprang in and struck from the side, the keen edge crunching against Sir George's body half way between hip and arm pit. That blow should have cleft the ribs into the lung, but instead, the blade shivered like glass. Jack, dazed, reeled back, the useless hilt falling from his nerveless hand.

Sir George recovered himself and thrust with a wild cry of triumph. But even as the blade sang through the air, straight toward Jack's defenseless breast, a great shadow fell between. Banway's blade was brushed aside with incredible ease.

Hollinster, crawling away like a snake with a broken back, saw Solomon Kane looming like a black cloud over Sir George Banway, while the Puritan's long rapier, inexorable as doom, forced the nobleman to break ground, fencing desperately.

In the light of the moon which frosted the long quick blades with silver, Hollinster watched that fight as he leaned over the fainting girl and tried with weak and fumbling hands to loosen her bonds. He had heard of Kane's remarkable sword play. Now he had an opportunity to see for himself and – born sword lover that he was – found himself wishing Kane faced a more worthy foe.

For though Sir George was an accomplished swordsman and had a name as a deadly duellist hereabouts, Kane merely toyed with him. With a great advantage in height, weight,

strength and reach, Kane had still other advantages – those of
skill and of speed. For all his size he was quicker than Banway.
As to skill, the nobleman was a novice in comparison. Kane
fought with an economy of motion and a lack of heat which
robbed his play of some brilliance – he made no wide
spectacular parries or long breath-taking lunges. But every
motion he made was the right one; he was never at loss, never
excited – a combination of ice and steel. In England and on
the Continent, Hollinster had seen more flashy, more brilliant
fencers than Kane, but he realized as he watched that he had
never seen one who was as technically perfect, as crafty, as
deadly, as the tall Puritan.

It seemed to him that Kane could have transfixed his
adversary at the first pass, but such was not the Puritan's
intention. He kept close in, his point ever threatening the
other's face, and as he kept the young nobleman ever on the
defensive, he talked in a calm passionless tone, never losing
the play for a second, as if tongue and arm worked far apart.

"No, no, young sir, you need not leave your breast open.
I saw Jack's blade shatter on your side and I will not risk my
steel, strong and pliant as it is. Well, well, never take shame,
sir; I have worn a steel mail under my shirt also, in my time,
myself, though methinks 'twas scarce as strong as yours, to so
turn a bullet at close range. However, the Lord in his infinite
justice and mercy hath so made man that his vitals be not all
locked up in his brisket. Would you were handier with the
steel, Sir George; I take shame in slaying you – but – well,
when a man sets foot on an adder he asks not its size."

These words were delivered in a serious and sincere
manner, not in a sardonic fashion. Jack knew that Kane did
not mean them as taunts. Sir George was white-faced; now his
hue grew ashy under the moon. His arm ached with weariness
and was heavy as lead; still this great devil in black pressed

him as hard as ever, nullifying his most desperate efforts with superhuman ease.

Suddenly Kane's brow clouded, as if he had an unpleasant task to do and would do it quickly.

"Enough!" he cried in his deep vibrant voice which chilled and thrilled his hearers. "This is an ill deed – let it be done quickly!"

What followed was too quick for the eye to follow. Hollinster never again doubted that Kane's sword play could be brilliant when he wished. Jack caught a flashing hint of a feint at the thigh – a sudden blinding flurry of bright steel – Sir George Banway lay dead at Solomon Kane's feet without twitching. A slight trickle of blood seeped from his left eye.

"Through the eye ball and into the brain," said Kane rather moodily, cleansing his point on which shone a single drop of blood. "He knew not what took him and died without pain. God grant all our deaths be as easy. But my heart is heavy within me, for he was little more than a youth, albeit an evil one, and was not my equal with the steel. Well, the Lord judge between him and me on the Judgment Day."

Mary whimpered in Jack's arms, coming out of her swoon. A strange glow was spreading over the land and Hollinster heard a peculiar crackling.

"Look! The house burns!"

Flames leaped from the black roof of the Banway manor

house. The departing pirates had set a blaze and now it sprang into full fury, dimming the moon. The sea shimmered gorily in the scarlet glare and the pirate ship which was beating out to open sea seemed to ride in a sea of blood. Her sails redly reflected the glow.

"She sails in an ocean of crimson blood!" cried Kane, all the latent superstition and poetry roused in him. "She sails in gore and her sails are bright with blood! Death and destruction follow her and Hell cometh after! Red be her ruin and black her doom!"

Then with a sudden change in mood, the fanatic bent over Jack and the girl.

"I would bind and dress your wounds, lad," said he gently, "but methinks they are not serious, and I hear the rattle of many hoofs across the moors and your friends will soon be about you. Out of travail cometh strength and peace and happiness, and mayhap your paths will run straighter for this night of horror."

"But who are you?" cried the girl, clinging to him. "I know not how to thank you —"

"Thou hast thanked me enough, little one," said the strange man tenderly. "'Tis enough to see thee well and delivered out of persecution. May thou thrive and wed and bear strong sons and rosy daughters."

"But who are you? Whence come you? What seek you? Whither do you go?"

"I am a landless man." A strange intangible, almost mystic look flashed into his cold eyes. "I come out of the sunset and into the sunrise I go, wherever the Lord doth guide my feet. I seek — my soul's salvation, mayhap. I came, following the trail of vengeance. Now I must leave you. The dawn is not far away and I would not have it find me idle. It may be I shall see you no more. My work here is done; the long red trail is ended. The man of blood is dead. But there be other men of blood, and other trails of revenge and retribution. I work the will of God. While evil flourishes and wrongs grow rank, while men are persecuted and women wronged, while weak things, human or animal, are maltreated, there is no rest for me beneath the skies, nor peace at any board or bed. Farewell!"

"Stay!" cried out Jack, rising, tears springing suddenly into his eyes.

"Oh wait, sir!" called Mary, reaching out her white arms.

But the tall form had vanished in the darkness and no sound came back of his going.

The Hills of the Dead

The Hills of the Dead

I
VOODOO

The twigs which N'Longa flung on the fire broke and crackled. The upleaping flames lighted the countenances of the two men. N'Longa, voodoo man of the Slave Coast, was very old. His wizened and gnarled frame was stooped and brittle, his face creased by hundreds of wrinkles. The red firelight glinted on the human finger-bones which composed his necklace.

The other was a white man and his name was Solomon Kane. He was tall and broad-shouldered, clad in black close garments, the garb of the Puritan. His featherless slouch hat was drawn low over his heavy brows, shadowing his darkly pallid face. His cold deep eyes brooded in the firelight.

"You come again, brother," droned the fetish-man, speaking in the jargon which passed for a common language of black man and white on the West Coast. "Many moons burn and die since we make blood-palaver. You go to the setting sun, but you come back!"

"Aye." Kane's voice was deep and almost ghostly. "Yours is a grim land, N'Longa, a red land barred with the black darkness of horror and the bloody shadows of death. Yet I have returned –"

N'Longa stirred the fire, saying nothing, and after a pause Kane continued.

"Yonder in the unknown vastness" – his long finger stabbed at the black silent jungle which brooded beyond the firelight – "yonder lie mystery and adventure and nameless terror. Once I dared the jungle – once she nearly claimed my bones. Something entered into my blood, something stole into my soul like a whisper of unnamed sin. The jungle! Dark and brooding – over leagues of the blue salt sea she has drawn me and with the dawn I go to seek the heart of her. Mayhap I shall find curious adventure – mayhap my doom awaits me. But better death than the ceaseless and everlasting urge, the fire that has burned my veins with bitter longing."

"She call," muttered N'Longa. "At night she coil like serpent about my hut and whisper strange things to me. *Ai ya!* The jungle call. We be blood-brothers, you and I. Me, N'Longa, mighty worker of nameless magic. You go to the jungle as all men go who hear her call. Maybe you live, more like you die. You believe in my fetish work?"

"I understand it not," said Kane grimly, "but I have seen you send your soul forth from your body to animate a lifeless corpse."

"Aye! Me N'Longa, priest of the Black God! Now watch, I make magic."

Kane gazed at the black man who bent over the fire, making even motions with his hands and mumbling incantations. Kane watched and he seemed to grow sleepy. A mist wavered in front of him, through which he saw dimly the form of N'Longa, etched black against the flames. Then all faded out.

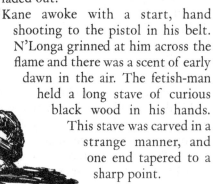

Kane awoke with a start, hand shooting to the pistol in his belt. N'Longa grinned at him across the flame and there was a scent of early dawn in the air. The fetish-man held a long stave of curious black wood in his hands. This stave was carved in a strange manner, and one end tapered to a sharp point.

"This voodoo staff," said N'Longa, putting it in the Englishman's hand. "Where your guns and long knife fail, this save you. When you want me, lay this on your breast, fold your hands on it and sleep. I come to you in your dreams."

Kane weighed the thing in his hand, highly suspicious of witchcraft. It was not heavy, but seemed hard as iron. A good weapon at least, he decided. Dawn was just beginning to steal over the jungle and the river.

II
Red Eyes

Solomon Kane shifted his musket from his shoulder and let the stock fall to the earth. Silence lay about him like a fog. Kane's lined face and tattered garments showed the effect of long bush travel. He looked about him.

Some distance behind him loomed the green, rank jungle, thinning out to low shrubs, stunted trees and tall grass. Some distance in front of him rose the first of a chain of bare, somber hills, littered with boulders, shimmering in the merciless heat of the sun. Between the hills and the jungle lay a broad expanse of rough, uneven grasslands, dotted here and there by clumps of thorn-trees.

An utter silence hung over the country. The only sign of life was a few vultures flapping heavily across the distant hills. For the last few days Kane had noticed the increasing number of these unsavory birds. The sun was rocking westward but its heat was in no way abated.

Trailing his musket he started forward slowly. He had no objective in view. This was all unknown country and one direction was as good as another. Many weeks ago he had plunged into the jungle with the assurance born of courage

and ignorance. Having by some miracle survived the first few weeks, he was becoming hard and toughened, able to hold his own with any of the grim denizens of the fastness he dared.

As he progressed he noted an occasional lion spoor but there seemed to be no animals in the grasslands – none that left tracks, at any rate. Vultures sat like black, brooding images in some of the stunted trees, and suddenly he saw an activity among them some distance beyond. Several of the dusky birds circled about a clump of high grass, dipping, then rising again. Some beast of prey was defending his kill against them, Kane decided, and wondered at the lack of snarling and roaring which usually accompanied such scenes. His curiosity was roused and he turned his steps in that direction.

At last, pushing through the grass which rose about his shoulders, he saw, as through a corridor walled with the rank waving blades, a ghastly sight. The corpse of a black man lay, face down, and as the Englishman looked, a great dark snake rose and slid away into the grass, moving so quickly that Kane was unable to decide its nature. But it had a weird human-like suggestion about it.

Kane stood over the body, noting that while the limbs lay awry as if broken, the flesh was not torn as a lion or leopard would have torn it. He glanced up at the whirling vultures and was amazed to see several of them skimming along close to the earth, following a waving of the grass which marked the flight of the thing which had presumably slain the black man. Kane wondered what thing the carrion birds, which eat only the dead, were hunting through the grasslands. But Africa is full of never-explained mysteries.

Kane shrugged his shoulders and lifted his musket again. Adventures he had had in plenty since he parted from N'Longa some moons agone, but still that nameless paranoid urge had driven him on and on, deeper and deeper into those trackless ways. Kane could not have analyzed this call; he would have attributed it to Satan, who lures men to their destruction. But it was but the restless turbulent spirit of the adventurer, the wanderer – the same urge which sends the gipsy caravans about the world, which drove the Viking galleys over unknown seas and which guides the flights of the wild geese.

Kane sighed. Here in this barren land seemed neither food nor water, but he had wearied unto death of the dank, rank venom of the thick jungle. Even a wilderness of bare hills was preferable, for a time at least. He glanced at them, where they lay brooding in the sun, and started forward again.

He held N'Longa's fetish stave in his left hand, and though his conscience still troubled him for keeping a thing so apparently diabolic in nature, he had never been able to bring himself to throw it away.

Now as he went toward the hills, a sudden commotion broke out in the tall grass in front of him, which was, in places, taller than a man. A thin, high-pitched scream

sounded and on its heels an earth-shaking roar. The grass
parted and a slim figure came flying toward him like a wisp of
straw blown on the wind – a brown-skinned girl, clad only in
a skirt-like garment. Behind her, some yards away but gaining
swiftly, came a huge lion.

The girl fell at Kane's feet with a wail and a sob, and lay
clutching at his ankles. The Englishman dropped the voodoo
stave, raised his musket to his shoulder and sighted coolly at
the ferocious feline face which neared him every instant.
Crash! The girl screamed once and slumped on her face. The
huge cat leaped high and wildly, to fall and lie motionless.

Kane reloaded hastily before he spared a glance at the
form at his feet. The girl lay as still as the lion he had just
slain, but a quick examination showed that she had only
fainted.

He bathed her face with water from his canteen and
presently she opened her eyes and sat up. Fear flooded her face
as she looked at her rescuer and she made to rise.

Kane held out a restraining hand and she cowered down,
trembling. The roar of his heavy musket was enough to
frighten any native who
had never
before seen
a white man,
Kane reflected.

The girl was a much
higher type than the
thick-lipped, bestial West
Coast negroes to whom
Kane had been used.
She was slim and finely
formed, of a deep brown

hue rather than ebony; her nose was
straight and thin-bridged, her lips
were not too thick. Somewhere in
her blood there was a strong
Berber strain.

Kane spoke to her in a river
dialect, a simple language he
had learned during his
wandering, and she replied
haltingly. The inland tribes
traded slaves and ivory to the
river people and were familiar
with their jargon.

"My village is there," she
answered Kane's question,
pointing to the southern jungle
with a slim, rounded arm. "My
name is Zunna. My mother
whipped me for breaking a cooking-kettle and
I ran away because I was angry. I am afraid;
let me go back to my mother!"

"You may go," said Kane, "but I will
take you, child. Suppose another lion came
along? You were very foolish to run away."

She whimpered a little. "Are you not a god?"

"No, Zunna. I am only a man, though the color of my
skin is not as yours. Lead me now to your village."

She rose hesitantly, eyeing him apprehensively through
the wild tangle of her hair. To Kane she seemed like some
frightened young animal. She led the way and Kane followed.
She indicated that her village lay to the southeast, and their
route brought them nearer to the hills. The sun began to sink
and the roaring of lions reverberated over the grasslands.

Kane glanced at the western sky; this open country was no place in which to be caught by night. He glanced toward the hills and saw that they were within a few hundred yards of the nearest. He saw what seemed to be a cave.

"Zunna," said he haltingly, "we can never reach your village before nightfall and if we bide here the lions will take us. Yonder is a cavern where we may spend the night –"

She shrank and trembled.

"Not in the hills, master!" she whimpered. "Better the lions!"

"Nonsense!" His tone was impatient; he had had enough of native superstition. "We will spend the night in yonder cave."

She argued no further, but followed him. They went up a short slope and stood at the mouth of the cavern, a small affair, with sides of solid rock and a floor of deep sand.

"Gather some dry grass, Zunna," commanded Kane, standing his musket against the wall at the mouth of the cave, "but go not far away, and listen for lions. I will build here a fire which shall keep us safe from beasts tonight. Bring some grass and any twigs you may find, like a good child, and we will sup. I have dried meat in my pouch and water also."

She gave him a strange, long glance, then turned away without a word. Kane tore up grass near at hand, noting how it was seared and crisp from the sun, and heaping it up, struck flint and steel. Flame leaped up and devoured the heap in an instant. He was wondering how he could gather enough grass to keep a fire going all night, when he was aware that he had visitors.

Kane was used to grotesque sights, but at first glance he started and a slight coldness traveled down his spine. Two black men stood before him in silence. They were tall and gaunt and entirely naked. Their skins were a dusty black, tinged with a gray, ashy hue, as of death. Their faces were different from any negroes he had seen. The brows were high and narrow, the noses huge and snout-like; the eyes were inhumanly large and inhumanly red. As the two stood there it seemed to Kane that only their burning eyes lived.

He spoke to them, but they did not answer. He invited them to eat with a motion of his hand, and they silently squatted down near the cave mouth, as far from the dying embers of the fire as they could get.

Kane turned to his pouch and began taking out the strips of dried meat which he carried. Once he glanced at his silent guests; it seemed to him that they were watching the glowing ashes of his fire, rather than him.

The sun was about to sink behind the western horizon. A red, fierce glow spread over the grasslands, so that all seemed like a waving sea of blood. Kane knelt over his pouch, and glancing up, saw Zunna come around the shoulder of the hill with her arms full of grass and dry branches.

As he looked, her eyes flared wide; the branches dropped from her arms and her scream knifed the silence, fraught with terrible warning. Kane whirled on his knee. Two great black forms loomed over him as he came up with the lithe motion of a springing leopard. The fetish stave was in his hand and he drove it through the body of the nearest foe with a force which sent its sharp point out between the negro's shoulders.

Then the long, lean arms of the other locked about him, and white man and black man went down together.

The talon-like nails of the black were tearing at his face, the hideous red eyes staring into his with a terrible threat, as Kane writhed about and, fending off the clawing hands with one arm, drew a pistol. He pressed the muzzle close against the black's side and pulled the trigger. At the muffled report, the negro's body jerked to the concussion of the bullet, but the thick lips merely gaped in a horrid grin.

One long arm slid under Kane's shoulders, the other hand gripped his hair. The Englishman felt his head being forced back irresistibly. He clutched at the other's wrist with both hands, but the flesh under his frantic fingers was as hard as wood. Kane's brain was reeling; his neck seemed ready to break with a little more pressure. He threw his body backward with one volcanic effort, breaking the deathly hold. The black was on him and the talons were clutching again. Kane found and raised the empty pistol, and he felt the black man's skull cave in like a shell as he brought down the long barrel with all his strength. And once again the writhing lips parted in fearful mockery.

And now a near panic clutched Kane. What sort of man was this, who still menaced his life with tearing fingers, after having been shot and mortally bludgeoned? No man, surely, but one of the sons of Satan! At the thought Kane wrenched and heaved explosively, and the close-locked combatants tumbled across the earth to come to a rest in the smoldering ashes before the cave mouth. Kane barely felt the heat, but the mouth of his foe gaped, this time in seeming agony. The frightful fingers loosened their hold and Kane sprang clear.

The black man with his shattered skull was rising on one hand and one knee when Kane struck, returning to the attack as a gaunt wolf returns to a wounded bison. From the side he leaped, landing full on the black giant's back, his steely arms seeking and finding a deadly wrestling hold; and as they went to the earth together he broke the negro's neck, so that the hideous dead face looked back over one shoulder. The black man lay still but to Kane it seemed that he was not dead even then, for the red eyes still burned with their grisly light.

The Englishman turned, to see the girl crouching against the cave wall. He looked for his stave; it lay in a heap of dust, among which were a few moldering bones. He stared, his brain reeling. Then with one stride he caught up the voodoo staff and turned to the fallen negro. His face set in grim lines as he raised it; then he drove it through the black breast. And before his eyes, the giant body crumbled, dissolving to dust as he watched horror-struck, even as had crumbled he through whom Kane had first thrust the stave.

III
Dream Magic

"Great God!" whispered Kane; "these men were dead! Vampires! This is Satan's handiwork manifested."

Zunna crawled to his knees and clung there.

"These be walking dead men, master," she whimpered. "I should have warned you."

"Why did they not leap on my back when they first came?" asked he.

"They feared the fire. They were waiting for the embers to die entirely."

"Whence came they?"

"From the hills. Hundreds of their kind swarm among the boulders and caverns of these hills, and they live on human life, for a man they will slay, devouring his ghost as it leaves his quivering body. Aye, they are suckers of souls!

"Master, among the greater of these hills there is a silent city of stone, and in the old times, in the days of my ancestors, these people lived there. They were human, but they were not as we, for they had ruled this land for ages and ages. The ancestors of my people made war on them and slew many, and their magicians made all the dead men as these were. At last all died.

"And for ages have they preyed on the tribes of the jungle, stalking down from the hills at midnight and at sunset to haunt the jungle-ways and slay and slay. Men and beasts flee them and only fire will destroy them."

"Here is that which will destroy them," said Kane grimly, raising the voodoo stave. "Black magic must fight black magic, and I know not what spell N'Longa put hereon, but –"

"You are a god," said Zunna decidedly. "No man could overcome two of the walking dead men. Master, can you not lift this curse from my tribe? There is nowhere for us to flee and the monsters slay us at will, catching wayfarers outside the village wall. Death is on this land and we die helpless!"

Deep in Kane stirred the spirit of the crusader, the fire of the zealot – the fanatic who devotes his life to battling the powers of darkness.

"Let us eat," said he; "then we will build a great fire at the cave mouth. The fire which keeps away beasts shall also keep away fiends."

Later Kane sat just inside the cave, chin rested on clenched fist, eyes gazing unseeingly into the fire. Behind in the shadows, Zunna watched him, awed.

"God of Hosts," Kane muttered, "grant me aid! My hand it is which must lift the ancient curse from this dark land. How am I to fight these dead fiends, who yield not to mortal weapons? Fire will destroy them – a broken neck renders them helpless – the voodoo stave thrust through them crumbles them to dust – but of what avail? How may I prevail against the hundreds who haunt these hills, and to whom human life-essence is Life? Have not – as Zunna says – warriors come against them in the past, only to find them fled to their high-walled city where no man can come against them?"

The night wore on. Zunna slept, her cheek pillowed on her round, girlish arm. The roaring of the lions shook the hills and still Kane sat and gazed broodingly into the fire. Outside, the night was alive with whispers and rustlings and stealthily soft footfalls. And at times Kane, glancing up from his meditations, seemed to catch the gleam of great red eyes beyond the flickering light of the fire.

Gray dawn was stealing over the grasslands when Kane shook Zunna into wakefulness.

"God have mercy on my soul for delving in barbaric magic," said he, "but demonry must be fought with demonry, mayhap. Tend ye the fire and awake me if aught untoward occur."

Kane lay down on his back on the sand floor and laid the voodoo staff on his breast, folding his hands upon it. He fell asleep instantly. And sleeping, he dreamed. To his slumbering self it seemed that he walked through a thick fog and in this fog he met N'Longa, true to life. N'Longa spoke, and the words were clear and vivid, impressing themselves on his consciousness so deeply as to span the gap between sleeping and waking.

"Send this girl to her village soon after sun-up when the lions have gone to their lairs," said N'Longa, "and bid her bring her lover to you at this cave. There make him lie down as if to slumber, holding the voodoo stave."

The dream faded and Kane awoke suddenly, wondering. How strange and vivid had been the vision, and how strange to hear N'Longa talking in English, without the jargon! Kane shrugged his shoulders. He knew that N'Longa claimed to possess the power of sending his spirit through space, and he himself had seen the voodoo man animate a dead man's body. Still –

"Zunna," said Kane, giving the problem up, "I will go with you as far as the edge of the jungle and you must go on to your village and return here to this cave with your lover."

"Kran?" she asked naïvely.

"Whatever his name is. Eat and we will go."

Again the sun slanted toward the west. Kane sat in the cave, waiting. He had seen the girl safely to the place where the jungle thinned to the grasslands, and though his conscience stung him at the thought of the dangers which might confront her, he sent her on alone and returned to the cave. He sat now, wondering if he would not be damned to everlasting flames for tinkering with the magic of a black sorcerer, blood-brother or not.

Light footfalls sounded, and as Kane reached for his musket, Zunna entered, accompanied by a tall, splendidly proportioned youth whose brown skin showed that he was of the same race as the girl. His soft dreamy eyes were fixed on Kane in a sort of awesome worship. Evidently the girl had not minimized the white god's glory in her telling.

He bade the youth lie down as he directed and placed the voodoo stave in his hands. Zunna crouched at one side, wide-eyed. Kane stepped back, half ashamed of this mummery and wondering what, if anything, would come of it. Then to his horror, the youth gave one gasp and stiffened!

Zunna screamed, bounding erect.

"You have killed Kran!" she shrieked, flying at the Englishman who stood struck speechless.

Then she halted suddenly, wavered, drew a hand languidly across her brow – she slid down to lie with her arms about the motionless body of her lover.

And this body moved suddenly, made aimless motions with hands and feet, then sat up, disengaging itself from the clinging arms of the still senseless girl.

Kran looked up at Kane and grinned, a sly, knowing grin which seemed out of place on his face somehow. Kane started. Those soft eyes had changed in expression and were now hard and glittering and snaky – N'Longa's eyes!

"*Ai ya*," said Kran in a grotesquely familiar voice. "Blood-brother, you got no greeting for N'Longa?"

Kane was silent. His flesh crawled in spite of himself. Kran rose and stretched his arms in an unfamiliar sort of way, as if his limbs were new to him. He slapped his breast approvingly.

"Me N'Longa!" said he in the old boastful manner. "Mighty ju-ju man! Blood-brother, not you know me, eh?"

"You are Satan," said Kane sincerely. "Are you Kran or are you N'Longa?"

"Me N'Longa," assured the other. "My body sleep in ju-ju hut on Coast many treks from here. I borrow Kran's body for while. My ghost travel ten days march in one breath; twenty days march in same time. My ghost go out from my body and drive out Kran's."

"And Kran is dead?"

"No, he no dead. I send his ghost to shadowland for a while – send the girl's ghost too, to keep him company; bimeby come back."

"This is the work of the Devil," said Kane frankly, "but I have seen you do even fouler magic – shall I call you N'Longa or Kran?"

"Kran – *kah!* Me N'Longa – bodies like clothes! Me N'Longa, in here now!" He rapped his breast. "Bimeby Kran live along here – then he be Kran and I be N'Longa, same like before. Kran no live along now; N'Longa live along this one fellow body. Blood-brother, I am N'Longa!"

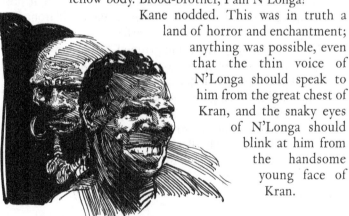

Kane nodded. This was in truth a land of horror and enchantment; anything was possible, even that the thin voice of N'Longa should speak to him from the great chest of Kran, and the snaky eyes of N'Longa should blink at him from the handsome young face of Kran.

"This land I know long time," said N'Longa, getting down to business. "Mighty ju-ju, these dead people! No, no need to waste one fellow time – I know – I talk to you in sleep. My blood-brother want to kill out these dead black fellows, eh?"

"'Tis a thing opposed to nature," said Kane somberly. "They are known in my land as vampires – I never expected to come upon a whole nation of them."

IV
THE SILENT CITY

"Now we find this stone city," said N'Longa.

"Yes? Why not send your ghost out to kill these vampires?" Kane asked idly.

"Ghost got to have one fellow body to work in," N'Longa answered. "Sleep now. Tomorrow we start."

The sun had set; the fire glowed and flickered in the cave mouth. Kane glanced at the still form of the girl, who lay where she had fallen, and prepared himself for slumber.

"Awake me at midnight," he admonished, "and I will watch from then until dawn."

But when N'Longa finally shook his arm, Kane awoke to see the first light of dawn reddening the land.

"Time we start," said the fetish-man.

"But the girl – are you sure she lives?"

"She live, blood-brother."

"Then in God's name, we can not leave her here at the mercy of any prowling fiend who might chance upon her. Or some lion might –"

"No lion come. Vampire scent still linger, mixed with man scent. One fellow lion he no like man scent and he fear the walking dead men. No beast come; and" – lifting the voodoo stave and laying it across the cave entrance – "no dead man come now."

Kane watched him somberly and without enthusiasm.

"How will that rod safeguard her?"

"That mighty ju-ju," said N'Longa. "You see how one fellow vampire go along dust alongside that stave! No vampire dare touch or come near it. I gave it to you, because outside Vampire Hills one fellow man sometimes meet a corpse walking in jungle when shadows be black. Not all walking dead men be here. And all must suck Life from men – if not, they rot like dead wood."

"Then make many of these rods and arm the people with them."

"No can do!" N'Longa's skull shook violently. "That ju-ju rod be mighty magic! Old, old! No man live today can tell how old that fellow ju-ju stave be. I make my blood-brother sleep and do magic with it to guard him, that time we make palaver in Coast village. Today we scout and run; no need it. Leave it here to guard girl."

Kane shrugged his shoulders and followed the fetish-man, after glancing back at the still shape which lay in the cave. He would never have agreed to leave her so casually, had he not believed in his heart that she was dead. He had touched her, and her flesh was cold.

They went up among the barren hills as the sun was rising. Higher they climbed, up steep clay slopes, winding their way through ravines and between great boulders. The hills were honeycombed with dark, forbidding caves, and these they passed warily, and Kane's flesh crawled as he thought of the grisly occupants therein. For N'Longa said:

"Them vampires, he sleep in caves most all day till sunset. Them caves, he be full of one fellow dead man."

The sun rose higher, baking down on the bare slopes with an intolerable heat. Silence brooded like an evil monster over the land. They had seen nothing, but Kane could have sworn at times that a black shadow drifted behind a boulder at their approach.

"Them vampires, they stay hid in daytime," said N'Longa with a low laugh. "They be afraid of one fellow vulture! No fool vulture! He know death when he see it! He pounce on one fellow dead man and tear and eat if he be lying or walking!"

A strong shudder shook his companion.

"Great God!" Kane cried, striking his thigh with his hat; "is there no end to the horror of this hideous land? Truly this land is dedicated to the powers of darkness!"

Kane's eyes burned with a dangerous light. The terrible heat, the solitude and the knowledge of the horrors lurking on either hand were shaking even his steely nerves.

"Keep on one fellow hat, blood-brother," admonished N'Longa with a low gurgle of amusement. "That fellow sun, he knock you dead, suppose you no look out."

Kane shifted the musket he had insisted on bringing and made no reply. They mounted an eminence at last and looked down on a sort of plateau. And in the center of this plateau was a silent city of gray and crumbling stone. Kane was smitten by a sense of incredible age as he looked. The walls and houses were of great stone blocks, yet they were falling into ruin. Grass grew on the plateau, and high in the streets of that dead city. Kane saw no movement among the ruins.

"That is their city – why do they choose to sleep in caves?"

"Maybe-so one fellow stone fall on them from roof and crush. Them stone huts, he fall down bimeby. Maybe-so they no like to stay together – maybe-so they eat each other, too."

"Silence!" whispered Kane; "how it hangs over all!"

"Them vampires no talk nor yell; they dead. They sleep in caves, wander at sunset and at night. Maybe-so them black fellow bush tribes come with spears, them vampires go to stone kraal and fight behind walls."

Kane nodded. The crumbling walls which surrounded that dead city were still high and solid enough to resist the attack of spearmen – especially when defended by these snout-nosed fiends.

"Blood-brother," said N'Longa solemnly, "I have mighty magic thought! Be silent a little while."

Kane seated himself on a boulder and gazed broodingly at the bare crags and slopes which surrounded them. Far away to the south he saw the leafy green ocean that was the jungle. Distance lent a certain enchantment to the scene. Closer at hand loomed the dark blotches that were the mouths of the caves of horror.

N'Longa was squatting, tracing some strange pattern in the clay with a dagger point. Kane watched him, thinking how easily they might fall victim to the vampires if even three or four of the fiends should come out of their caverns.

And even as he thought it, a black and horrific shadow fell across the crouching fetish-man.

Kane acted without conscious thought. He shot from the boulder where he sat like a stone hurled from a catapult, and his musket stock shattered the face of the hideous black thing who had stolen upon them. Back and back Kane drove his inhuman foe staggering, never giving him time to halt or launch an offensive, battering him with the onslaught of a frenzied tiger.

At the very edge of the cliff the vampire wavered, then pitched back over, to fall for a hundred feet and lie writhing on the rocks of the plateau below. N'Longa was on his feet pointing; the hills were giving up their dead.

Out of the caves they were swarming, the terrible black silent shapes; up the slopes they came charging and over the boulders they came clambering, and their red eyes were all turned toward the two humans who stood above the silent city. The caves belched them forth in an unholy judgment day.

N'Longa pointed to a crag some distance away and with a shout started running fleetly toward it. Kane followed. From behind boulders black-taloned hands clawed at them, tearing their garments. They raced past caves, and mummied monsters came lurching out of the dark, gibbering silently, to join in the pursuit.

The dead hands were close at their back when they scrambled up the last slope and stood on a ledge which was the top of the crag. The fiends halted silently a moment, then came clambering after them. Kane clubbed his musket and smashed down into the red-eyed faces, knocking aside the upleaping hands. They surged up like a black wave; he swung his musket in a silent fury that matched theirs. The black wave broke and wavered back; came on again.

He – could – not – kill – them! These words beat on his

brain like a sledge on an anvil as he shattered wood-like flesh and dead bone with his smashing swings. He knocked them down, hurled them back, but they rose and came on again. This could not last – what in God's name was N'Longa doing? Kane spared one swift, tortured glance over his shoulder. The fetish-man stood on the highest part of the ledge, head thrown back, arms lifted as if in invocation.

Kane's vision blurred to the sweep of hideous black faces with red, staring eyes. Those in front were horrible to see now, for their skulls were shattered, their faces caved in and their limbs broken. But still they came on and those behind reached across their shoulders to clutch at the man who defied them.

Kane was red but the blood was all his. From the long-withered veins of those monsters no single drop of warm red blood trickled. Suddenly from behind him came a long piercing wail – N'Longa! Over the crash of the flying musket-stock and the shattering of bones it sounded high and clear – the only voice lifted in that hideous fight.

The black wave washed about Kane's feet, dragging him down. Keen talons tore at him, flaccid lips sucked at his wounds. He reeled up again, disheveled and bloody, clearing a space with a shattering sweep of his splintered musket. Then they closed in again and he went down.

"This is the end!" he thought, but even at that instant the press slackened and the sky was suddenly filled with the beat of great wings.

Then he was free and staggered up, blindly and dizzily, ready to renew the strife. He halted, frozen. Down the slope the black horde was fleeing and over their heads and close at their shoulders flew huge vultures, tearing and rending avidly, sinking their beaks in the dead black flesh, devouring the vampires as they fled.

Kane laughed, almost insanely.

"Defy man and God, but you may not deceive the vultures, sons of Satan! They know whether a man be alive or dead!"

N'Longa stood like a prophet on the pinnacle and the great black birds soared and wheeled about him. His arms still waved and his voice still wailed out across the hills. And over the skylines they came, hordes on endless hordes – vultures, vultures, vultures! come to the feast so long denied them. They blackened the sky with their numbers, blotted out the sun; a strange darkness fell on the land. They settled in long dusky lines, diving into the caverns with a whir of wings and a clash of beaks. Their talons tore at the black horrors which these caves disgorged.

Now all the vampires were fleeing to their city. The vengeance held back for ages had come down on them and their last hope was the heavy walls which had kept back the desperate human foes. Under those crumbling roofs they might find shelter. And N'Longa watched them stream into the city, and he laughed until the crags re-echoed.

Now all were in and the birds settled like a cloud over the doomed city, perching in solid rows along the walls, sharpening their beaks and claws on the towers.

And N'Longa struck flint and steel to a bundle of dry leaves he had brought with him. The bundle leaped into instant flame and he straightened and flung the blazing thing far out over the cliffs. It fell like a meteor to the plateau beneath, showering sparks. The tall grass of the plateau leaped aflame.

From the silent city beneath them Fear flowed in unseen waves, like a white fog. Kane smiled grimly.

"The grass is sere and brittle from the drouth," he said; "there has been even less rain than usual this season; it will burn swiftly."

Like a crimson serpent the fire ran through the high dead grass. It spread and it spread and Kane, standing high above, yet felt the fearful intensity of the hundreds of red eyes which watched from the stone city.

Now the scarlet snake had reached the walls and was rearing as if to coil and writhe over them. The vultures rose on heavily flapping wings and soared reluctantly. A vagrant gust of wind whipped the blaze about and drove it in a long red sheet around the wall. Now the city was hemmed in on all sides by a solid barricade of flame. The roar came up to the two men on the high crag.

Sparks flew across the wall, lighting in the high grass in the streets. A score of flames leaped up and grew with terrifying speed. A veil of red cloaked streets and buildings, and through this crimson, whirling mist Kane and N'Longa saw hundreds of black shapes scamper and writhe, to vanish suddenly in red bursts of flame. There rose an intolerable scent of decayed flesh burning.

Kane gazed, awed. This was truly a hell on earth. As in a nightmare he looked into the roaring red cauldron where black insects fought against their doom and perished. The flames leaped a hundred feet in air, and suddenly above their roar sounded one bestial, inhuman scream like a shriek from across nameless gulfs of cosmic space, as one vampire, dying, broke the chains of silence which had held him for untold centuries. High and haunting it rose, the death cry of a vanishing race.

Then the flames dropped suddenly. The conflagration had been a typical grass fire, short and fierce. Now the plateau showed a blackened expanse and the city a charred and smoking mass of crumbling stone. Not one corpse lay in view, not even a charred bone. Above all whirled the dark swarms of the vultures, but they, too, were beginning to scatter.

Kane gazed hungrily at the clean blue sky. Like a strong sea wind clearing a fog of horror was the sight to him. From somewhere sounded the faint and far-off roaring of a distant lion. The vultures were flapping away in black, straggling lines.

V
PALAVER SET!

Kane sat in the mouth of the cave where Zunna lay, submitting to the fetish-man's bandaging.

The Puritan's garments hung in tatters about his frame; his limbs and breast were deeply gashed and darkly bruised, but he had had no mortal wound in that deathly fight on the cliff.

"Mighty men, we be!" declared N'Longa with deep approval. "Vampire city be silent now, sure 'nough! No walking dead man live along these hills."

"I do not understand," said Kane, resting chin on hand. "Tell me, N'Longa, how have you done things? How talked you with me in my dreams; how came you into the body of Kran; and how summoned you the vultures?"

"My blood-brother," said N'Longa, discarding his pride in his pidgin English, to drop into the river language understood by Kane, "I am so old that you would call me a liar if I told you my age. All my life I have worked magic, sitting first at the feet of mighty ju-ju men of the south and the east; then I was a slave to the Buckra – the white man – and learned more. My brother, shall I span all these years in a moment and make you understand with a word, what has taken me so long to learn? I could not even make you understand how these vampires have kept their bodies from decay by drinking the lives of men.

"I sleep and my spirit goes out over the jungle and the rivers to talk with the sleeping spirits of my friends. There is a mighty magic on the voodoo staff I gave you – a magic out of the Old Land which draws my ghost to it as a white man's magnet draws metal."

Kane listened unspeaking, seeing for the first time in N'Longa's glittering eyes something stronger and deeper than the avid gleam of the worker in black magic. To Kane it seemed almost as if he looked into the far-seeing and mystic eyes of a prophet of old.

"I spoke to you in

dreams," N'Longa went on, "and I made a deep sleep come over the souls of Kran and of Zunna, and removed them to a far dim land, whence they shall soon return, unremembering. All things bow to magic, blood-brother, and beasts and birds obey the master words. I worked strong voodoo, vulture-magic, and the flying people of the air gathered at my call.

"These things I know and am a part of, but how shall I tell you of them? Blood-brother, you are a mighty warrior, but in the ways of magic you are as a little child lost. And what has taken me long dark years to know, I may not divulge to you so you would understand. My friend, you think only of bad spirits, but were my magic always bad, should I not take this fine young body in place of my old wrinkled one and keep it? But Kran shall have his body back safely.

"Keep the voodoo staff, blood-brother. It has mighty power against all sorcerers and serpents and evil things. Now I return to the village on the Coast where my true body sleeps. And what of you, my blood-brother?"

Kane pointed silently eastward.

"The call grows no weaker. I go."

N'Longa nodded, held out his hand. Kane grasped it. The mystical expression had gone from the dusky face and the eyes twinkled snakily with a sort of reptilian mirth.

"Me go now, blood-brother," said the fetish-man, returning to his beloved jargon, of which knowledge he was prouder than all his conjuring tricks. "You take care – that one fellow jungle, she pluck your bones yet! Remember that voodoo stave, brother. *Ai ya*, palaver set!"

He fell back on the sand, and Kane saw the keen sly expression of N'Longa fading from the face of Kran. His flesh crawled again. Somewhere back on the Slave Coast, the body of N'Longa, withered and wrinkled, was stirring in the ju-ju hut, was rising as if from a deep sleep. Kane shuddered.

Kran sat up, yawned, stretched and smiled. Beside him the girl Zunna rose, rubbing her eyes.

"Master," said Kran apologetically, "we must have slumbered."

Hawk of Basti

(Fragment)

Hawk of Basti

"Solomon Kane!"

The interlapping branches of the great trees rose in mighty arches, hundreds of feet above the moss-carpeted earth, making a Gothic twilight among the giant trunks. Was this witchcraft? Who, in this heathen forgotten land of shadowy mysteries, broke the brooding silence to shout the name of a strange wanderer?

Kane's cold eyes roved among the trees; one lean iron hand hardened on the carved sharp-pointed stave he carried, the other hovered near one of the flintlock pistols he wore.

Then from among the shadows stepped a bizarre figure. Kane's eyes widened slightly. A white man it was, strangely clad. A silken loincloth was all of his garments, and he wore curious sandals on his feet. Armlets of gold and a heavy golden chain about his neck increased the barbarity of his appearance, as well as the hoop-like rings in his ears. But while the other ornaments were of curious and unfamiliar workmanship, the earrings were such as Kane had seen hundreds of times in the ears of European seamen.

The man was scratched and bruised as if he had been racing through thick woods recklessly, and there were shallow gashes on his limbs and body that no thorn or bramble could have made. In his right hand he held a short curved sword, dyed a sinister red.

"Solomon Kane, by the howling hounds of Hell!" exclaimed this man, glaring in amazement, as he approached the staring Englishman. "Keelhaul me from Satan's craft, but you gave me a start! I thought to be the only white man for a thousand miles!"

"I had thought the same of myself," answered Kane. "But I know you not."

The other laughed harshly.

"I wonder not thereat," quoth he. "Belike I'd scarce know myself should I meet myself suddenly. Well, Solomon, my sober cutthroat, it's been many a year since I gazed on that sombre face of yours, but I'd know it in Hades. Come – have you forgotten the brave old days when we harried the Dons from the Azores to Darien and back again? Cutlass and carronade! By the bones of the saints, ours was a red trade! You've not forgotten Jeremy Hawk!"

Recognition glimmered in Kane's cold eyes as a shadow passes across the surface of a frozen lake.

"I remember; we did not sail on the same ship, though. I was with Sir Richard Grenville. You sailed with John Bellefonte."

"Aye!" cried Hawk with an oath. "I'd give the crown I've lost to live those days again! But Sir Richard's at the bottom of the sea, and Bellefonte's in Hell, and many of the bold brethren are swinging in chains or feeding the fishes with good English flesh. Tell me, my melancholy murderer, does

good Queen Bess still rule old England?"

"It's been many moons since I left our native shores," answered Kane. "She sat firmly on her throne when I sailed."

He spoke shortly and Hawk stared at him curiously. "You never loved the Tudors, eh, Solomon?"

"Her sister harried my people like beasts of prey," answered Kane harshly. "She herself has lied to and betrayed the folk of my faith – but that's neither here nor there. What do you here?"

Hawk, Kane noticed, from time to time turned his head and stared back in the direction from which he had come, in an attitude of close listening, as if he expected pursuit.

"It's a long story," he answered. "I'll tell it briefly – you know there were high words between Bellefonte and others of the English captains –"

"I've heard he became no better than a common pirate," Kane said bluntly.

Hawk grinned wickedly. "Why, so they said. At any rate, away to the Main we sailed, and by Satan's eyes, we lived like kings among the isles, preying on the plate ships and treasure galleons. Then came a Spanish war-ship and harried us sore. A bursting cannon shot sent Bellefonte to his master, the Devil, and I, as first mate, became captain. There was a French rogue named La Costa who opposed me – well, I hanged La Costa to the main-yards and squared sails for the south. We gave the war-ship the slip at last, and made for the Slave Coast for a cargo of black ivory. But our luck went with Bellefonte. We piled on a reef in a heavy fog and when the mist cleared a hundred war-canoes full of naked howling devils were swarming about us.

"We fought for half a day and when we had beaten them off, we found ourselves nearly out of powder, half our men dead and the ship ready to slip off the reef where she hung

and sink under our feet. There were but two things to do – take to sea in open boats or come ashore. And there was but one boat the bombards of the war-ship had left unshattered. Some of the crew piled into it and the last we saw of them, they were rowing westward. The rest of us got ashore on rafts.

"By the black gods of Hades! It was madness – but what else was there for us to do? The jungles swarmed with blood-lusting blacks. We marched northward hoping to come upon a barracoon where slavers came, but they cut us off and we turned due eastward perforce. We fought every step of the way; our band melted like mist before the sun. Spears and savage beasts and venomous serpents took their fearful toll. At last I alone faced the jungle that had swallowed all my men. I eluded the blacks. For months I travelled alone and all but unarmed in this hostile land. At last I came out upon the shores of a great lake and saw the walls and towers of an island kingdom rising before me."

Hawk laughed fiercely. "By the bones of the saints! It sounds like a tale of Sir John Mandeville! I found a strange people upon the islands – black folk and a curious and ungodly race who ruled over them. They had never seen a

white man before. In my youth I wandered about with a band of thieves who masked their real characters by tumbling and juggling. By virtue of my skill at sleight o' hand, I impressed the people. They looked on me as a god – all except old Agara, their priest – and he could not explain away my white skin.

"They made a fetish of me and old Agara secretly offered to make me a high priest. I appeared to acquiesce and learned many of his secrets. I feared the old vulture at first for he could make magic that made my sleight o' hand seem childish – but the black people were strongly drawn to me.

"The lake is called Nyayna; the isles thereon are named the Isles of Ra and the main island is called Basti; the brown masters call themselves Khabasti and the black slaves are named Masutos.

"The life of these black people is wretched indeed. They have no will of their own save the desires of their cruel masters. They are more brutally treated than the Indians of Darien are treated by the Spanish. I have seen black women flogged to death and black men crucified for the slightest of faults. The cult of the Khabasti is a dark and bloody one, which they brought with them from whatever foul land they came from. On the black altar in the temple of the Moon, each week a howling victim dies beneath old Agara's dagger – always a black sacrifice, a strong young lad or a virgin. Nor is that the worst – before the dagger brings relief from suffering, the victim is mutilated in ways hideous to mention – the Holy Inquisition pales before the tortures inflicted by Basti's priests – yet so hellish is their art that the gibbering, mowing, blind and skinless creature lives until the final thrust of the dagger speeds him or her beyond the reach of the brown-skinned devils."

Hawk's covert glance showed him that deep volcanic fires were beginning to smolder coldly in Kane's strange eyes. His expression became more darkly brooding than ever, as he motioned the buccaneer to continue.

"No Englishman could look on the daily agonies of the poor wretches without pity. I became their champion as soon as I learned the language and I took the part of the black people. Then old Agara would have slain me, but the black folk rose and slew the fiend who held the throne. Then they begged me to remain and rule them. I did so. Under my rule Basti prospered, both the brown folk and the black. But old Agara, who had slunk away to some secret hiding place, was working in the shadows. He plotted against me and finally even turned many of the black people against their deliverer. The poor fools! Yesterday he came out in the open and in a pitched battle, the streets of Basti ran red. But old Agara prevailed with his evil magic, and most of my adherents were cut down. We retreated in canoes to one of the lesser islands and there they came upon us, and again we lost the fight. All of my henchmen were slain or taken – and God help those taken alive! – only I escaped. They have hunted me like wolves since. Even now they are hard on my track. They will not rest until they slay me, if they have to first follow me across the continent."

"Then we should waste no time in talk," said Kane, swiftly, but Hawk smiled coldly.

"Nay – the moment I glimpsed you through the trees and realized that by some strange whim of Fate I had met a man of my own race, I saw that again I should wear the golden gem-set circlet that is the crown of Basti. Let them come – we will go and meet them!

"Harkee, my bold Puritan, what I did before, I did unarmed, by sheer craft o' head. Had I a firearm, I had been ruler in Basti at this hour. They never heard of powder. You have two pistols – enough to make us kings a dozen times over – but would you had a musket."

Kane shrugged his shoulders. Needless to tell Hawk of the fiendish battle in which his musket had been splintered; even now he wondered if that ghastly episode had not been a vision of delirium.

"I have weapons enow," said he, "though my supply of powder and shot be limited."

"Three shots will put us on the throne of Basti," quoth Hawk. "How, my brave broadbrim, wilt chance it with an old comrade?"

"I will aid you in all that it be my power," answered Kane sombrely. "But I wish no earthly throne of pride and vanity. If we bring peace to a suffering race and punish evil men for their cruelty, it is enough for me."

They made a strange contrast, those two, standing there in the twilight of that great tropic forest. Jeremy Hawk was as tall as Solomon Kane and like him was rangy and powerful – steel springs and whalebone. But where Solomon was dark, Jeremy Hawk was blond. Now he was burned to light bronze by the sun, and his tangled yellow locks fell over his high narrow forehead. His jaw, masked by a yellow stubble, was lean and aggressive, and his thin gash of a mouth was cruel. His grey eyes were gleaming and restless, full of wild glitterings and shifting lights. His nose was thin and aquiline and his whole face was that of a bird of prey. He stood, leaning slightly forward in

his usual attitude of fierce eagerness, nearly naked, gripping his reddened sword.

Facing him stood Solomon Kane, likewise tall and powerful, in his worn boots, tattered garments and featherless slouch hat, girt with pistols, rapier and dagger, with his powder-and-shot pouch slung to his belt. There was no hint of likeness between the wild, reckless hawk's face of the buccaneer and the sombre features of the Puritan, whose dark pallor rendered his face almost corpse-like. Yet in the tigerish litheness of the pirate, in the wolfish appearance of Kane the same quality was apparent. Both of these men were born rovers and killers, curst with a paranoid driving urge that burned them like a quenchless fire and never gave them rest.

"Give me one of your pistols," exclaimed Hawk, "and half your powder and shot. They will soon be upon us – by Judas, we won't await them! We'll go to meet them! Leave it all to me – one shot and they will fall down and worship us. Come! And as we go, tell me how you come to be here."

"I have wandered for many moons," said Kane, half reluctantly. "Why I am here I know not – but the jungle called me across many leagues of blue sea and I came. Doubtless the same Providence which hath guided my steps all my years has led me hither for some purpose which my weak eyes have not yet seen."

"You carry a strange stick," said Hawk as they moved with long swinging stride beneath the huge arches.

Kane's eyes drifted to the stave in his right hand. It was as long as a sword, hard as iron and sharpened at the smaller end. The other end was carved in the shape of a cat's head, and all up and down the stave were strange wavering lines and curious carvings.

"I doubt not but that it is a thing of black magic and

sorcery," said Kane sombrely. "But in time past it hath prevailed mightily against beings of darkness and it is a goodly weapon. It was given me by a strange creature – one N'Longa, a fetish man of the Slave Coast, whom I have seen perform nameless and ungodly feats. Yet beneath his black and wrinkled hide beats the heart of a true man, I doubt not."

"Hark!" Hawk halted, stiffening suddenly. From ahead of them sounded the tramp of many sandaled feet – faint as a wind in the tree-tops, yet, keen-eared as hunting hounds, both he and his companion heard and translated it.

"There's a glade just ahead," grinned Hawk fiercely. "We'll await them there –"

And so Kane and the ex-king of Basti stood in plain view at one side of the glade when a hundred men burst from the other side, like a pack of wolves on a hot trail. They stopped in amazement, struck speechless at the sight of he who had been fleeing for his life and who now faced them with a cruel, mocking smile – and at the sight of his silent companion.

As for Kane, he gazed at them in wonder. Half of them were negroes, stocky burly fellows, with the barrel chests and short legs of men who spend much of their time in canoes. They were naked and armed with heavy spears. It was the others who arrested the Englishman's attention. These were tall, well-formed men whose regular features and straight black hair showed

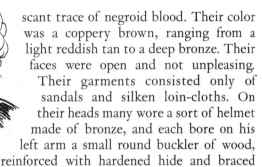

scant trace of negroid blood. Their color was a coppery brown, ranging from a light reddish tan to a deep bronze. Their faces were open and not unpleasing. Their garments consisted only of sandals and silken loin-cloths. On their heads many wore a sort of helmet made of bronze, and each bore on his left arm a small round buckler of wood, reinforced with hardened hide and braced with copper nails. Their arms were curved swords similar to that borne by Hawk, polished wooden maces and light battle-axes. Some carried heavy bows of evident power and quivers of long barbed arrows.

And it came forcibly to Solomon Kane that somewhere he had seen men much like these, or pictures of men like them. But where he could not say. They halted in the midst of the glade, to gaze uncertainly at the two white men.

"Well," said Hawk, mockingly, "you have found your king – have you forgotten your duty to your ruler? – down on your knees, dogs!"

A well-built young warrior at the head of the men spoke passionately and Kane started as he realized that he understood the language. It was much akin to the numerous Bantu dialects, many of which Kane had picked up in his travels, though some of the words were unintelligible to him and had a tang of peculiar antiquity.

"Red-handed murderer!" exclaimed the youth, his dark cheeks flushing in anger. "You dare to mock us? I know not who this man is but our quarrel is not with him; it is your head that we will take back to Agara with us – seize him –"

His own hand went back with the javelin he carried and in that instant Hawk aimed deliberately and fired. The

heavy-bored pistol crashed deafeningly and in the smoke
Kane saw the young warrior drop like a log. The effect on the
rest was just as Kane had seen it be on savages in many other
lands. Their weapons slipped from nerveless hands and they
stood frozen, gaping like frightened children. Some of the
black men cried out and dropped to their knees or flat on their
faces.

The distended eyes of all were drawn as by a magnet to
the silent corpse. At the close range the heavy ball had
literally shattered the youth's skull – had blasted out his
brains. And while his comrades stood like sheep, Hawk struck
while the iron was hot.

"Down, dogs!" he
cried sharply, striding
forward and striking a
warrior to his knees with a
blow of his open hand.
"Shall I loose the thunders of
death upon you all, or will
you receive me again as your
rightful king?"

Dazed, brains numbed,
the brown men sank to
their knees. The black men
wriggled prostrate on their
bellies and whimpered.
Hawk placed his heel on the
neck of the nearest warrior
and grinned savagely and
triumphantly at Kane.

"Arise," said he,
with a contemptuous
kick. "But none

forget I am king! Will ye return to Basti and fight for me, or will ye all die here?"

"We will fight for you, master," came the answering chorus. Hawk grinned again.

"Retaking the throne is easier than even I thought," said he. "Rise now – leave that carrion where it has fallen. I am your king and this is Solomon Kane my comrade. He is a terrible magician and even if you should slay me – who am immortal! – he will blast you all out of existence."

Men are sheep, thought Solomon, as he saw the warriors, brown and black, meekly forming themselves according to Hawk's orders. They formed short ranks, three abreast, and in the center walked Kane and Hawk.

"No fear of a spear in the back," said the buccaneer to Kane. "They are cowed – see the dazed look in their eyes? Yet be on guard."

Then calling to a man who had the appearance of a chief, he ordered him to walk between himself and Kane.

The Return of
Sir Richard Grenville

The Return of
Sir Richard Grenville

One slept beneath the branches dim,
    Cloaked in the crawling mist,
And Richard Grenville came to him
    And plucked him by the wrist.

No nightwind shook the forest deep
    Where the shadows of Doom were spread,
And Solomon Kane awoke from sleep
    And looked upon the dead.

He spake in wonder, not in fear:
    "How walks a man who died?
"Friend of old times, what do ye here,
    "Long fallen at my side?"

"Rise up, rise up," Sir Richard said,
    "The hounds of Doom are free;
"The slayers come to take your head
    "To hang on the ju-ju tree.

"Swift feet press the jungle mud
    "Where the shadows are grim and stark,
"And naked men who pant for blood
    "Are racing through the dark."

And Solomon rose and bared his sword,
    And swift as tongue could tell,
The dark spewed forth a painted horde
    Like shadows out of Hell.

His pistols thundered in the night,
  And in that burst of flame
He saw red eyes with hate alight,
  And on the figures came.

His sword was like a cobra's stroke
  And death hummed in its tune;
His arm was steel and knotted oak
  Beneath the rising moon.

But by him sang another sword,
  And a great form roared and thrust,
And dropped like leaves the screaming horde
  To writhe in bloody dust.

Silent as death their charge had been,
  Silent as night they fled;
And in the trampled glade was seen
  Only the torn dead.

And Solomon turned with outstretched hand,
  Then halted suddenly,
For no man stood with naked brand
  Beneath the moon-lit tree.

Wings in the Night

Wings in the Night

I

THE HORROR ON THE STAKE

Solomon Kane leaned on his strangely carved staff and gazed in scowling perplexity at the mystery which spread silently before him. Many a deserted village Kane had seen in the months that had passed since he turned his face east from the Slave Coast and lost himself in the mazes of jungle and river, but never one like this. It was not famine that had driven away the inhabitants, for yonder the wild rice still grew rank and unkempt in the untilled fields. There were no Arab slave-raiders in this nameless land – it must have been a tribal war that devastated the village, Kane decided, as he gazed somberly at the scattered bones and grinning skulls that littered the space among the rank weeds and grasses. These bones were shattered and splintered and Kane saw jackals and a hyena furtively slinking among the ruined huts. But why had the slayers left the spoils? There lay war spears, their shafts crumbling before the attacks of the white ants. There lay shields, moldering in the rains and sun. There lay the cooking-pots, and about the neck-bones of a shattered skeleton glistened a necklace of gaudily painted pebbles and shells – surely rare loot for any savage conqueror.

He gazed at the huts, wondering why the thatch roofs of so many were torn and rent, as if by taloned things seeking entrance. Then something made his cold eyes narrow in startled unbelief. Just outside the moldering mound that was once the village wall towered a gigantic baobab tree, branchless for sixty feet, its mighty bole too large to be gripped and scaled. Yet in the topmost branches dangled a

skeleton,
apparently
impaled on a broken
limb. The cold hand of
mystery touched the shoulder of Solomon
Kane. How came those pitiful remains in
that tree? Had some monstrous ogre's
inhuman hand flung them there?

Kane shrugged his broad shoulders and
his hand unconsciously touched the black
butts of his heavy pistols, the hilt of his
long rapier, and the dirk in his belt. Kane
felt no fear as an ordinary man would feel,
confronted with the Unknown and
Nameless. Years of wandering in
strange lands and warring with
strange creatures had melted
away from brain, soul and body
all that was not steel and
whalebone. He was tall and
spare, almost gaunt, built with
the savage economy of the wolf.

Broad-shouldered, long-armed, with nerves of ice and thews
of spring steel, he was no less the natural killer than the born
swordsman.

The brambles and thorns of the jungle had dealt hardly
with him; his garments hung in tatters, his featherless slouch
hat was torn and his boots of Cordovan leather were
scratched and worn. The sun had baked his chest and limbs to
a deep bronze but his ascetically lean face was impervious to
its rays. His complexion was still of that strange dark pallor
which gave him an almost corpse-like appearance, belied only
by his cold, light eyes.

And now Kane, sweeping the village once more with his searching gaze, pulled his belt into a more comfortable position, shifted to his left hand the cat-headed stave N'Longa had given him, and took up his way again.

To the west lay a strip of thin forest, sloping downward to a broad belt of savannas, a waving sea of grass waist-deep and deeper. Beyond that rose another narrow strip of woodlands, deepening rapidly into dense jungle. Out of that jungle Kane had fled like a hunted wolf with pointed-toothed men hot on his trail. Even now a vagrant breeze brought faintly the throb of a savage drum which whispered its obscene tale of hate and blood-hunger and belly-lust across miles of jungle and grassland.

The memory of his flight and narrow escape was vivid in Kane's mind, for only the day before had he realized too late that he was in cannibal country, and all that afternoon in the reeking stench of the thick jungle, he had crept and run and hidden and doubled and twisted on his track with the fierce hunters ever close behind him, until night fell and he gained and crossed the grasslands under cover of darkness. Now in the late morning he had seen nothing, heard nothing of his pursuers, yet he had no reason to believe that they had abandoned the chase. They had been close on his heels when he took to the savannas.

So Kane surveyed the land in front of him. To the east, curving from north to south ran a straggling range of hills, for the most part dry and barren, rising in the south to a jagged black skyline that reminded Kane of the black hills of Negari. Between him and these hills stretched a broad expanse of

gently rolling country, thickly treed, but nowhere approaching the density of a jungle. Kane got the impression of a vast upland plateau, bounded by the curving hills to the east and by the savannas to the west.

Kane set out for the hills with his long, swinging, tireless stride. Surely somewhere behind him the black demons were stealing after him, and he had no desire to be driven to bay. A shot might send them flying in sudden terror, but on the other hand, so low they were in the scale of humanity, it might transmit no supernatural fear to their dull brains. And not even Solomon Kane, whom Sir Francis Drake had called Devon's king of swords, could win in a pitched battle with a whole tribe.

The silent village with its burden of death and mystery faded out behind him. Utter silence reigned among these mysterious uplands where no birds sang and only a silent macaw flitted among the great trees. The only sounds were Kane's cat-like tread, and the whisper of the drum-haunted breeze.

And then Kane caught a glimpse among the trees that made his heart leap with a sudden, nameless horror, and a few moments later he stood before Horror itself, stark and grisly. In a wide clearing, on a rather bold incline stood a grim stake, and to this stake was bound a thing that had once been a black man. Kane had rowed, chained to the bench of a Turkish galley, and he had toiled in Barbary vineyards; he had battled red Indians in the New Lands and had languished in the dungeons of Spain's Inquisition. He knew much of the fiendishness of man's inhumanity, but now he shuddered and grew sick. Yet it was not so much the ghastliness of the mutilations, horrible as they were, that shook Kane's soul, but the knowledge that the wretch still lived.

For as he drew near, the gory head that lolled on the butchered breast lifted and tossed from side to side, spattering blood from the stumps of ears, while a bestial, rattling whimper drooled from the shredded lips.

Kane spoke to the ghastly thing and it screamed unbearably, writhing in incredible contortions, while its head jerked up and down with the jerking of mangled nerves, and the empty, gaping eye-sockets seemed striving to see from their emptiness. And moaning low and brain-shatteringly it huddled its outraged self against the stake where it was bound and lifted its head in a grisly attitude of listening, as if it expected something out of the skies.

"Listen," said Kane, in the dialect of the river-tribes. "Do not fear me – I will not harm you and nothing else shall harm you any more. I am going to loose you."

Even as he spoke Kane was bitterly aware of the emptiness of his words. But his voice had filtered dimly into the crumbling, agony-shot brain of the black man. From between splintered teeth fell words, faltering and uncertain, mixed and mingled with the slavering droolings of imbecility. He spoke a language akin to the dialects Kane had learned from friendly river-folk on his wanderings, and Kane gathered that he had been bound to the stake for a long time – many moons, he whimpered in the delirium of approaching death; and all this time, inhuman, evil things had worked their monstrous will upon him. These things he mentioned by name, but Kane could make nothing of it for he used an unfamiliar term that sounded like *akaana*. But these things had not bound him to the stake, for the torn wretch slavered the name of Goru, who was a priest and who had drawn a cord too tight about his legs – and Kane wondered that the memory of this small pain should linger through the red mazes of agony that the dying man should whimper over it.

And to Kane's horror, the black spoke of his brother who had aided in the binding of him, and he wept with infantile sobs, and moisture formed in the empty sockets and made tears of blood. And he muttered of a spear broken long ago in some dim hunt, and while he muttered in his delirium, Kane gently cut his bonds and eased his broken body to the grass. But even at the Englishman's careful touch, the poor wretch writhed and howled like a dying dog, while blood started anew from a score of ghastly gashes, which, Kane noted, were more like the wounds made by fang and talon than by knife or spear. But at last it was done and the bloody, torn thing lay on the soft grass with Kane's old slouch hat beneath its death's-head, breathing in great, rattling gasps.

Kane poured water from his canteen between the mangled lips, and bending close, said: "Tell me more of these devils, for by the God of my people, this deed shall not go unavenged, though Satan himself bar my way."

It is doubtful if the dying man heard. But he heard something else. The macaw, with the curiosity of its breed, swept from a near-by grove and passed so close its great wings fanned Kane's hair. And at the sound of those wings, the butchered black man heaved upright and screamed in a voice that haunted Kane's dreams to the day of his death: "The wings! The wings! They come again! Ahhhh, mercy, *the wings*!"

And the blood burst in a torrent from his lips and so he died.

Kane rose and wiped the cold sweat from his forehead. The upland forest shimmered in the noonday heat. Silence lay over the land like an enchantment of dreams. Kane's brooding eyes ranged to the black, malevolent hills crouching in the distance and back to the far-away savannas. An ancient curse lay over that mysterious land and the shadow of it fell across the soul of Solomon Kane.

Tenderly he lifted the red ruin that had once pulsed with life and youth and vitality, and carried it to the edge of the glade, where arranging the cold limbs as best he might, and shuddering once again at the unnamable mutilations, he piled stones above it till even a prowling jackal would find it hard to get at the flesh below.

And he had scarcely finished when something jerked him back out of his somber broodings to a realization of his own position. A slight sound – or his own wolf-like instinct – made him whirl. On the other side of the glade he caught a movement among the tall grasses – the glimpse of a hideous black face, with an ivory ring in the flat nose, thick lips parted to reveal teeth whose filed points were apparent even at that distance, beady eyes and a low slanting forehead topped by a mop of frizzly hair. Even as the face faded from view Kane leaped back into the shelter of the ring of trees which circled the glade, and ran like a deer-hound, flitting from tree to tree and expecting each moment to hear the exultant clamor of the braves and to see them break cover at his back.

But soon he decided that they were content to hunt him down as certain beasts track their prey, slowly and inevitably. He hastened through the upland forest, taking advantage of every bit of cover, and he saw no more of his pursuers; yet he *knew*, as a hunted wolf knows, that they hovered close behind him, waiting their moment to strike him down without risk to their own hides. Kane smiled bleakly and without mirth. If it was to be a test of endurance, he would see how savage thews compared with his own spring-steel resilience. Let night come and he might yet give them the slip. If not – Kane knew in his heart that the savage essence of the Anglo-Saxon which chafed at his flight, would make him soon turn at bay, though his pursuers outnumbered him a hundred to one.

The sun sank westward. Kane was hungry, for he had not eaten since early morning when he wolfed down the last of his dried meat. An occasional spring had given him water, and once he thought he glimpsed the roof of a large hut far away through the trees. But he gave it a wide berth. It was hard to believe that this silent plateau was inhabited, but if it were, the natives were doubtless as ferocious as those hunting him. Ahead of him the land grew rougher, with broken boulders and steep slopes as he neared the lower reaches of the brooding hills. And still no sight of his hunters except for faint glimpses caught by wary backward glances – a drifting shadow, the bending of the grass, the sudden straightening of a trodden twig, a rustle of leaves. Why should they be so cautious? Why did they not close in and have it over?

Night fell and Kane reached the first long slopes which led upward to the foot of the hills which now brooded black and menacing above him. They were his goal, where he hoped to shake off his persistent foes at last, yet a nameless aversion warned him away from them. They were pregnant with hidden evil, repellent as the coil of a great sleeping serpent, glimpsed in the tall grass.

Darkness fell heavily. The stars winked redly in the thick heat of the tropic night. And Kane, halting for a moment in an unusually dense grove, beyond which the trees thinned out on the slopes, heard a stealthy movement that was not the night wind – for no breath of air stirred the heavy leaves. And even as he turned, there was a rush in the dark, under the trees. A shadow that merged with the shadows flung itself on Kane with a bestial mouthing and a rattle of iron, and the Englishman, parrying by the gleam of the stars on the weapon, felt his assailant duck into close quarters and meet him chest to chest. Lean wiry arms locked about him, pointed teeth gnashed at him as Kane returned the fierce grapple. His tattered shirt ripped beneath a jagged edge, and by blind chance Kane found and pinioned the hand that held the iron knife, and drew his own dirk, flesh crawling in anticipation of a spear in the back.

But even as the Englishman wondered why the others did not come to their comrade's aid, he threw all of his iron muscles into the single combat. Close-clinched they swayed and writhed in the darkness, each striving to drive his blade into the other's flesh, and as the superior strength of the white man began to assert itself, the cannibal howled like a rabid dog, tore and bit. A convulsive spin-wheel of effort pivoted them out into the starlit glade where Kane saw the ivory nose-ring and the pointed teeth that snapped beast-like at his throat. And simultaneously he forced back and down the hand that gripped his knife-wrist, and drove the dirk deep into the black ribs. The warrior screamed and the raw acrid scent of blood flooded the night air. And in that instant Kane was stunned by a sudden savage rush and beat of mighty wings that dashed him to earth, and the black man was torn from his grip and vanished with a scream of mortal agony. Kane leaped to his feet, shaken to his foundation. The dwindling scream of the wretched black sounded faintly *and from above him.*

Straining his eyes into the skies he thought he caught a glimpse of a shapeless and horrific Thing crossing the dim stars − in which the writhing limbs of a human mingled namelessly with great wings and a shadowy shape − but so quickly it was gone, he could not be sure.

And now he wondered if it were not all a nightmare. But groping in the grove he found the ju-ju stave with which he had parried the short stabbing spear which lay beside it. And here, if more proof was needed, was his long dirk, still stained with blood.

Wings! Wings in the night! The skeleton in the village of torn roofs − the mutilated black man whose wounds were not made with knife or spear and who died shrieking of wings. Surely those hills were the haunt of gigantic birds who made humanity their prey. Yet if birds, why had they not wholly devoured the black man on the stake? And Kane knew in his heart that no true bird ever cast such a shadow as he had seen flit across the stars.

He shrugged his shoulders, bewildered. The night was silent. Where were the rest of the cannibals who had followed him from their distant jungle? Had the fate of their comrade frightened them into flight? Kane looked to his pistols. Cannibals or no, he went not up into those dark hills that night.

Now he must sleep, if all the devils of the Elder World

were on his track. A deep roaring to the westward warned
him that beasts of prey were a-roam, and he walked rapidly
down the rolling slopes until he came to a dense grove some
distance from that in which he had fought the cannibal. He
climbed high among the great branches until he found a thick
crotch that would accommodate even his tall frame. The
branches above would guard him from a sudden swoop of any
winged thing, and if savages were lurking near, their clamber
into the tree would warn him, for he slept lightly as a cat. As
for serpents and leopards, they were chances he had taken a
thousand times.

Solomon Kane slept and his dreams were vague, chaotic,
haunted with a suggestion of pre-human evil and which at
last merged into a vision vivid as a scene in waking life.
Solomon dreamed he woke with a start, drawing a pistol – for
so long had his life been that of the wolf, that reaching for a
weapon was his natural reaction upon waking suddenly. And
his dream was that a strange, shadowy thing had perched
upon a great branch close by and gazed at him with greedy,
luminous yellow eyes that seared into his brain. The dream-
thing was tall and lean and strangely misshapen, so blended
with the shadows that it seemed a shadow itself, tangible only
in the narrow yellow eyes. And Kane dreamed he waited,
spellbound, while uncertainty came into those eyes and then
the creature walked out on the limb as a man would walk,
raised great shadowy wings, sprang into space and vanished.
Then Kane jerked upright, the mists of sleep fading.

In the dim starlight, under the arching Gothic-like
branches, the tree was empty save for himself. Then it had
been a dream, after all – yet it had been so vivid, so fraught
with inhuman foulness – even now a faint scent like that
exuded by birds of prey seemed to linger in the air. Kane
strained his ears. He heard the sighing of the night-wind, the

whisper of the leaves, the far-away roaring of a lion, but naught else. Again Solomon slept – while high above him a shadow wheeled against the stars, circling again and again as a vulture circles a dying wolf.

II

The Battle in the Sky

Dawn was spreading whitely over the eastern hills when Kane woke. The thought of his nightmare came to him and he wondered again at its vividness as he climbed down out of the tree. A near-by spring slaked his thirst and some fruit, rare in these highlands, eased his hunger.

Then he turned his face again to the hills. A finish fighter was Solomon Kane. Along that grim skyline dwelt some evil foe to the sons of men, and that mere fact was as much a challenge to the Puritan as had ever been a glove thrown in his face by some hot-headed gallant of Devon.

Refreshed by his night's sleep, he set out with his long easy stride, passing the grove that had witnessed the battle in the night, and coming into the region where the trees thinned at the foot of the slopes. Up these slopes he went, halting for a moment to gaze back over the way he had come. Now that he was above the plateau, he could easily make out a village in the distance – a cluster of mud-and-bamboo huts with one unusually large hut a short distance from the rest on a sort of low knoll.

And while he gazed, with a sudden rush of grisly wings the terror was upon him! Kane whirled, galvanized. All signs had pointed to the theory of a winged thing that hunted by night. He had not expected attack in broad daylight – but here a bat-like monster was swooping at him out of the very eye of the rising sun. Kane saw a spread of mighty wings, from which glared a horribly human face; then he drew and fired with unerring aim and the monster veered wildly in midair and came whirling and tumbling out of the sky to crash at his feet.

Kane leaned forward, pistol smoking in his hand, and gazed wide-eyed. Surely this thing was a demon out of the black pits of hell, said the somber mind of the Puritan; yet a leaden ball had slain it. Kane shrugged his shoulders, baffled; he had never seen aught to approach this, though all his life had fallen in strange ways.

The thing was like a man, inhumanly tall and inhumanly thin; the head was long, narrow and hairless – the head of a predatory creature. The ears were small, close-set and queerly pointed. The eyes, set in death, were narrow, oblique and of a strange yellowish color. The nose was thin and hooked, like the beak of a bird of prey, the mouth a wide cruel gash, whose thin lips, writhed in a death snarl and flecked with foam, disclosed wolfish fangs.

The creature, which was naked and hairless, was not unlike a human being in other ways. The shoulders were broad and powerful, the neck long and lean. The arms were long and muscular, the thumb being set beside the fingers after the manner of the great apes. Fingers and thumbs were armed with heavy hooked talons. The chest was curiously misshapen, the breastbone jutting out like the keel of a ship, the ribs curving back from it. The legs were long and wiry with huge,

hand-like, prehensile feet, the great toe set opposite the rest like a man's thumb. The claws on the toes were merely long nails.

But the most curious feature of this curious creature was on its back. A pair of great wings, shaped much like the wings of a moth but with a bony frame and of leathery substance, grew from its shoulders, beginning at a point just back and above where the arms joined the shoulders, and extending half-way to the narrow hips. These wings, Kane reckoned, would measure some eighteen feet from tip to tip.

He laid hold on the creature, involuntarily shuddering at the slick, hard leather-like feel of the skin, and half lifted it. The weight was little more than half as much as it would have been in a man the same height – some six and a half feet. Evidently the bones were of a peculiar bird-like structure and the flesh consisted almost entirely of stringy muscles.

Kane stepped back, surveying the thing again. Then his dream had been no dream after all – that foul thing or another like it had in grisly reality lighted in the tree beside him – a whir of mighty wings! A sudden rush through the sky!

Even as Kane whirled he realized he had committed the jungle-farer's unpardonable crime — he had allowed his astonishment and curiosity to throw him off guard. Already a winged fiend was at his throat and there was no time to draw and fire his other pistol. Kane saw, in a maze of thrashing wings, a devilish, semi-human face — he felt those wings battering at him — he felt cruel talons sink deep into his breast; then he was dragged off his feet and felt empty space beneath him.

The winged man had wrapped his limbs about the Englishman's legs, and the talons he had driven into Kane's breast muscles held like fanged vises. The wolf-like fangs drove at Kane's throat but the Puritan gripped the bony throat and thrust back the grisly head, while with his right hand he strove to draw his dirk. The bird-man was mounting slowly and a fleeting glance showed Kane that they were already high above the trees. The Englishman did not hope to survive this battle in the sky, for even if he slew his foe, he would be dashed to death in the fall. But with the innate ferocity of the fighting Anglo-Saxon he set himself grimly to take his captor with him.

Holding those keen fangs at bay, Kane managed to draw his dirk and he plunged it deep into the body of the monster. The bat-man veered wildly and a rasping, raucous screech burst from his half-throttled throat. He floundered wildly, beating frantically with his great wings, bowing his back and twisting his head fiercely in a vain effort to free it and sink home his deadly fangs. He sank the talons of one hand agonizingly deeper and deeper into Kane's breast muscles, while with the other he tore at his foe's head and body. But the Englishman, gashed and bleeding, with the silent and tenacious savagery of a bulldog sank his fingers deeper into the lean neck and drove his dirk home again and again, while

far below awed eyes watched the fiendish battle that was raging at that dizzy height.

They had drifted out over the plateau, and the fast-weakening wings of the bat-man barely supported their weight. They were sinking earthward swiftly, but Kane, blinded with blood and battle-fury, knew nothing of this. With a great piece of his scalp hanging loose, his chest and shoulders cut and ripped, the world had become a blind, red thing in which he was aware of but one sensation – the bulldog urge to kill his foe. Now the feeble and spasmodic beating of the dying monster's wings held them hovering for an instant above a thick grove of gigantic trees, while Kane felt the grip of claws and twining limbs grow weaker and the slashing of the talons become a futile flailing.

With a last burst of power he drove the reddened dirk straight through the breastbone and felt a convulsive tremor

run through the creature's frame. The great wings fell limp –
and victor and vanquished dropped headlong and plummet-
like earthward.

Through a red wave Kane saw the waving branches
rushing up to meet them – he felt them flail his face and tear
at his clothing, as still locked in that death-clinch he rushed
downward through leaves which eluded his vainly grasping
hand; then his head crashed against a great limb and an
endless abyss of blackness engulfed him.

III
THE PEOPLE IN THE SHADOW

Through colossal, black basaltic corridors of night, Solomon
Kane fled for a thousand years. Gigantic winged demons,
horrific in the utter darkness, swept over him with a rush of
great bat-like pinions and in the blackness he fought with
them as a cornered rat fights a vampire-bat, while fleshless
jaws drooled fearful blasphemies and horrid secrets in his
ears, and the skulls of men rolled under his groping feet.

Solomon Kane came back suddenly from the land of
delirium and his first sight of sanity was that of a fat, kindly
black face bending over him. Kane saw he was in a roomy,
clean and well-ventilated hut, while from a cooking-pot
bubbling outside wafted savory scents. Kane realized he was
ravenously hungry. And he was strangely weak, and the hand
he lifted to his bandaged head shook and its bronze was
dimmed.

The fat man and another, a tall, gaunt, grim-faced
warrior, bent over him, and the fat man said: "He is awake,
Kuroba, and of sound mind." The gaunt man nodded and
called something which was answered from without.

"What is this place?" asked Kane, in a language he had learned, akin to the dialect the black had used. "How long have I lain here?"

"This is the last village of Bogonda." The fat black pressed him back with hands gentle as a woman's. "We found you lying beneath the trees on the slopes, badly wounded and senseless. You have raved in delirium for many days. Now eat."

A lithe young warrior entered with a wooden bowl full of steaming food and Kane ate ravenously.

"He is like a leopard, Kuroba," said the fat man admiringly. "Not one in a thousand would have lived with his wounds."

"Aye," returned the other. "And he slew the akaana that rent him, Goru."

Kane struggled to his elbows. "Goru?" he cried fiercely. "The priest who binds men to stakes for devils to eat?"

And he strove to rise so that he could strangle the fat man, but his weakness swept over him like a wave, the hut swam dizzily to his eyes and he sank back panting, where he soon fell into a sound, natural sleep.

Later he awoke and found a slim young girl, named Nayela, watching him. She fed him, and feeling much stronger, Kane asked questions which she answered shyly but intelligently. This was Bogonda, ruled by Kuroba the chief and Goru the priest. None in Bogonda had ever seen or heard of a white man before. She counted the days Kane had lain helpless, and he was amazed. But such a battle as he had been through was enough to kill an ordinary man. He wondered that no bones had been broken, but the girl said the branches had broken his fall and he had landed on the body of the akaana. He asked for Goru, and the fat priest came to him, bringing Kane's weapons.

"Some we found with you where you lay," said Goru, "some by the body of the akaana you slew with the weapon which speaks in fire and smoke. You must be a god — yet the gods bleed not and you have just all but died. Who are you?"

"I am no god," Kane answered, "but a man like yourself, albeit my skin be white. I come from a far land amid the sea, which land, mind ye, is the fairest and noblest of all lands. My name is Solomon Kane and I am a landless wanderer. From the lips of a dying man I first heard your name. Yet your face seemeth kindly."

A shadow crossed the eyes of the shaman and he hung his head.

"Rest and grow strong, oh man, or god or whatever you be," said he, "and in time you will learn of the ancient curse that rests upon this ancient land."

And in the days that followed, while Kane recovered and grew strong with the wild beast vitality that was his, Goru and Kuroba sat and spoke to him at length, telling him many curious things.

Their tribe was not aboriginal here, but had come upon the plateau a hundred and fifty years before, giving it the name of their former home. They had once been a powerful tribe in Old Bogonda, on a great river far to the south. But tribal wars broke their power, and at last before a concerted uprising, the whole tribe gave way, and Goru repeated legends of that great flight of a thousand miles through jungle and swampland harried at every step by cruel foes.

At last, hacking their way through a country of ferocious cannibals, they found themselves safe from man's attack – but prisoners in a trap from which neither they nor their descendants could ever escape. They were in the horror-country of Akaana, and Goru said his ancestors came to understand the jeering laughter of the man-eaters who had hounded them to the very borders of the plateau.

The Bogondi found a fertile country with good water and plenty of game. There were numbers of goats and a species of wild pig that throve here in great abundance. At first the black people ate these pigs, but later they spared them for a very good reason. The grasslands between plateau and jungle swarmed with antelopes, buffaloes and the like, and there were many lions. Lions also roamed the plateau, but Bogonda meant "Lion-slayer" in their tongue and it was not many moons before the remnants of the great cats took to the lower levels. But it was not lions they had to fear, as Goru's ancestors soon learned.

Finding that the cannibals would not come past the savannas, they rested from their long trek and built two villages – Upper and Lower Bogonda. Kane was in Upper Bogonda; he had seen the ruins of the lower village. But soon they found that they had strayed into a country of nightmares with dripping fangs and talons. They heard the beat of mighty wings at night, and saw horrific shadows cross the stars and loom against the moon. Children began to disappear and at last a young hunter strayed off into the hills, where night overtook him. And in the gray light of dawn a mangled, half-devoured corpse fell from the skies into the village street and a whisper of ogreish laughter from high

above froze the horrified onlookers. Then a little later the full
horror of their position burst upon the Bogondi.

At first the winged men were afraid of the black people.
They hid themselves and ventured from their caverns only at
night. Then they grew bolder. In the full daylight, a warrior
shot one with an arrow, but the fiends had learned they could
slay a human and its death scream brought a score of the
devils dropping from the skies, who tore the slayer to pieces
in full sight of the tribe.

The Bogondi then prepared to leave that devil's country
and a hundred warriors went up into the hills to find a pass.
They found steep walls, up which a man must climb
laboriously, and they found the cliffs honeycombed with caves
where the winged men dwelt.

Then was fought the first pitched battle between men
and bat-men and it resulted in a crushing victory for the
monsters. The bows and spears of the black people proved
futile before the swoops of the taloned fiends, and of all that
hundred that went up into the hills, not one survived; for the
akaanas hunted down those that fled and dragged down the
last one within bowshot of the upper village.

Then it was that the Bogondi, seeing they could not hope
to win through the hills, sought to fight their way out again
the way they had come. But a great horde of cannibals met
them in the grasslands and in a great battle that lasted nearly
all day, hurled them back, broken and defeated. And Goru
said while the battle raged, the skies were thronged with
hideous shapes, circling above and laughing their fearful
mirth to see men die wholesale.

So the survivors of those two battles, licking their
wounds, bowed to the inevitable with the fatalistic
philosophy of the black man. Some fifteen hundred men,
women and children remained, and they built their huts,

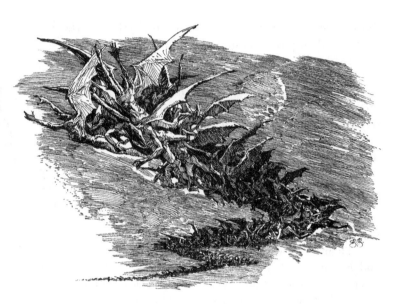

tilled the soil and lived stolidly in the shadow of the nightmare.

In those days there were many of the bird-people, and they might have wiped out the Bogondi utterly, had they wished. No one warrior could cope with an akaana, for he was stronger than a human, he struck as a hawk strikes, and if he missed, his wings carried him out of reach of a counter-blow. Here Kane interrupted to ask why the blacks did not make war on the demons with arrows. But Goru answered that it took a quick and accurate archer to strike an akaana in midair at all and so tough were their hides that unless the arrow struck squarely it would not penetrate. Kane knew that the blacks were very indifferent bowmen and that they pointed their shafts with chipped stone, bone or hammered iron almost as soft as copper; he thought of Poitiers and Agincourt and wished grimly for a file of stout English archers – or a rank of musketeers.

But Goru said the akaanas did not seem to wish to destroy the Bogondi utterly. Their chief food consisted of the little pigs which then swarmed the plateau, and young goats. Sometimes they went out on the savannas for antelope, but they distrusted the open country and feared the lions. Nor did they haunt the jungles beyond, for the trees grew too close for the spread of their wings. They kept to the hills and the plateau – and what lay beyond those hills none in Bogonda knew.

The akaanas allowed the black folk to inhabit the plateau much as men allow wild animals to thrive, or stock lakes with fish – for their own pleasure. The bat-people, said Goru, had a strange and grisly sense of humor which was tickled by the sufferings of a howling human. Those grim hills had echoed to cries that turned men's hearts to ice.

But for many years, Goru said, once the Bogondi learned not to resist their masters, the akaanas were content to snatch up a baby from time to time, or devour a young girl strayed from the village or a youth whom night caught outside the walls. The bat-folk distrusted the village; they circled high above it but did not venture within. There the Bogondi were safe until late years.

Goru said that the akaanas were fast dying out; once there had been hope that the remnants of his race would outlast them – in which event, he said fatalistically, the cannibals would undoubtedly come up from the jungle and put the survivors in the cooking-pots. Now he doubted if there were more than a hundred and fifty akaanas altogether. Kane asked him why did not the warriors then sally forth on a great hunt and destroy the devils utterly, and Goru smiled a bitter smile and repeated his remarks about the prowess of the bat-people in battle. Moreover, said he, the whole tribe of Bogonda numbered only about four hundred souls now, and the bat-people were their only protection against the cannibals to the west.

Goru said the tribe had thinned more in the past thirty years than in all the years previous. As the numbers of the akaanas dwindled, their hellish savagery increased. They seized more and more of the Bogondi to torture and devour in their grim black caves high up in the hills, and Goru spoke of sudden raids on hunting-parties and toilers in the plantain fields and of the nights made ghastly by horrible screams and gibberings from the dark hills, and blood-freezing laughter that was half human; of dismembered limbs and gory grinning heads flung from the skies to fall in the shuddering village, and of grisly feasts among the stars.

Then came drouth, Goru said, and a great famine. Many of the springs dried up and the crops of rice and yams and plantains failed. The gnus, deer and buffaloes which had formed the main part of Bogonda's meat diet withdrew to the jungle in quest of water, and the lions, their hunger overcoming their fear of man, ranged into the uplands. Many of the tribe died and the rest were driven by hunger to eat the pigs which were the natural prey of the bat-people. This angered the akaanas and thinned the pigs. Famine, Bogondi and the lions destroyed all the goats and half the pigs.

At last the famine was past, but the damage was done. Of all the great droves which once swarmed the plateau, only a remnant was left and these were wary and hard to catch. The Bogondi had eaten the pigs, so the akaanas ate the Bogondi. Life became a hell for the black people, and the lower village, numbering now only some hundred and fifty souls, rose in revolt. Driven to frenzy by repeated outrages, they turned on their masters. An akaana lighting in the very streets to steal

a child was set on and shot to death with arrows. And the
people of Lower Bogonda drew into their huts and waited for
their doom.

And in the night, said Goru, it came. The akaanas had
overcome their distrust of the huts. The full flock of them
swarmed down from the hills, and Upper Bogonda awoke to
hear the fearful cataclysm of screams and blasphemies that
marked the end of the other village. All night Goru's people
had lain sweating in terror, not daring to move, harkening to
the howling and gibbering that rent the night; at last these
sounds ceased, Goru said, wiping the cold sweat from his
brow, but sounds of grisly and obscene feasting still haunted
the night with demon's mockery.

In the early dawn Goru's people saw the hell-flock
winging back to their hills, like demons flying back to hell
through the dawn, and they flew slowly and heavily, like
gorged vultures. Later the people dared to steal down to the
accursed village, and what they found there sent them
shrieking away; and to that day, Goru said, no man passed
within three bowshots of that silent horror. And Kane nodded
in understanding, his cold eyes more somber than ever.

For many days after that, Goru said, the people waited in
quaking fear, and finally in desperation of fear, which breeds
unspeakable cruelty, the tribe cast lots and the loser was
bound to a stake between the two villages, in hopes the
akaanas would recognize this as a token of submission so that
the people of Bogonda might escape the fate of their kinsmen.
This custom, said Goru, had been borrowed from the
cannibals who in old times worshipped the akaanas and
offered a human sacrifice at each moon. But chance had shown
them that the akaana could be killed, so they ceased to
worship him – at least that was Goru's deduction, and he

explained at much length that no mortal thing is worthy of real adoration, however evil or powerful it may be.

His own ancestors had made occasional sacrifices to placate the winged devils, but until lately it had not been a regular custom. Now it was necessary; the akaanas expected it, and each moon they chose from their waning numbers a strong young man or a girl whom they bound to the stake. Kane watched Goru's face closely as he spoke of his sorrow for this unspeakable necessity, and the Englishman realized the priest was sincere. Kane shuddered at the thought of a tribe of human beings thus passing slowly but surely into the maws of a race of monsters.

Kane spoke of the wretch he had seen, and Goru nodded, pain in his soft eyes. For a day and a night he had been hanging there, while the akaanas glutted their vile torture-lust on his quivering, agonized flesh. Thus far the sacrifices had kept doom from the village. The remaining pigs furnished sustenance for the dwindling akaanas, together with an occasional baby snatched up, and they were content to have their nameless sport with the single victim each moon.

A thought came to Kane.

"The cannibals never come up into the plateau?"

Goru shook his head; safe in their jungle, they never raided past the savannas.

"But they hunted me to the very foot of the hills."

Again Goru shook his head. There was only one cannibal; they had found his footprints. Evidently a single warrior, bolder than the rest, had allowed his passion for the chase to overcome his fear of the grisly plateau and had paid the penalty. Kane's teeth came together with a vicious snap which ordinarily took the place of profanity with him. He was stung by the thought of fleeing so long from a single enemy. No wonder that enemy had followed so cautiously, waiting until

dark to attack. But, asked Kane, why had the akaana seized
the black man instead of himself – and why had he not been
attacked by the bat-man who alighted in his tree that night?

The cannibal was bleeding, Goru answered; the scent
called the bat-fiend to attack, for they scented raw blood as
far as vultures. And they were very wary. They had never
seen a man like Kane, who showed no fear. Surely they had
decided to spy on him, take him off guard before they struck.

Who were these creatures? Kane asked. Goru shrugged
his shoulders. They were there when his ancestors came, who
had never heard of them before they saw them. There was no
intercourse with the cannibals, so they could learn nothing
from them. The akaanas lived in caves, naked like beasts; they
knew nothing of fire and ate only fresh raw meat. But they
had a language of a sort and acknowledged a king among
them. Many died in the great famine when the stronger ate
the weaker. They were vanishing swiftly; of late years no
females or young had been observed among them. When these
males died at last, there would be no more akaanas; but
Bogonda, observed Goru, was doomed already, unless – he
looked strangely and wistfully at Kane. But the Puritan was
deep in thought.

Among the swarm of native legends he had heard on his
wanderings, one now stood out. Long, long ago, an old, old ju-
ju man had told him, winged devils came flying out of the
north and passed over his country, vanishing in the maze of
the jungle-haunted south. And the ju-ju man related an old,
old legend concerning these creatures – that once they had
abode in myriad numbers far on a great lake of bitter water
many moons to the north, and ages and ages ago a chieftain
and his warriors fought them with bows and arrows and slew
many, driving the rest into the south. The name of the chief
was N'Yasunna and he owned a great war canoe with many

oars driving it swiftly through the bitter water.

And now a cold wind blew suddenly on Solomon Kane, as if from a Door opened suddenly on Outer gulfs of Time and Space. For now he realized the truth of that garbled myth, and the truth of an older, grimmer legend. For what was the great bitter lake but the Mediterranean Ocean and who was the chief N'Yasunna but the hero Jason, who conquered the harpies and drove them – not alone into the Strophades Isles but into Africa as well? The old pagan tale was true then, Kane thought dizzily, shrinking aghast from the strange realm of grisly possibilities this opened up. For if this myth of the harpies were a reality, what of the other legends – the Hydra, the centaurs, the chimera, Medusa, Pan and the satyrs? All those myths of antiquity – behind them did there lie and lurk nightmare realities with slavering fangs and talons steeped in shuddersome evil? Africa, the Dark Continent, land of shadows and horror, of bewitchment and sorcery, into which all evil things had been banished before the growing light of the western world!

Kane came out of his reveries with a start. Goru was tugging gently and timidly at his sleeve.

"Save us from the akaanas!" said Goru. "If you be not a god, there is the power of a god in you! You bear in your hand the mighty ju-ju stave which has in times gone by been the scepter of fallen empires and the staff of mighty priests. And you have weapons which speak death in fire and smoke – for our young men watched and saw you slay two akaanas. We will make you king – god – what you will! More than a moon has passed since you came into Bogonda and the time for the sacrifice is gone by, but the bloody stake stands bare. The akaanas shun the village where you lie; they steal no more babes from us. We have thrown off their yoke because our trust is in you!"

Kane clasped his temples with his hands. "You know not what you ask!" he cried. "God knoweth it is in my deepest heart to rid the land of this evil, but I am no god. With my pistols I can slay a few of the fiends, but I have but a little powder left. Had I great store of powder and ball, and the musket I shattered in the vampire-haunted Hills of the Dead, then indeed would there be a rare hunting. But even if I slew all these fiends, what of the cannibals?"

"They too will fear you!" cried old Kuroba, while the girl Nayela and the lad, Loga, who was to have been the next sacrifice, gazed at him with their souls in their eyes. Kane dropped his chin on his fist and sighed.

"Yet will I stay here in Bogonda all the rest of my life if ye think I be protection to the people."

So Solomon Kane stayed at the village of Bogonda of the Shadow. The people were a kindly folk, whose natural sprightliness and fun-loving spirits were subdued and saddened by long dwelling in the Shadow. But now they had taken new heart by the white man's coming and it wrenched Kane's heart to note the pathetic trust they placed in him. Now they sang in the plantain fields and danced about the fires, and gazed at him with adoring faith in their eyes. But Kane, cursing his own helplessness, knew how futile would be his fancied protection if the winged fiends swept suddenly out of the skies.

But he stayed in Bogonda. In his dreams the gulls wheeled above the cliffs of old Devon carved in the clean, blue, wind-whipped skies, and in the day the call of the unknown lands beyond Bogonda clawed at his heart with fierce yearning. But he abode in Bogonda and racked his brains for a plan. He sat and gazed for hours at the ju-ju stave, hoping in desperation that black magic would aid him, where the white man's mind failed. But N'Longa's ancient gift gave him no aid. Once he had summoned the Slave Coast shaman to him across leagues of intervening space – but it was only when confronted with supernatural manifestations that N'Longa could come to him, and these harpies were not supernatural.

The germ of an idea began to grow at the back of Kane's mind, but he discarded it. It had to do with a great trap – and how could the akaanas be trapped? The roaring of lions played a grim accompaniment to his brooding meditations. As man dwindled on the plateau, the hunting beasts who feared only the spears of the hunters were beginning to gather. Kane laughed bitterly. It was not lions, that might be hunted down and slain singly, that he had to deal with.

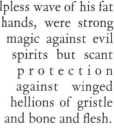

At some little distance from the village stood the great hut of Goru, once a council hall. This hut was full of many strange fetishes which, Goru said with a helpless wave of his fat hands, were strong magic against evil spirits but scant protection against winged hellions of gristle and bone and flesh.

IV
THE MADNESS OF SOLOMON

Kane woke suddenly from a dreamless sleep. A hideous medley of screams burst horrific in his ears. Outside his hut, people were dying in the night, horribly, as cattle die in the shambles. He had slept, as always, with his weapons buckled on him. Now he bounded to the door, and something fell mouthing and slavering at his feet to grasp his knees in a convulsive grip and gibber incoherent pleas. In the faint light of a smoldering fire near by, Kane in horror recognized the face of the youth Loga, now frightfully torn and drenched in blood, already freezing into a death mask. The night was full of fearful sounds, inhuman howlings mingled with the whisper of mighty wings, the tearing of thatch and a ghastly demon-laughter. Kane freed himself from the locked dead arms and sprang to the dying fire. He could make out only a confused and vague maze of fleeing forms, and darting shapes, the shift and blur of dark wings against the stars.

He snatched up a brand and thrust it against the thatch of his hut – and as the flame leaped up and showed him the scene he stood frozen and aghast. Red, howling doom had fallen on Bogonda. Winged monsters raced screaming through her streets, wheeled above the heads of the fleeing people, or tore apart the hut thatches to get at the gibbering victims within.

With a choked cry the Englishman woke from his trance of horror, drew and fired at a darting flame-eyed shadow which fell at his feet with a shattered skull. And Kane gave tongue to one deep, fierce roar and bounded into the melee, all the berserk fury of his heathen Saxon ancestors bursting into terrible being.

Dazed and bewildered by the sudden attack, cowed by

long years of submission, the Bogondi were incapable of combined resistance and for the most part died like sheep. Some, maddened by desperation, fought back, but their arrows went wild or glanced from the tough wings while the devilish agility of the creatures made spear-thrust and ax-stroke uncertain. Leaping from the ground they avoided the blows of their victims and sweeping down upon their shoulders dashed them to earth, where fang and talon did their crimson work.

Kane saw old Kuroba, gaunt and blood-stained, at bay against a hut wall with his foot on the neck of a monster who had not been quick enough. The grim-faced old chief wielded a two-handed ax in great sweeping blows that for the moment held back the screeching onset of half a dozen of the devils. Kane was leaping to his aid when a low, pitiful whimper checked him. The girl Nayela writhed weakly, prone in the bloody dust, while on her back a vulture-like thing crouched and tore. Her dulling eyes sought the face of the Englishman in anguished appeal. Kane ripped out a bitter oath and fired point-blank. The winged devil pitched backward with an abhorrent screeching and a wild flutter of dying wings and Kane bent to the dying girl, who whimpered and kissed his hands with uncertain lips as he cradled her head in his arms. Her eyes set.

Kane laid the body gently down, looking for Kuroba. He saw only a huddled cluster of grisly shapes that sucked and tore at something between them. And Kane went mad. With a scream that cut through the inferno he bounded up, slaying even as he rose. Even in the act of lunging up from bent knee he drew and thrust, transfixing a vulture-like throat. Then whipping out his rapier as the thing floundered and twitched in its death struggles, the raging Puritan charged forward seeking new victims.

On all sides of him the people of Bogonda were dying hideously. They fought futilely or they fled and the demons coursed them down as a hawk courses a hare. They ran into the huts and the fiends rent the thatch or burst the door, and what took place in those huts was mercifully hidden from Kane's eyes. And to the frantic white man's horror-distorted brain it seemed that he alone was responsible. The black folk had trusted him to save them. They had withheld the sacrifice and defied their grim masters and now they were paying the horrible penalty and he was unable to save them. In the agony-dimmed eyes turned toward him Kane quaffed the black dregs of the bitter cup. It was not anger or the vindictiveness of fear. It was hurt and a stunned reproach. He was their god and he had failed them.

Now he ravened through the massacre and the fiends avoided him, turning to the easy black victims. But Kane was not to be denied. In a red haze that was not of the burning hut, he saw a culminating horror; a harpy gripped a writhing naked thing that had been a woman and the wolfish fangs gorged deep. As Kane sprang, thrusting, the bat-man dropped his yammering, mowing prey and soared aloft. But Kane dropped his rapier and with the bound of a blood-mad panther caught the demon's throat and locked his iron legs about its lower body.

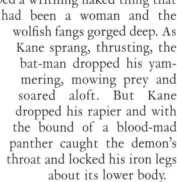

Again he found himself battling in midair, but

this time only above the roofs of the huts. Terror had entered
the cold brain of the harpy. He did not fight to hold and slay;
he wished only to be rid of this silent, clinging thing that
stabbed so savagely for his life. He floundered wildly,
screaming abhorrently and thrashing with his wings, then as
Kane's dirk bit deeper, dipped suddenly sidewise and fell
headlong.

The thatch of a hut broke their fall, and Kane and the
dying harpy crashed through to land on a writhing mass on
the hut floor. In the lurid flickering of the burning hut
outside, that vaguely lighted the hut into which he had fallen,
Kane saw a deed of brain-shaking horror being enacted – red
dripping fangs in a yawning gash of a mouth, and a crimson
travesty of a human form that still writhed with agonized
life. Then in the maze of madness that held him, his steel
fingers closed on the fiend's throat in a grip that no tearing of
talons or hammering of wings could loosen, until he felt the
horrid life flow out from under his fingers and the bony neck
hung broken.

And still outside the red madness of slaughter
continued. Kane bounded up, his hand closing blindly on the
haft of some weapon, and as he leaped from the hut a harpy

soared from under his very feet. It was an ax that Kane had snatched up, and he dealt a stroke that spattered the demon's brains like water. He sprang forward, stumbling over bodies and parts of bodies, blood streaming from a dozen wounds, and then halted baffled and screaming with rage.

The bat-people were taking to the air. No longer would they face this white-skinned madman who in his insanity was more terrible than they. But they went not alone into the upper regions. In their lustful talons they bore writhing, screaming forms, and Kane, raging to and fro with his dripping ax, found himself alone in a corpse-choked village.

He threw back his head to shriek his hate at the fiends above him and he felt warm, thick drops fall into his face, while the shadowy skies were filled with screams of agony and the laughter of monsters. And Kane's last vestige of reason snapped as the sounds of that ghastly feast in the skies filled the night and the blood that rained from the stars fell into his face. He gibbered to and fro, screaming chaotic blasphemies.

And was he not a symbol of Man, staggering among the tooth-marked bones and severed grinning heads of humans, brandishing a futile ax, and screaming incoherent hate at the grisly, winged shapes of Night that make him their prey, chuckling in demoniac triumph above him and dripping into his mad eyes the pitiful blood of their human victims?

V

THE WHITE-SKINNED CONQUEROR

A shuddering, white-faced dawn crept over the black hills to shiver above the red shambles that had been the village of Bogonda. The huts stood intact, except for the one which had sunk to smoldering coals, but the thatches of many were torn. Dismembered bones, half or wholly stripped of flesh, lay in the streets, and some were splintered as though they had been dropped from a great height.

It was a realm of the dead where was but one sign of life. Solomon Kane leaned on his blood-clotted ax and gazed upon the scene with dull, mad eyes. He was grimed and clotted with half-dried blood from long gashes on chest, face and shoulders, but he paid no heed to his hurts.

The people of Bogonda had not died alone. Seventeen harpies lay among the bones. Six of these Kane had slain. The rest had fallen before the frantic dying desperation of the black people. But it was poor toll to take in return. Of the four-hundred-odd people of Upper Bogonda, not one had lived to see the dawn. And the harpies were gone – back to their caves in the black hills, gorged to repletion.

With slow, mechanical steps Kane went about gathering up his weapons. He found his sword, dirk, pistols and the ju-ju stave. He left the main village and went up the slope to the great hut of Goru. And there he halted, stung by a new horror. The ghastly humor of the harpies had prompted a delicious jest. Above the hut door stared the severed head of Goru. The fat cheeks were shrunken, the lips lolled in an aspect of horrified idiocy, and the eyes stared like a hurt child. And in those dead eyes Kane saw wonder and reproach.

Kane looked at the shambles that had been Bogonda, and he looked at the death mask of Goru. And he lifted his clenched fists above his head, and with glaring eyes raised and writhing lips flecked with froth, he cursed the sky and the earth and the spheres above and below. He cursed the cold stars, the blazing sun, the mocking moon and the whisper of the wind. He cursed all fates and destinies, all that he had loved or hated, the silent cities beneath the seas, the past ages

and the future eons. In one soul-shaking burst of blasphemy he cursed the gods and devils who make mankind their sport, and he cursed Man who lives blindly on and blindly offers his back to the iron-hoofed feet of his gods.

Then as breath failed he halted, panting. From the lower reaches sounded the deep roaring of a lion and into the eyes of Solomon Kane came a crafty gleam. He stood long, as one frozen, and out of his madness grew a desperate plan. And he silently recanted his blasphemy, for if the brazen-hoofed gods made Man for their sport and plaything, they also gave him a brain that holds craft and cruelty greater than any other living thing.

"There you shall bide," said Solomon Kane to the head of Goru. "The sun will wither you and the cold dews of night will shrivel you. But I will keep the kites from you and your eyes shall see the fall of your slayers. Aye, I could not save the people of Bogonda, but by the God of my race, I can avenge them. Man is the sport and sustenance of titanic beings of Night and Horror whose giant wings hover ever above him. But even evil things may come to an end – and watch ye, Goru."

In the days that followed Kane labored mightily, beginning with the first gray light of dawn and toiling on past sunset, into the white moonlight till he fell and slept the sleep of utter exhaustion. He snatched food as he worked and he gave his wounds absolutely no heed, scarcely being aware that they healed of themselves. He went down into the lower levels and cut bamboo, great stacks of long, tough stalks. He cut thick branches of trees, and tough vines to serve as ropes. And with this material he reinforced the walls and roof of Goru's hut. He set the bamboos deep in the earth, hard against the wall, and interwove and twined them, binding them fast with the vines that were pliant and tough as cords.

The long branches he made fast along the thatch, binding them close together. When he had finished, an elephant could scarcely have burst through the walls.

The lions had come into the plateau in great quantities and the herds of little pigs dwindled fast. Those the lions spared, Kane slew, and tossed to the jackals. This racked Kane's heart, for he was a kindly man and this wholesale slaughter, even of pigs who would fall prey to hunting beasts anyhow, grieved him. But it was part of his plan of vengeance and he steeled his heart.

The days stretched into weeks. Kane toiled by day and by night, and between his stints he talked to the shriveled, mummied head of Goru, whose eyes, strangely enough, did not change in the blaze of the sun or the haunt of the moon, but retained their life-like expression. When the memory of those lunacy-haunted days had become only a vague nightmare, Kane wondered if, as it had seemed to him, Goru's dried lips had moved in answer, speaking strange and mysterious things.

Kane saw the akaanas wheeling against the sky at a distance, but they did not come near, even when he slept in the great hut, pistols at hand. They feared his power to deal death with smoke and thunder. At first he noted that they flew sluggishly, gorged with the flesh they had eaten on that red night, and the bodies they had borne to their caves. But as the weeks passed they appeared leaner and leaner and ranged far afield in search of food. And Kane laughed, deeply and madly. This plan of his would never have worked before, but now there were no humans to fill the bellies of the harpy-folk. And there were no more pigs. In all the plateau there were no creatures for the bat-people to eat. Why they did not range east of the hills, Kane thought he knew. That must be a region of thick jungle like the country to the west. He saw them fly into the grassland for antelopes and he saw the lions take toll of them. After all, the akaanas were weak beings among the hunters, strong enough only to slay pigs and deer – and humans.

At last they began to soar close to him at night and he saw their greedy eyes glaring at him through the gloom. He judged the time was ripe. Huge buffaloes, too big and ferocious for the bat-people to slay, had strayed up into the plateau to ravage the deserted fields of the dead black people. Kane cut one of these out of the herd and drove him, with shouts and volleys of stones, to the hut of Goru. It was a tedious, dangerous task, and time and again Kane barely escaped the surly bull's sudden charges, but persevered and at last shot the beast before the hut.

A strong west wind was blowing and Kane flung handfuls of blood into the air for the scent to waft to the harpies in the hills. He cut the bull to pieces and carried its quarters into the hut, then managed to drag the huge trunk itself inside. Then he retired into the thick trees near by and waited.

He had not long to wait. The morning air filled suddenly with the beat of many wings and a hideous flock alighted before the hut of Goru. All of the beasts – or men – seemed to be there, and Kane gazed in wonder at the tall, strange creatures, so like to humanity and yet so unlike – the veritable demons of priestly legend.

They folded their wings like cloaks about them as they walked upright and they talked to one another in a strident crackling voice that had nothing of the human in it. No, these things were not men, Kane decided. They were the materialization of some ghastly jest of Nature – some travesty of the world's infancy when Creation was an experiment. Perhaps they were the offspring of a forbidden and obscene mating of man and beast; more likely they were a freakish offshoot on the branch of evolution – for Kane had long ago dimly sensed a truth in the heretical theories of the ancient philosophers, that Man is but a higher beast. And if Nature made many strange beasts in the past ages, why should she not have experimented with monstrous forms of mankind? Surely Man as Kane knew him was not the first of his breed to walk the earth, nor yet to be the last.

Now the harpies hesitated, with their natural distrust for a building, and some soared to the roof and tore at the thatch. But Kane had builded well. They returned to earth and at last, driven beyond endurance by the smell of raw blood and the sight of the flesh within, one of them ventured inside. In an instant all were crowded into the great hut, tearing ravenously at the meat, and when the last one was within, Kane reached out a hand and jerked a long vine which tripped the catch that held the door he had built. It fell with a crash and the bar he had fashioned dropped into place. That door would hold against the charge of a wild bull.

Kane came from his covert and scanned the sky. Some hundred and forty harpies had entered the hut. He saw no more winging through the skies, and believed it safe to suppose he had the whole flock trapped. Then with a cruel, brooding smile, Kane struck flint and steel to a pile of dead leaves next the wall. Within sounded an uneasy mumbling as the creatures realized that they were prisoners. A thin wisp of smoke curled upward and a flicker of red followed it; the whole heap burst into flame and the dry bamboo caught.

A few moments later the whole side of the wall was ablaze. The fiends inside scented the smoke and grew restless. Kane heard them cackling wildly and clawing at the walls. He grinned savagely, bleakly and without mirth. Now a veer of the wind drove the flames around the wall and up over the thatch – with a roar the whole hut caught and leaped into flame. From within sounded a fearful pandemonium. Kane heard bodies crash against the walls, which shook to the impact but held. The horrid screams were music to his soul, and brandishing his arms, he answered them with screams of fearful, soul-shaking laughter. The cataclysm of horror rose unbearably, paling the tumult of the flames. Then it dwindled to a medley of strangled gibbering and gasps as the flames ate in and the smoke thickened. An intolerable scent of burning flesh pervaded the atmosphere, and had there been room in Kane's brain for aught else than insane triumph, he would have shuddered to realize that the scent was of that

nauseating and indescribable odor that only human flesh emits when burning.

From the thick cloud of smoke Kane saw a mowing, gibbering thing emerge through the shredding roof and flap slowly and agonizingly upward on fearfully burned wings. Calmly he aimed and fired, and the scorched and blinded thing tumbled back into the flaming mass just as the walls crashed in. To Kane it seemed that Goru's crumbling face, vanishing in the smoke, split suddenly in a wide grin and a sudden shout of exultant human laughter mingled eerily in the roar of the flames. But the smoke and an insane brain play queer tricks.

Kane stood with the ju-ju stave in one hand and the smoking pistol in the other, above the smoldering ruins that hid forever from the sight of man the last of those terrible, semi-human monsters whom another white-skinned hero had banished from Europe in an unknown age. Kane stood, an unconscious statue of triumph – the ancient empires fall, the dark-skinned peoples fade and even the demons of antiquity gasp their last, but over all stands the Aryan barbarian, white-skinned, cold-eyed, dominant, the supreme fighting man of the earth, whether he be clad in wolf-hide and horned helmet, or boots and doublet – whether he bear in his hand battle-ax or rapier – whether he be called Dorian, Saxon or Englishman – whether his name be Jason, Hengist or Solomon Kane.

Kane stood and the smoke curled upward into the morning sky, the roaring of foraging lions shook the plateau, and slowly, like light breaking through mists, sanity returned to him.

"The light of God's morning enters even into dark and lonesome lands," said Solomon Kane somberly. "Evil rules in the waste lands of the earth, but even evil may come to an end. Dawn follows midnight and even in this lost land the shadows shrink. Strange are Thy ways, oh God of my people, and who am I to question Thy wisdom? My feet have fallen in evil ways but Thou hast brought me forth scatheless and hast made me a scourge for the Powers of Evil. Over the souls of men spread the condor wings of colossal monsters and all manner of evil things prey upon the heart and soul and body of Man. Yet it may be in some far day the shadows shall fade and the Prince of Darkness be chained forever in his hell. And till then mankind can but stand up stoutly to the monsters in his own heart and without, and with the aid of God he may yet triumph."

And Solomon Kane looked up into the silent hills and felt the silent call of the hills and the unguessed distances beyond; and Solomon Kane shifted his belt, took his staff firmly in his hand and turned his face eastward.

The Footfalls Within

The Footfalls Within

Solomon Kane gazed somberly at the black woman who lay dead at his feet. Little more than a girl she was, but her wasted limbs and staring eyes showed that she had suffered much before death brought her merciful relief. Kane noted the chain galls on her limbs, the deep crisscrossed scars on her back, the mark of the yoke on her neck. His cold eyes deepened strangely, showing chill glints and lights like clouds passing across depths of ice.

"Even into this lonesome land they come," he muttered. "I had not thought —"

He raised his head and gazed eastward. Black dots against the blue wheeled and circled.

"The kites mark their trail," muttered the tall Englishman. "Destruction goeth before them and death followeth after. Wo unto ye, sons of iniquity, for the wrath of God is upon ye. The cords be loosed on the iron necks of the hounds of hate and the bow of vengeance is strung. Ye are proud-stomached and strong, and the people cry out beneath your feet, but retribution cometh in the blackness of midnight and the redness of dawn."

He shifted the belt that held his heavy pistols and the keen dirk, instinctively touched the long rapier at his hip, and went stealthily but swiftly eastward. A cruel anger burned in his deep eyes like blue volcanic fires burning beneath leagues of ice, and the hand that gripped his long, cat-headed stave hardened into iron.

After some hours of steady striding, he came within hearing of the slave train that wound its laborious way through the jungle. The piteous cries of the slaves, the shouts and curses of the drivers, and the cracking of the whips came plainly to his ears. Another hour brought him even with them, and gliding along through the jungle parallel to the trail taken by the slavers, he spied upon them safely. Kane had fought Indians in Darien and had learned much of their woodcraft.

More than a hundred blacks, young men and women, staggered along the trail, stark naked and made fast together by cruel yoke-like affairs of wood. These yokes, rough and heavy, fitted over their necks and linked them together, two by two. The yokes were in turn fettered together, making one long chain. Of the drivers there were fifteen Arabs and some seventy black warriors, whose weapons and fantastic apparel showed them to be of some eastern tribe – one of those tribes

subjugated and made Moslems and allies by the conquering
Arabs.

Five Arabs walked ahead of the train with some thirty of
their warriors, and five brought up the rear with the rest of
the black Moslems. The rest marched beside the staggering
slaves, urging them along with shouts and curses and with
long, cruel whips which brought spurts of blood at almost
every blow. These slavers were fools as well as rogues,
reflected Kane – not more than half of the slaves would
survive the hardships of that trek to the coast. He wondered
at the presence of these raiders, for this country lay far to the
south of the districts usually frequented by the Moslems. But
avarice can drive men far, as the Englishman knew. He had
dealt with these gentry of old. Even as he watched, old scars
burned in his back – scars made by Moslem whips in a
Turkish galley. And deeper still burned Kane's unquenchable
hate.

He followed, shadowing his foes like a ghost, and as he
stole through the jungle, he racked his brain for a plan. How
might he prevail against that horde? All the Arabs and many
of the blacks were armed with guns – long, clumsy firelock
affairs, it is true, but guns just the same, enough to awe any
tribe of natives who might oppose them. Some carried in
their wide girdles long, silver-chased pistols of more effective
pattern – flintlocks of Moorish and Turkish make.

Kane followed like a brooding ghost and his rage and
hatred ate into his soul like a canker. Each crack of the whips
was like a blow on his own shoulders. The heat and cruelty of
the tropics play queer tricks with white men. Ordinary
passions become monstrous things; irritation turns to a
berserker rage; anger flames into unexpected madness and
men kill in a red mist of passion, and wonder, aghast,
afterward.

The fury Solomon Kane felt would have been enough at any time and in any place to shake a man to his foundation; now it assumed monstrous proportions, so that Kane shivered as if with a chill, iron claws scratched at his brain and he saw the slaves and the slavers through a crimson mist. Yet he might not have put his hate-born insanity into action had it not been for a mishap.

One of the slaves, a slim young girl, suddenly faltered and slipped to the earth, dragging her yoke-mate with her. A tall, hook-nosed Arab yelled savagely and lashed her viciously. Her yoke-mate staggered partly up, but the girl remained prone, writhing weakly beneath the lash, but evidently unable to rise. She whimpered pitifully between her parched lips, and the other slavers came about, their whips descending on her quivering flesh in slashes of red agony.

A half-hour of rest and a little water would have revived her, but the Arabs had no time to spare. Solomon, biting his arm until his teeth met in the flesh as he fought for control, thanked God that the lashing had ceased and steeled himself for the swift flash of the dagger that would put the child beyond torment. But the Arabs were in a mood for sport. Since the girl would fetch them no profit on the market block,

they would utilize her for their pleasure – and the humor of their breed is such as to turn men's blood to icy water.

A shout from the first whipper brought the rest crowding around, their bearded faces split in grins of delighted anticipation, while the black warriors edged nearer, their brutish eyes gleaming. The wretched slaves realized their masters' intentions and a chorus of pitiful cries rose from them.

Kane, sick with horror, realized, too, that the girl's was to be no easy death. He knew what the tall Moslem intended to do, as he stooped over her with a keen dagger such as the Arabs used for skinning game. Madness overcame the Englishman. He valued his own life little; he had risked it without thought for the sake of a negro baby or a small animal. Yet he would not have premeditatedly thrown away his one hope of succoring the wretches in the train. But he acted without conscious thought. A pistol was smoking in his hand and the tall butcher was down in the dust of the trail with his brains oozing out, before Kane realized what he had done.

He was almost as astonished as the Arabs, who stood frozen for a moment and then burst into a medley of yells. Several threw up their clumsy firelocks and sent their heavy balls crashing through the trees, and the rest, thinking no doubt that they were ambushed, led a reckless charge into the jungle. The bold suddenness of that move was Kane's undoing. Had they hesitated a moment longer he might have faded away unobserved, but as it was he saw no choice but to meet them openly and sell his life as highly as he could.

And indeed it was with a certain ferocious satisfaction that he faced his howling attackers. They halted in sudden amazement as the tall, grim Englishman stepped from behind his tree, and in that instant one of them died with a bullet from Kane's remaining pistol in his heart. Then with yells of savage rage they flung themselves on their lone defier. Kane placed his back against a huge tree and his long rapier played a shining wheel about him. Three blacks and an Arab were hacking at him with their heavy curved blades while the rest milled about, snarling like wolves, as they sought to drive in blade or ball without maiming one of their own number.

The flickering rapier parried the whistling simitars and the Arab died on its point, which seemed to hesitate in his heart only an instant before it pierced the brain of a black swordsman. Another ebon warrior, dropping his sword and leaping in to grapple at close quarters, was disemboweled by the dirk in Kane's left hand, and the others gave back in sudden fear. A heavy ball smashed against the tree close to Kane's head and he tensed himself to spring and die in the thick of them. Then their sheikh lashed them on with his long whip and Kane heard him shouting fiercely for his warriors to take the infidel alive. Kane answered the command with a sudden cast of his dirk, which hummed so close to the sheikh's head that it slit his turban and sank deep in the shoulder of one behind him.

The sheikh drew his silver-chased pistols, threatening his own men with death if they did not take the white man, and they charged in again desperately. One of the black men ran full upon Kane's sword and an Arab behind the fellow, with the craft of his race, thrust the screaming wretch suddenly forward on the weapon, driving it hilt-deep in his writhing body, fouling the blade. Before Kane could wrench it clear, with a yell of triumph the pack rushed in on him and bore him down by sheer weight of numbers. As they grappled him from all sides, the Puritan wished in vain for the dirk he had thrown away. But even so, his taking was none too easy.

Blood spattered and faces caved in beneath his iron-hard fists that splintered teeth and shattered bone. A black warrior reeled away disabled from a vicious drive of knee to groin. Even when they had him stretched out and piled man-weight on him until he could no longer strike with fists or foot, his long lean fingers sank fiercely through a black beard to lock about a corded throat in a grip that took the power of three strong men to break and left the victim gasping and green-faced.

At last, panting from the terrific struggle, they had him bound hand and foot and the sheikh, thrusting his pistols back into his silken sash, came striding to stand and look down at his captive. Kane glared up at the tall, lean frame, at the hawk-like face with its black curled beard and arrogant brown eyes.

"I am the sheikh Hassim ben Said," said the Arab. "Who are you?"

"My name is Solomon Kane," growled the Puritan in the sheikh's own language. "I am an Englishman, you heathen jackal."

The dark eyes of the Arab flickered with interest.

"Sulieman Kahani," said he, giving the Arabesque equivalent of the English name, "I have heard of you – you have fought the Turks betimes and the Barbary corsairs have licked their wounds because of you."

Kane deigned no reply. Hassim shrugged his shoulders.

"You will bring a fine price," said he. "Mayhap I will take you to Stamboul, where there are shahs who would desire such a man among their slaves. And I mind me now of one Kemal Bey, a man of ships, who wears a deep scar across his face of your making and who curses the name of Englishman. He will pay me a high price for you. And behold, oh Frank, I do you the honor of appointing you a separate guard. You shall not walk in the yoke-chain but free save for your hands."

Kane made no answer, and at a sign from the sheikh, he was hauled to his feet and his bonds loosened except for his hands, which they left bound firmly behind him. A stout cord was looped about his neck and the other end of this was given into the hand of a huge black warrior who bore in his free hand a great curved simitar.

"And now what think ye of my favor to you, Frank?" queried the sheikh.

"I am thinking," answered Kane in a slow, deep voice of menace, "that I would trade my soul's salvation to face you and your sword, alone and unarmed, and to tear the heart from your breast with my naked fingers."

Such was the concentrated hate in his deep resounding voice, and such primal, unconquerable fury blazed from his terrible eyes, that the hardened and fearless chieftain blanched and involuntarily recoiled as if from a maddened beast.

Then Hassim recovered his poise and with a short word to his followers, strode to the head of the cavalcade. Kane noted, with thankfulness, that the respite occasioned by his capture had given the girl who had fallen a chance to rest and revive. The skinning knife had not had time to more than touch her; she was able to reel along. Night was not far away. Soon the slavers would be forced to halt and camp.

The Englishman perforce took up the trek, his black
guard remaining a few paces behind with his huge blade ever
ready. Kane also noted with a touch of grim vanity, that three
more blacks marched close behind, muskets ready and
matches burning. They had tasted his prowess and they were
taking no chances. His weapons had been recovered and
Hassim had promptly appropriated all except the cat-headed
ju-ju staff. This had been contemptuously cast aside by him
and taken up by one of the blacks.

The Englishman was presently aware that a lean, gray-
bearded Arab was walking along at his side. This Arab seemed
desirous of speaking but strangely timid, and the source of
his timidity seemed, curiously enough, the ju-ju stave which
he had taken from the black man who had picked it up, and
which he now turned uncertainly in his hands.

"I am Yussef the Hadji," said this Arab suddenly. "I have
naught against you. I had no hand in attacking you and would
be your friend if you would let me. Tell me, Frank, whence
comes this staff and how comes it into your hands?"

Kane's first inclination was to consign his questioner to
the infernal regions, but a certain sincerity of manner in the
old man made him change his mind and he answered: "It was
given me by my blood-brother – a black magician of the Slave
Coast, named N'Longa."

The old Arab nodded and muttered in his beard and
presently sent a black running forward to bid Hassim return.
The tall sheikh presently came striding back along the slow-
moving column, with a clank and jingle of daggers and sabers,
with Kane's dirk and pistols thrust into his wide sash.

"Look, Hassim," the old Arab thrust forward the stave,
"you cast it away without knowing what you did!"

"And what of it?" growled the sheikh. "I see naught but

a staff – sharp-pointed and with the head of a cat on the other end – a staff with strange infidel carvings upon it."

The older man shook it at him in excitement: "This staff is older than the world! It holds mighty magic! I have read of it in the old iron-bound books and Mohammed – on whom peace! – himself hath spoken of it by allegory and parable! See the cat-head upon it? It is the head of a goddess of ancient Egypt! Ages ago, before Mohammed taught, before Jerusalem was, the priests of Bast bore this rod before the bowing, chanting worshippers! With it Musa did wonders before Pharaoh and when the Yahudi fled from Egypt they bore it with them. And for centuries it was the scepter of Israel and Judah and with it Sulieman ben Daoud drove forth the conjurers and magicians and prisoned the efreets and the evil genii! Look! Again in the hands of a Sulieman we find the ancient rod!"

Old Yussef had worked himself into a pitch of almost fanatic fervor but Hassim merely shrugged his shoulders.

"It did not save the Jews from bondage nor this Sulieman from our captivity," said he; "so I value it not as much as I esteem the long thin blade with which he loosed the souls of three of my best swordsmen."

Yussef shook his head. "Your mockery will bring you to no good end, Hassim. Some day you will meet a power that will not divide before your sword or fall to your bullets. I will keep the staff, and I warn you – abuse not the Frank. He has borne the holy and terrible staff of

Sulieman and Musa and the Pharaohs, and who knows what magic he has drawn therefrom? For it is older than the world and has known the terrible hands of strange, dark pre-Adamite priests in the silent cities beneath the seas, and has drawn from an Elder World mystery and magic unguessed by humankind. There were strange kings and stranger priests when the dawns were young, and evil was, even in their day. And with this staff they fought the evil which was ancient when their strange world was young, so many millions of years ago that a man would shudder to count them."

Hassim answered impatiently and strode away with old Yussef following him persistently and chattering away in a querulous tone. Kane shrugged his mighty shoulders. With what he knew of the strange powers of that strange staff, he was not one to question the old man's assertions, fantastic as they seemed. This much he knew – that it was made of a wood that existed nowhere on earth today. It needed but the proof of sight and touch to realize that its material had grown in some world apart. The exquisite workmanship of the head, of a pre-pyramidal age, and the hieroglyphics, symbols of a language that was forgotten when Rome was young – these, Kane sensed, were additions as modern to the antiquity of the staff itself, as would be English words carved on the stone monoliths of Stonehenge.

As for the cat-head – looking at it sometimes Kane had a peculiar feeling of alteration; a faint sensing that once the pommel of the staff was carved with a different design. The dust-ancient Egyptian who had carved the head of Bast had merely altered the original figure, and what that figure had been, Kane had never tried to guess. A close scrutiny of the staff always aroused a disquieting and almost dizzy suggestion of abysses of eons, unprovocative to further speculation.

The day wore on. The sun beat down mercilessly, then screened itself in the great trees as it slanted toward the horizon. The slaves suffered fiercely for water and a continual whimpering rose from their ranks as they staggered blindly on. Some fell and half crawled, and were half dragged by their reeling yoke-mates. When all were buckling from exhaustion, the sun dipped, night rushed on, and a halt was called. Camp was pitched, guards thrown out, and the slaves were fed scantily and given enough water to keep life in them – but only just enough. Their fetters were not loosened but they were allowed to sprawl about as they might. Their fearful thirst and hunger having been somewhat eased, they bore the discomforts of their shackles with characteristic stoicism.

Kane was fed without his hands being untied and he was given all the water he wished. The patient eyes of the slaves watched him drink, silently, and he was sorely ashamed to guzzle what others suffered for; he ceased before his thirst was fully quenched. A wide clearing had been selected, on all sides of which rose gigantic trees. After the Arabs had eaten and while the black Moslems were still cooking their food, old Yussef came to Kane and began to talk about the staff again. Kane answered his questions with admirable patience, considering the hatred he bore the whole race to which the Hadji belonged, and during their conversation, Hassim came striding up and looked down in contempt. Hassim, Kane ruminated, was the very symbol of militant Islam — bold, reckless, materialistic, sparing nothing, fearing nothing, as sure of his own destiny and as contemptuous of the rights of others as the most powerful Western king.

"Are you maundering about that stick again?" he gibed. "Hadji, you grow childish in your old age."

Yussef's beard quivered in anger. He shook the staff at his sheikh like a threat of evil.

"Your mockery little befits your rank, Hassim," he snapped. "We are in the heart of a dark and demon-haunted land, to which long ago were banished the devils from Arabia. If this staff, which any but a fool can tell is no rod of any world we know, has existed down to our day, who knows what other things, tangible or intangible, may have existed through the ages? This very trail we follow — know you how old it is? Men followed it before the Seljuk came out of the East or the Roman came out of the West. Over this very trail, legends say, the great Sulieman came when he drove the demons westward out of Asia and prisoned them in strange prisons. And will you say —"

A wild shout interrupted him. Out of the shadows of the jungle a black came flying as if from the hounds of Doom. With arms flinging wildly, eyes rolling to display the whites and mouth wide open so that all his gleaming teeth were visible, he made an image of stark terror not soon forgotten. The Moslem horde leaped up, snatching their weapons, and

Hassim swore: "That's Ali, whom I sent to scout for meat —
perchance a lion —"

But no lion followed the black man who fell at Hassim's
feet, mouthing gibberish, and pointing wildly back at the
black jungle whence the nerve-strung watchers expected
some brain-shattering horror to burst.

"He says he found a strange mausoleum back in the
jungle," said Hassim with a scowl, "but he cannot tell what
frightened him. He only knows a great horror overwhelmed
him and sent him flying. Ali, you are a fool and a rogue."

He kicked the groveling black viciously, but the other
Arabs drew about him in some uncertainty. The panic was
spreading among the black warriors.

"They will bolt in spite of us," muttered a bearded Arab,
uneasily watching the blacks who milled together, jabbered
excitedly and flung fearsome glances over the shoulders.
"Hassim, 'twere better to march on a few miles. This is an evil
place after all, and though 'tis likely the fool Ali was frighted
by his own shadow — still —"

"Still," jeered the sheikh, "you will all feel better when
we have left it behind. Good enough; to still your fears I will
move camp — but first I will have a look at this thing. Lash up
the slaves; we'll swing into the jungle and pass by this
mausoleum; perhaps some great king lies there. The blacks
will not be afraid if we all go in a body with guns."

So the weary slaves were whipped into wakefulness and
stumbled along beneath the whips again. The black warriors
went silently and nervously, reluctantly obeying Hassim's
implacable will but huddling close to their white masters.
The moon had risen, huge, red and sullen, and the jungle was
bathed in a sinister silver glow that etched the brooding trees
in black shadow. The trembling Ali pointed out the way,
somewhat reassured by his savage master's presence.

And so they passed through the jungle until they came to a strange clearing among the giant trees – strange because nothing grew there. The trees ringed it in a disquieting symmetrical manner and no lichen or moss grew on the earth, which seemed to have been blasted and blighted in a strange fashion. And in the midst of the glade stood the mausoleum. A great brooding mass of stone it was, pregnant with ancient evil. Dead with the death of a hundred centuries it seemed, yet Kane was aware that the air *pulsed* about it, as with the slow, unhuman breathing of some gigantic, invisible monster.

The black Moslems drew back, muttering, assailed by the evil atmosphere of the place. The slaves stood in a patient, silent group beneath the trees. The Arabs went forward to the frowning black mass, and Yussef, taking Kane's cord from his ebon guard, led the Englishman with him like a surly mastiff, as if for protection against the unknown.

"Some mighty sultan doubtless lies here," said Hassim, tapping the stone with his scabbard-end.

"Whence come these stones?" muttered Yussef uneasily.

"They are of dark and forbidding aspect. Why should a great sultan lie in state so far from any habitation of man? If there were ruins of an old city hereabouts it would be different –"

He bent to examine the heavy metal door with its huge lock, curiously sealed and fused. He shook his head forebodingly as he made out the ancient Hebraic characters carved on the door.

"I can not read them," he quavered, "and belike it is well for me I can not. What ancient kings sealed up, is not good for men to disturb. Hassim, let us hence. This place is pregnant with evil for the sons of men."

But Hassim gave him no heed. "He who lies within is no son of Islam," said he, "and why should we not despoil him of the gems and riches that undoubtedly were laid to rest with him? Let us break open this door."

Some of the Arabs shook their heads doubtfully but Hassim's word was law. Calling to him a huge black who bore a heavy hammer, he ordered him to break open the door.

As the black swung up his sledge, Kane gave a sharp exclamation. Was he mad? The apparent antiquity of this brooding mass of stone was proof that it had stood undisturbed for thousands of years. *Yet he could have sworn that he heard the sound of footfalls within.* Back and forth they padded, as if something paced the narrow confines of that grisly prison in a never-ending monotony of movement. A cold hand touched the spine of Solomon Kane. Whether the sounds registered on his conscious ear or on some unsounded deep of soul or sub-feeling, he could not tell, but he *knew* that somewhere within his consciousness there re-echoed the tramp of monstrous feet from within that ghastly mausoleum.

"Stop!" he exclaimed. "Hassim, I may be mad, but I hear the tread of some fiend within that pile of stone."

Hassim raised his hand and checked the hovering hammer. He listened intently, and the others strained their ears in a silence that had suddenly become tense.

"I hear nothing," grunted a bearded giant.

"Nor I," came a quick chorus. "The Frank is mad!"

"Hear ye anything, Yussef?" asked Hassim sardonically.

The old Hadji shifted nervously. His face was uneasy.

"No, Hassim, no, yet —"

Kane decided he must be mad. Yet in his heart he knew he was never saner, and he knew somehow that this occult keenness of the deeper senses that set him apart from the Arabs came from long association with the ju-ju staff that old Yussef now held in his shaking hands.

Hassim laughed harshly and made a gesture to the black. The hammer fell with a crash that re-echoed deafeningly and shivered off through the black jungle in a strangely altered cachinnation. Again – again – and again the hammer fell, driven with all the power of the rippling black muscles and the mighty ebon body. And between the blows Kane still heard that lumbering tread, and he who had never known fear as men know it, felt the cold hand of terror clutching at his heart.

This fear was apart from earthly or mortal fear, as the

sound of the footfalls was apart from mortal tread. Kane's fright was like a cold wind blowing on him from outer realms of unguessed Darkness, bearing him the evil and decay of an outlived epoch and an unutterably ancient period. Kane was not sure whether he heard those footfalls or by some dim instinct sensed them. But he was sure of their reality. They were not the tramp of man or beast; but inside that black, hideously ancient mausoleum some nameless *thing* moved with soul-shaking and elephantine tread.

The great black sweated and panted with the difficulty of his task. But at last, beneath the heavy blows the ancient lock shattered; the hinges snapped; the door burst inward. And Yussef screamed. From that black gaping entrance no tiger-fanged beast or demon of solid flesh and blood leaped forth. But a fearful stench flowed out in billowing, almost tangible waves and in one brain-shattering, ravening rush, whereby the gaping door seemed to gush *blood*, the Horror was upon them. It enveloped Hassim, and the fearless chieftain, hewing vainly at the almost intangible terror, screamed with sudden, unaccustomed fright as his lashing simitar whistled only through stuff as yielding and unharmable as air, and he felt himself lapped by coils of death and destruction.

Yussef shrieked like a lost soul, dropped the ju-ju stave and joined his fellows who streamed out into the jungle in mad flight, preceded by the howling black warriors. Only the black slaves fled not, but stood shackled to their doom, wailing their terror. As in a nightmare of delirium Kane saw Hassim swayed like a reed in the wind, lapped about by a gigantic pulsing red Thing that had neither shape nor earthly substance. Then as the crack of splintering bones came to him, and the sheikh's body buckled like a straw beneath a stamping hoof, the Englishman burst his bonds with one volcanic effort and caught up the ju-ju stave.

Hassim was down, crushed and dead, sprawled like a broken toy with shattered limbs awry, and the red pulsing Thing was lurching toward Kane like a thick cloud of blood in the air, that continually changed its shape and form, and yet somehow *trod* lumberingly as if on monstrous legs!

Kane felt the cold fingers of fear claw at his brain but he braced himself, and lifting the ancient staff, struck with all his power into the center of the Horror. And he felt an unnamable, immaterial substance meet and give way before the falling staff. Then he was almost strangled by the nauseous burst of unholy stench that flooded the air, and somewhere down the dim vistas of his soul's consciousness re-echoed unbearably a hideous formless cataclysm that he knew was the death-screaming of the monster. For it was down and dying at his feet, its crimson paling in slow surges like the rise and receding of red waves on some foul coast. And as it paled, the soundless screaming dwindled away into cosmic distances as though it faded into some sphere apart and aloof beyond human ken.

Kane, dazed and incredulous, looked down on a shapeless, colorless, all but invisible mass at his feet which he knew was the corpse of the Horror, dashed back into the black realms from whence it had come, by a single blow of the staff of Solomon. Aye, the same staff, Kane knew, that in the hands of a mighty king and magician had ages ago driven the monster into that strange prison, to bide until ignorant hands loosed it again upon the world.

The old tales were true then, and King Solomon had in truth driven the demons westward and sealed them in strange places. Why had he let them live? Was human magic too weak in those dim days to more than subdue the devils? Kane shrugged his shoulders in wonderment. He knew nothing of magic, yet he had slain where that other Solomon had but imprisoned.

And Solomon Kane shuddered, for he had looked on Life that was not Life as he knew it, and had dealt and witnessed Death that was not Death as he knew it. Again the realization swept over him, as it had in the dust-haunted halls of Atlantean Negari, as it had in the abhorrent Hills of the Dead, as it had in Akaana – that human life was but one of a myriad forms of existence, that worlds existed within worlds, and that there was more than one plane of existence. The planet men call the earth spun on through the untold ages, Kane realized, and as it spun it spawned Life, and living things which wriggled about it as maggots are spawned in rot and corruption. Man was the dominant maggot now – why should he in his pride suppose that he and his adjuncts were the first maggots – or the last to rule a planet quick with unguessed life?

He shook his head, gazing in new wonder at the ancient gift of N'Longa, seeing in it at last, not merely a tool of black magic, but a sword of good and light against the powers of inhuman evil forever. And he was shaken with a strange reverence for it that was almost fear. Then he bent to the Thing at his feet, shuddering to feel its strange mass slip through his fingers like wisps of heavy fog. He thrust the staff beneath it and somehow lifted and levered the mass back into the mausoleum and shut the door.

Then he stood gazing down at the strangely mutilated body of Hassim, noting how it was smeared with foul slime and how it had already begun to decompose. He shuddered again, and suddenly a low timid voice aroused him from his somber cogitations. The slaves knelt beneath the trees and watched with great patient eyes. With a start he shook off his strange mood. He took from the moldering corpse his own pistols, dirk and rapier, making shift to wipe off the clinging foulness that was already flecking the steel with rust. He also took up a quantity of powder and shot dropped by the Arabs in their frantic flight. He knew they would return no more. They might die in their flight, or they might gain through the interminable leagues of jungle to the coast; but they would not turn back to dare the terror of that grisly glade.

Kane came to the black slaves and after some difficulty released them.

"Take up these weapons which the warriors dropped in their haste," said he, "and get you home. This is an evil place. Get ye back to your villages and when the next Arabs come, die in the ruins of your huts rather than be slaves."

Then they would have knelt and kissed his feet, but he, in much confusion, forbade them roughly. Then as they made preparations to go, one said to him: "Master, what of thee? Wilt thou not return with us? Thou shalt be our king!"

But Kane shook his head.

"I go eastward," said he. And so the tribespeople bowed to him and turned back on the long trail to their own homeland. And Kane shouldered the staff that had been the rod of the Pharaohs and of Moses and of Solomon and of nameless Atlantean kings behind them, and turned his face eastward, halting only for a single backward glance at the great mausoleum that other Solomon had built with strange arts so long ago, and which now loomed dark and forever silent against the stars.

The Children of Asshur
(Fragment)

The Children of Asshur

I

Solomon Kane started up in the darkness, snatching at the weapons which lay on the pile of skins that served him as a crude pallet. It was not the mad drum of the tropic rain on the leaves of the hut-roof which had wakened him, nor the bellowing of the thunder. It was the screams of human agony, the clash of steel that cut through the din of the tropical storm. Some sort of a conflict was taking place in the native village in which he had sought refuge from the storm, and it sounded much like a raid in force. As Solomon groped for his sword, he wondered what bushmen would raid a village in the night and in such a storm as this. His pistols lay beside his sword but he did not take them up, knowing that they would be useless in such a torrent of rain, which would wet their priming instantly.

He had laid down fully clad, save for his slouch hat and cloak, and without stopping for them, he ran to the door of the hut. A ragged streak of lightning which seemed to rip the sky open showed him a chaotic glimpse of struggling figures in the spaces between the huts, dazzlingly glinting back from flashing steel. Above the storm he heard the shrieks of the black people and deep-toned shouts in a language unfamiliar to him. Springing from the hut he sensed the presence of one in front of him, and even then another thunderous burst of fire ripped across the sky, limning all in a weird blue light. In that flashing instant Solomon thrust savagely, felt the blade bend double in his hand and saw a heavy sword swinging for his head. A burst of sparks, brighter than the lightning, exploded before his eyes, then blackness darker than the jungle night engulfed him.

Dawn was spreading pallidly over the dripping jungle reaches when Solomon Kane stirred and sat up in the ooze before the hut. Blood had caked on his scalp and his head ached slightly. Shaking off a slight grogginess, he rose. The rain had long ceased, the skies were clear. Silence lay over the village, and Kane saw that it was in truth a village of the dead. Corpses of men, women and children lay strewn everywhere – in the streets, in the doorways of the huts, inside the huts, some of which had been literally ripped to pieces, either in search of cowering victims, or in sheer wantonness of destruction. They had not taken many prisoners, Solomon decided, whoever the unknown raiders might be. Nor had they taken the spears, axes, cooking pots and plumed head-pieces of their victims, this fact seeming to argue a raid by a race superior in culture and artizanship to the crude villagers. But they had taken all the ivory they could find, and they had taken, Kane discovered, his rapier, and his dirk, pistols and powder-and-shot pouches. And they had taken his staff, the sharp-pointed strangely carved, cat-headed stave, which his friend, N'Longa, the West Coast witch-man, had given him, as well as his hat and cloak.

Kane stood in the center of the desolated village, brooding over the matter, strange speculations running at random through his mind. His conversation with the natives of the village, into which he had made his way the night before out of the storm-beaten jungle, gave him no clue as to the nature of the raiders. The natives themselves had known little about the land into which they had but recently come, driven over a long trek by a rival, more powerful tribe. They had been a simple, good-natured people, who had welcomed him into their huts and given him freely of their humble goods. Kane's heart was hot with wrath against their unknown destroyers, but even deeper than that burned his unquenchable curiosity, the curse of the white man.

For Kane had looked on mystery in the night and the storm. That vivid flame of lightning had showed him, etched momentarily in its glare, a fierce, black-bearded face – the face of a white man. Yet according to sanity there could be no white men, not even Arab raiders, within hundreds and hundreds of miles. Kane had had no time to observe the man's dress, but he had a vague impression that the figure was clad strangely and bizarrely. And that sword which, striking glancingly and flat, had struck him down, surely that had been no crude native weapon.

Kane glanced at the crude mud wall which surrounded the village, at the bamboo gates which now lay in ruins, hewn to pieces by the raiders. The storm had apparently greatly abated when the raiders marched forth, for he made out a broad trampled track leading out of the broken gate and into the jungle.

Kane picked up a crude native axe that lay nearby. If any of the unknown slayers had fallen in the battle, their bodies had been carried away by their companions. Leaves pieced together made him a makeshift hat to protect his head from the force of the sun. Then Solomon Kane went through the broken gate and into the dripping jungle, following the spoor of the unknown.

Under the giant trees the tracks became clearer, and Kane made out that most of them were of sandals – a type of sandal, likewise, that was strange to him. The rest were of bare feet, showing that some prisoners had been taken. They must have had a long start of him, for though he travelled without pause, swinging along tirelessly on his rangy legs, he never sighted the column that day.

He ate of the food he had brought from the ruined village, and pressed on without halting, consumed by anger and by desire to solve the mystery of that lightning-limned face – more, the raiders had taken his weapons, and in that dark land, a man's weapons were his life. The day wore on. As the sun sank, the jungle gave way to forest-land, and at twilight Kane came out on a rolling, grass-grown, tree-dotted plain, and saw, far across it, what appeared to be a low-lying range of hills. The tracks led straight out across the plain, and Kane believed the raiders' goal was those low, even hills.

He hesitated; across the grass-lands came the thunderous roaring of lions, echoed and re-echoed from a score of different points. The great cats were beginning to stalk their prey, and it would be suicide to venture across that vast open space, armed with only an axe. Kane found a giant tree and, clambering into it, settled himself in a crotch as comfortably as he might. Far out across the plain he saw a point of light twinkling among the hills. Then on the plain, approaching the hills, he saw other lights, a twinkling fire-set serpentine that moved toward the hills, now scarcely visible against the stars along the horizons. It was the column of raiders and their slaves, he realized, bearing torches and travelling swiftly. The torches were no doubt to keep off the lions, and Kane decided that their goal must be very near at hand if they risked a night march on those carnivora-haunted grass-lands. As he watched, he saw the twinkling fire-points move upward, and for awhile they glittered among the hills, then he saw them no more.

Speculating on the mystery of it all, Kane slept, while the night winds whispered dark secrets of ancient Africa among the leaves, and lions roared beneath his tree, lashing their tufted tails as they gazed upward with hungry fire-lit eyes.

Again dawn lighted the land with rose and gold, and Solomon descended from his perch and took up his journey. He ate the last of the food he had brought, drank from a stream that looked fairly pure, and speculated on the chance of finding food among the hills. If he did not find it, he might be in a precarious position, but Kane had been hungry before – aye, and starving, and freezing and weary. His rangy, broad-shouldered frame was hard as iron, pliant as steel.

So he swung boldly out across the savannas, watching warily for lurking lions, but slackening not his pace. The sun climbed to the zenith and dipped westward. As he approached the low range, it began to grow in distinctness. He saw that instead of rugged hills, he was approaching a low plateau that rose abruptly from the surrounding plain and appeared to be level. He saw trees and tall grass on the edges, but the cliffs seemed barren and rough. However, they were at no point more than seventy or eighty feet in height, as far as he could see, and he anticipated no great difficulty in surmounting them.

As he came up to them he saw that they were almost solid rock, though overlaid by a fairly thick stratum of soil. Boulders had tumbled down in many places and he saw that an active man could scale the cliffs in many places. But he saw something else – a broad road which wound up the steep pitch of the precipice, and up which led the spoors he was following.

He went up, and noted the excellent workmanship of the road, which was no mere animal path, or even a native trail, but had been cut into the cliff with consummate skill, and was paved and balustraded with smoothly cut blocks of stone.

Wary as a wolf, he avoided the road, and further on found a less steep slope, up which he went. It was unstable footing, and boulders that seemed to poise on the slope threatened to roll down upon him, but he accomplished the task without undue hazard and came out over the edge of the cliff.

He stood on a rugged, boulder-strewn slope, which pitched off rather steeply onto a flat expanse. From where he stood, he saw the broad plateau spread out beneath his feet, carpeted with green lush grass. And in the midst – he blinked his eyes and shook his head, thinking he looked on some mirage or hallucination. No! It was still there! A massive walled city, rearing in the midst of the grassy plain!

He saw the battlements, the towers beyond, and small figures moving about on the battlements. On the other side of the city he saw a small lake, on the shores of which stretched luxuriant gardens and fields, and meadow-like expanses filled with grazing cattle.

Amazement at the sight held him frozen for an instant, then the clink of an iron

heel on a stone brought him quickly about to face the man who had come from among the boulders. This man was broad-built and powerful, almost as tall as Kane, and heavier. His bare arms bulged with muscles and his legs were like knotted iron pillars. His face was a duplicate of that Kane had seen in the lightning flash — fierce, black-bearded, the face of a white man, with arrogant intolerant eyes and a predatory hooked nose. From his bull-throat to his knees he was clad in a corselet of iron scales, and on his head was an iron helmet. A metal-braced shield of hardwood and leather was on his left arm, a dagger in his girdle, a short heavy iron mace in his hand.

All this Kane saw in a glance as the man roared and leaped. The Englishman realized in that instant that there was to be no such thing as a parley. It was to be a battle to the death. As a tiger leaps, he sprang to meet the warrior, launching his axe with all the power of his rangy frame. The warrior caught the blow on his shield, the axe-edge turned, the haft splintered in Kane's hand, and the buckler shattered. Carried by the momentum of his savage lunge, Kane's body crashed against his foe, who dropped the useless shield and, staggering, grappled with the Englishman. Straining and gasping they reeled on hard-braced feet, and Kane snarled like a wolf as he felt the full power of his foe's strength. The armor hampered the Englishman, and the warrior had shortened his grasp on the iron mace and was ferociously striving to crash it on Kane's bare head.

The Englishman was striving to pinion the warrior's arm, but his clutching fingers missed, and the mace crashed sickeningly against his bare head; again it fell, as a fire-shot mist clouded Kane's vision, but his instinctive wrench avoided it, though it half-numbed his shoulder, ripping the skin so that the blood started in streams.

Maddened, Kane lunged fiercely against the stalwart body of the mace-wielder, and one blindly grasping hand closed on the dagger-hilt at the warrior's girdle – ripped it forth and stabbed blindly and savagely.

Close-locked, the fighters staggered backward, the one stabbing in venomous silence, the other striving to tear his arm free so that he might crash home one destroying blow. The warrior's short half-hindered blows glanced from Kane's head and shoulders, ripping the skin and bringing blood in streams, sending red lances of agony across the Englishman's clouding brain. And still the dagger in his lunging hand glanced from the iron scales that guarded his foe's body.

Blinded, dazed, fighting on instinct alone as a wounded wolf fights, Kane's teeth snapped fang-like into the great bull's throat of his foe, tearing the flesh horrifyingly, and bringing a burst of flooding blood and an agonized roar from his victim. The lashing mace faltered as the warrior flinched back, and then they reeled on the edge of a low precipice and pitched, rolling headlong close-clinched. At the foot of the slope they brought up, Kane uppermost. The dagger in his hand glittered high above his head and flashed downward, sinking hilt-deep in the warrior's throat, and

Kane's body pitched forward with the blow and he lay senseless above his slain enemy.

They lay in a widening pool of blood, and in the sky specks appeared, black against the blue, wheeling and circling and dropping lower.

Then from among the defiles appeared men similar in apparel and appearance to he who lay dead beneath Kane's senseless body. They had been attracted by the sound of the battle, and now they stood about discussing the matter in harsh guttural tones. Their black servants stood about silent.

They dragged the forms apart and discovered that one was dead, one probably dying. Then after some discussion, they made a litter of their spears and sword-slings, made their blacks lift the bodies and carry them. Then all set out toward the city which gleamed in the midst of the grassy plain.

II

Again consciousness returned to Solomon Kane. He was lying on a couch covered with finely dressed skins and furs, in a large chamber, whose floor, walls and ceiling were of stone. There was one window, heavily barred, and one doorway, outside which Kane saw standing a stalwart warrior much like the man he had slain. Then Kane discovered another thing; golden chains were on his wrists, neck and ankles. These were linked together in an intricate pattern, and were made fast to a ring set in the wall, with a strong silver lock.

Kane found that his wounds had been bandaged, and as he pondered over his situation, a black man entered with food and a kind of purple wine. Kane made no attempt at conversation, but ate the food offered and drank deeply. Then he slept, and the wine must have been drugged, for when he wakened, hours later, he found that the bandages had been changed, and there was a different guard outside the door – a man of the same type as the former soldier, however – muscular, black-bearded and clad in armor.

This time, when he awakened, he felt strong and refreshed, and decided that when the black entered again, he would seek to learn something of the curious environs into which he had fallen. The scruff of leather sandals on the tilings announced the approach of someone, and Kane sat up on his couch as a group of figures entered the chamber.

There were a clump of men with robes, inscrutable, shaven faces and shaven heads in the background, behind them the rangy black who had brought the food; these stayed in the background. Before them stood a figure which dominated the whole scene – a tall man whose garments were of silk, bound by a golden-scaled girdle. His blue-black hair and beard were curiously curled, his hawk-nosed face cruel and predatory; the arrogance of the eyes, which Kane had noticed as characteristic of the unknown race, was in this man much more strongly evident than in the others. On his head was a curiously carved circlet of gold, in his hand a golden wand. The attitude of the rest toward him was one of cringing servility, and Kane believed that he looked upon either the king or the high priest of the city.

Beside this personage stood a shorter, fatter man, with shaven face and head, clad in robes much like those worn by the lesser persons in the background, but much more costly. In his hand he bore a scourge composed of six thongs made fast to a jewel-set handle. The thongs ended in triangular shaped bits of metal, and the whole represented as savage an implement of punishment as Kane had ever looked upon. The man who bore this had small shifty, crafty eyes, and his whole attitude was a mixture of fawning servility toward the man with the sceptre, and intolerant despotism toward lesser beings.

Kane gave back their stare, trying to place an elusive sense of familiarity. There was something in the features of these people which vaguely suggested the Arab, yet they were strangely unlike any Arabs he had ever seen. They spoke together, and their language, at times, had a fantastically familiar sound. But he could not define these faint stirrings of half-memory.

At last the tall man with the sceptre turned and strode majestically forth, followed by his slavish companions, and Kane was left alone. After a time the fat shaven man returned with half a dozen soldiers and acolytes. Among these was the young black man who brought Kane's food, and a tall sombre figure, naked but for a loin cloth, who bore a great key at his girdle. The soldiers ringed Kane, javelins ready, while this man unlocked the chains from the ring in the wall. Then they surrounded him and, holding to his chains, indicated that he was to march with them. Surrounded by his captors, Kane emerged from the chamber into what appeared to be a series of wide galleries winding about the interior of the vast structure. Tier by tier they mounted, and turned at last into a chamber much like that he left, and similarly furnished. Kane's chains were made fast to a ring in the stone wall near the single window. He could stand upright or lie or sit on the skin-piled couch, but he could not move half a dozen steps in any direction. Wine and food were placed at his disposal, then they left him, and Kane noticed that neither was the door bolted nor a guard placed before it. He decided that they considered his chains sufficient to keep him safe, and after testing them, he realized that they were right. Yet there was another reason for their apparent carelessness, as he was to learn.

Kane looked out the window, which was larger than the other had been, and not so thickly barred. He was looking out over the city from a considerable height. He looked down on narrow streets, broad avenues flanked by what seemed to be columns and carven stone lions, and on wide expanses of flat-roofed houses, on many of which canopies seemed to argue that people basked under their shade. Much of the buildings seemed to be of stone, much of sun-dried bricks. There was a massiveness about their architecture that was vaguely repellent – a sombre heavy motif that seemed to suggest a sullen and slightly inhuman character of the builders.

He saw that the wall which surrounded the city was tall, thick and upheld towers spaced at regular intervals. He saw armored figures moving sentinel-like along the wall, and meditated upon the war-like aspect of this people. The streets and market-places below him offered a colorful maze as the richly clad people moved in an ever-shifting panorama.

As for the building which was his prison, Kane naturally could make out but little of its nature. Yet below him he saw a series of massive tiers descending like giant stair-steps. It must be, he decided, with a rather unpleasant sensation, built much like the fabled Tower of Babel, one tier above another.

He turned his attention back to his chamber. The walls were rich in mural decorations, carvings painted in various colors, well-tinted and blended. Indeed the art was of as high standard as any Kane had ever seen in Asia or Europe. Most of the scenes were of war or the hunt – powerful men with black beards, often curled, in armor, slaying lions and driving other warriors before them. Some of these other warriors were naked black men, others somewhat like their conquerors. The human figures were not as well depicted as those of the beasts, seemingly conventionalized to a point that often lent them a somewhat wooden aspect. But the lions were portrayed with vivid realism. Some of the scenes showed the black-bearded slayers in chariots, drawn by fire-breathing steeds, and Kane felt again that strange sense of familiarity, as if he had seen these scenes, or similar scenes, before. These chariots and horses, he noted, were inferior in life-likeness to the lions; the fault was not in  conventionalizing but in the artist's ignorance of his subject, Kane decided, noting mistakes that seemed extremely incongruous, considering the skill with which they were portrayed.

Time passed swiftly as he pored over the carvings, and presently the silent black man entered with food and wine.

As he set down the viands, Kane spoke to him in a dialect of the bush-tribes, to one of the divisions of which he believed the man belonged, noting the tribal scars on his features. The dull face lighted slightly and the man answered in a tongue similar enough for Kane to understand him.

"What city is this?"

"Ninn, bwana."

"Who are these people?"

The dull black shook his head in doubt.

"They be very old people, bwana. They have dwelt here very long time."

"Was that their king who came to my chamber with his men?"

"Yes, bwana, that be King Asshur-ras-arab."

"And the man with the lash?"

"Yamen, the priest, bwana Persian."

"Why do you call me that?" asked Kane, nonplussed.

"So the masters name you, bwana –" The black shrank back and his black skin turned ashy as the shadow of a tall figure fell across the doorway. The shaven-headed half-naked giant Shem entered and the black man fell to his knees, wailing his terror. Shem's mighty fingers closed about the black throat and Kane saw the wretched black's eyes protruding, his tongue thrust from his gaping mouth. His body writhed and threshed unavailingly, his hands clawed weakly and more weakly at the iron wrists. Then he went limp in his slayer's hands and as Shem released him, his corpse slumped loosely to the floor. Shem smote his hands together and a pair of giant blacks entered. Their faces turned ashy at the sight of their companion's corpse, but at a gesture from Shem, they callously laid hold of the dead man's feet and dragged him forth.

Shem turned at the door and his opaque implacable eyes met Kane's gaze, as if in warning. Hate drummed in Kane's temples, and it was the grim eyes of the murderer which fell before the cold fury in the Englishman's glare. Shem went noiselessly forth, leaving Kane to his meditations.

When food was next brought to Kane, it was brought by a rangy young black of genial and intelligent appearance.

Kane made no effort to speak to him; apparently the masters did not wish for their slave to learn anything about them, for some reason or another.

How many days Kane remained in the high-flung chamber, he did not know; each day was exactly like the last and he lost count of time. Sometimes Yamen the priest came and looked upon him with a satisfied air that made Kane's eyes turn red with the killer's lust; sometimes Shem noiselessly appeared and as noiselessly disappeared. Kane's eyes were riveted to the key that swung from the silent giant's girdle. Could he but once get within reach of the fellow – but Shem was careful to stay out of his reach unless Kane was surrounded by warriors with ready javelins.

Then one night to his chamber came Yamen the priest with Shem and some fifty acolytes and soldiers. Shem unlocked Kane's chains from the wall, and between two columns of soldiers and priests the Englishman was escorted along the winding galleries, lighted by flaring torches set in the niches along the walls, and borne in the hands of the priests.

By the light Kane observed again the carven figures marching everlastingly around the massive walls of the galleries. Many were life-size, some dimmed and somewhat defaced as with age. Most of these, Kane noted, portrayed men in chariots drawn by horses, and he decided that the later, imperfect figures of steeds and chariots had been copied from these older carvings. Apparently there were no horses or chariots in the city now. Various racial distinctions were evident in the human figures – the hooked noses and curled black beards of the dominant race were plainly distinguished. Their opponents were sometimes black men, sometimes men somewhat like themselves, and occasionally tall rangy men with unmistakable Arab features. Kane was startled to note, too, that in some of the older scenes, men were depicted whose apparel and features were entirely different from those of their enemies. They always appeared in battle with the other race, and not always in retreat as in the case of the others. These frequently seemed to be having the best of the fight, and it was significant, Kane thought, that nowhere were these men portrayed as slaves. But what interested him was the familiarity about their features. No vague misplaced feeling about that familiarity! Those carven features were like the countenance of a friend in a strange land to the wanderer. But for their strange, barbaric arms and apparel they might have been Englishmen, with their Aryan features and yellow locks. They rode horses and rode like the wind.

Somewhere, in the long, long ago, Kane knew, the ancestors of the men of Ninn had warred with men kin to his own ancestors – but in what age and what land, he could not know. Certainly the scenes were not laid in the country that was now the home-land of the Ninnites, for these scenes showed wide fertile plains, grassy hills and wide rivers that wound through fertile plains. Aye, and great cities, like Ninn, but strangely unlike. And suddenly Kane remembered where he had seen similar carvings, wherein kings with black curled beards slew lions from chariots – on crumbling pieces of masonry that marked the site of a long forgotten city in Mesopotamia he had seen them, and men had told him those ruins were all that remained of Nineveh the Bloody, the accursed of God.

Now the Englishman and his captors had reached the ground-tier of the great temple, and they passed between huge squat columns, carven as were the walls, until they came to a vast circular space between the massive wall and the flanking pillars. Apparently cut from the stone of the mighty wall sat a colossal idol, whose carven features were as devoid of human weakness and kindness as the face of a Stone Age monster.

Facing the idol, on a stone throne in the shadow of the pillars, sat the King Asshur-ras-arab, the firelight flickering on his strongly chiseled face so that at first Kane thought that it was an idol that sat on that throne.

Before the god, facing the king's throne, there was another, smaller throne, before which stood a brazier on a golden tripod; coals glowed in the brazier and smoke curled languorously upward.

A flowing robe of shimmering green silk was put upon Kane, hiding his tattered, worn and stained garments and the golden chains. He was motioned to sit in the throne before the brazier, and he did so. Then his ankles and wrists were locked cunningly to the throne, hidden by the folds of the silken robe. Then the lesser priests and the soldiers melted away, leaving only Kane, the priest Yamen, and the king upon his throne. Back in the shadows among the tree-like columns Kane occasionally glimpsed a glint of metal, like fire-flies in the dark. The soldiers still lurked there, out of sight. He sensed that some sort of a stage had been set; somehow he got a suggestion of charlatanry in the whole procedure.

Now Asshur-ras-arab lifted the golden wand and struck once upon a gong that hung near his throne, and a full mellow note like a distant chime echoed among the dim reaches of the shadowy temple. Along the dusky avenue between the columns came a group of men whom Kane realized must be the nobles of that fantastic city. They were tall men, black-bearded and haughty of bearing, clad in shimmering silk and gleaming gold. And among them walked one in golden chains, a youth whose attitude seemed a mixture of apprehension and defiance.

All knelt before the king, bowing their heads to the floor, and at a word from him, rose and faced the god and the Englishman before the god. Now Yamen, with the firelight glinting on his shaven head and evil eyes, so that he looked like a paunchy demon, cried out a sort of weird chant and flung a handful of powder into the brazier. Instantly a greenish smoke billowed upward, half-veiling Kane's face. The Englishman gagged; the smell and taste were unpleasant in the extreme. He felt groggy, drugged. His brain reeled like a drunken man's and he tore savagely at his chains. Only half conscious of what he said, unaccustomed oaths ripped from his lips.

He was dimly aware that Yamen cried out fiercely at his curses, and leaned forward in an attitude of listening. Then the powder burned out, the smoke waned away, and Kane sat groggily and bewilderedly on the throne. Yamen turned toward the king and bending low, straightened again and with his arms outstretched, spoke in a sonorous tone. The king solemnly repeated his words, and Kane saw the face of the noble prisoner go white. Then his companions seized his arms, and the band marched slowly away, their footfalls coming back eerily through the shadowy vastness.

Like silent ghosts the soldiers came from the shadows

and unchained him. Again they grouped themselves about
Kane and led him up and up through the shadowy galleries to
his chamber, where again Shem locked
his chains to the wall. Kane sat
on his couch, chin on his fist,
striving to find some motive in all
the fantastic actions he had witnessed. And presently he realized
that there was undue stir in the
streets below.

He looked out the window.
Great fires blazed in the market-
place and the figures of men,
curiously foreshortened, came and
went. They seemed to be busying
themselves about a figure in the
center of the market-place, but
they clustered about it so thickly
he could make nothing of it. A
circle of soldiers ringed the group;
the firelight glanced on their
armor. About them clamored a
disorderly mob, yelling and shouting.
Suddenly a scream of frightful agony
cut through the din, and the shouting
died away for an instant, to be renewed with
more force than before. Most of the clamor sounded like
protest, Kane thought, though mingled with it was the sound
of jeers, taunting howls and devilish laughter. And all
through the babble rang those ghastly, intolerable shrieks.

A swift pad of naked feet sounded on the tiles and the
young black, Sula, rushed in and thrust his head into the
window, panting with excitement. The firelight from without

shone on his ebon face and white rolling eyeballs.

"The people strive with the spearmen," he exclaimed, forgetting, in his excitement, the order not to converse with the strange captive. "Many of the people loved well the young prince Bel-lardath – oh, bwana, there was no evil in him! Why did you bid the King have him flayed alive?"

"I!" exclaimed Kane, taken aback and dumbfounded. "I said naught! I do not even know this prince! I have never seen him."

Sula turned his head and looked full into Kane's face.

"Now I know what I have secretly thought, bwana," he said in the Bantu tongue Kane understood. "You are no god, nor mouthpiece of a god, but a man, such as I have seen before the men of Ninn took me captive. Once before, when I was small, I saw men cast in your mold, who came with their black servants and slew our warriors with weapons which spoke with fire and thunder."

"Truly I am but a man," answered Kane, dazedly, "but what – I do not understand. What is it they do in yonder market-place?"

"They are skinning prince Bel-lardath alive," answered Sula. "It has been talked freely among the market-places that the king and Yamen hated the prince, who is of the blood of Abdulai. But he had many followers among the people, especially among the Arbii, and not even the king dared sentence him to death. But when you were brought into the temple, secretly, none in the city knowing of it, Yamen said you were the mouthpiece of the gods. And he said Baal had revealed to him that prince Bel-lardath had roused the wrath of the gods. So they brought him before the oracle of the gods –"

Kane swore sickly. How incredible – how ghastly – to think that his lusty English oaths had doomed a man to a horrible death. Aye – crafty Yamen had translated his random words in his own way. And so the prince, whom Kane had never seen before, writhed beneath the skinning knives of his executioners in the market-place below, where the crowd shrieked or jeered.

"Sula," he said, "what do these people call themselves?"

"Assyrians, bwana," answered the black absently, staring in horrified fascination at the grisly scene below.

III

In the days that followed Sula found opportunities from time to time to talk with Kane. Little he could tell the Englishman of the origin of the men of Ninn. He only knew that they had come out of the east in the long, long ago, and had built their massive city on the plateau. Only the dim legends of his tribe spoke of them. His people lived in the rolling plains far to the south and had warred with the people of the city for untold ages. His people were called Sulas, and they were strong and war-like, he said. From time to time they made raids on the Ninnites, and occasionally the Ninnites returned the raid – in such a raid Sula was captured – but not often did they venture far from the plateau. Though of late, Sula said, they had been forced to range further afield in search of slaves, as the black people shunned the grim plateau and generation by generation moved further back into the wilderness.

The life of a slave of Ninn was hard, Sula said, and Kane believed him, seeing the marks of lash, rack and brand on the young black's body. The drifting ages had not softened the spirit of the Assyrians, nor modified their fierceness, a byword in the ancient East.

Kane wondered much at the presence of this ancient

people in this unknown land, but Sula could tell him nothing. They came from the east, long, long ago – that was all Sula knew. Kane knew now why their features and language had seemed remotely familiar. Their features were the original Semitic features, now modified in the modern inhabitants of Mesopotamia, and many of their words had an unmistakable likeness to certain Hebraic words and phrases.

Kane learned from Sula that not all of the inhabitants were of one blood; they did not mix with their black slaves, or if they did, the offspring of such a union was instantly put to death, but there was more than one strain in the race. The dominant strain, Sula learned, was Assyrian; but there were some of the people, both common people and nobles, whom Sula said were "Arbii," much like the Assyrians, yet differing somewhat. Then there were "Kaldii," who were magicians and soothsayers, but they were held in no great esteem by the true Assyrians. Shem, Sula said, and his kind were Elamites, and Kane started at the biblical term. There were not

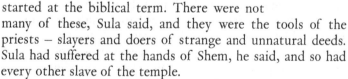

many of these, Sula said, and they were the tools of the priests – slayers and doers of strange and unnatural deeds. Sula had suffered at the hands of Shem, he said, and so had every other slave of the temple.

And it was this same Shem on whom Kane kept hungry eyes riveted. At his girdle hung the golden key that meant liberty. But, as if he read the meaning in the Englishman's cold eyes, Shem walked with care, a dark sombre giant with a grim carven face, and came not within reach of the captive's long steely arms, unless accompanied by armed guards.

Never a day passed but Kane heard the crack of the scourge, the screams of agonized slaves beneath the brand, the lash, or the skinning knife. Ninn was a veritable Hell, he reflected, ruled by the demoniac Asshur-ras-arab and his crafty and lustful satellite, Yamen the priest. The king was high priest as well, as had been his royal ancestors in ancient Nineveh. And Kane realized why they called him a Persian, seeing in him a resemblance to those wild old Aryan tribesmen who had ridden down from their mountains to sweep the Assyrian empire off the earth. Surely it was fleeing those yellow-haired conquerors that the people of Ninn had come into Africa.

And so the days passed and Kane abode as a captive in the city of Ninn. But he went no more to the temple as an oracle. Then one day there was confusion in the city. Kane heard the trumpets blaring upon the wall, and the roll of kettle-drums. Steel clanged in the streets and the sound of men marching rose to his eyrie. Looking out, over the wall, across the plateau, he saw a horde of naked black men approaching the city in loose formation. Their spears flashed in the sun, their head-pieces of ostrich-plumes floated in the breeze, and their yells came faintly to him.

Sula rushed in, his eyes blazing.

"My people!" he exclaimed. "They come against the men of Ninn! My people are warriors! Bogaga is war-chief — Katayo is king. The war-chiefs of the Sulas hold their honors by the might of their hands, for any man who is strong enough to slay him with his naked hands, becomes war-chief in his place! So Bogaga won the chieftainship, but it will be many a day before any slays him, for he is the mightiest chieftain of them all!"

Kane's window afforded a better view over the wall than any other, for his chamber was in the top-most tier of Baal's temple. To his chamber came Yamen, with his grim guards, Shem and another sombre Elamite. They stood out of Kane's reach, looking through one of the windows.

The mighty gates swung wide; the Assyrians were marching out to meet their enemies. Kane reckoned that there were fifteen hundred armed warriors; that left three hundred still in the city, the bodyguard of the king, the sentries, and house-troops of the various noblemen. The host, Kane noted, was divided into four divisions; the center was in the advance, consisting of six hundred men, while each flank or wing was composed of three hundred. The remaining three hundred marched in compact formation behind the center, between the wings, so the whole presented an appearance of this figure:

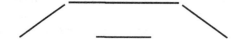

The warriors were armed with javelins, swords, maces and short heavy bows. On their backs were quivers bristling with shafts.

They marched out on the plain in perfect order, and took up their position, apparently awaiting the attack. It was not slow in coming. Kane estimated that the blacks numbered at least three thousand warriors, and even at that distance he

could appreciate their splendid stature and courage. But they had no system or order of warfare. In one great ragged disorderly horde they rushed onward, to be met by a withering blast of arrows that ripped through their bull-hide shields as though they had been made of paper.

The Assyrians had slung their shields about their necks and were drawing and loosing methodically, not in regular volleys as the archers of Crécy and Agincourt had loosed, but steadily and without pause, nevertheless. With reckless courage the black men hurled themselves forward, into the teeth of the fearful hail; Kane saw whole lines melt away, and the plain became carpeted with the dead, but the blacks hurled themselves forward, wasting their lives like water. Kane marveled at the perfect discipline of the Semitic soldiers, who went through their motions as coolly as if they were on the drill-ground. The wings had moved forward, their foremost tips connecting with the ends of the center, presenting an unbroken front. The men in the company between the wings maintained their place, unmoving, not yet having taken any part in the battle.

The black horde was broken, staggering back under the deadly fire, against which flesh and blood could not stand. The great ragged crescent had broken to bits, and from the fire of the right flank and the center, the black men were falling back disorderly, hounded by the ranging shafts of the white warriors. But on the left flank, a frothing mob of perhaps four hundred warriors had burst through the fearful barrage and, yelling like fiends, they shocked against the Assyrian wing. But before the spears clashed, Kane saw the company in reserve between the wings wheel and march in double quick time to support the threatened wing. Against that double wall of six hundred mailed war-men, the onslaught staggered, broke and reeled backward.

Swords flashed among the spears and Kane saw the naked black men falling like grain before the reaper as the javelins and swords of the Assyrians mowed them down. Not all the corpses on the bloody ground were those of black men, but where one Assyrian lay dead or wounded, ten Sulas had died.

Now the black men were in full flight across the plain, and the iron ranks moved forward in quick but orderly pace, loosing at every step, hunting the vanquished across the plateau, plying the dagger on the wounded. They took no prisoners. Sulas did not make good slaves, as Solomon was instantly to see.

In Kane's chamber, the watchers were crowded at the windows, eyes glued in fascination on the wild and gory scene. Sula's chest heaved with passion; his eyes blazed with the blood-lust of the savage, as the shouts and the slaughter and the spears of his tribesmen fired all the slumbering ferocity in his savage soul.

With the yell of a blood-mad panther, he sprang on the backs of his masters. Before any could lift a hand, he snatched the dagger from Shem's girdle and plunged it to the hilt between Yamen's shoulders. The priest shrieked like a wounded woman and went to his knees, blood spurting, and the Elamites closed with the raging slave. Shem sought to seize his wrist, but the other Elamite and Sula whirled into a deadly embrace, plying their knives which were in an instant red to the hilt. Eyes glaring, froth on their lips, they rolled and tumbled, slashing and stabbing. Shem, seeking to catch Sula's wrist, was struck by the hurtling bodies and knocked violently aside. He lost his footing and sprawled against Kane's couch.

And before he could move, the chained Englishman was on him like a great cat. At last the moment he had waited for had come! Shem was within his reach! Even as Shem sought to rise, Kane's knee smote him in the breast, breaking his ribs, and Kane's iron fingers locked in his throat. Kane scarcely was aware of the terrible, wild-beast struggles of the Elamite as he sought in vain to break that grasp. A red mist veiled the Englishman's sight and through it he saw horror growing in Shem's inhuman eyes – saw them distend and turn blood-shot – saw the mouth gape and the tongue protrude as the shaven head was bent back at a horrible angle – then Shem's neck snapped like a heavy branch and the straining body went limp in Kane's hands.

The Englishman snatched at the key in the dead man's girdle, and an instant later stood up free, feeling a wild surge of exultation sweep over him as he flexed his unhampered limbs. He glanced about the chamber; Yamen was gurgling out his life on the tiles, and Sula and the other Elamite lay dead, locked in each others' iron arms, literally slashed to pieces.

Kane ran swiftly from the chamber. He had no plan, except to escape from the temple he had grown to hate as a man hates Hell. He ran down the winding galleries, meeting no one. Evidently the servants of the temple had been massed on the walls, watching the battle. But on the lower tier, he came face to face with one of the temple guards. The man gaped at him

stupidly — and Kane's fist crashed against his black-bearded jowl, stretching him senseless. Kane snatched up his heavy javelin. A thought had come to him that perhaps the streets were practically deserted as the people watched the battle, and he could make his way across the city and scale the wall on the side next the lake.

He ran through the pillar-forested temple and out the mighty portal. He saw a scattering of people who shrieked and fled at the sight of the strange figure emerging from the grim temple. Kane hurried down the street in the direction of the opposite gate. He saw few people. Then as he turned down a side street, thinking to take a short cut, he heard a thunderous roar.

Ahead of him he saw four black slaves bearing a richly ornamented litter, such as nobles rode in. The occupant was a young girl, whose jewel-bedecked garments showed her importance and wealth. And now around the corner came roaring a great tawny shape. A lion, loose in the city streets!

The blacks dropped the litter and fled, shrieking, while the people on the housetops screamed. The girl cried out once, scrambling up in the very path of the charging monster. She stood facing it, frozen with terror.

Kane, at the first roar of the beast, had experienced a fierce satisfaction. So hateful had Ninn become to him that the thought of a wild beast raging through its streets and devouring its cruel inhabitants had given the Puritan an indisputable satisfaction. But now, as he saw the pitiful figure of the girl facing the man-eater, he felt a pang of pity for her, and acted.

As the lion launched himself through the air, Kane hurled the javelin with all the power of his iron frame. Just behind the mighty shoulder it struck, transfixing the tawny body. A deafening roar burst from the beast which spun

sidewise in mid-air, as though it had encountered a solid wall, and instead of the rending claws, it was the heavy shaggy shoulder that smote the frail figure of its victim, hurling her aside as the great beast crashed to the earth.

Kane, forgetful of his own position, sprang forward and lifted the girl, to ascertain if she were injured. This was easy, as her garments, like the garments of most of the Assyrian noble-women, were so scanty as to consist more of ornaments than covering. Kane assured himself that she was only bruised and badly frightened.

He helped her to her feet, and then was aware that a throng of curious people had surrounded him. He turned to press through them, and they made no effort to stop him, when suddenly a priest appeared and yelled something, pointing at him. The people instantly fell back, but half a dozen armored soldiers came forward, javelins ready. Kane faced them, red fury seething in his soul, ready to leap among them and do what damage he could with his naked hands before he died, when down the stones of the street sounded the tramp of marching men, and a company of soldiers swung into view, their spears red from the recent strife.

The girl cried out and ran forward to fling her arms about the stalwart neck of the young officer in command and there followed a rapid fire of conversation which Kane naturally could not understand. Then the officer spoke curtly to the guards, who drew back, and advanced toward Kane, his empty hands outstretched, a smile on his lips. His manner was friendly in the extreme and the Englishman realized that he was trying to express his gratitude for his rescue of the girl, who was no doubt either his sister or his sweetheart. The priest frothed and cursed, but the young noble answered him shortly, and made motions for Kane to accompany him. Then as the Englishman hesitated, suspicious, he drew his own sword and extended it to Kane, hilt foremost. Kane took the weapon; it might have been the form of courtesy to have refused it, but Kane was unwilling to take chances, and he felt much more secure with a weapon in his hand.

Solomon Kane's Homecoming

Solomon Kane's Homecoming

The white gulls wheeled above the cliffs,
    the air was slashed with foam,
The long tides moaned along the strand
    when Solomon Kane came home.
He walked in silence strange and dazed
    through the little Devon town,
His gaze, like a ghost's come back to life,
    roamed up the streets and down.

The people followed wonderingly
    to mark his spectral stare,
And in the tavern silently
    they thronged about him there.
He heard as a man hears in a dream
    the worn old rafters creak,
And Solomon lifted his drinking-jack
    and spoke as a ghost might speak:

"There sat Sir Richard Grenville once;
    in smoke and flame he passed,
"And we were one to fifty-three,
    but we gave them blast for blast.
"From crimson dawn to crimson dawn,
    we held the Dons at bay.
"The dead lay littered on our decks,
    our masts were shot away.

"We beat them back with broken blades,
          till crimson ran the tide;
"Death thundered in the cannon smoke
          when Richard Grenville died.
"We should have blown her hull apart
          and sunk beneath the Main."
The people saw upon his wrists
          the scars of the racks of Spain.

"Where is Bess?" said Solomon Kane.
          "Woe that I caused her tears."
"In the quiet churchyard by the sea
          she has slept these seven years."
The sea-wind moaned at the window-pane,
          and Solomon bowed his head.
"Ashes to ashes and dust to dust,
          and the fairest fade," he said.

His eyes were mystical deep pools
          that drowned unearthly things,
And Solomon lifted up his head
          and spoke of his wanderings.
"Mine eyes have looked on sorcery
          in the dark and naked lands,
"Horror born of the jungle gloom
          and death on the pathless sands.

"And I have known a deathless queen
          in a city old as Death,
"Where towering pyramids of skulls
          her glory witnesseth.
"Her kiss was like an adder's fang,
          with the sweetness Lilith had,
"And her red-eyed vassals howled for blood
          in that City of the Mad.

"And I have slain a vampire shape
    that sucked a black king white,
"And I have roamed through grisly hills
    where dead men walked at night.
"And I have seen heads fall like fruit
    in the slaver's barracoon,
"And I have seen winged demons fly
    all naked in the moon.

"My feet are weary of wandering
    and age comes on apace;
"I fain would dwell in Devon now,
    forever in my place."
The howling of the ocean pack
    came whistling down the gale,
And Solomon Kane threw up his head
    like a hound that snuffs a trail.

A-down the wind like a running pack
    the hounds of the ocean bayed,
And Solomon Kane rose up again
    and girt his Spanish blade.
In his strange cold eyes a vagrant gleam
    grew wayward and blind and bright,
And Solomon put the people by
    and went into the night.

A wild moon rode the wild white clouds,
    the waves in white crests flowed,
When Solomon Kane went forth again
    and no man knew his road.
They glimpsed him etched against the moon,
    where clouds on hilltop thinned;
They heard an eery echoed call
    that whistled down the wind.

Solomon Kane's Homecoming
(Variant)

Solomon Kane's Homecoming
(Variant)

The white gulls wheeled above the cliffs,
    the wind was slashed with foam,
The long tides moaned along the strand
    when Solomon Kane came home.
He walked in silence through the streets
    of the little Devon town,
The folk all followed whispering
    all up the streets and down.

They whispered of his sun-bronzed hue
    and his deep strange stare;
They followed him into the tavern
    and thronged about him there.
He heard, as a man hears in a dream,
    the old worn rafters creak,
And Solomon lifted his drinking jack
    and spoke as a ghost might speak:

"Where are the lads that gathered here
    so many years ago?
"Drake and Hawkins and Oxenham,
    Grenville and Leigh and Yeo?
"Was it so long ago," said Kane,
    "sat Richard Grenville there?
"The dogs of Spain," said Solomon Kane,
    "by God, we fought them fair!

"For a day and a night and a day again
        we held their fleet at bay,
"Till their round shot riddled us through and through
        and ripped our masts away.
"Where is Bess?" said Solomon Kane.
        "It racked me hard to go –
"But I heard the high tide grate the keel
        and I heard the sea-wind blow.

"I left her – though it racked my heart
        to see the lass in tears –"
"In the quiet churchyard by the sea
        she has slept these seven years."
The sea-wind moaned at the window pane
        and Solomon bowed his head.
"Ashes to ashes, dust to dust,
        and the fairest fade," he said.

His eyes were mystical deep pools
        that drown unearthly things,
And Solomon lifted up his head
        and spoke of his wanderings.
"My feet have tracked a bloody way
        across the trackless sands,
"Mine eyes have looked on sorcery
        in the dark and naked lands.

"And I have known a deathless queen
        in a city old as Death;
"Her smile was like a serpent's kiss,
        her kiss was Lilith's breath.
"And I have roamed in grisly hills
        where dead men walked by night,
"And I have seen a tattered corpse
        stand up to blast men's sight.

"And I have heard the death-chant rise
    in the slaver's barracoon,
"And I have seen a winged fiend fly,
    all naked, in the moon.
"My feet are weary of wandering
    and age comes on apace –
"I fain would dwell in Devon now,
    forever in my place."

The shouting of the ocean-winds
    went whistling down the gale,
And Solomon Kane raised up his head
    like a hound that snuffs the trail.
A-down the winds like a running pack,
    the hounds of the ocean bayed,
And Solomon Kane rose up again
    and girt his Spanish blade.

Hands held him hard but the vagrant gleam
    in his eyes grew blind and bright,
And Solomon Kane put by the folk
    and went into the night.
A wild moon rode in the wild white clouds,
    the waves their white crests showed
When Solomon Kane went forth again,
    and no man knew his road.

They saw him etched against the moon
    on the hill in clouds that thinned,
They heard an eery, echoed call
    that whistled down the wind.
Out of the tavern into the night
    went Solomon Kane once more,
He heard the clamor of the winds,
    he had harked to the ocean's roar.

Appendices

A Short Biography of
Robert E. Howard

by Rusty Burke

Robert Ervin Howard (1906-1936) ranks among the greatest writers of
adventure stories. The creator of Conan the Cimmerian, Kull of
Atlantis, Solomon Kane, Bran Mak Morn, Francis X. Gordon ("El
Borak"), Sailor Steve Costigan, Breckenridge Elkins, and many other
memorable characters, Howard, during a writing career that spanned
barely a dozen years, had well over a hundred stories published in the
pulp magazines of his day, chiefly *Weird Tales*, but including *Action
Stories*, *Argosy*, *Fight Stories*, *Oriental Stories*, *Spicy Adventure*, *Sport Story*,
Strange Detective, *Thrilling Adventure*, *Top Notch*, and a number of others.
His stories consistently proved popular with the readers, for they are
powerfully vivid adventures, with colorful, larger-than-life heroes and
compelling, rivetting prose that grabs the reader from the first
paragraph and sweeps him along to the thrilling conclusion. So great
was the appeal of Howard's storytelling that it continues to capture
new generations of readers and inspire many of the finest writers of
fantasy and adventure.

Robert E. Howard was born on January 22, 1906, in the "fading
little ex-cowtown" of Peaster, Texas, in Parker County, just west of
Fort Worth. The Howards were living at the time in neighboring Palo
Pinto County, on the banks of Dark Valley Creek. Robert's father, Dr.
Isaac Mordecai Howard, presumably moved his wife temporarily to the
larger community of Peaster so that she would have readier access to
medical care when her pregnancy came to term. Hester Jane Ervin
Howard, Robert's mother, did not enjoy robust health, to put it
mildly: there was a history of tuberculosis in her family, and Mrs.
Howard was sickly for much of Robert's life. Isaac Howard was a
country doctor, a profession which entails frequent lengthy absences
from home. Thus he may have wished to be certain that his wife of two
years, experiencing her first pregnancy in her mid-thirties, would have
adequate medical attention when she delivered their first, and as it
happened, only child.

Isaac Howard seems to have been possessed of a combination of
wanderlust and ambition that led him to move his family frequently in

search of better opportunities. By the time he was eight, Robert had lived in at least seven different, widely scattered Texas towns. Finally, in 1915, the family moved to the community of Cross Cut, in Brown County, and they would live in this vicinity, with moves to Burkett (in Coleman County) in 1917 and finally to Cross Plains (Callahan County) in 1919, for the rest of Robert's and his mother's lives.

Cross Plains in the 1920s was a small town of approximately 2000 souls, give or take a thousand, but like much of the Central West Texas region, it went through periodic oil booms. Two town-site booms, in particular, brought hundreds, perhaps thousands, of temporary inhabitants who set up camps just outside the town limits, jammed the hotels to capacity, and rented rooms or beds in private homes. The lease men, riggers, drillers, tool dressers, and roughnecks who followed the oil were followed in their turn by those who sought to exploit them for profit, from men or women who set up temporary hamburger stands to feed them, to gamblers and prostitutes who provided "recreation," to thugs, thieves and con men who simply preyed on them. An oil boom could transform a sleepy little community into a big city in no time at all, in those days: when oil was discovered in Ranger, Texas (about 40 miles from Cross Plains) in 1917, the population increased from 1,000 to 30,000 in less than a year, and similar growth was reported in nearby Breckinridge. Cross Plains never saw anything like that kind of growth, but certainly the few thousand who did come transformed it into a wilder and rowdier town than usual. One resident recalls her family driving into town on Saturday night just to watch people, hoping fights would break out. They were rarely disappointed. Of the atmosphere in a boom town, Howard wrote: "I'll say one thing about an oil boom: it will teach a kid that Life's a pretty rotten thing about as quick as anything I can think of." Just as quickly as the town grew, however, it could decline: when the oil played out, the speculators and oil-field workers and their camp-followers moved on. The influence of this boom-and-bust cycle on Howard's later ideas about the growth and decline of civilization has often been overlooked.

Bob Howard attended the local high school, where he was remembered as polite and reserved, and to make pocket money he worked at a variety of jobs, including hauling trash, picking up and delivering laundry for dry-cleaners, clerking in stores, loading freight at the train station, etc. He had some close friends among the local boys, but there seem to have been none who shared his literary interests.

Bob's literary interests had probably been encouraged from an early age by his mother, an ardent poetry lover. He was an avid reader, claiming even to have raided schoolhouses during the summer in his quest for books. While this story is probably hyperbolic, it does give an indication of his thirst for reading material, which was a rare commodity in the communities in which the Howards lived, most of which had no libraries, much less bookstores. Bob seems to have had an extraordinary ability to read quickly and to remember what he had read. His friends recall their astonishment at his ability to pick up a book in the library or a store or someone's house, to quickly turn the pages and run his eyes over them, faster than they thought anyone could actually be reading, and later to be able to relate to them with perfect clarity what he had read. His library, presented by his father to Howard Payne College after his death, reveals the breadth of his interests: history and fiction are dominant, but also represented are biography, sports, poetry, anthropology, Texana, and erotica. Near the end of his life he wrote to H.P. Lovecraft:

"My favorite writers are A. Conan Doyle, Jack London, Mark Twain, Sax Rohmer, Jeffery Farnol, Talbot Mundy, Harold Lamb, R.W. Chambers, Rider Haggard, Kipling, Sir Walter Scott, [Stanley] Lane-Poole, Jim Tully, Ambrose Bierce, Arthur Machen, Edgar Allan Poe, and H.P. Lovecraft. For poetry, I like Robert W. Service, Kipling, John Masefield, James Elroy Flecker, [Robert] Vansittart, Sidney Lanier, Edgar Allan Poe, the Benets – Stephen Vincent better than William Rose – Walter de la Mare, Rupert Brooke, Siegfried Sassoon, Francis Ledwedge, Omar Khayyam, Joe Moncure March, Nathalia Crane, Henry Herbert Knibbs, Lord Dunsany, G.K. Chesterton, Bret Harte, Oscar Wilde, Longfellow, Tennyson, Swinburne, [George Sylvester] Viereck, Alfred Noyes, and Lovecraft."

In addition to his reading, Bob Howard had a passion for oral story-telling. It is well attested that he frequently told his stories aloud as he typed them: his neighbors reported that they sometimes had difficulty sleeping at night because of the racket Howard was making. His youthful buddies in Cross Cut remember that he liked to have them all play out stories he made up, and the literary friends of his adulthood recall being often enthralled by the stories he would tell when they were together. He seemed never to tire of telling stories, though he generally would not relate a tale he was actually writing: he told Novalyne Price that once the story was told, he had difficulty getting it on paper. Sometimes, however, his oral stories were the inspiration or basis for the stories he would write. He loved, too, to listen to others tell stories: in his letters he relates how as a young boy he was thrilled and terrified by the tales of the family's cook, a former slave, and those of his grandmother. Novalyne Price remembers him sitting riveted by the stories of her grandmother, and that he loved to find old-timers who could relate tales of pioneer days. It may well be the quality of the oral story, the well-spun yarn, that makes Howard's stories so enthralling.

Howard seems to have determined upon a literary career at an early age. In a letter to H.P. Lovecraft he says that his first story was written when he was "nine or ten," and a former postmistress at Burkett recalls that he began writing stories about this time and expressed an intention of becoming a writer. He submitted his first story for professional publication when he was but 15, and his first professional sale, "Spear and Fang," was made at age 18. Howard always insisted that he chose writing as his profession simply because it gave him the freedom to be his own boss:

"I've always had a honing to make my living by writing, ever since I can remember, and while I haven't been a howling success in that line, at least I've managed for several years now to get by without grinding at some time clock-punching job. There's freedom in this game; that's the main reason I chose it."

Whatever his reasons, once Howard had determined upon his path, he kept at it.

The Cross Plains school only went through tenth grade during Bob Howard's day, but he needed to complete the eleventh grade to qualify for college admission. Therefore, in the fall of 1922 Bob and his mother moved to Brownwood, a larger town that served as the county seat for Brown County, so that he could finish high school there. It was there that he met Truett Vinson and Clyde Smith, who would remain his friends until the end of his life: they were the first of his friends to share and encourage his interest in literature and writing. Smith, in particular, shared much of Howard's literary taste, and the two encouraged each other in writing poetry. Also at Brownwood High, Howard enjoyed his first appearances as a published author: two of his stories won cash prizes and publication in the high school paper, *The Tattler*, December 22, 1922, and three more were printed during the spring term.

After his graduation from high school, Howard returned to Cross Plains. His father, in particular, wanted him to attend college, perhaps hoping that he, too, would become a physician. But Bob had little aptitude for and no interest in science. He also claimed a passionate hatred for school. As he wrote later to Lovecraft: "I hated school as I hate the memory of school. It wasn't the work I minded; I had no trouble learning the tripe they dished out in the way of lessons – except arithmetic, and I might have learned that if I'd gone to the trouble of studying it. I wasn't at the head of my classes – except in history – but I wasn't at the foot either. I generally did just enough work to keep from flunking the courses, and I don't regret the loafing I did. But what I hated was the confinement – the clock-like regularity of everything; the regulation of my speech and actions; most of all the idea that someone considered himself or herself in authority over me, with the right to question my actions and interfere with my thoughts."

Although he did eventually take courses at the Howard Payne commercial school, these were business courses – stenography, typing, and a program in bookkeeping; despite his interest in history, anthropology, and literature, Howard never took college courses in these subjects. During the period from his high school graduation in spring of 1923 to his completion of the bookkeeping program in the spring of 1927, he continued writing. While he finally made his first professional sale during this period, when *Weird Tales* accepted "Spear and Fang," he also accumulated many rejection slips. Further, because most of his early sales were to *Weird Tales*, which paid upon publication, rather than acceptance, he found that the money was not coming in as he might have liked. He therefore took a variety of jobs during these years. He tried reporting oil-field news, but found he did not like interviewing people he did not know or like about a topic that did not interest him. He tried stenography, both in a law office and as an independent public stenographer, but found he was not particularly good at it and did not like it. He worked as an assistant to an oil-field geologist, and while he did enjoy the work, he one day collapsed in the fearsome Texas summer heat, which led him to fear that he had heart problems (it was later learned that his heart had a mild tendency to race under stress), so he was just as glad when the survey ended and the geologist left town. He spent several months as a soda jerk and counterman at Robertson's Drug Store, a job that he actively detested, and which required so much of his time that he had little left over for writing or recreation. Thus he made a pact with his father: he would take the course in bookkeeping at the Howard Payne Academy, following which he would have one year to try to make a success of his writing. If at the end of that year he was not making it, he would try to find a bookkeeping job.

During the summer of 1927, Bob Howard met Harold Preece, who would be an important friend and correspondent for the next few years. It was Preece who encouraged Bob's interest in Irish and Celtic history and legend: he had earlier shown some interest in the subject, and now, inspired by Preece's enthusiasm, it would become an active passion. He also met, the same weekend, Booth Mooney, who would become the editor of a literary circular, *The Junto*, to which Howard, Preece, Clyde Smith, Truett Vinson, and others contributed over a period of about two years.

After completing the bookkeeping course, Howard set about in earnest the business of becoming a writer. By early 1928, it was clear that he was going to be able to succeed in this, and indeed he never again worked at any other job. *Weird Tales* had published two Howard stories in 1925, one in 1926, and one (plus two poems) in 1927. In 1928 they would publish four stories (including the first Solomon Kane tale, "Red Shadows") and five poems. From January 1928 until his death in

June 1936, Howard stories or verse appeared in nearly three of every four issues of *Weird Tales*.

Several critics have noted that Howard's writing can be divided into "periods." Though they overlap to a degree, these periods, which seemed to last two to three years each, may reveal something about Howard's writing style and methods. The most well-defined periods are those during which he wrote boxing stories, culminating in the Steve Costigan series; heroic fantasy stories, culminating with Conan; oriental adventure stories, culminating with the El Borak tales; and western stories – he was still "in" this period at his death. A close reading of Howard's letters and stories, and placement of these along a timeline, reveals that he would develop an interest in a subject, read about it avidly, immerse himself in it so thoroughly that he virtually adopted a new identity (a persona, the "voice" through which a writer speaks, not to be confused with the writer's own personality), whereupon he would begin, at first tentatively and then with increasing confidence and vigor, to write about the subject in this new "voice." While something of the pattern can be seen from his early writing, it is most vivid beginning with his "boxing" persona, Steve Costigan.

Howard's passion for boxing is attested as early as age nine. He boxed with his friends at any opportunity, and in his late teens may have occasionally assisted in promoting fights at local clubs in Cross Plains. While working at the soda fountain at Robertson's Drug Store, he developed a friendship with one oil-field worker who introduced him to the amateur fighters at the local ice house, and he became a frequent participant in these bouts. Between 1925 (at the latest) and 1928, he put himself through a weight and strength program, and took on really heroic proportions. He read avidly about prizefighters, and attended fights whenever and wherever he could. By early 1929 he had begun writing and submitting boxing stories, though his first efforts mingled boxing with weird themes. (This was another of his patterns: when trying out a new literary field, he would often use characters, settings or themes with which he was already comfortable.) With the first Steve Costigan story, "The Pit of the Serpent," in the July 1929 *Fight Stories*, he had found a market that would prove as steady for him as *Weird Tales*, at least until the Depression knocked out *Fight Stories* and its companion magazine, *Action Stories*, in 1932.

The same weekend he met Harold Preece in Austin, Howard had bought a copy of G.K. Chesterton's book-length epic poem, *The Ballad of the White Horse*, which brings together Celts, Romanized Britons, and Anglo-Saxons under King Alfred in a battle of Christians against the heathen Danish and Norse invaders of the 9th century. Howard enthusiastically praised the poem in letters to Clyde Smith, sharing lengthy passages. It apparently inspired him to begin work on "The Ballad of King Geraint," in which he brings together representatives of various Celtic peoples of early Britain in a valiant "last stand" against the invading Angles, Saxons, and Jutes. Chesterton's idea of "telescoping history," that "it is the chief value of legend to mix up the centuries while preserving the sentiment," must have appealed to Howard greatly, for this is precisely what he did in many of his fantasy adventures, particularly in his creation of Conan's Hyborian Age, in which we find represented many different historical eras and cultures, from medieval Europe (Aquilonia and Poitain) to the American frontier (the Pictish Wilderness and its borderlands), from Cossacks (the Kozaki) to Elizabethan pirates (the Free Brotherhood). Howard "mix(ed) up the centuries while preserving the sentiment": this "telescoping" allowed him to portray what he saw as universal elements of human nature and historical patterns, as well as giving him virtually all of human history for a playground.

When Howard discovered that Harold Preece shared his enthusiasm for matters Celtic, he entered into his "Celtic" phase with his customary brio. His letters to Preece and to Clyde Smith from 1928 to 1930 are full of discussions of Irish history, legend, and poetry – he even taught himself a smattering of Irish Gaelic, and began exploring his genealogy in earnest. Irish and Celtic themes came to dominate his poetry, and by 1930 he was ready to try out this new persona with fiction. In keeping with his general tendency to use older work as a springboard to the new, he first introduced an Irish character into a story featuring two earlier creations – Cormac of Connacht is often overlooked as one of the "Kings of the Night," overshadowed by the teaming up of Bran Mak Morn and King Kull, but the story is told from the Irish king's point of view. During 1930 Howard wrote a number of stories featuring Gaelic heroes, nearly all of them outlawed by clan and country.

In June 1930 Howard received a letter from Farnsworth Wright informing him that *Weird Tales* planned to launch a companion magazine dealing with oriental fiction, and asking him to contribute. This request rekindled the author's avid interest in the Orient, particularly the Middle East, and he produced some of his finest stories for the new magazine (originally titled *Oriental Stories*, later *Magic Carpet*). But while these stories were set during the Crusades, or periods of Mongol or Islamic conquests, they inevitably featured Celtic heroes.

Also in June 1930, Howard wrote to Farnsworth Wright in praise of H.P. Lovecraft's "The Rats in the Walls," which had just been reprinted in *Weird Tales*. In the letter, he noted the use of a phrase in Gaelic, suggesting that Lovecraft might hold to a minority view on the settling of the British Isles. Wright sent the letter on to Lovecraft, who frankly had not supposed when he wrote the story that anyone would notice the liberty he had taken with his archaic language. He wrote to Howard to set the record straight, and so began what is surely one of the great correspondence cycles in all of fantasy literature. For the next six years, Howard and Lovecraft debated the merits of civilization versus barbarism, cities and society versus the frontier, the mental versus the physical, art versus commerce, and other subjects. At first Howard was very deferential to Lovecraft, whom he (like many of his colleagues) considered the pre-eminent writer of weird fiction of the day. But gradually Howard came to assert his own views more forcefully, and eventually could even direct withering sarcasm toward Lovecraft's views, as when he noted how "civilized" Italy was in bombing Ethiopia.

These letters provide a vast store of information on Howard's travels and activities during these years, as well as his views on many subjects, and in them we see the development of the persona that would come increasingly to dominate Howard's fiction and letters in the last part of his life, "The Texian" (a term used for Texans prior to statehood). Lovecraft, and later August Derleth, with whom Howard also began corresponding, strongly encouraged Howard's growing interests in regional history and lore, as did E. Hoffmann Price, with whom Howard was already corresponding in 1930 and who was the only writer of the *Weird Tales* group to actually meet him in person. It is unfortunate that this persona did not have a chance to develop fully by the time of Howard's death. The evidence of his letters suggests that he might have become a great western writer.

Even before Howard bought his own car in 1932, he and his parents had made many trips to various parts of Texas, to visit friends and relatives, and for his mother's health, which was in serious decline. After he bought his car, he continued to travel with his parents, but made a few trips with his friends, such as Lindsey Tyson and Truett Vinson. His travels ranged from Fort Worth to the Rio Grande Valley, from the East Texas oil fields to New Mexico. His letters to Lovecraft contain a good deal of description and discussion of the geography and history of these places, and are highly entertaining in their own right, apart from being windows into Howard's life.

In 1934, a new schoolteacher arrived in Cross Plains, who was to become a major force in Bob Howard's life. Bob had met Novalyne Price a little over a year previously, when introduced to her by their mutual friend Clyde Smith. Upon moving to Cross Plains, Novalyne made several attempts to call Bob, only to be told by his mother that he could not come to the phone, or was out of town. At last tiring of these excuses, she talked her cousin into giving her a ride to the Howard home, where she was greeted stand-offishly by his father but warmly by Bob. This was the beginning of a sometimes romantic, sometimes stormy relationship. For the first time, Bob had someone locally who shared his interests – and she was a woman! But his closeness to his mother, particularly his insistence upon attending to her in her illness, which Novalyne thought he should hire a nurse to do, rankled Novalyne, as did his refusal to attend social events. Marriage often entered their minds, and was even occasionally discussed – but the two never entertained the same feelings at the same time. When she would think she was in love, he would insist he needed his freedom. When he thought he was ready for love, she saw only the differences in their attitudes toward socializing. They were two headstrong, passionate, assertive personalities, which made for an interesting relationship, but one that was impossible to sustain. In the spring of 1936, Novalyne was accepted into the graduate program in education at Louisiana State, and left Cross Plains.

Through 1935 and 1936, Howard's mother's health was in rapid decline. More and more frequently Robert had to take her to sanitariums and hospitals, and even though Dr. Howard received a courtesy discount on services, the medical bills began to mount. Bob was faced with a dilemma: his need for money was more pressing than ever, but he had little time in which to write. *Weird Tales* owed him around $800, and payments were slow. Dr. Howard, his own meager savings exhausted, moved his practice to his home, so that patients came in and out all day and night. Father and son finally tried hiring women to nurse and keep house, further filling the house with people. Bob could find no time to be alone with his writing. This, and the despair he felt as his mother inexorably slid toward death, created enormous stress for the young writer. He resurrected an apparently long-standing plan not to outlive his mother.

This was no impulsive act. For years, he had told associates such as Clyde Smith that he would kill himself were it not that his mother needed him. Much of his poetry, most of it written during the 1920s and early 1930s, clearly and forcefully reflects his suicidal ideation. He was not at all enamored with life for its own sake, seeing it only as weary, gruelling toil at the behest of others, with scant chance of success and precious little freedom. A 1931 letter to Farnsworth Wright contains several statements of common Howard themes: "Like the average man, the tale of my life would merely be a dull narration of drab monotony and toil, a grinding struggle against poverty. . . . I'll say one thing about an oil boom; it will teach a kid that life's a pretty rotten thing about as quick as anything I can think of. . . . Life's not worth living if somebody thinks he's in authority over you. . . . I'm merely one of a huge army, all of whom are bucking the line one way or another for meat for their bellies. . . . Every now and then one of us finds the going too hard and blows his brains out, but it's all in the game, I reckon."

His letters frequently express the feeling that he was a misfit in a cold and hostile world: "The older I grow the more I sense the senseless unfriendly attitude of the world at large." In nearly all his fiction, the characters are misfits, outcasts, aliens in a world that is hostile to them. One wonders if the early childhood experience of being uprooted on a regular basis, as Dr. Howard gambled on one boom town after another – the Howards had at least eight different residences, scattered all over Texas, before Robert was nine years old – may have contributed to this feeling of being an outsider in an inhospitable land.

In some of his letters to Lovecraft he expressed another variation on this theme: the feeling that he was somehow born out of his proper time. He frequently bemoaned the fate that had him born too late to have participated in the taming of the frontier. "I only wish I had been born earlier – thirty years earlier, anyway. As it was I only caught the tag end of a robust era, when I was too young to realize its meaning. When I look down the vista of the years, with all the 'improvements', 'inventions' and 'progress' that they hold, I am infinitely thankful that I am no younger. I could wish to be older, much older. Every man wants to live out his life's span. But I hardly think life in this age is worth the effort of living. I'd like to round out my youth; and perhaps the natural vitality and animal exuberance of youth will carry me to middle age. But good God, to think of living the full three score years and ten!"

Howard also seems to have had an abhorrence of the idea of growing old and infirm. A month before his death he'd written to August Derleth: "Death to the old is inevitable, and yet somehow I often feel that it is a greater tragedy than death to the young. When a man dies young he misses much suffering, but the old have only life as a possession and somehow to me the tearing of a pitiful remnant from weak fingers is more tragic than the looting of a life in its full rich prime. I don't want to live to be old. I want to die when my time comes, quickly and suddenly, in the full tide of my strength and health."

For a young man, Howard seems to have had an exaggerated sense of growing old. When he was only 24 he wrote to Harold Preece, "I am haunted by the realization that my best days, mental and physical, lie behind me." Novalyne Price recalls that during the time they were dating, in 1934–35, Bob often said that he was in his "sere and yellow leaf," echoing a phrase from Macbeth: "I have lived long enough, my way of life | Is fal'n into the sere, the yellow leaf . . ."

Also in his May 1936 letter to Derleth, Howard mentioned that "I haven't written a weird story for nearly a year, though I've been contemplating one dealing with Coronado's expedition on the Staked Plains in 1541." This suggests that "Nekht Semerkeht" may well have been the last story Howard started, and if so, it is of interest here, in that it dwells upon the idea of suicide. "The game is not worth the candle," thinks the hero, de Guzman:

"'Oh, of course we are guided *solely* by reason, even when reason tells us it is better to die than to live! It is not the intellect we boast that bids us live—and kill to live—but the blind unreasoning beast-instinct.'

"Hernando de Guzman did not try to deceive himself into believing there was some intellectual reason, then, why he should not give up the agonizing struggle and place the muzzle of his pistol to his head; quit an existence whose savor had long ago become less than its pain."

And in the end, it may be that stress played an important role in his decision to take his own life. His mother's worsening illness had necessitated frequent absences from home, to take her to medical facilities in other parts of the state, and even when the Howards were home, Bob had little uninterrupted time, or peace, in which to write. He worried constantly about his mother. It may be that a complex array of forces coalesced to convince him of the futility of existence, and to impel him to take a long-contemplated course of action.

Howard planned for his death very carefully. He made arrangements with his agent, Otis Kline, for the handling of his stories in the event of his death. He carefully put together the manuscripts he had not yet submitted to *Weird Tales* or the Kline agency, with instructions on where they were to be sent. He borrowed a gun, a .380 Colt automatic, from a friend who was unaware of his plans. Dr. Howard may have hidden Bob's own guns, aware of what he might be contemplating. He said that he had seen his son make preparations on earlier occasions when it appeared Mrs. Howard might die. He said that he was trying to keep an eye on his son, but that he did not expect him to act before his mother died.

Hester Howard sank into her final coma about the 8th of June, 1936. On the 10th, Bob went to Brownwood and purchased a cemetery lot for three burials, with perpetual care. He asked Dr. J.W. Dill, who had come to be with Dr. Howard during his wife's final illness, whether anyone had been known to live after being shot through the brain. Unaware of Bob's plan, the doctor told him that such an injury meant certain death.

Dr. Howard related that Robert had disarmed him of his intentions the night before, assuming "an almost cheerful attitude": "He came to me in the night, put his arm around me and said, buck up, you are equal to it, you will go through it all right." He did not know, he said, that on the morning of the 11th, Robert asked the nurse attending Mrs. Howard if she thought his mother would ever regain consciousness, and that the nurse had told him she would not.

He then left the room, and was next seen leaving the house and getting into his car. The cook he and his father had hired said later that, looking through the kitchen window, she saw him raise his hands in prayer, though what looked to her like prayer may have been holding up the gun to get it ready. She heard a shot, and saw Robert slump over the steering wheel. She screamed. Dr. Howard and Dr. Dill ran out to the car and carried Bob back into the house. Both were country doctors, and they knew that no one could live with the kind of injury Bob had sustained. He had shot himself above the right ear, the bullet emerging on the left side.

Robert Howard's robust health allowed him to survive this terrible wound for almost eight hours. He died at about 4:00 in the afternoon, Thursday, June 11, 1936, without ever regaining consciousness. His mother died the following day, also without regaining consciousness. A double funeral was held on June 14, and the mother and son were transported to Brownwood for burial.

In Robert's room, a four line couplet was reportedly found on his typewriter:

> All fled, all done
> So lift me on the pyre.
> The feast is over
> And the lamps expire.

Gary Gianni

Gary Gianni graduated from The Chicago Academy of Fine Art in 1976. From there, he worked for the Chicago Tribune as an illustrator and Network Television News as a courtroom sketch artist. His artwork has appeared in numerous magazines, children's books and paperbacks.

1990 marked his debut in the illustrated graphic novel field with adaptations of *The Tales of O. Henry* and *20,000 Leagues Under the Sea* for the Classics Illustrated series.

At Dark Horse Comics, he wrote and drew *Indiana Jones and the Shrine of the Sea Devil*, collaborated with such major writers as Harlan Ellison and Andrew Vachss and teamed up with Michael Kaluta to work on the enduring pulp hero, The Shadow. He is the creator of *Corpus Monstrum Mysteries* running as a back-up feature in Mike Mignola's *Hellboy*.

Gianni says: "I have always wanted to produce a book that may stand the test of time. I hope somebody could pick this thing up and say, oh, this is a very classically, traditionally illustrated book. It doesn't look like it's rooted in the 1990s when it was done. I tried to stay away from things that might pinpoint when it was actually produced. That way, maybe it'll always have some merit, like the old Harryhausen films, the old *Thief of Baghdad*. They have certain qualities to them because the people really cared about what they were doing. I care about Howard and I have grown to care for Kane, hopefully this will have that same feel as those masters of genres."

Al Williamson said of Gianni, "He is a wonderful artist, he brings to his work the feeling and love of the great pulp illustrators." Scott Gustafson compares his work with the old Brandywine painting tradition of N.C.Wyeth with his "sheer love of drawing."

Gary's work harks back to the golden age of illustrating, to people like Vierge, Clement Coll, Booth and Krenkel.

In 1997, his illustrations won him The Eisner Award for Best Short Story, *Heroes*, in *Batman: Black and White*, for DC Comics.

Notes on the Original Howard Text

The texts for this edition of *The Savage Tales of Solomon Kane* were prepared by Rusty Burke and David Gentzel, with the assistance of Glenn Lord, Rob Jones, Bill Cavalier, and Steve Trout. The stories which appeared in *Weird Tales* have been carefully checked against the magazine appearances; the whereabouts of the typescripts for these stories is unknown, and they are presumed lost. Other stories have been checked against Howard's original typescripts, provided by Lord, or against the first known publication, when typescripts were unavailable. Every effort has been made to present the text as written by Robert E. Howard, as faithfully as practicable.

Deviations from original sources are detailed in these textual notes. In the following notes, page, line, and word numbers are given as follows: 21.3.2, indicating page 21, third line, second word. Story titles, chapter titles, and breaks before and after chapter headings or titles are not counted; in poems, only text lines are counted. The page/line number will be followed by the reading in the original source, or a statement indicating the type of change made.

Two types of changes are not detailed here. We have standardized chapter numbering and titling; Howard's and *Weird Tales'* practices varied. Standard *Weird Tales* practice was to italicize non-English words, such as m'sieu or senhor, except when they were followed by a proper name. We have not italicized these words, following Howard's own practice.

Skulls in the Stars

Originally appeared in *Weird Tales*, January 1929. No changes were made for this appearance.

The Right Hand of Doom

Text taken from typescript, provided by Glenn Lord. 21.3.2: no hyphen in "high pitched"; 21.8.1: comma after "voice"; 21.13.11: "end of noose"; 22.3.8: comma after "boasted"; 22.9.10: "That" capitalized; 22.19.7: comma after "resentfully"; 22.24.2: no hyphen in "long stemmed"; 23.1.4: no comma after "tomorrow"; 23.10: four asterisks mark section break; 24.1.10: comma after "in"; 24.3.4: no hyphen in "evil visaged"; 24.9.6: comma after "hairy"; 24.12.7: "spell bound" as two words; 24.13.10: "up" repeated; 24.14.2: "bed stead" as two words; 24.16.8: "the" for "a"; 24.28.1-2: "human hand" in capitals; 25.22.1: comma after "gasped"; 25.25: four asterisks mark section break; 26.15.7: "a" omitted ("as man that"); 27.13.2: comma after "Kane"

Red Shadows

Originally appeared in *Weird Tales*, August 1928. 37.28.1: "mephistophelean"; 40.8.7: comma after "idly"; 47.4.7: "hog-like" hyphenated at line break; similar constructions elsewhere in the story (e.g., "catlike") not hyphenated; 52.3.12: "rôle"; 52.4.8: omits closing quotation marks; 52.8.7: closing quotation marks omitted; 56.19.10: "is" is not capitalized; 58.6.1: "swaying"; 69.19.4: "man-like" hyphenated at line break; similar constructions elsewhere in the story (e.g., "catlike") not hyphenated

Rattle of Bones

Originally appeared in *Weird Tales*, June 1929. 79.24.5: "the" omitted

The Castle of the Devil

Text taken from typescript, provided by Glenn Lord. 87.15.5: period after "garb"; 87.16.4: comma after "horse"; 87.19.7: there is a blank space in the typescript, indicating that a place name was to be filled in later ("Genoa" added by Lord); 87.21.2: comma after "voice"; 87.27.1: "Where-ever"; 88.1.4: "over-tax"; 88.15.6: "You" capitalized; 88.18.4: following "soldiery" is the word "in," followed by a blank space indicating a place-name to be filled in later; 88.18.9: following "going to" there is a blank space, indicating a place name to be filled in later ("Genoa" added by Lord); 88.18.10: "to" not in typescript; 88.26.2: "t'is"; 88.29.7: "t'is"; 89.5.3: comma after "mildly"; 89.11.3: "You" capitalized; 89.15.6: a hyphen rather than a period follows "impatience"; 89.18.1: no opening quotation marks; 89.19.9: comma after "grimly"; 89.26.6: comma after "Kane"; 89.30.9: "way farers" as two words; 90.2.1: "so-journs"; 90.8.9: comma after "somberly"; 90.14.8: comma after "suddenly"; 90.15.2: "T'is"; 90.18.9: "But" capitalized

Death's Black Riders

Originally appeared in *The Howard Collector*, volume 2, number 4 (whole number 10), Spring 1968. No changes have been made for this publication.

The Moon of Skulls

Originally appeared in *Weird Tales*, June and July 1930 (two-part serial). 107.19.6: "swordsman"; 111.18.11: "pæan"; 122.26.5: "Taferel"; 123.8.7: omits "for"; 128.2.1: comma after "muttered"; 133.21.11: closing quotation marks omitted; 133.31.9: comma after "said"; 166.11.1: "hour"

The One Black Stain

Originally appeared in *The Howard Collector*, volume 1, number 2 (whole number 2), Spring 1962. 173.14.5: "sombre"; 174.12.3: "sombrely"; 175.16.3: "sombre." The typescript from which *The Howard Collector* version was taken was not located in time for this publication. Three other drafts of the poem exist, and all three conform to the American spelling, "somber." We have accordingly used this spelling. Otherwise the text is identical with that in *The Howard Collector*.

The Blue Flame of Vengeance

Text taken from typescript, provided by Bill Cavalier. This story was revised by another author for its first publication; when the Howard-only version was first published, it was retitled "Blades of the Brotherhood." We have restored Howard's original title. 179, heading: no period after "corpses," period after "Kane"; 179.7.4: no hyphen in "blue eyed"; 180.1.3: "the" not capitalized; 180.7.2: no hyphen in "black eyed"; 180.12.1: comma after "oath"; 180.12.9: "T'is"; 180.16.3: comma after "steel"; 180.19.4: comma after "Rupert"; 180.23.7: no apostrophe in "an"; 181.3.11: "drift wood" as two words; 181.13.5: no hyphen in "gilt work"; 181.15.8: "home spun" as two words; 182.5.6: no hyphen in "sweat plastered"; 182.9.7: no hyphen in "moss grown"; 182.13.7: "sea-ward"; 182.14.5: no hyphen in "deep-throated"; 182.20.5: "It's" capitalized; 182.20.8: "villian"; 182.26.1: comma after "fell"; 182.28.4: comma after "passionately"; 183.14.1: no apostrophe in "An"; 183.22.8: no em-dash after "teeth!"; 183.27.4: comma after "Randel"; 183.30.8: comma after "other"; 184.11.1: "T'would"; 184.12.3: "THAT" all caps; 184.12.5: "t'will"; 185.9.3: "surplous"; 185.26.8: no hyphen in "smooth shaven"; 185.28.6: no hyphen in "corpse like"; 185.30.4: "vitallity"; 186.14.4: "this waist"; 186.26.9: "On" capitalized; 187.27.10: no apostrophe in "ships"; 187.29.1: "T'is"; 187.30.1: comma after "Kane"; 188.28.1: "were" for "where"; 188.32.7: comma after "sombrely"; 189.12.6: no hyphen in "dream haunted"; 190.8.7: "villiany"; 190.12.4: comma after "clothes"; 190.20.6: comma after "he"; 190.28.8: no hyphen in "evil visaged"; 191.8.4: no hyphen in "boulder torn"; 191.26.1: comma after "whisper"; 192.1.2: "as" omitted; 192.17.8: no hyphen in "sticky looking"; 192.28.1: "devided"; 193.8.9: "evidene"; 193.9.4: no hyphen in "jewel hilted"; 193.9.8: no hyphen in "silver chased"; 193.15.7: no hyphen in "silver buckled"; 193.29.7: no hyphen in "broad shouldered"; 194.4.1: "resplendant"; 194.4.3: no hyphen in "gold work"; 194.5.1: no hyphen in "scroll worked"; 194.15.2: "lips"; 194.21.3: comma after "words"; 194.32.2: "t'is"; 194.32.3: "YOUR" all caps; 194.33.1: "JACK" all caps; 195.9.8: "dissaray"; 195.13.6: comma after "jack"; 195.16.2: no hyphen in "black hearted"; 195.17.5: comma after "effort"; 195.18.5: no hyphen in "white livered"; 195.19.10: no apostrophe in "an"; 195.23.7: comma after "admiringly"; 195.27.6: comma after "rat"; 196.4.4: "weared"; 196.5.1: "tow"; 196.6.2: "jovialty" followed by a comma; 196.14.2: no apostrophe in "its"; 196.19.7: "How" capitalized; 196.20.5: "missal"; 196.21.4: comma after "aloud"; 196.21.7: "writtin"; 196.25.8: "hairsute"; 196.26.2: comma after "glee"; 196.30.5: "t'is"; 197.10.1: "down hearted" as two words; 197.11.1: no apostrophe in "havent"; 197.20.1: no apostrophe in "Its"; 197.23.6: comma after "back"; 197.25.5: "THAT" all caps; 197.28.6: comma after "up"; 198.4.9: "You" capitalized; 198.8.3: comma after "direly"; 198.20.2: no hyphen in "low drawn"; 198.22.7: comma after "tonelessly"; 200.10.1: "cut throat" as two words; 202.14.4: comma after "Fishhawk"; 202.16.6: comma after "it"; 202.21.3: double quotation marks before and after "The Flying Heart"; 202.28.7: "her"; 203.1.1-6: "YES, I, YOU DAMNED BLACK SWINE!" all caps; 203.16.2: "For" capitalized; 203.18.9: "You'd" capitalized; 203.21.9: "And" capitalized; 203.27.8: "YOU" all caps; 204.3.2: comma after "armor"; 204.7.5: "But" capitalized; 204.10.1: comma after "somberly"; 204.11.6: comma after "triumphantly"; 204.11.7: no apostrophe in "An"; 204.23.4: "by-word"; 205.17.5: comma after "muttered"; 206.5.8: comma after "approach"; 206.7.2: "AM" all caps; 206.8.1: comma after "somberly"; 206.10.3: "But" capitalized; 206.11.4: "BLOOD" all caps; 206.14.5: no hyphen in "down turned"; 206.16.3: no hyphen in "steel spring"; 209.28.9: "blood stained" as two words; 210.14.2: no comma after "Hollinster"; 210.15.3: no hyphen in "trance like"; 210.28.2: "soullfully"; 211.7.1: "T'is"; 211.17.5: no comma after "Jack"; 211.27.6: comma after "requested"; 212.19.4: no hyphen in "red hot"; 213.4.3: no hyphen in "self reproaches"; 213.5.11: comma after "youth"; 213.14.4: comma after "brought"; 213.22.3: "be" omitted; 214.5.7: comma after "brow"; 214.13.9: no hyphen in "evil looking"; 214.15.4: comma after "house"; 214.15.6: "was"; 214.17.1: "recieved"; 215.11.11: no hyphen in "long boat"; 215.13.1: "boat load" as two words; 215.25.4: "NO" all caps; 215.25.8: comma after "rasp"; 215.29.9: "sun-rise"; 216.25.1: no hyphen in "blood blinded"; 216.29.11: no comma after "Jack"; 217.13.11: comma after "himself"; 218.6.5: no hyphen in "breath taking"; 218.14.1: "adversary"; 218.23.4: "t'was"; 218.23.9: "your's"; 218.31.9: no hyphen in "white faced"; 219.6.5: comma after "hearers"; 219.23.4: comma after "blood"; 220.4.5: comma after "sea"; 220.7.8: comma after "him"; 220.9.1: "distruction"; 220.14.2: "But" capitalized; 220.19.10: comma after "him"; 220.22.3: comma after "tenderly"; 220.22.4: "T'is"; 220.27.5: comma after "man"; 220.27.6: "a" lower case; 220.28.7: comma after "eyes"; 220.29.8: "where-ever"

The Hills of the Dead
Originally appeared in *Weird Tales*, August 1930. 240.18.5: "he" not capitalized; 244.32.2: "easy"; 252.2.10: "remove"; 252.17.5: "blood brother" not hyphenated here, though it is elsewhere in the story

Hawk of Basti
Text taken from typescript, provided by Glenn Lord. Originally untitled, titled by Lord. 257.3.8: no hyphen in "moss carpeted"; 257.5.2: "witch-craft"; 257.9.6: no hyphen in "sharp pointed"; 257.10.8: "flint lock" as two words; 257.13.4: "loin cloth" as two words; 257.14.6: "Arm-lets"; 258.1.3: "ear-rings"; 258.2.9: "sea-men"; 258.10.3: comma after "Englishman"; 258.10.4: "Keel haul" as two words; 258.13.9: comma after "Kane"; 258.16.6: comma after "he"; 258.17.7: "suddenly" followed by em-dash rather than period; 258.17.8: "well" not capitalized; 258.18.3: "cut-throat"; 258.29.6: comma after "oath"; 259.2.1: no apostrophe in "Its"; 259.3.2: comma after "Kane"; 259.3.6: "in"; 259.7.3: comma after "harshly"; 259.13.1: no apostrophe in "Its"; 259.13.6: comma after "answered"; 260.20.4: "barricoon"; 260.25.6: comma after "I"; 260.30.3: comma after "fiercely"; 261.31.1: no hyphen in "brown skinned"; 262.31.10: "fire-arm"; 263.5.7: "Though" capitalized; 263.9.1: comma after "Hawk"; 263.8.5: "broad-brim"; 263.11.1: comma after "sombrely"; 263.18.3: "whale-bone"; 264.15.9: "And" capitalized; 264.17.3: no apostrophe in "wont"; 264.21.1: comma after "reluctantly"; 265.1.4: comma after "sombrely"; 265.9.7: no hyphen in "keen eared"; 265.11.8: comma after "fiercely"; 265.31.4: no hyphen in "well formed"; 266.9.5: "re-enforced"; 266.19.5: "You" capitalized; 266.20.9: no question mark after "ruler"; 266.22.2: no hyphen in "well built"; 266.25.2: no comma after "dialects"; 266.28.1: no hyphen in "Red handed";

266.29.4: comma after "anger"; 267.1.1: no hyphen in "heavy bored"; 267.10.1: "litterally"; 267.17.5: comma after "hand"; 267.33.1: comma after "kick"; 268.6.1: comma after "he"

The Return of Sir Richard Grenville
Text taken from typescript provided by Glenn Lord. Originally untitled, titled by Lord.

Wings in the Night
Originally appeared in *Weird Tales*, July 1932. 287.30.2: both instances of "breast-bone" occur at line breaks (see also 292.33.4); 291.15.9: "bird-man" hyphenated at line break 292.33.4: both instances of "breast-bone" occur at line breaks (see also 287.32.2); 301.20.3: "bow-shots" hyphenated at line break; elsewhere (see 297.21.4) "bowshot" is not hyphenated; 306.24.3: comma after "fetishes"; 306.25.1: no comma after "which"; 307.27.11: "mêlée"; 313.14.1: no hyphens in "four hundred odd"; 320.11.13: "plays"

The Footfalls Within
Originally appeared in *Weird Tales*, September 1931. 332.2.8: comma after "he"; 332.3.7: "shas"; 344.29.5: "alredy"

The Children of Asshur
Text taken from original typescript, provided by Glenn Lord. Originally untitled, titled by Lord. 350.1.4: no hyphen in "deep toned"; 350.11.7: "set"; 350.14.8: comma after "clear"; 350.15.9: comma after "truth"; 350.20.1: "wantoness"; 350.28.6: no hyphen in "sharp pointed"; 250.30.1: no comma after "witch-man"; 351.9.7: comma after "that"; 351.14.9: comma after "sanity"; 351.15.3: "no"; 351.18.8: "strikingly"; 351.30.5: "make-shift"; 352.7.4: comma after "column"; 352.14.1: comma after "twilight"; 352.14.8: "grassgrown" as one word; 352.22.11-12: comma after "tree" rather than "and"; 352.31.9: comma after "hand"; 352.32.8: "grass-land"; 353.6.3: comma after "tails"; 353.21.6: comma after "plain"; 354.1.7: "excellence"; 354.3.9: "consumate"; 354.10.6: no hyphen in "boulder strewn"; 354.15.3: "halluciation"; 354.28.3: comma after "expanses"; 355.12.2: comma after "eyes"; 355.15.1: "hard-wood"; 355.25.9: comma after shield; 355.26.1: no comma after "and"; 356.7.1: no comma after "Maddened"; 356.11.2: no comma after "close-locked"; 357.3.12: comma after "sky"; 357.6.8: "similiar"; 358.12.8: "back-ground"; 358.24.6: "high-priest"; 359.3.10: "illusive"; 359.13.7: "accolytes"; 359.18.2-3: comma after "him" rather than "and"; 359.21.3: comma after "galleries"; 359.23.9: "similiarly"; 359.25.5: "could" omitted; 360.3.2: "than" repeated; 360.13.3: no hyphen in "flat roofed"; 360.20.7: "repellant"; 360.24.4: "toweres"; 360.29.2: "far"; 361.3.2: no hyphen in "well tinted"; 361.5.9: "powerfully"; 361.17.2: "lion"; 361.28.3: "devisions"; 362.17.4: "Kane's"; 362.21.4: no apostrophe in "slayers"; 362.22.2: "loosly"; 362.27.9: "impacable"; 363.19.6: "accolytes"; 363.25.8: "nitches"; 363.32.7: comma after "chariots"; 364.7.2: "and"; 364.13.9: comma after "him"; 364.17.9: comma after "apparel"; 364.29.1: "beard"; 365.4.5: comma after

"space"; 365.11.3: "fire-light"; 365.15.4: no comma after "another"; 365.18.3: "langurously"; 365.21.5: comma after "garments"; 366.2.4: "gang"; 366.13.9: "fire-light"; 366.17.5: no hyphen in "half veiling"; 366.21.1: "concious"; 367.2.11: comma after "galleries"; 367.12.6: no hyphen in "market place" (two words); 367.14.2: "fore-shortened"; 367.33.6: "fire-light"; 368.1.9: "eye-balls"; 368.2.6: "spear-men"; 368.4.3-4: comma after "captive," "many" lower-case; 368.7.7: "dumfounded"; 368.12.7-8: comma after "understood," "you" lower-case; 368.13.2: "mouth-piece"; 368.22.1-2: comma after "Sula," "it" lower-case; 368.26.1: "sentance"; 368.28.4: "mouth-piece"; 369.6.9: period rather than question mark after "themselves"; 369.18-19: in the typescript, which is double-spaced, the phrase "in such a raid Sula was captured" is inserted between lines which begin "raids on the Ninnites" and "often did they venture" – it is flush with the left margin, and no indication is given as to where in the text it was to be inserted; 369.28.1: "by-word"; 370.23.4: no comma after "Kaldii"; 371.11.6: "high-priest"; 371.31.4-5: comma after "exclaimed," "they" lower-case; 372.16.2: "devided"; 372.16.5: "devisions"; 372.32.9: "numbered" omitted; 373.1.5: "statue"; 373.2.7: "war-fare"; 373.8.6: No accent in "Crecy"; 373.28.1-2: comma after "barrage" rather than "and"; 373.30.6: comma after "wings"; 374.15.1: no hyphen in "blood lust"; 375.5.5: "it" omitted; 375.30.3: "face" omitted; 375.31.4: "temple-guards"; 376.14.8: comma after "slaves"; 376.20.5: "house-tops"; 376.24.9: comma after "him"; 376.26.4: comma after "inhabitants"; 378.1.2: "him"; 378.2.11: comma after "hands"; 378.10.1: no comma after "guards"; 378.19.9: "curtesty"

Solomon Kane's Homecoming

Originally appeared in *Fanciful Tales*, volume 1, number 1, Fall 1936. 381.7.9: period after "life"; 382.10.6: no period after "tears"; 383.7.3: "bave"; 383.12.4: comma after "place"; 383.18.2: "huonds"

Solomon Kane's Homecoming (Variant)

Text taken from typescript, provided by Glenn Lord. The typescript is in four-line stanzas; we have divided the lines. 387.22.1: "Sat" capitalized; 387.24.1: "By" capitalized; 388.4.5: closing quotation mark after "away."; 388.5.3: comma rather than question mark after "Bess"; 388.11.4: "church-yard"; 388.13.7: "window-pane"; 389.13.1: no hyphen in "Adown"; 389.18.7: no comma after "bright"; 389.23.6: no comma after "again"